A Matter of Interpretation

ELIZABETH MAC DONALD

Fairlight Books

First published by Fairlight Books 2019

Fairlight Books
Summertown Pavilion, 18-24 Middle Way, Oxford, OX2 7LG

A CIP catalogue record for this book is available from the British Library

1 2 3 4 5 6 7 8 9 10

ISBN 978-1-912054-70-1

www.fairlightbooks.com

Printed and bound in Great Britain

Jacket design by Leo Nickolls

For my husband, Luca,
and my son, David,
who has grown with this novel.
For my parents,
Marcus and Mairéad,
without whom none of this
would have been possible.

My heart can take on any form:
A meadow for gazelles,
A cloister for monks,
For the idols, sacred ground,
Ka'ba for the circling pilgrim,
The tables of the Torah,
The scrolls of the Quran.

My creed is Love;
Wherever its caravan turns along the way,
That is my belief,
My faith.

—Ibn Arabī

Palermo,
Kingdom of Sicily

I

February AD *1230*

The restive shuffling of feet and sporadic coughing compete with an expectant silence. Few of the monks gathered in the church of San Giovanni degli Eremiti for Terce followed by Mass have managed to lose themselves in prayerful contemplation. Surreptitiously they observe the abbot, who is seated to the right of the altar, his head bowed. Why has he not begun the Office?

Their eyes flick to the empty stall nearest the altar. The Scot is keeping them waiting again. There is some nudging, some whispering. It stops as soon as the abbot raises his head. The creaking of the heavy wooden door at the entrance stills the congregation; the abbot rises from his seat and moves to the centre of the altar. But under cover of the hoods of their cowls, most monks' eyes swivel to scrutinise the latecomer. The silence is complete as Canon Michael Scot strides up the nave, cleaving the air before him, his outlandishly long legs rapidly covering its length. He stops at his empty stall, bows, blesses himself, and takes his place.

All eyes now turn to the abbot, but he just extends his hands, palms upturned, and begins the prayer. The desultory response that greets his invocation bespeaks a certain disgruntlement among the monks assembled in their stalls.

Terce is followed by Mass. As he prepares for the consecration, the abbot stands with his back to the congregation, a dark silhouette against the bright east-facing window behind the altar. The monks stand and bow their heads. But one of the youngest, as he lowers his dark, tonsured head respectfully, cannot resist taking a sidelong look at The Scot. A newly arrived novice from the Sicilian interior, he has never come into contact with anyone so bizarrely foreign as this elderly cleric. It all exerts a peculiar pull over him: the faded red beard; the immense height; the pale eyes, which have never failed to provoke an involuntary shiver on those few occasions when they have come to rest on him; and then there's the aura of controversy that shadows him like a tainted, sulphurous cloud. The Scot too has got to his feet, and yes, as a sign of respect at the moment of the consecration, has removed that absurd contraption from his head – a shiny metal skullcap that otherwise never leaves it, and which has given rise to endless speculation among the monks. What can it be for? And why does the abbot permit it? The bell tinkles as the Host is raised. The young monk, caught by an impetus of conscience, closes his eyes.

A hoarse cry rips through this dense silence, followed by the clanging of metal. There is a moment of incredulity; heads jerk back up, glances fly from one face to another, then pandemonium breaks loose.

The Scot lies crumpled and still on the stone flagging of the church floor, the metal skullcap rocking frenetically just beyond the reach of his outstretched fingers. The monks swarm around him in a babbling crescendo of consternation. The abbot, his hands still raised in the act of consecration, has half turned to look behind him. Slowly he lowers his hands and turns back to face the large crucifix on the altar; then, blessing himself, he partakes of a solitary Holy Communion.

He descends from the altar and intimates to the monks to let him through. A hush falls as they comply, parting to reveal the motionless figure on the ground. Blood is seeping from a wound on his head. 'Give us some air,' says the abbot, his voice sharp with impatience.

Reluctantly, the monks draw back. The abbot gets to his knees, his fingers reach out to probe Canon Michael Scot's neck. There is a tense moment, and then his face relaxes. 'Yes, thank the Lord, there is still a pulse.'

A sudden groan from the bleeding figure on the ground startles the craning monks. The Scot's eyes open and roll back into his head; he shudders uncontrollably.

A monk screams. 'He is possessed!'

'A demon!'

The huddle of monks falls apart; two of them turn and run from the church.

The abbot is about to give the order for a pallet to be brought, on which Canon Michael can be conveyed to the infirmary, when his eye falls on a rectangular brick a little way from the injured cleric. It is blood-spattered. The remaining monks' eyes follow his, back to The Scot's head. The abbot seems to steel himself, his hands clench, and then, slowly, he raises his eyes to the ceiling of the church. His intake of breath is a sibilant hiss; a gasp runs through the monks. Above their unsuspecting heads, there is a small black hole, the one left by the now blood-smeared brick, which some twist of fate decreed should come loose and hurtle down with devilish speed, smashing into The Scot's uncovered skull.

[illegible]

II

The four towers of the Norman Palace rise challengingly into the night sky. From this, the highest point in Palermo, the blazing torches atop each one shower a lava of sparks into the night breeze that can be seen all over the city. La Greca, La Pisana, La Joaria and La Kirimbi: each bears its own name and presides over one of the four wings of the seat of the kings of Sicily. Their names are redolent of the many strands that have gone into making this kingdom one of the wonders of Christendom. Byzantine Greeks, with their mastery of rite and rhetoric; hard-headed, enterprising merchants from the emerging city-states up north in mainland Italy; and the Saracens, bringing their love of gardens, fountains and patios.

The chancellery is situated in the palace wing presided over by La Greca. It has been thrown into a feverish burst of activity. The announcement of a visitation from the emperor has fallen on the scribes, notaries and functionaries there with the ominous suddenness of a declaration of war. Even now the emperor is making his way to the chancellery for the inspection. By rights the working day should be over; indeed, some of the scribes had already put their work away. But it has to be retrieved from desks, cupboards and presses, and a queasy nervousness slithers through not a few stomachs.

Giovanni da Messina leans up against the large, sloping wooden desk at which he carries out his duties as a newly appointed notary in the legal branch of the court administration. He surveys the scurrying to and fro with a certain detached smugness. His own papers are in order; it is a point of honour with him to carry out his duties as if an inspection were always in the offing. He fully understands the import of this visitation, as do the other anxious-looking clerks scuttling around him. His eyes follow one young scribe, who is attempting to add to the pitifully few scraps of parchment on his desk. They point to very modest levels of activity. The scribe removes a weightier sheaf of documents from the press containing older, completed assignments. He pauses in an agony of indecision, then slowly places it at the bottom of his own scant pile. Giovanni da Messina shifts from one foot to another. The risk, of course, is that the young scribe will not be able to account for work he did not personally carry out.

Suddenly silence falls. Frederick II, Holy Roman Emperor, enters briskly, escorted by six heavily armed guards, and all heads incline in an act of homage.

The emperor's penetrating eyes take their time in surveying the assembled functionaries. 'News has just reached us that the Ghibelline party, having suitably chastised the pope with an enforced two-year exile in Perugia, has decided to allow him to return to Rome. As a mark of papal gratitude, his Holiness appears to be willing to desist in his attempts to destroy the empire and now wishes to sue for peace. This will, of course, necessitate a change in our policies. A number of new directives must therefore be drawn up and issued forthwith.'

Giovanni da Messina reflects with a touch of pride that his mentor, Pier delle Vigne, in his capacity as the emperor's chief secretary, has had a crucial role in this.

The emperor takes a step forward. 'In the coming weeks, I shall have need of your hard work. And, of course, your absolute loyalty.' There is a pause as the blue eyes observe the carefully impassive faces.

'But first things first. Who,' he enquires crisply, 'was charged with organising the invitations for Saturday's banquet?'

'I was, your Majesty,' the young scribe replies, his voice unnaturally high.

'I see. So it is your fault that an invitation to the banquet was not extended to Master Michael Scot.'

The scribe swallows. 'No, your Majesty. That is,' – his voice sinks to a whisper – 'I was advised that an invitation would not be necessary.'

The stillness intensifies. The emperor's eyes narrow. 'Your whittling down of the invitation list has been zealous.' He turns to finger the paltry number of documents on the scribe's desk. 'But it is ill-judged; you would have done better to apply yourself here, where there is call for it.'

Chastened into silence, the scribe looks at the floor.

'I am greatly desirous of Master Scot's presence at the banquet in two days' time. Despite your evident expectation that he would no longer be with us, you will send him an invitation immediately. And I will get to the bottom of this unseemly haste to be rid of Master Michael Scot.' His voice rises, brushing over the chancellery like a nettle sting. 'Loyalty first and foremost.'

'Yes, your Majesty,' the bowed heads reply dutifully.

Giovanni da Messina also keeps his eyes firmly on the floor. He is personally responsible for having brought the news of The Scot's accident to the chancellery, a feat that has garnered him credit among his fellow functionaries. He is well aware, however, that at present it would do nothing to advance his cause with the emperor. But, unlike the scribe, he had known what needed to be done. He had also known to whom he could turn. Brother Gerardo, his contact at the monastery of San Giovanni degli Eremiti, had immediately filled him in on all the details, offsetting the abbot's attempt to ensure this debacle remain a secret. After all, the whole thing reeks of Divine retribution.

According to Brother Gerardo, The Scot was unconscious for all of yesterday, only to unexpectedly revive early this Thursday morning. To be sure, it is not at all the news they either expected or wished for. In this the emperor is right: such great store had been set by an entirely different outcome. But the emperor does not know this shameless master of the black arts as they do. And now, against all the odds, he is showing signs of pulling through. He has been sleeping fitfully for most of the day, apparently, with the abbot a vigilant presence at his bedside.

'Since you have not been fatiguing yourself excessively,' the emperor turns back to the scribe, his lip curling, 'you had better bestir yourself now and take down this missive to Master Michael Scot. He is to receive and reply to it immediately.'

A prod from behind galvanises the scribe into action and he moves to retrieve his stylus and wax tablet from the sloping desk. The emperor folds his arms, inserting his hands into the voluminous sleeves of his robe. He proceeds to dictate a short communication, inviting Master Michael Scot, should his health permit it, to a private audience after the banquet. 'Now show me what you have produced.'

Rapidly he peruses the tablet; an exclamation of annoyance breaks the tense silence, followed by a clatter as the tablet is tossed onto the desk. Minatory eyes swivel back to the scribe.

'Is this the way to spell my name?' The emperor's finger jabs at the discarded tablet.

The scribe blanches. His hand trembling, he picks it up and looks at the signature. *Frederik*. His mouth opens, but no sound comes out. With a slowness born of dread, he replaces the tablet on the desk.

The emperor waves a hand at one of the armed guards. His voice falls to a chilling hiss. 'Off with the thumb.' He looks contemptuously at the appalled scribe. 'At least you will have no further occasion to offend me with your ineptitude.'

Blood spurts in glistening scarlet globs across the opaque sheen of the waxen tablet. The stump falls to the floor and, as if in a final regretful paroxysm of life, rolls with grotesque speed under another desk. All eyes slew back to the wretched scribe, taking in the silent 'O' formed by his open mouth as he regards his butchered hand, the hand he will never write with again. Whimpers of pain and shock escape him, promptly suffocated lest worse befall him, and his muffled sobbing recedes down the corridor as he is led away.

The emperor surveys the room a final time before taking his leave. No eyes meet his. 'See that this missive gets to Master Michael Scot as quickly as possible. I will not tolerate slacking or incompetence. You have been warned.'

In the commotion that follows, Giovanni da Messina manages to retrieve the wax tablet from the desk and check its contents. He listens impassively as the notary beside him wrings his hands and bewails the fate that could be meted out to any of them. 'Even so,' he murmurs, 'it's not the moment for slacking.' The notary is startled into wary silence. Swiftly da Messina heads to the press and removes a blank sheet of parchment as well as the imperial seal. One hand smooths the sheet out on the nearest desk and the other reaches for a quill. 'Leave this to me,' he says quietly.

III

Pier delle Vigne is making his way laboriously along the road skirting the city walls. Hindered by his girth and the darkness, he is already in a lather of sweat. Despite this, he pulls his cloak tighter around him, for he does not wish to be recognised on this business. He distracts himself from the sense of fatigue by reflecting with pleasure on the comfort offered by his new kidskin shoes. At a discreet distance follows Giovanni da Messina, whose delicate task it is not to overtake the elder man (seniority being owed its due), while simultaneously avoiding any appearance of dawdling. He too is heavily cloaked.

The muted red dome surmounting the squat white-stoned campanile of San Giovanni degli Eremiti emerges from the darkness, so, without turning his head, delle Vigne crosses the road. Through the shadows ahead he can now make out the other four red domes on the roof of the block-like form of the church. He picks his way over the uneven dusty surface of the entrance and heads for the adjoining monastery. The kidskin of his shoes is not sturdy enough for the sharp stones scattered round the forecourt, an arrangement that is a little too rustic for his taste, and his mouth twists in disapproval. His pace slows further as he begins the ascent to the monastery, and da Messina draws alongside him.

'The monks really should do something about cleaning this entrance up,' mutters delle Vigne. 'These Cistercians may pride themselves on their capacity for hard work, and the tilling and sowing and weeding are all very commendable in their way. But here is a job that needs to be done, yet continues to be disgracefully neglected.'

'Indeed,' replies da Messina. 'The forecourt has been like this for as long as I can remember. And it's not as if they can be lacking in money: between the church and the monastery and the emperor's endowments, their wealth is rivalled only by the Benedictine abbey of Monreale.'

Delle Vigne pauses to regain his breath. He does not want to present himself puffing and wheezing to the abbot, and incapable of speech. He runs probing fingers over the soles of his shoes to see how they are bearing up. These indeed are shoes that bespeak the prestige of his new appointment as the emperor's chief secretary. A far cry from his barefooted childhood, and all the more satisfying for that.

As one of the most senior of the court's functionaries, it is not his task to make the journey to the monastery. But in cases like this, his instincts have always served him well: no piece of information, no matter how trivial or seemingly insignificant, really goes to waste. And he has been listening and hoarding – a word here, an indiscretion there, the outpourings of anger, the vituperative whisperings of envy. Certainly, what has befallen The Scot is sending ripples of curiosity, benign and otherwise, round the court. He needs to know if The Scot – that unwanted, soothsaying harbinger of doom – is about to meet his Maker. Imperial policy depends upon it.

A gust of chill wind shreds the tattered remains of a cloud covering the moon, and the iron studs on the large wooden door to the monastery come into focus. To the side, the carved white arches of the cloisters under the moonlight are like frozen waves fading into the surrounding blackness. There has still been no reply to the urgent missive Giovanni da Messina delivered here yesterday, from the emperor to The Scot, summonsing him to a private audience after Saturday's banquet in the Green Hall. This further instance of undeserved courtesy on the part of the emperor to The Scot would normally have irked delle Vigne beyond measure, but his instinct tells him that the lack of a reply is an admission of weakness from the monastery. That is why he himself has come up here like any common underling. Depending on the outcome of these very events, the balance of power between the chancellery and monastery may undergo a significant shift. He closes his eyes tightly. So much is at stake here.

This particular struggle is a microcosm of the greater struggle his emperor is waging against the tyranny of Pope and Church: if he, Pier delle Vigne, can tip the balance in favour of the emperor in this instance, it will represent a reassuring portent of defeat for the Church in the wider context. With his dark sorcery, that upstart necromancer has gained a stranglehold on the emperor's mind – if only it could be loosened, along with the pernicious influence he has gained on imperial policy. The survival of the empire depends on it.

Da Messina, noting that his mentor has regained a measure of composure, solicitously steps up to the main entrance and lifts the knocker, giving a sharp double rap on the heavy wooden door. There is no answer. Impatiently, he raps again, three times. Still no answer. Delle Vigne bids him to lift the knocker yet again when a key begins to rattle in the lock from the inside. Slowly, the door is pulled back and Brother Gerardo's surly face appears. Momentary surprise registers at the sight of no less a personage than Pier delle Vigne, the emperor's chief secretary, and his sidekick da Messina, but the customary frown rapidly descends.

'This is not a permitted time for visitors,' he grumbles, beckoning them inside with a curt gesture of his large hand. 'I was making my way back from Vespers when I heard you from the cloister banging on the door.' Brother Gerardo's eyes flick back over his shoulder to make sure the abbot is not in the vicinity; he is in breach of the rule of monastic silence by talking. His voice is low when he adds, 'I've already told everything I know to da Messina. I have not seen The Scot since the accident and only have the infirmarian's word to go on.' He replaces the large key on the ring attached to his habit and pulls the door to.

They survey each other as best they can, their outlines indistinct in the gloom of the vestibule.

'So he has regained consciousness,' murmurs Pier delle Vigne, shooting a glance at da Messina, 'against all prognostications.'

Brother Gerardo clicks his tongue and mutters, 'The devil looks after his own.'

'You mentioned that he had lost a lot of blood and was slipping away,' probes da Messina.

Brother Gerardo shrugs. 'What can I tell you? Slipping away or not, he's still giving us as much trouble as he can.'

'And yet...' Pier delle Vigne pauses, and then says resolutely, 'There has been no reply to the emperor's summons. I have been sent to ascertain why. Please advise the abbot that I need to talk to him.'

Brother Gerardo heaves a sigh. 'That means I'll have to light the torches here in the vestibule.' Pier delle Vigne watches him stump sullenly away. Ah, the pleasures of the religious life. He feels his way slowly along the walls, out towards the rectangular white-stoned cloister as Brother Gerardo reappears and lights a couple of torches on the wall.

His task accomplished, he then heads off without another word to fetch the abbot. When his retreating steps can no longer be heard on the flagstones, delle Vigne turns quickly to da Messina and whispers, 'Go now,' and watches his cloaked figure melt silently into the darkness in the wake of Brother Gerardo.

In the dim moonlight delle Vigne can make out the palm tree standing at each of the cloister's four corners. A pleasing spectacle in its harmonious simplicity. But the harmony of the monastery begins and ends here with this illusion of beauty and grace. He had been right to get away from the clerics who had overseen his childhood education. A bright and promising student he had been, ever eager to learn. He knew they had seen another religious in the making, despite the relentless insults that had been his lot as the illegitimate offspring of an adulteress. And he had not led them to believe anything to the contrary, biding his time until he had acquired as good an education as was possible under them. That completed, and having come of age, he had abandoned the Cathedral School and his poverty-stricken past in Capua forever.

The realisation that the religious life was not for him had come early, more from a dislike of the acrimonious hypocrisies engendered by its all-too-futile attempts to live up to the Christian ideal than from any real scruple about vocation. There had, of course, been those who did not even try to measure up. The vagaries of human nature had visited themselves on him with daily monotony as he battled with the ambition, pride and petty spitefulness of his fellow students – to say nothing of the masters – in the suffocating confines of the Cathedral School.

He remembers it all very well, and it still rankles. Out in the world it is easier to suffer human failings, as there is less of the chafing that concentrated contact with deluded consciences leads to. He is his own man now: the emperor's court offers every opportunity for an educated layperson like him to make his way in life. The religious have no monopoly of learning here. The emperor wouldn't allow it.

And that is why the empire is so crucial. Without it, there would be nothing to offset the tyranny of the Church. Pier delle Vigne clasps his hands behind his back and rises up on the balls of his feet. Up and down, up and down, in an attempt to shake off the feeling of foreboding that washes over him at the recollection of his recent encounter with that soothsaying necromancer. It had been deeply unpleasant. It is also most unfortunate that Giovanni da Messina should have witnessed the scene, for it has placed him in a regrettably vulnerable position with the younger man. He is under no illusion that their alliance would vanish like snow in the March sun if da Messina deemed it to be politically opportune. He sighs. It is imperative to establish the extent to which The Scot's rantings have compromised him; he will now have to keep a watchful eye on da Messina as well. One more thing on the lengthening list of problems that he will need to address.

His thoughts, snagged on the thorn of unwelcome recollection, strain to move on from the galling memory. But it will not leave him be. The clash with The Scot occurred a week past, yet the anxiety it caused is unabated. The doubt niggles that his present actions are about as useful as bolting the entrance door after a hurricane has blown the rest of the house down.

His informants had told him that the emperor had cleared his engagements for a whole afternoon to consult with The Scot on the latest horoscope. The opportunity was too good to pass up, so da Messina and he had set off for The Scot's vacant study. Da Messina managed to pick the lock on the door. Once inside they located the press where The Scot kept his materials, and removed a bundle of his horoscopes. They had been bent over them, quietly debating the import of the reams of calculations and squiggles, when a chilling voice from behind brought them up short.

'What can you two weasels mean by forcing an entry into my study and rifling through my private writings?'

Finding himself uncharacteristically speechless, he had turned to Giovanni da Messina for support. But one glance at the ashen countenance beside him revealed the necessity of extricating himself from this hornet's nest by his own devices.

'The emperor has urgent need of your horoscopes before sending off a dispatch to Rome,' he replied with as much defiance as he could muster.

'So without as much as a by-your-leave,' retorted The Scot, his voice ominously quiet, 'you break in here and spy on confidential matters.'

'Time is of the essence.'

'Isn't it always...'

The hairs on the back of his neck had risen as he noted the deepening of the voice. Immediately, he took a few paces away from The Scot, as did da Messina. The unnerving grey eyes followed him, latched onto his own and held them in a searing beam that liquefied his innards. He knew the sinister power wielded by those eyes. He knew that he mustn't look into them; knew that he must distract himself.

'Who are you,' he had cried, 'to create such despair in his Majesty's heart with these,' – his hand flapped weakly at the astrological chart – 'these deluded maunderings?' Bolstered by the sound of his own voice, despite its unnaturally high pitch, even to his own ears, he managed to tear his eyes away and fix them on the wooden tabletop.

'And who are you to take such liberties with what is not yours?'

'How dare you! I shall report this slander to his Majesty.'

'Ah – but slander it is not.'

And with that, The Scot had lunged forward and grabbed hold of his hands. He had been so shocked by this that no sound escaped him. Slack-jawed, da Messina groped his way round to the opposite side of the table. Pier delle Vigne cried out as The Scot twisted his hands palm upwards.

'Observe these protuberances,' said The Scot, pressing on the plump mounds at the base of delle Vigne's thumbs. 'What do you think they represent?' He had felt The Scot's eyes boring into him and struggled to resist some fatal compulsion to return their gaze.

'I'll tell you what they represent,' continued The Scot, his grip tightening. 'They represent testicles. Or is it eyes?' The Scot closed his own eyes and, frowning in concentration, his head began to sway.

Repulsed, yet unable to contain himself, delle Vigne had glanced up at the pale face, whose closed eyes were intent on reeling in a hidden answer. 'What have we here?' The Scot's voice was an icy murmur, 'What have we here?'

Suddenly, horrifyingly, those ghostly eyes had opened and stared balefully down at him. He felt the strength drain from his legs.

'Your eyes,' stated The Scot, flinging his hands back down, 'which you shall lose most painfully.'

Delle Vigne had rubbed his wrists and tried to still the trembling in his legs.

'Listen carefully, weasel, and know that I see you for what you are. I have seen confirmation of it in the future.' The Scot seemed to grow taller and his declaiming voice rose, filling the small room with a pulsating anger. 'You will lose those eyes as a punishment for treason! For those eyes stoke the greed that will lead you to thievery and knavery of such heinousness, that you will not stop at committing treason.'

Shaken, delle Vigne had stared at The Scot in silence. A quick glance in da Messina's direction showed him crumpled over the table. 'Falsehoods!' he cried, his own voice rising. 'Like everything else that spews from your deranged mouth.'

'I wonder whether his Majesty will take the same view,' replied The Scot.

'But,' he shot back, 'we all know the view that his Majesty takes of your dabblings in black magic.'

The Scot shrugged.

Rapidly, he had roused da Messina and they had left the study.

Steps can be heard treading softly behind him. Pier delle Vigne takes a deep breath and composes himself. He peers into the darkness. The abbot is approaching.

IV

Hugo de Clermont, abbot of San Giovanni degli Eremiti and personal confessor to the emperor, has been disagreeably surprised by Brother Gerardo's announcement that both Pier delle Vigne and Giovanni da Messina are waiting for him in the vestibule. There must indeed be a great deal at stake if the emperor's chief secretary, accompanied by that minion of mischief, Giovanni da Messina, have seen fit to come all the way out to the monastery at this late hour. As he walks along the corridor he bows his head and says a quick prayer for guidance.

A sense of apprehension insinuates itself. He wonders how it goes with Canon Michael Scot. He notes the sense of protectiveness that takes hold of him whenever he thinks of this difficult, prickly man. Certainly, it was not always so. He did not like him when first he met him, but time has changed that. He knew from the beginning that, apart from any personal considerations, it would be very difficult to insert Canon Michael into the contemplative context of the Cistercian monastery. But the emperor had ordered him to do so, and he had been forced to obey. There had been times indeed when he found himself making a conscious effort to suppress the word 'cuckoo', for it was wont to dart into his mind with uncharitable frequency at the beginning of their acquaintance. And in truth, he cannot say what his sentiments for Canon Michael are even now; all he knows is that the man is a presence in his life he has come to value. In the monastery the passing of time is a purgatorial honing of dross. But the abbot has stayed the course; he has done right by Canon Michael.

And now this latest calamity. On top of a mind already darkened by severe melancholy has come this new blow. It seems like an accident, albeit a bizarre one; but the abbot senses that it is useless to take comfort in appearances. He must now face whatever trouble has issued from the chancellery. And that missive from the emperor has to be dealt with, but he hopes that his delay in answering has managed to gain them some time. He consoles himself with the reflection that, while Canon Michael is still worryingly weak – he has been plagued from early this Friday morning, from as soon as he regained consciousness indeed, with a severe headache – it is altogether astounding that he has managed to rally at all. God willing, he will pull through.

A footfall in the shadowy corridor heralds the abbot's arrival. As he observes his lack of stature and the portly demeanour, Pier delle Vigne finds himself wondering, and not for the first time, what it is that gives the man such an aura of gravitas. Then he takes in the pristine condition of the habit, despite its homespun roughness, and the clean whiteness of the tunic. The contrast with the slovenly Brother Gerardo could not be more marked.

'You wished to see me?' enquires Hugo de Clermont, coming to a halt before Pier delle Vigne. 'And where is your – er – your... assistant?'

'My Lord Abbot,' says Pier delle Vigne, bowing. 'Giovanni da Messina had to return to the Norman Palace.' The abbot's mouth settles into a thin line. 'It is a matter of urgency,' continues delle Vigne, regaining an upright position, 'that you provide me with a reply to the missive summonsing The Scot to the emperor's presence tomorrow, Saturday.'

The abbot's eyebrows rise. 'You mean to say you've come chasing up here in the dark merely to hear me confirm that *Canon* Michael Scot,' – the abbot enunciates the title and name in a barely veiled rebuke – 'is honoured by his Majesty's invitation and will be in attendance at the ordained time and place?'

Pier delle Vigne clears his throat and looks down, his eyes coming to rest on the abbot's sandals. They are of common cowhide and look very much the worse for wear. Fortified in this knowledge, he looks up once again and meets the challenge in the abbot's pale blue eyes. 'I was wondering,' he says, holding the abbot's eyes, 'or rather, we were all wondering, how the patient is.'

'Allow me to allay any fears that may have afflicted you on that score,' the abbot replies, with the veneer of condescending courtesy that never fails to rile Pier delle Vigne. 'I am delighted to be able to inform you that he is coming along splendidly.'

'Such an extraordinary thing to have happened,' Pier delle Vigne murmurs, shaking his head. He pauses. 'While I would never make so bold as to attribute it to the hand of Providence—'

'As, of course, is your duty as a Christian,' the abbot interrupts. His eyes have become more hooded. 'Otherwise, you run the risk of falling into heresy. You are aware of that, are you not?'

'Naturally. And, I repeat, I myself would never link what has befallen The Scot with the hand of Providence. Unfortunately, not everyone at court is as well informed, theologically and factually, as I am. There are those who feel that his imminent death, regrettable as it may be, is an ineluctable act of God. And you cannot blame them.'

'Oh, but I can – and I do.' The abbot's eyes are vitreous. 'You may inform them that they sin grievously in attributing to the source of all good any harm that has come to a son on whom He has shown such favour.' Hugo de Clermont's hand enfolds the crucifix hanging from his neck. His tone becomes disdainful. 'And then there is the culpable malice of those who spread such falsehoods.

Canon Michael Scot is not dying. Thank the good Lord, he will be with us for a long while yet.'

'Ah.' Pier delle Vigne glances at him and his eyes narrow speculatively. 'Nevertheless, it will not be easy to scotch the rumours. I shall need to see for myself that The Scot is not about to—'

'That will not be possible.'

'With all due respect, I have been charged with ascertaining personally—'

'That may be so.' The abbot's expression is haughty. 'But it is the emperor who requires to be informed here. And as his confessor, I shall no doubt see him sooner than you or anyone else in the chancellery.'

'So The Scot will not be present at the banquet or the audience with the emperor – despite the summons.'

'You misunderstand me; I said no such thing. The invitation extended to Canon Scot comes – and in this at least you are correct – from the emperor himself. So it is to the emperor that Canon Scot's reply must be directed.' The abbot's eyelids lower, as if to shield his eyes from some disagreeable sight. 'He certainly does not require you as an intermediary in his communications with his Imperial Majesty: they have been communicating quite successfully without you for nearly as many years as are on your shoulders.'

A dull flush mottles Pier delle Vigne's cheeks. Without another word, he turns on his heel and heads for the door.

Hugo de Clermont's eyes narrow with distaste. A vexatious spirit, if ever there was one. Then a large, awkward form sidling along the outer reaches of the vestibule in the flickering light of the torches obtrudes upon his attention. He sighs at length, and the figure quickens its pace. Its haste and hunched shoulders denote an unseemly need to reach the safety of the door porter's cubicle before attracting undue attention.

'Brother Gerardo,' he calls.

The figure stops, and then turns round slowly. 'Yes, Father Abbot?'

That wheedling tone, the ingratiating servility. The abbot schools his face to blankness as Brother Gerardo draws up. 'I have been reflecting on your needs, Brother Gerardo.' Satisfaction and wariness battle it out on the coarse face in front of him. 'And I have reached the conclusion that as every monk deserves a change of duties and this is doubly true of the door porter.' Wariness begins to gain the upper hand. 'I am transferring you to the kitchen.'

'But Father Ab—'

'You are wasted out here on your own in so much solitude. You will gain from the company of the other monks.' The abbot notes the clenched hands, the jutting jaw, and reflects that the benefit will be sadly unilateral. But what alternative has he got?

'That will be all, Brother Gerardo. Tomorrow morning you will start in the kitchens. Brother Tommaso will tell you what your duties are.'

The abbot frowns. A hectic end to this Friday. Pier delle Vigne sent packing and Brother Gerardo dispatched to the kitchens. He does not delude himself that The Scot has severed the hydra of probing tentacles issuing from the chancellery, intent on unearthing information in a bid to extend its control over the monastery. But he may have gained some valuable time.

Or has he?

Suddenly he is brought up short by a sense of unease. Did da Messina really return to the palace? Brother Gerardo saw him enter, but was not there to see him leave. And why indeed would Canon Michael's accident have warranted a visit from the chief secretary of the chancellery... Was this meeting just a ruse to distract him?

His sense of unease deepens, sending prickles of fear over his skin. He sets off in the direction of the infirmary. What if all this has something to do with the visions that Canon Michael had begun to recount to him not five days past? His pace quickens as another thought comes close on its heels. Canon Michael mentioned these visions just two days before his accident.

*

The door to the infirmary is wide open, framing a pit of utter darkness. The abbot steps within and his nose is assailed by the acrid smoke of a recently quenched candle in the heavy air. Helplessly, he returns to the corridor.

'Infirmarian!' his voice breaks the silence. 'Infirmarian, where are you?'

His ears pick up the sound of approaching steps in the echoing gloom. 'Father Abbot...' comes a voice, 'here I am!' A dim glow at the end of the corridor marks the arrival of the infirmarian who, thank God, is bearing a candle.

'Where had you got to?' Vexation makes Hugo de Clermont curt.

'I—I had to check some supplies,' the infirmarian defends himself. 'I haven't been gone long at all.' The abbot snatches the candle he is holding and steps back inside the infirmary. The infirmarian remains outside. Holding the candle aloft, Hugo de Clermont's eyes dart to Canon Michael's pallet, but it is empty.

'The Lord have mercy on us!' Shielding the candle with his hand, the abbot rushes over. Canon Michael has fallen to the ground on the far side and, for the second time in as many days, the abbot finds him collapsed on the floor. He turns back to the shadowed figure hovering at the door. 'Move, you fool!' he cries. 'Help me get Canon Michael back onto his pallet.'

As the infirmarian reluctantly approaches, he goes to the table in the centre of the room where the candle has fallen over in its holder. This might explain why it had gone out. But, then again, why would it have fallen over in the first place? He lights it with his own candle and sets it upright in the holder. Some mischief has been afoot here.

The infirmarian looks fearfully around him as shadows jump over the walls with their movements. The abbot takes Canon Michael's upper body, taking care to support his head, while the infirmarian takes his legs. They manage to lift him back onto the pallet which, the infirmarian notes with undiminished wonder, is too short to accommodate the outlandishly long frame of The Scot.

'Well?' presses the abbot. 'Is he alive?'

The infirmarian shoots him a glance. Under the abbot's stern gaze he lifts The Scot's wrist and checks for his pulse. 'He is,' says the infirmarian, his voice barely above a whisper. 'But he has lost consciousness again.'

'I can see that,' snaps the abbot.

Gingerly, the infirmarian replaces the motionless arm back down on the pallet. 'The pulse is weak,' he murmurs, and then places a hand on The Scot's forehead. 'And he is burning up with a fever.' He removes his hand and adds, 'But yes, he is still alive.'

Hugo de Clermont grasps the crucifix hanging from his neck. 'No thanks to you.' He glares at the infirmarian, who looks down at the floor in silence. 'I forbid you to leave your post like this again. If you contravene this express order, know that I shall bring it to the attention of the emperor and hand you over to him to be punished in whatever way he sees fit.' He glances down at the unconscious man. 'Now go and fetch an extra blanket for Canon Scot.'

'And perhaps a cold compress to lower the fever? His bandaging may need adjusting.'

'Indeed.' The abbot shakes his head as he watches the infirmarian scuttle out of the door, and then looks back down at Canon Michael. Is it his imagination, or is there some movement in the eyelids? He moves closer and bends down. Yes – yes, there is a flickering. He makes the sign of the cross on Canon Michael's forehead and calls his name.

Slowly the eyes open. The gaze is blank; the abbot calls his name again. Canon Michael's face creases in a grimace of pain. 'Where am I?' His voice has the dry rasp of someone who has a parching thirst. 'What happened?'

The abbot places his hand on Canon Michael's shoulder. 'What can you remember? I found you on the floor here beside your pallet.' He glances hurriedly at the infirmary door. 'Tell me quickly before the infirmarian returns.'

Michael Scot closes his eyes again and frowns. Slowly he shakes his head. 'I can remember nothing.' He takes a deep breath and winces.

'Do not trouble yourself about this yet. The infirmarian will make you comfortable,' the abbot pats his bony shoulder, 'and I will stay with you through the night.' He pauses for a moment. 'But Michael, should you remember anything that might help us, set it in writing. I will leave your writing materials close to hand. Sleep now and see if the night brings its own counsel.'

†

Confessio
February AD 1230

A long time dreaded, in the end it took but a moment for the vision and the horoscope to come to pass. Death has placed a hand on my shoulder; it behoves me, Michael Scot, to turn and face him.

A lifetime bends before the scythe, and I see now with bitterness what a meagre sheaf it will yield. For what has this life of mine been but an unheeded sequence of events that distracted my mind from its obsessions. To have been reduced to so paltry a thing. And now when it is too late my heart aches with the burden of what might have been. The priceless beauty of what is to be thieved from me; the fragility of a life. I am one who foresaw his own death.

A life of learning. A life spent wandering the labyrinthine paths of knowledge and the arcane. What has it all been for? An ignorant fool I was at its inception; a presumptuous fool in its living. And the greatest proof of my deserving these epithets to be found in its ending. As for dying, we all die. It is indeed true that I saw how; but the real question is when. And the answer to this, despite all my horoscopes and learning, continues to elude me.

Outside the window of this infirmary, the expectant hush of an early spring evening falls over the monastery. There is so much of beauty in the natural world: twilight advances and the sky is a vast iris petal of golden moon hanging in indigo silence. But what does it signify now? Silence without and silence within. Only You have the answer to my question. You only can break down this wall of silence and bring some kind of balm to my soul. But You mock me with Your remoteness, and I writhe like a worm in salt.

I have spent my life stalking other men's greatness, to the point where any claim I may have had to it myself has evaporated. Is this how You repay Your faithful servants? For by assigning such an ignoble end to my life, You have made a mockery of all that precedes it. Am I nothing more to You than the pagan Euripides, smitten by the hand of divine wrath, struck dead by that stone falling from the sky on his head? He, too, an exile in a land not his own, this island prison of Sicily, in flight from the Lord knows what, his useless flight brought to an abrupt end.

A risible end.

And so the horoscope was indeed true in its predictions. It augurs ill then for the other visions I had, just six days past, of the emperor and his empire. I feel death closing in around me, poisonously sweet, and have not the desire to fight it off. Salmon-like, I feel I must begin the long haul back to my place of birth; over the sea and numberless roads shall I wend my way northwards to die.

After a lifetime in foreign lands, grant me, I beseech You, this final mercy of death in the place I once called home.

V

Michael Scot places the quill back on the table and blows on the sheet of parchment. His head throbs and his vision has blurred. He turns and extinguishes the candle that he had stuck onto the table, but this worsens the throbbing. He gets to his feet unsteadily, then puts a hand to his head and presses on the bandaging. Everything blackens before his eyes, but he must find the strength to retrieve the sheet of parchment and put it away safely in the press beside his bed. If it fell into the wrong hands, it would be sufficient to bring a charge of heresy down on his head. And, although he knows he is dying, and is therefore beyond the reach of a death sentence, still it would be another wearisome trial to have to face at this juncture. Indeed, he won't show this record of his final thoughts even to the abbot. The infirmary has fallen into silent shadow. That fool of an infirmarian fears being left on his own with him and has taken himself off again. If he has another seizure like the one he had this morning, there will be no one to stop the worst of it.

Outside it is almost dark. A solitary blackbird chirrups loudly from the highest branch of a nearby tree, a last salute to the dying day. He inches his way forward along the side of his pallet, then opens the press and carefully places the sheet of parchment at the back of it. Gingerly, he lowers himself onto the narrow pallet. Relief washes over him, even though he cannot stretch out fully.

His eyelids grow heavy. Ah, if only he could sleep. But the

images pursue him relentlessly. Since he regained consciousness, the flow of memories has been incessant, dogging his every waking breath, haunting his dreams.

At least when he had been unconscious he had not had to contend with these memories. Is there to be no let-up from them? All those far-off events, locked away somewhere: like demons they have rebelled and risen up to torment him. They encircle him in a taunting dance, prodding him until he is overcome with regrets and remorse; then they metamorphose horribly into crow-like visions of what is coming. Past and future stalk each other, the one jeering, the other despairing.

How could it have come to this?

Closing his eyes, he cups the crown of his head again and moans softly. The pain is intermittent, but thank the Lord it has not erupted into the agonising headache he had for most of yesterday. He makes the sign of the cross and his lips begin the *Our Father.* His breathing comes more evenly now and the sense of oppression begins to ease. But he cannot summon the concentration necessary to ponder the words as he ought.

The whispering is closing in around him now. A crackling rips through his head, bringing searing pain. He whimpers.

'Fear not, Canon Michael. I will assist you.'

He cannot turn his head, cannot even open his eyes. 'Father Abbot, is that you?'

'Yes, Michael, it is.' The abbot looks around him. He lets a few drops of wax fall from the candle he is carrying onto the small table to his left, then fixes another candle in it and lights the wick. 'Where is the infirmarian?'

With impeccable timing, the infirmarian steps back into the infirmary. He is bearing a compress and some cordial. 'Father Abbot, I absented myself so I could procure these medicaments for Canon Scot.'

The abbot's mouth settles into a thin line. 'Help me to make Canon Scot more comfortable.'

This accomplished, the infirmarian proceeds to bathe Michael Scot's forehead with cooling water; then he administers the cordial, which the patient swallows in a surprisingly docile fashion.

Propped up on the narrow infirmary pallet, Michael Scot stares listlessly at his hands. The abbot sits down on the stool at the foot of the pallet and watches as, with painful slowness, Canon Michael brings his eyes to bear on his own. What, he wonders, is the peace of God? Where is it to be found? This elusive dynamic that he spends most of his time trying to disseminate within this monastery of San Giovanni degli Eremiti. If, in all these years, he had managed to make even the smallest breach in the invisible wall separating the divine from the earthly, to let even a trickle of this healing essence through, he would gladly give it all to the gaunt man in front of him, the stillness of his posture belied by the haunted intensity of the eyes.

'The peace of our Lord be with you, Canon Michael,' murmurs the abbot.

Michael Scot looks away, back down at his hands. No reply disturbs the air. The abbot's hand enfolds the crucifix on his chest. Those grey eyes. What once had been flashes of quicksilver are now murky.

'How are you feeling?' The abbot stands up to get a better look at the bandage around Canon Michael's head. The bleeding has been staunched, but there has been a disconcerting deterioration in his face and general demeanour. The cheeks are suddenly sunken, while the unkempt tufts of white hair, hidden under that metal skullcap, day and night, for the past three years, are now visible again. Their disarray underlines a deeper aura of defeat.

The abbot recalls the shock of his first glimpse of the skullcap. How his remonstrations with the man had been useless. The benign properties of the metal, Canon Michael had stated with slow deliberation, served to keep his severe headaches in check and were crucial to his well-being. The abbot had been sceptical of these sudden headaches, but faced with Canon Michael's mounting obduracy, he had given way. For a time the skullcap had passed unnoticed beneath the hood of his cowl, but inevitably it was spotted, giving rise to comment and then rife speculation. The abbot had been obliged to let slip details in certain quarters in order to offset the more inimical conjectures. And this in its turn had given rise to jealousy among the monks that the abbot had seen fit once again to make an exception of Canon Scot.

With the benefit of hindsight, if he had it all to do again, would he still make the same choices? Has he been as fair as he ought to with his monks, or has he indeed let his better judgement be clouded by his respect and, latterly, sympathy for this outsider?

When he looks back up, Michael Scot is observing him.

The silence grows heavy and the abbot is moved to break it. 'Canon Michael, I am glad to see that your injury is healing.'

Michael Scot slowly folds his arms. He raises an eyebrow. 'And what brings you to that happy conclusion?'

'The dressing on your head is clean,' the abbot replies evenly. 'The bleeding has stopped.'

A frown settles on Michael Scot's face. 'Mars was in Aries in my sixth house; there's nothing to be done for a head injury.'

'Look here, Canon Michael,' the abbot says briskly, removing a missive from his pocket, 'the emperor desires news of you.'

Michael Scot looks up and the abbot hands him the piece of parchment. He reads it and then nods slowly.

'The emperor wishes you to come before him in the Green Hall, after which he invites you to a private audience. Are you well enough to sustain this?' The abbot pauses. 'It is an untimely request, but one that cannot well be evaded.'

'I will do what I must. The vipers' nest has to be faced.'

The abbot notes that the copious sweating has abated.

'You see,' Michael Scot's voice becomes more urgent, 'I must speak to the emperor. But before I do that,' – his eyes briefly meet those of Hugo de Clermont – 'I must speak with you, Father Abbot.'

'Speak, Canon Michael. Tell me what is troubling you.'

There is a brief silence, then Michael Scot says, 'I need your help and advice. You know I do.'

The abbot's stomach gives a lurch, but he keeps his expression impassive. 'I do, Canon Michael, I do. Let us resume the talk we started this Monday past in the library. You can open your heart to me,' he adds, his hand enfolding the crucifix, 'for nothing is ever so serious that it cannot be brought before the Lord.'

'Ah – but these are matters that I have already brought before the Lord. And I find myself wondering now how much is ours to choose and how much is preordained.'

The abbot stares fixedly at him. Then his eyes dart over to the infirmarian, who is endeavouring to look busy over by the window.

The abbot raises his forefinger to his lips. He calls out to the infirmarian. 'You may leave,' he tells him. 'Do not return until I summon you.'

'I refer,' takes up Michael Scot, 'to the skullcap first of all, and then to the visions I mentioned to you last Monday concerning the emperor and his empire.' He looks up at the abbot, but their eyes do not quite meet. He shakes his head slowly. 'Such vistas of ruination…'

The abbot closes his eyes, then runs a hand over the white stubble on his face. 'One thing at a time, Canon Michael. Let us start with the skullcap.'

'The skullcap is quite clear to me now; but understanding of the visions is still cloudy.'

'Start from the beginning and omit nothing.'

Michael Scot sighs. 'I have known for three years that the cause of my death would be a stone falling on my head. I first saw it in a vision.' The abbot's eyes widen, but he says nothing. 'I had been engaged in carrying out a horoscope for the emperor and could not resist doing one for myself. I broke one of the first rules of astrology and looked into my own future. Would that I had not.'

'And that is why you took to wearing the metal skullcap?'

Michael Scot nods slowly. 'And what a ludicrous attempt to avoid the inevitable it has turned out to be. I would have been better off knowing nothing. That way, at least, I could have saved myself the humiliation of cowering my way through these past three years.'

As Canon Michael speaks, Hugo de Clermont reflects on the bizarre occurrence. Certainly, it defies any rational explanation. It is unsettling enough that Canon Michael should have seen this in a horoscope; but he has come to appreciate – albeit most unwillingly – that what Canon Michael sees, through whatever glass darkly, is usually the truth in some form. What really troubles him, therefore, is not that the event foreseen should actually have come to pass. No. Rather is it the *manner* in which it did. For it must have depended on such a great coincidence of timing. Half a minute later and the skullcap would have been back on, and in all likelihood far less damage done. Most disquieting. Best to say nothing of this for the moment. 'Well,' he says bracingly in reply to Michael Scot, 'the worst has indeed happened: the stone has fallen, the skullcap was of no use – and yet you are still with us.'

Michael Scot glances sharply at the abbot. 'Be that as it may,' he says, 'the injury will nevertheless be working its mischief inside my skull. Death could come at any moment.'

'The same could be said for all of us.'

Michael Scot shrugs.

'But the visions,' pursues the abbot, 'let us return to them.'

'Ah – the visions.' Michael Scot closes his eyes. 'As I told you, the visions seem to show that the emperor's hopes for his empire will come to naught. I saw city after city in the north of Italy laying down a challenge and, siege after siege, the emperor's power inexorably eroded. The Lombard League gaining the upper hand. And the betrayal by his son in Germany. Treason from unexpected quarters at court. The dragon in Rome, hoarding power and breathing fire, laying waste the emperor's plans. And then the emperor himself—'

Michael Scot's voice cracks. Fleetingly, the assessing, unblinking gaze of a six-year-old orphan passes before his eyes.

'What of the emperor?' urges the abbot.

'An untimely death awaits him, too. In a city of the flower. Florence probably, before gates of iron.'

Silence falls on the infirmary. This is information of a different calibre. Being in possession of it places Canon Michael Scot in grave danger. What is to be done?

'The time has come,' Michael Scot says, breaking the silence. 'There is so little of it left. I must go.'

'Go? Go where?'

'Home.'

The abbot observes him for a moment. 'Home, you say.' The bristles on his face make a rasping sound as he rubs them meditatively. 'This,' he says eventually, 'may indeed be the best solution. But for the moment you are in no fit condition to take on the physical hardship such a journey entails.' Or the mental strain, he adds silently to himself. 'However, the idea is a good one, and I will see what can be done to assist you.'

'I ask this in the name of the goodwill that has existed between us over these long, difficult years, for truly I shall not ask anything else of you.' Some of the old fire flickers through Michael Scot's eyes. 'Release me that I may return home to die.'

The abbot's eyes close for a moment. Were the content of these visions to come to light, Canon Michael would make such enemies for himself, both in the Church and the imperial administration, that he would find himself facing a double charge: of heresy for speaking of the pope in such terms; and treason for sabotaging the emperor's imperial plans.

With a sense of grave misgiving, the scene in the library early on Monday morning comes back to him. Canon Michael had intimated there was something urgent he wished to tell him, and they had gone to the library to talk undisturbed.

Time was pressing, as they were due in church for Terce, and Canon Michael had been brief. But barely had he been apprised of the gist of these visions when out of the corner of his eye he had seemed to glimpse a hooded figure slip quietly out of the door. He had thought they were alone. It is true that they had spoken softly, but even so, enough had been said to compromise them. He had followed the figure as quickly as he could, but the corridor outside the library was empty, as was the surrounding area.

Whoever it was had been in a hurry to make good their escape.

Dangerous times, reflects the abbot. But if Canon Michael were indeed suddenly to disappear – and only he and the emperor needed to know where to – it would put him beyond the reach of the court administration. First, however, these ruinous predictions should be secretly entrusted to the emperor, who would then be in a position to combat them. The abbot nods. 'You have my blessing, Michael.'

He stands up and goes over to the door. 'Infirmarian,' he calls out into the dark corridor. 'Step back in.' The infirmarian reappears and the abbot directs him to assess Canon Scot's state of health. Is he well enough to withstand a trip to the Norman Palace? The infirmarian checks the patient's pulse and temperature. 'He is very weak,' he tells the abbot, 'but I shall give him some more cordial. At present he has no headache, so if he is wrapped up well, and does not stay from his bed too long, he may bear up.'

'Very well,' replies the abbot. He helps Canon Michael up from the pallet. 'The banquet has already begun in the Green Hall. After which I shall accompany you to the private audience in King Ruggero's chamber.' He grips his arm. 'Let us go now.'

It will not be an easy encounter. Between them they will have to steer a course over perilous terrain, sidestepping the quicksand of political treason by pointing the emperor in the direction of will-o'-the-wisp visions.

VI

'It's a question of loyalty,' states Pier delle Vigne. 'Not just a question of increased taxes. The emperor has need of more monies for his campaigns, and the onus is on the barons to show their loyalty through financial support.'

Don Ruggero hawks loudly and spits onto the rush-strewn floor of the Green Hall, causing Pier delle Vigne to turn on his heel and walk off.

'I would not be so intemperate in my treatment of our friend,' murmurs Don Filippo. 'He is very powerful, you know.'

Don Ruggero shrugs. 'Powerful thanks to what is not his.'

Don Filippo looks up at him. The northern skin, hardened by exposure to the southern sun, is rough and leathery. Red cheeks latticed with veins, one of which bears a long purple scar. Deep lines furrowing his forehead. Crows' feet round the eyes, etched palely against the tan. Eyes used to squinting into the glare of the Mediterranean sunlight. A face that looks older than its forty-two years. But the vitality is that of a man in his prime. Ever the bluff soldier, he is like a fish out of water in the intricacies of court protocol. Don Filippo places a restraining hand on Don Ruggero's arm. 'Powerful and dangerous. For he is also greedy. And sooner or later he will find a way to feed his greed. You mark my words.'

Both sets of eyes settle on Pier delle Vigne and silently observe his progress through the assembled guests.

Don Ruggero sketches a bow and moves off to one of the laden tables. He helps himself to a goblet of wine mixed with water, and knocks back two mouthfuls. Insufferable. Each time he comes to one of these confounded banquets, he vows it will be his last, and yet, here he is again. Well, there is nothing for it – he must find out about these latest developments from Rome. Unlike that scribbling sycophant, delle Vigne, if the emperor has plans to be on the move again with his army, it will affect him directly.

His mind turns to the recent devastating flood in Rome. The famine and pestilence it has brought in its wake have broken down the defences of the inhabitants, and they have been clamouring for the pope to return from Perugia, where they had effectively forced him into exile. Don Ruggero swirls the wine round in the goblet and takes another mouthful. An enforced sojourn of almost two years at this stage. Now the flood has been making the pro-imperial Romans wonder whether they have not brought down an act of divine retribution on their heads. From all accounts, his Holiness is not inclined to waste this opportunity and has made his way back in all haste to the Papal See.

He appears to have set aside his anti-imperial campaign, heretics now being the new target for papal chastisement. Against these enemies of Christendom, Pope Gregory IX is now expending his considerable energies; word has it that he might even sue for peace with the emperor and make him an ally in this latest battle.

It is difficult to know how much store to set by these rumours. Events following the emperor's return from his victorious crusade are still very fresh in Don Ruggero's mind. He scans the assembled courtiers in the Green Hall and sees a considerable number of knights who fought with him alongside the emperor on his return from Jerusalem. How ironic that they had not even had to unsheathe their swords in the Holy Land, only to find themselves on their return fighting for survival in a Sicily overrun by marauding papal troops.

Don Ruggero takes a final mouthful from the goblet and puts it down on the table. His eye lights on Goffredo Lo Clerico. Now here's someone from whom it might be possible to get some sense. Lo Clerico is a senior notary in the chancellery: a life spent compiling documents behind the scenes means that he just might favour him with a dispassionate evaluation of the situation in Rome.

He is about to beckon Lo Clerico over, when an image of his young wife, Adelasia, materialises in his mind's eye, and his half-raised hand falls back down to his side. She stands there as he saw her this morning, smiling shyly at him, a hand resting on her swollen belly. She is carrying his third child.

His first two sons are practically strangers to him, their childhoods fleeting by as campaign followed on campaign. Never before has home seemed like such an oasis to Don Ruggero. He has maintained the family tradition of loyalty to the crown, coming always to the emperor's aid in his various struggles: against the insurgent barons, then in clearing the land of the rebellious Saracens, and ultimately in his crusade to Jerusalem. He has spent his life fighting for the order that the emperor's rule brings with it; his own home – castle and estate – would benefit now from a strong guiding hand. God willing, there will be a respite from military campaigns. As he raises his hand again to beckon to Goffredo Lo Clerico, he becomes aware of silence falling over the Green Hall like ice extending a crippling grip over a pond, except for one high-pitched, wavering voice that continues with a certain nervous determination.

Don Ruggero glances over at the diminutive Don Filippo: the old man has kept up a stream of comments that are reverberating round the silent hall. Surely observations of such startling banality as he is directing at Goffredo Lo Clerico do not deserve the effort he is investing in their enunciation. More especially as his interlocutor's eyes have swung away towards the door. Don Ruggero's do likewise.

There stands Master Michael Scot.

*

Framed by the shadowy doorway, Michael Scot's tall figure is enveloped in a forbidding black cloak. As he steps forward into the Green Hall, the flickering orange of the torchlight falls with mottled intermittency on the darkness of the cloak, and he seems to elongate grotesquely. A murmur runs through the courtiers, a few of whom take a step backwards.

Hugo de Clermont, abbot of San Giovanni degli Eremiti, appears from behind him and calmly surveys the multitude of courtiers. His eye comes to rest on Pier delle Vigne, who elects not to hold it. With slow deliberation both men make their way up towards the throne and take a stand to the right of it.

In a powerful swell, a deluge of voices now washes through the hall, drowning out Don Filippo's tremulous falsetto. Michael Scot helps himself to water.

And then, in another sudden switch, a hush descends. Heads begin to bow in obeisance. The emperor walks briskly into the hall, a noontime sun followed in his progress to the throne by a field of sunflowers.

In a respectful silence the emperor seats himself and composes his rich garments. In truth, he is rather dwarfed by the throne. It is, however, a consideration that his subjects do not permit themselves to dwell on; the awe that his rule has instilled in them precludes it. The Saracens showed no such delicacy of scruple when they came in contact with him in Jerusalem. They evaluated him as being short of stature and lacking in hair. Had his Imperial Highness been put up for sale in the slave market, they surmised, he would hardly have fetched the price of a mangy camel. These failings passed rapidly into the background when they had occasion to test the brilliance of his mind. It is very much in evidence in the astute enamel blue eyes that pass over his courtiers.

'Master Scot!' he says loudly. The silence intensifies and quivers in inquisitive expectancy. He extends his right hand and Michael Scot moves forward. Under the watchful eyes of the courtiers, The Scot comes to a standstill in front of the throne. Slowly, he falls onto one knee – the left one, notes Pier delle Vigne – and then raises the extended hand to his lips, kissing the large ring on the fourth finger. The emperor rises.

'Most esteemed among my learned men,' he says loudly, his voice directed at the courtiers. Then his eye falls back onto the bowed head below him. He places a hand on Michael Scot's shoulder. 'Indeed I am glad to see you here this evening.'

A spasm passes over Pier delle Vigne's face.

Swiftly, the emperor helps Master Scot to his feet. 'We shall adjourn to King Ruggero's chamber after the banquet for a talk.'

Michael Scot bows as a murmur builds up among the courtiers.

*

They make an incongruous picture, Don Filippo muses: the older man towering over the younger, despite his stoop, and the apparent frailty of the younger belied by the evident support he is giving to the older.

It makes Don Filippo very uneasy to see the way Master Scot is treated by the courtiers. This is what induced him to draw attention to himself in such an ill-advised fashion just now. It cannot be right that these rumours and hostilities follow the man like a swarm of buzzing flies. Despite his life's mission of discretion in all things, it was fitting that there be some splinter in the wall of silence that greeted Master Scot. Above all, following this terrible accident. He is glad therefore of the emperor's demonstration of regard for the man. But then, this will only have served to fan the flames of envy in quarters where they had already been crackling hungrily. What age is Master Scot now, he wonders. He must be tipping fifty-five.

From the height of his seventy-five years, he feels an almost paternal interest in this man who has made such a lasting impression on Palermo.

His acquaintance with Master Michael Scot goes back a decade. It was to his large town house that Master Scot was sent to lodge following his return to Palermo from Toledo in 1220. Don Filippo had been very put out by this high-handed invasion of his property and privacy, above all by such an outlandish foreigner. How could this fail to draw attention to him? But his duties as courtier had to be carried out, even at the cost of going against his deepest inclinations.

Don Filippo has a horror of doing the wrong thing and being seen to do the wrong thing. Of standing out. Of drawing the envious or malevolent attention of men to himself, and thus setting in motion the workings of blind and callous fate. He comes of a long-established family of landed gentry. The family's prime objective has always been that of maintaining the status quo, for there is too much to be lost for any notions of change to be entertained: the family title and standing, a large estate out near Cefalù, the beautiful house in Palermo. This was instilled in Don Filippo from the beginning. He was the only boy in a family of girls, so it fell to him to husband the family's prestige and wealth.

And this he has done exceptionally well. He has lost nothing that was entrusted to him. In such violent times, it often seems like a miracle to have got this far unscathed. For this he is very thankful. The fewer enemies you make, the fewer nasty surprises you lay up for yourself. If life is like taking a bull by the horns, he has inched his discreet way round it, bit by bit, until now he stands in sight of the end.

Certainly, he has not gained anything either. He has never married. He has no children. It is his nephew who will inherit the fruits of so much painstaking prudence. His nephew is already running the estate, while he lives quietly in town. A nephew he hardly ever sees and with whom he has nothing in common.

He watches as Master Scot makes his way to the banqueting table. Immediately to the emperor's right sits Hugo de Clermont, and to his right, Master Michael Scot. His appearance is disconcertingly haggard; his prime is well gone, too.

How different a figure he is now from the man who made his triumphant return to the court in Palermo from Toledo. Master Michael Scot had successfully carried out the emperor's injunction to bring the erudition of Aristotle to a knowledge-starved Christendom. For the ten years between 1210 and 1220, he had buried himself in the writings of the Moors, and from these gleaned and translated the lost works of Aristotle.

It had been an epic task.

But what has become of these translations? Don Filippo shakes his head and reflects that they are probably languishing in some dark corridor of the administration, tucked away in an even darker cupboard. It is hard to say why.

And this must have been hard for Master Scot to bear. Certainly, the direction his restless, enquiring mind has taken over this past decade cannot be considered felicitous. While Don Filippo does not condone the behaviour of the courtiers, he can see all too well how it has come about. For who can forget the sight of Master Michael Scot upon his return from Toledo, entering the Green Hall before the assembled court in Moorish garb?

The consternation brought on by this sight – a man of the Church attired like a Mohammedan – has followed in Master Scot's wake like a shadow of iniquity, a shadow that has obscured the brilliance of his achievements. For man is ever ready to be stirred up in the abomination of the allegedly scandalous rather than setting himself to an analysis of the facts.

The facts in this case are not easily ascertainable. It would take somebody of goodwill to give himself the trouble of uncovering them, but where Master Michael Scot is concerned, goodwill is in very short supply. And at some stage over this last decade, the rumour that Master Scot's uncanny proficiency in drawing up horoscopes was due to the devilish use he had made of Moorish sorcery, became accepted as fact.

The court had delivered its judgment on him.

VII

'A word, my Lord Abbot, if you have a moment.'

Something about the intentness of Don Filippo's eyes gives Hugo de Clermont pause for thought. 'Of course,' he replies. Don Filippo turns to Canon Michael and salutes him warmly. 'I am glad to see you here this evening, Master Scot.' He places a hand on his shoulder. 'May I wish you a speedy and complete recovery.' The shadow of a smile flickers over Michael Scot's face. He nods, and then looks away.

Turning back to the abbot, Don Filippo says, 'Let us adjourn to that corner. We shall be in full view of everyone, but we shall not be overheard.' The abbot's ears prick up and he follows Don Filippo through the throng of courtiers.

Their backs to the walls, Don Filippo takes his place at Hugo de Clermont's side, so that they do not stand facing one another, but look together out on the sea of faces before them in the Green Hall. The older man's voice barely rises above a discreet murmur.

'I have just overheard a conversation,' starts Don Filippo, 'which I think you need to be made aware of immediately.' He proceeds to recount the gist of an exchange that has just taken place between Pier delle Vigne and Giovanni da Messina, his expression throughout, as he surveys the courtiers milling about the Green Hall, an unchanging one of unperturbed equanimity.

He had been standing behind a column minding his own

business and, through no fault of his own other than that occasioned by a lack of girth and height, was not noticed by the two functionaries. They were discussing the imminent arrival – for he was expected at the banquet – of the Grand Master of the Teutonic Knights. 'Apparently, he is carrying intelligence of the rapprochement delle Vigne is pushing for between the emperor and the pope.' Don Filippo pauses in his account to smile pleasantly at an acquaintance to his right, inclining his head. 'But what I believe you'll find of particular interest,' he takes up, 'is the use that delle Vigne intends to make of the Grand Master's communication.'

Taking care not to turn towards Don Filippo, Hugo de Clermont asks, 'And what might that be?'

'They intend to place Canon Scot in an entirely unfavourable light by highlighting how the controversy surrounding him, both as a translator of material tainted with heresy and as a proficient in the dark arts, represents the single greatest obstacle to a successful conclusion of the process delle Vigne has set in train.'

The abbot takes care that his expression not alter. 'Is that so...'

Don Filippo catches another courtier's eyes and smiles benignly. 'His assistant then offered his congratulations on having laid a trap for Master Scot that not even his skill as a necromancer could extricate him from. They mentioned something about turning the tables on him. Something about the treasonous nature of his – er – his soothsaying. How it undermines morale...' Don Filippo's voice trails away.

The abbot digests this in silence. Don Filippo continues to survey the procession of courtiers before them with studied detachment. Eventually, the abbot says, 'This is timely news, for which I thank you. I am in your debt.'

'Think nothing of it, my Lord Abbot. I had the good fortune to be in the right place at the right time. And then, with old age comes the invisibility of the unthreatening; it might surprise you how people mislay their discretion.'

Michael Scot's eyes desultorily observe the yammering crowd of courtiers. He has placed himself as far away from them as he can, since the last thing he wants is for their noisy chattering to set off another headache. He starts to yawn, but it dies in his throat as his eye comes to light on Giovanni da Messina who, in an act of uncharacteristic bonhomie, has just clapped another functionary on the back. Michael Scot stares. There is nothing exceptional in such a gesture, but a dim sensation of déjà vu has flashed through his mind. Why would that be?

His eyes latch on to the lackey now, following his movements. They hone in on the man's face, examining his expressions. From this remove, he cannot hear what he is saying, but the demeanour is all pompous complacency, with a hint of barely suppressed pugnaciousness. Da Messina is beginning to show himself in his true colours. What has made him feel so secure?

And then the memory washes over him. The merest flash, but enough to place the déjà vu. For he now remembers the sudden darkness in the infirmary last night; he remembers the hand coming out of the darkness and a blow being administered to him; remembers his feeble struggle with the two hands pressing a cloth into his nose and mouth; and – yes – he remembers the faint outline of the figure looming over him. He remembers, too, the liquefying sense of relief at the sound of approaching steps hurrying over the flagstones of the echoing corridor outside. And then the hands releasing their hold and the shove that made him fall heavily to the floor.

What devilment had been afoot?

He calls the abbot over and relates what his memory has recovered. 'And,' he adds, 'there is something else you should know about that pair of weasels.' He relates how he had come on them rifling through his horoscopes in his study, and the vision that had come to him of Pier delle Vigne having his eyes plucked out for treason.

'Did you relate this vision to delle Vigne?'

'I did.'

The abbot's eyes widen. He takes a moment to compose himself and then turns to Canon Michael. 'This is worse than I feared.'

Michael Scot's eyes close in a grimace of pain, 'I feel another seizure coming on.'

The abbot takes in the shivering that now grips Canon Michael. He must act immediately.

No one can witness this or they are undone. Keeping his head lowered, he scans that Green Hall, sees that they are not being observed at that moment, and takes Canon Michael under the elbow. He steers him rapidly in the direction of the nearest door. 'Fortitude,' he urges, 'now is the moment for fortitude.'

The darkness of the corridor is a blessed relief. It is dimly lit by just a couple of torches. Michael Scot groans softly. 'Come this way,' the abbot presses him. 'I can bring you to the room where I sometimes hear the emperor's confession. I have the key with me.' The clamour of voices from the Green Hall recedes as they progress down the corridor, at the end of which the abbot turns right. He extracts a key from his pocket and uses it to gain access to the first room on the left.

The abbot removes a candle and taper from the shelf just inside the door and returns to the corridor. From a nearby torch he lights the candle. With its dim light, he walks back into the room and closes the door. He guides Michael Scot over to a settle by the wall.

'Lie down now, Canon Michael. I can only hope that I am doing the right thing leaving you here – I feel that you will be out of harm's way.' The abbot joins his hands as if he were about to pray, but he brings them to his lips and pauses. 'I believe that we are both now in danger. You, Canon Michael, for the risk you pose to delle Vigne, and me, on account of what delle Vigne must have guessed I know. I have to return to the Green Hall and persuade the emperor that it is a matter of the utmost urgency for him to speak to you before he concedes an audience to delle Vigne.' The abbot shakes his head. 'Delle Vigne has been plotting assiduously and I fear that, if the emperor should speak first to him, it will go exceedingly ill for us.' Removing the key to the room from his pocket, he holds it up to Michael Scot. 'It is not safe for you to return to the infirmary. So, to avoid any further danger, I am going to lock the door after me. Until I come back and free you, you will not be able to get out; but more to the point, neither will any ill-intentioned person be able to get in.'

He walks over to the door. 'I have left you some water,' he points to a jug and goblet on the nearby table, 'and I have also taken the precaution of removing your personal writings from the press beside your pallet in the infirmary. We don't want them falling into the wrong hands. You will find everything on the table.' He pauses, raises his hand in a blessing, and adds, 'I will come for you when it is time. Be of good hope, Canon Michael.'

The key turns in the lock from the outside.

*

He feels so hot; the sweat is running into his eyebrows and down his temples. Whispered phrases wheel round, the whispering dropping on him like snowflakes fizzling onto the molten lead of his head. He attempts to wipe the sweat away, but realizes that he is shivering. Unbearably cold. Only now does Michael Scot admit how much the effort of parading himself in front of the court has taken out of him. Slowly, terrified to upset whatever precarious balance still separates him from plummeting into the agony of a seizure, he eases his way fully onto the settle. The silence and the warm glow from the candle are restful. Please God this will get no worse; once again, were the seizure to return, there would be no one to see him through it. He struggles to clear his mind of all thoughts. No whispering welter of thoughts. Nothing that will tip him over into a seizure.

Michael Scot sighs, a faint, ragged exhalation. The stillness of the room soothes him and he is grateful for this. He lets himself be cradled by it for a long while. He rejoices in the sense of torpor that creeps over him, knowing that as it advances, so do the chances of a seizure retreat. As he pulls back from the brink, his mind wanders off, falling into a reverie. Gradually, the thoughts resurface and begin to scatter in eddying circles, like fallen leaves toyed with by the autumn wind.

If he were to die here, now, this very evening – what would his life have amounted to?

He keeps his eyes closed and lets himself hover above some formless chasm. The past stretches away into unreachable darkness; will anything speak to him from it? And gradually it comes to him, with a bittersweet sense of loss, that there is no surge; no wave of knowing; no losing of himself in some guiding current of awareness.

It is gone.

Alone on a shoreline, he stands looking out on the swell of the ocean and sees the bright streak of horizon grow dim. What now? What is left to him?

With a great effort he withdraws his gaze from the horizon, bringing it to bear on his hands. Each holds a manuscript. He raises them to eye level: the manuscript in his right hand bears the title *De anima* and the names Aristotle and Averroës; that in his left, *At-Tasrif* and the name Albucasis. His translation, and medicine.

In the advancing twilight he sits down on the sandy shoreline, the only sound the sigh of lapping waves, and places both manuscripts before him on his lap. He looks to the left. Medicine. That two-edged sword: safeguard of life and destroyer of life. Ah, but it had taken him decades before he finally gave in and set to its study. He had resisted its pull until he was thirty-seven; but there had been good reasons for this, of course.

He twitches, not at all sure he wants this memory, not now.

His eyes open and he stares unseeingly in front of him. No – if he were to die here, now, tonight, he needs to make his peace with the chaos. And he can count only on his strength, for every other force has abandoned him.

Medicine. When finally he had given in, a highroad had unfurled leading him to the position of emperor's physician. But it had not been his first choice. Ever since he was a child medicine had been a shadowy force in his head, both preserver and destroyer of life, an unraveller of destinies. His mother was a healer and he had become a physician. And here he is, sitting under a death sentence after a stone has dropped on his head; what then is he to make of the malevolent, brutal force of stones in his mother's destiny...

His eyes [illegible] and he [illegible] in front of him. No— [illegible]
[illegible] to make his [illegible]
[illegible]. And he [illegible]
[illegible]

[illegible] had [illegible]
[illegible] but [illegible]
[illegible]
[illegible] of life
[illegible] and he [illegible]
[illegible]
[illegible]
[illegible]

Scotia

VIII

AD 1183

What is home? Where is it to be found? He too had been born in a particular place, at a particular time, to certain parents. But his parents had been taken from him and the place had never felt like home. He had spent his childhood being found blameworthy because of an accident of birth; always looked at askance because of his provenance; having to justify his every action purely because of this accident of birth. This is what home was to him, a place where he was kept at arm's length, and this is what he escaped from. Yet he has never managed to put enough miles between himself and this pain, which at most has been quieted, but never extinguished.

His father was from the Borders; his mother from the Highlands. What accident of fate had brought about their meeting? She must have loved him, for she left all that was dear to her and followed his father to his own part of the country.

They had never let her forget her outsider status. Why had she been perceived as such a threat? It was true she was self-contained, but – and it always gives him a pang – he can still feel the spark of kindness that leaped from her silver-grey eyes as they came to rest on him. The quiet empathy that emanated from her in her dealings with the sick.

In the midst of the industrious seeking after prosperity and influence of her husband's family, her retiring ways won her no allies. There had always been those that attributed her continuing attachment to solitary walks as evidence of wilful pride. Then it became a peculiarity. He could not put a finger on the moment when it had eventually been ascribed to something more sinister.

She earned some respite for herself when she managed to heal an elderly relative. The family physician had failed to get rid of a fever that had debilitated the man to the point almost of unconsciousness. Then she had come forward with a poultice and cordial, applied the one and helped him drink the other. A miracle! A miracle! they had shouted, when the man was restored fully to health.

That had been the beginning of it. Every time the family and then the village had need of a healing, they went to her. And all the while the physician had nurtured his rancorous dislike of her.

The family and the villagers who crowded to her door, did so with reluctance. Their hostility towards the woman grew proportionately with their need. With all the malice of his belittled status, the physician sneered at them and at her. How could she, a mere uncouth Highlander, know any of this? And why were they such fools as to trust her?

Then Michael's father had been killed participating in a raid on a neighbouring territory. The death of his father left him a prey not only to grief, but to some nameless dread, the weight of which fell on his boyish heart like a pall.

His mother no longer had a man to defend her. Gradually, she found herself isolated. The clans-people's grudging respect was now too laced with hostility to permit regular contact; a volatile sentiment that seemed ever ready to explode into something else. Slowly, the small boy had watched the spark drain from his mother's eye, powerless to prevent it. More and more she kept to herself.

When it was born, the baby had seemed healthy. The firstborn son of one of her dead husband's kin. She had not been present at the birth or been called upon, but she heard that it had been a long and difficult lying-in. The mother's life in the balance. The father distraught. The infant handed out immediately to a wet nurse. The new mother had fallen into a fever-induced sleep from which she rarely awoke. But his own mother had awoken in the night with a scream; she had had one of her visions. She hastened to see the infant boy: hers was the only voice counselling a herb poultice to eliminate blockages. Scorn was poured on the idea. The infant was crying lustily, even if he hadn't as yet suckled. She had come back repeatedly and silently wrung her hands as every attempt to offer her herbs was rebuffed. Finally, the door was slammed in her face. The new mother, having recovered some strength, had come to hear of her visits and was fretting in case she had hexed the infant.

The little body was found in its crib, stone cold and blue round the mouth.

They had come looking for her, the father and the wet nurse's family, trailed by the villagers. The word 'witch' had echoed menacingly outside the door. And then it had started. They broke down the door and dragged her out by the hair, screaming. Terrified, he had hidden in the clothes chest under the stairs. The roaring and the yells reached him, interspersed with her screams, until the screams came no more.

They had stoned her. Her face so disfigured that he was not let look at her body when it was buried.

He was eight years old when it happened.

His father's family had looked after him, they had done their duty by the boy. But it was from them he learned the extent to which he must have taken after his mother. Mostly through silence. The eyes that followed him everywhere. The disapproving silence that would fall following an observation on his part. The awkward act of kindness that shrivelled into confused or hostile silence when it encountered his silver-grey eyes. What was given to him with one hand was always taken away with the other; what his blood entitled him to, his blood also rendered him unworthy of.

Second sight. For so long he had wanted no part of it, as it brought only misery and destruction. But as he had come to realise, while he was indeed his father's son, of the prosperous Scots of Fife, even more was he his mother's, with her gift for healing and discernment.

Mathematics then, and not medicine, had been his chosen path of study. Here his intuitive grasp of the discipline was all he needed to forge ahead, and his brilliance became apparent to his masters at the school attached to the local church. Putting all taint of visions and discernment behind him, he had left Scotland at a precocious age, headed for Oxford University. He was taken under the Church's wing, and he willingly gave himself up to the ascetic rigour of the cleric's life.

In Oxford, during the Trivium, he had made himself noted in Grammar, Logic and Rhetoric. Mathematical renown had followed him from his school studies. And so, as the University of Paris offered the best course in mathematics, he was advised to proceed to the Quadrivium there. His mentor, and fellow Premonstratensian, would be no less a personage than Stephen de Provins, advisor to the pope on matters of orthodoxy.

But before leaving for Paris had come that chance meeting with a returning crusader. The figure of Hugo de Rocelin stands out in his memory as large as life now as it had seemed to him then, a young man of twenty, flush with the triumph of his first public recognition as a young man of brilliance.

It was 1195 and he had just graduated, coming first in his year. De Rocelin, the father of one of his fellow students, had come back from the Third Crusade. Into the hushed, cloistered confines of Oxford University had come this crusader, seemingly invincible on his battle horse, bearing tales of the wonders and terrors that lay beyond the sea.

With him had come the names of Richard the Lionheart. And Saladin. The Levant and the holy city of Jerusalem. Evocations of great expanses of barren desert; oases and date-laden palm trees.

It had started with the retaking of Jerusalem by Saladin in 1187.

The Third Crusade had got under way in 1189. De Rocelin had sailed to mild-climed France and then on to the island of Sicily, a bridge to the Levant with its flowering, many-hued gardens and heat-filled summers. The crusaders had seized the cities of the Levantine coast, Tyre, Acre and Jaffa, and gained inland territories as well. But they had not managed to wrest Jerusalem from Muslim control.

He had been honoured, said Hugo de Rocelin, to fight for a great and brave king; but even more, it had been his privilege to fight at a time when his foe was of equal stature. For the world, said Hugo de Rocelin, was a far greater and more mysterious place than he had suspected. And he had found courtesy where least he had thought to in the bravery and mercy shown by the great Saladin, whose words after his conquest of Jerusalem in 1187 had stayed with him: 'Victory is changing the heart of your opponents with gentleness and kindness.' There had been no massacres; whoever wanted to leave had been afforded safe passage and the right to worship in one's own faith had been upheld. Two giants among men – his king and his adversary – had achieved victory and suffered defeat; but the proof of their greatness lay in their rejection of wanton destruction.

For his own part the Lionheart had worked out a three-year treaty, ensuring safe passage for any pilgrim that visited the Holy Land. Despite his losses, Saladin had kept Jerusalem.

And that, de Rocelin had said, would be the root of the next crusade. For there would most certainly be another crusade.

The stories that de Rocelin told put him in mind, for the first time, of travel as an adventure, not just mere escape. Now he began to keenly anticipate his good fortune in securing a place at Paris University: here was the chance to put the narrow confines of his childhood home behind him and embark on a journey in the world of learning. A world of study and calculations, mathematics and astronomy, where logical reasonings were the motivating force of interaction.

Paris, France

IX

AD 1200

After two days of rioting, an autumn fog had descended on the *Montagne Sainte-Geneviève*, bringing an unreal silence to the Latin Quarter. At the top of the street winding down to the *Ile de la Cité*, Michael Scot stopped and peered. He could see no further than twenty paces ahead, but it was sufficient to make out the massive shadowy form of the barricade a little further down the hill. If it was still manned by the provost's guards, he would not be able to get past; only last night two students that shared lodgings with him near the abbey had been set upon by the night watch, severely beaten, and taken away to the provost's palace. Luckily, a third had managed to give them the slip and make it back to their lodgings, and he had explained to Michael Scot how to sidestep the barricade and go about his business.

If the rumours were right, once they had quelled the riot the provost's guards had returned to the palace; but he could not afford to take a chance and get caught. His meeting with Canon Stephen de Provins had already been delayed by two days and, knowing the older man as a stickler for form, there wasn't much leeway before his limited supply of patience ran out and their meeting postponed indefinitely. His future depended on what de Provins would tell him at this meeting – he had to get there this morning.

On either side of its effluence-filled central channel, the fog-shrouded street in front of him was littered with the debris of the struggle that had raged between students and citizenry. Splintered wood – smashed up furniture, logs, sticks and clubs – was scattered over its grimy cobblestoned surface. Here and there lay shattered crockery from the inn at the centre of the brawl. Michael Scot picked his way through them for a short stretch and then turned off into a narrow lane to the left.

This lane was not paved and his shoes slid on the filthy mud, nearly causing him to lose his footing. His hand shot out, coming to rest on the house-front within arm's reach. Indeed, the lane was barely wider than the span of his two arms and the tall, overhanging houses lining both sides of it all but blocked out the little light visible from the narrow strip of sky far above the noisome gloom.

Michael Scot lifted his habit and new black graduate's robe and proceeded carefully until he got to the first turn right. Circumspectly, he took a quick look round the corner, ascertained that this lane too was empty, and set off along the narrow track running parallel with the main street. The smell of burning wood coming from the houses on both sides was not unwelcome; it gave a sensation of warmth that offset the damp and fog all around him and covered other and worse odours.

He could see the river banks down ahead now. God willing, he would be in the library with Canon de Provins before the bells struck nine o'clock.

A knock broke the still silence in the library of Notre Dame's School of Theology. It was empty except for one small figure poring over a manuscript. Canon Stephen de Provins raised his head, looked at length at the door in front of him, and in a thin, high voice eventually uttered the monosyllable, 'Come.'

The door opened promptly to reveal Michael Scot. As the young Scotsman stooped to come in under the lintel, de Provins tried to quell the sense of irritation that coursed through him at the sight of Michael Scot in his new Master's gown. Ordinarily, the starkness of the white clerical habit and black gown should have mortified any earthly vanities, but in Master Scot's case it contrived to underline an aura of vigour. His former student always seemed to bring an element of the unruly with him: the very air seemed to surge, things seemed to happen faster. Too fast, indeed. Brilliance there was aplenty; but also waywardness. And Ecclesia was a stern mother who required humility and obedience from her sons. As his mentor, therefore, it was de Provins' duty to apply the necessary checks to the otherwise untrammelled ambition of the newly graduated Michael Scot, also known here in the Schools as Michael the Mathematician.

Stephen de Provins observed the long-limbed frame covering the space between them in three incisive steps and sat back into his chair, finding comfort in the feel of solid wood against his back. 'Well met, Master Scot.'

Michael Scot knelt before the older man, whose thin, white hands fluttered in a blessing over his head. 'Congratulations on your *licence*,' said de Provins. As Michael Scot stood up, Stephen de Provins found himself in the rather disagreeable position of having to tilt his neck backwards to an uncomfortable degree so as to maintain eye contact with the man. Blinking rapidly, he indicated that Michael Scot take the chair on the far side of the table.

Closing the manuscript, Stephen de Provins said, 'It must have been difficult for you to get here.'

'Not really.' Michael Scot shrugged. 'The barricades put up by the provost's guards are still in place all right, and there are a few of them doing the rounds even now, keeping students and the citizenry apart.' His face broke into a smile. 'But my students had tipped me off and I managed to avoid running into them.'

The wool of Michael Scot's habit dipped as he spread his legs; he placed his arms on the armrests and settled comfortably into the chair, which suddenly seemed too slight to contain him. De

Provins formed a pyramid with his hands, gently drumming the fingers together as his impassive eyes regarded his former student. No, as he had expected, there would be no apology from Master Scot for the tardiness of his arrival. And there he was, already referring with calm assurance to *his* students. The strange, ghostly light of this foggy day played with the red in the young man's beard and caught the silver in his eyes. But the eyebrows were dark and his hair was brown. Darkness in light, lightness in dark. So many contrasting shades in one physiognomy. The word 'unbiddable' came out of nowhere. 'Students,' replied de Provins, looking away into the middle distance, 'are not always models of good behaviour. While the citizenry, for the most part, is regrettably uncouth.'

Michael Scot caught the flicker in the older man's eyes.

'Almost as uncouth as the Scots,' de Provins concluded, 'but not quite. Of course, you must be well used to this kind of barbarity.'

What de Provins gave with one hand, he always took away with the other. Michael Scot turned his head away and looked out of the window. Sunlight had begun to palely illuminate the fog swirling like dragon's breath outside. A wind was getting up. 'Barbarity takes many guises,' he replied. 'Unfortunately, it seldom recognises itself as such.'

De Provins stood up and moved round the table beside Michael Scot's chair. His hand hovered close to the young Scotsman's shoulder, but fell short of actually touching it. 'There, there,' he murmured, not quite managing to rid his voice of an underlying relish, 'don't take it amiss. It was just a little jest.'

'Of course,' replied Michael Scot, 'and I congratulate you.' One eyebrow arched and he turned back to look at de Provins. 'For, rightly or wrongly, a sense of humour is not normally associated with a professor of Theology.'

Nettled, despite himself, de Provins compressed his lips. 'Be that as it may,' he replied, walking over to the window, 'it is precisely in my capacity as professor of Theology, as opposed to any alleged possession of a sense of humour, that I have the ear of the pope – and hence the capacity to help you in your future career.' De Provins sniffed and resumed his meditative finger-drumming.

'And that is why you have summoned me for this talk.'

'Indeed.' The finger-drumming ceased. 'I need to talk to you about new developments here in the Schools, and I have news for you about a position.' He started to pace up and down the room. Michael Scot looked down, fixing his eyes on his feet so he would not be distracted by de Provins' restless pacing. It was as he had imagined. He was facing a choice: either to continue his studies here in Paris, proceeding to a doctorate in theology under de Provins, and then staying on to lecture as a Master. Or accepting this new position, whatever it was. He folded his hands in his lap and willed himself into watchful stillness.

'Make no mistake,' commenced de Provins, the sudden tinny quality in his voice alerting Michael Scot that his mentor was now in the declaiming mode he reserved for lectures, so something of import was about to be communicated. 'Great deeds are afoot here in the Schools in Paris. It is a new century and change is in the air.' De Provins paused to tuck his hands into the wide sleeves of his habit and then resumed his pacing. The upshot of the all-too-frequent rioting between students and an easily exasperated citizenry, he explained, was that the Schools were about to get a charter from King Philippe which would create a new, self-governing entity, the *universitas*. 'The apparently banal brawl,' he observed, coming to a standstill, 'of not three days past between a Paris innkeeper and a German student, has brought things to a head between the chancellor and the provost. As you may be aware, they are representatives, respectively, of the archbishop and the king. Or, seen another way, of the two branches of power, the ecclesiastical and the secular, both of which have a stake in the Schools.'

De Provins paused. 'I feel myself to be removed from this,' he took up, his voice dropping to a more reflective murmur. 'Because above and beyond my position as professor of Theology, I am personal advisor to his Holiness. That means I have no part in the play for power here in Paris, I merely report on it.' He resumed his pacing. 'But report on it, I shall. These are very interesting developments and it is his Holiness' particular care that, if they be endowed with intelligence, the sheep in Mother Ecclesia's flock, no matter what their provenance or poverty, may find a way to put it to the greater good.' His voice regained in volume. 'His Holiness will be informed of the proceedings here so that he can decide which side has the best interests of the Lord's flock of sheep at heart, and lend them his support. This, however, might take some time. And the Lord's time is not mere mortals' time. Change is indeed in the air, but the fullness of time is needed before the greater good can be discerned.'

Silence fell in the library. Michael Scot did not stir and kept his gaze on his feet. Stephen de Provins walked slowly back over to the window. Once again he made a pyramid of his fingers and rested his lower lip on it. Master Scot and *his* students. For all the arrogance of this assumption, it was true that he already had a following in the Schools. Michael the Mathematician. He, de Provins, had seen with his own eyes how the young Scotsman held sway over his class of students. He had stepped into one of Master Scot's lectures and been struck by the enrapt silence in which the students hung on his every word. Undoubtedly, the man had a gift for teaching; this would stand him in good stead in this new position.

'The next step in your life,' de Provins took up, 'may not necessarily be in Paris. I took the liberty of informing his Holiness of the brilliance of your results in mathematics, and a position has been found for you as tutor to the young King Frederick of Sicily.'

De Provins abruptly turned to look at Michael Scot. 'How would you feel about that, Master Scot?'

'Sicily, you say?' Keeping his face impassive, Michael Scot rapidly took stock of his situation. It was clear that de Provins was pushing for Sicily, but he was also aware that were he to state outright what his preference was, de Provins – even against his own carefully laid plans – might instead grasp the opportunity to instil some humility in him by forcing him to take the other option. Staying on in Paris was the safer of the two, but if de Provins had decided that another course of action was more appropriate, there was no point in outstaying his welcome here. For that again, staying on in Paris meant theology and a life dedicated to its teaching. He did not want that. Whatever his interests, his talents lay elsewhere. First and foremost, mathematics. And Natural Philosophy. But talent was not a word that de Provins allowed him to use.

Hugo de Rocelin suddenly resurfaced in Michael Scot's memory, bringing with him images of the sun, heat, beauty and wonder. Yes – this was what he wanted. He wanted to travel to the ends of the earth, he wanted to see the mysterious places he had only heard tell of. He wanted to see the world in all its variety and learn about it. And he wanted to do this far from a stifling presence such as de Provins.

Better, however, to keep de Provins in the dark on this. 'What do you advise?' he asked, meekly.

De Provins' eyes flickered, not unappreciatively. 'Education,' he replied, 'is crucial – not only for the poor and ignorant – but also for sovereigns. Just as the Church has sponsored you in your studies, it will be your task now to further the Church's interest in a future emperor. Indeed, your future path might be not unlike my own. I collaborate with the pope in matters of orthodoxy, while you will be a tutor to his Highness, King Frederick of Sicily, in whom, as his ward, the pope takes a special interest. His Holiness is also acting as regent for the child. You will be his tutor in mathematics and natural philosophy. As a future ruler, he will have need of a guiding force in his life that his orphaned status left open to Mother Church. Before she died, the child's mother, the Norman Constance d'Hauteville, called on the pope to be his guardian, thus ensuring that the German relations of the child's father could have no claim to the Sicilian throne.'

Michael Scot nodded. Keeping a bland expression on his face, he reflected on just how valuable this move might prove to be. It meant that the pope could effectively move to keep the two parts of the empire – German and Sicilian – from uniting and becoming a threat to the papacy, which, at least geographically, found itself caught in the middle. It also meant that his own role in forming the young king's mind would be very important, for the papacy would want to ensure that it did not find itself having to contend with another enemy.

De Provins observed the silent Michael Scot, on whom a pale ray of sunlight now fell as the autumn sun finally broke through the fog outside, causing the grey eyes to glitter. Momentarily unsettled, de Provins blinked. 'Well, Master Scot, I am waiting for your answer.' Michael Scot stood up, the upper part of his body retreating back into shadow, and the effect dissipated.

So he was going to the Kingdom of Sicily. New horizons were opening up. 'Thank you for the interest you have taken in me,' he said. He smiled broadly and de Provins again had the unnerving sensation of being caught up in a surge of energy. 'I am grateful also to his Holiness for entrusting me with the education of his ward. I hope to prove myself worthy of it.'

De Provins resisted the temptation to smile back at Michael Scot. He had a disagreeable feeling that at some point the reins of the situation had slipped from his grasp. Looking down at the tonsured brown hair on the Scotsman's head bowed in readiness for his blessing, his eyes narrowed.

He would draft a letter to Di Monteforte in Palermo, apprising him of Master Scot's arrival.

Palermo, Kingdom of Sicily

X

AD 1201

A frail child of six years was ushered into the library by his scholastic supervisor, Tebaldo Francesco di Monteforte. Michael Scot took in the small face on which dirt and freckles did not manage to hide its pallor; the matted red hair; the grubby clothes hanging loosely on the scrawny limbs; the penetrating blue eyes.

'Your Majesty,' said di Monteforte, beckoning at the child to move forward, 'this is another tutor. As well as your other subjects, Master Scot is here to teach you mathematics and natural philosophy.' He turned to Michael Scot and said, 'His Majesty, King Frederick of Sicily.'

The pity the child's appearance excited quickly showed itself to be misplaced the moment Michael Scot's eyes came to rest on him and, in an unexpected reversal of roles, he found himself the object of their unblinking scrutiny.

He bowed and the child immediately asked, 'Where do you come from?'

'Scotland.'

'I have never heard of it.'

'You are not alone in that, your Majesty,' interjected di Monteforte. 'I was relieved to hear,' he added, glancing at Michael Scot, 'that you were educated at the Schools in Paris under Canon de Provins, as opposed to whatever passes for education in Scotland.'

Michael Scot turned slowly to observe di Monteforte. He had journeyed so far, truly to the ends of the earth, and yet there was something drearily familiar in the import of what di Monteforte had just said to him.

'Well then,' said the child, 'let us ask Master Scot for lessons in Geography as well. The world is a big place, I want to know it.'

'You already have enough on your plate,' replied di Monteforte 'without Geography. Besides,' he added, 'it is not your place to decide what you are to study.'

A fleeting glance passed between the child and his new tutor. 'However,' said Michael Scot, 'difficult as it may be to believe now, the day will come when that privilege shall be yours.'

In the months that followed this first meeting, Michael Scot found out that by the age of four the child had lost both his German father, Henry VI of Swabia, and his Norman mother, Constance d'Hauteville. He also perceived that for all the small boy's distinguished lineage there was no one to see to it that he was washed and fed properly. Motherless and fatherless, he had been left to fend for himself. The solitude had driven him to frequenting the children he came across on his wanderings round the streets of Palermo, and contenting himself with whatever sporadic adult kindness their parents sent his way.

And what a wonder the city seemed to Michael Scot. At twenty-five, he was well travelled, having seen Edinburgh, London, Oxford, Paris and Bologna – but Palermo...

He had come to the remote corners of the earth and in Palermo found marvels beyond believing. It was true there was also turbulence that not even the pope's authority could quell: the barons were exploiting their own personal fiefdoms with no thought to a unified kingdom, and incursions were also being made by the Germans, anxious to regain power in Sicily.

But alongside this political upheaval were the gardens, the

fountains, the courtyards; the palm trees, the sun, the wine, the food. So many different races, languages, creeds. Such breadth of learning.

Gradually he got his bearings, was initiated into the codes governing existence in this faraway land, and learned to perceive the same substance of the human heart at work behind the strange foreign exteriors. As time passed he came to realise that Frederick's upbringing, while neglectful and harsh, had also been eclectic. The boy had lived on his wits from such a young age that he was not inclined to sit passively at lessons; his prodigious intelligence and formidable character called for a formation that went beyond the usual rote of sanctioned learning.

*

The months turned into years, and Michael Scot watched as the future Holy Roman Emperor transformed from little more than a street urchin into a youth marked out for greatness.

Not falling foul of his heresy-obsessed ecclesiastical superior, Tebaldo Francesco di Monteforte, had been trickier. As the bishop of Palermo's assistant, he was zealous in his implementation of orthodoxy, especially where the education of the young king was concerned. Michael Scot had had to be very careful.

One phrase in particular he associated with the cleric's nit-picking vitriol: *A child-groom in the hands of a widow-bride*, for this was his scornful summing up of the fourteen-year-old Frederick's impending nuptials.

A child-groom in the hands of a widow-bride. First came the haggling as Pope Innocent III, Frederick's guardian, stepped in to oversee the match. Dangling the bait in the courts of Christendom, his Holiness let it be known that Frederick might one day be Holy Roman Emperor... He then obtained for the boy the hand of Constancia, daughter of the King of Aragon – an advantageous match for the Church, uniting as it did two bastions of Christendom. On a personal level, however, it was rather more ambiguous.

'Master Scot,' Frederick said one day at lessons, out of the blue, 'did you know that my future wife – the woman who has been so carefully selected for me – is eleven years my senior?'

He slowly nodded his head.

'And,' continued the youth, his voice betraying just the slightest tremor, 'she is already a widow.'

His intended, deemed Tebaldo Francesco di Monteforte, his lip curling in derision, was certainly no blushing maiden: twenty-five, well past her prime, and a widow to boot. And the boy as frail and slight at fourteen as his premature birth to an aged mother had presaged. A child-groom in the hands of a widow-bride.

As Frederick's tutor it was his duty to get through the areas of study that had been prescribed for the young king. He was careful to do this, as he had no wish to incur the wrath of his ecclesiastical superiors. Bit by bit, however, he had also incorporated discussions of topics more vulnerable to accusations of heresy. It was a risk he would not have run with anyone of lesser intelligence, but the flowering of the youth's mind more than compensated him. The cathedral library revealed itself to be an unexpected treasure trove where he found a store of manuscripts that seemed to have been largely forgotten. They contained material that fired both his own imagination and Frederick's, opening up horizons with a range of authors and translators that fed their ever-growing interest in the natural world. Then, concealed in an out-of-the-way corner of the library, came a life-changing opportunity to contribute to the course of learning. What a great stroke of good fortune that had been – a manuscript on Natural Philosophy in a Saracen translation. Ah, the joy that fell on him like a bright cloud, making him oblivious to his surroundings, his hands reverently turning the pages, the febrile attempt to scan the Arabic, the excitement that made them shake as the gist, and then the author, of the material began to sink in. He immediately grasped its potential for expanding the confines of knowledge; he also saw that it might assist his pupil in this difficult time of transition.

Aristotle... A part of his history of animals, brought to Michael Scot by Providence through a Saracen translation. What was this magnificent receptacle of learning doing shut up in these dark recesses, this obscurity?

He discussed it with his pupil. Through it, he might initiate him into the ways of nature, remove some of the fear from his impending marriage and the intimate relations it would entail. He could foster the youth's nascent interest in the workings of the world surrounding him. The young king was particularly eager to learn about the Saracen pursuit of falconry: what were a falcon's habits and disposition? How was it to be trained to hunt? To do this he needed to acquire the *novo sapere*, the new scientific knowledge of which Aristotle was undisputed master. Michael Scot and his pupil talked of how this new knowledge was still the preserve of the Saracens and a fearful whisper on the lips of Christians.

'Perhaps,' said Michael Scot, 'this precious material should now be translated into Latin. This manuscript was hidden away out of sight like a shameful secret, yet it ought to be known.'

'Agreed,' replied Frederick. 'Soon I will be of age, it is a question of months now. If I am old enough to be married off, I am old enough to decide what knowledge it is worthy to seek after.'

He turned to Michael Scot, who was glad of the animation he saw in the youth's eyes. 'You and I understand each other on this score, Master Scot. I shall commission you to carry out the translation into Latin of the Arabic versions of Aristotle. We must have this *novo sapere* here in Christendom.'

The Latins, explained Michael Scot, had long been familiar with Aristotle's writings on logic, but his writings on Natural Philosophy were as yet largely unknown. And it was rumoured that the Moors had recovered his lost writings on physics. That they had them in their possession. Indeed, they had even dared to gloss these priceless pages with commentaries which, they claimed, were more valuable than the original. 'So that the best thing to do,' said Michael Scot, 'would be to go to Spain, where it is easier to find Arabic versions of this body of work.'

'I shall miss you sorely, Master Scot – but I want you to go on a quest for knowledge, for the *novo sapere*,' cried Frederick. His eyes shone. 'I have a vision of greatness for my kingdom. I am counting on you to help me make Sicily illustrious.'

XI

AD 1209

Shortly after the young King Frederick had revealed his hopes for the translation venture to Michael Scot, there was a visitation from Tebaldo Francesco di Monteforte. While Michael Scot knew that he had done well to give free rein to Frederick's intellectual brilliance, listening to him spar with di Monteforte brought home with a jolt the extent to which he had perilously exposed them both. Driven by his passion for falconry, Frederick put it to di Monteforte that Aristotle's *novo sapere* should be available throughout Christendom.

'You should content yourself with the knowledge that God, in His wisdom, has seen fit to extend to you,' di Monteforte had intoned, tucking his hands inside the sleeves of his habit. His face took on a supercilious expression. 'Surely the assimilation of centuries of learning is enough to keep even your Majesty occupied.'

'Undoubtedly,' Frederick had replied. 'And far be it from me to wish for more than it is my given lot to expect.' Here he had glanced at Master Scot, who had not failed to see the glint in the young king's eye, cast down quickly however in modest contemplation of the floor. 'But if the assimilation of the past is not just to become a sterile exercise, surely its purpose must be that of providing a speculative basis on which to build for the future?'

Di Monteforte had started slightly at these words; his mouth opened and then shut again. Eventually, he opined, 'We are mere mortal – nay, sinful – creatures, to whom it is given only to see the past. Christian teaching builds on the unassailable tradition that the past affords us. It is sufficient for the soul's well-being to stick to that.'

Michael Scot saw Frederick open his mouth to reply, but before anything imprudent could emerge from it, he himself said placatingly, 'You speak the truth, Don Tebaldo. We ask your understanding of our foolish pride – that of a master in his pupil, and of a youth in the first flush of his intellectual vigour.' He cast a quelling glance in Frederick's direction. 'Well do we know that the Kingdom of Heaven is for the pure in heart, and that Mother Church's teachings are the only means of getting there.'

Di Monteforte nodded slowly. 'Indeed,' he said. 'The sin of pride and its rotten fruit, ambition, have led you both astray. Know that humility will get you further than the devilish sophistry of some long-dead pagan.'

'You refer to Aristotle, I presume.'

'I do. I trust you have not been corrupting the young king's mind with blasphemous impieties from that heathen – the taint of which cannot but imperil his immortal soul.'

Michael Scot regarded the man for a moment. Something in the complacent arrogance of his expression made his eyes narrow. He had been about to murmur a suitably humble disclaimer, had even wanted to; but, with a will of their own, entirely different words now found their way out of his mouth like cinders hissing into the cool silence between them. 'Our Heavenly Father enjoys the benefits of eternity. Who are you to place a limit on the gifts of knowledge he can bestow on us by harking always to tradition and the past?'

There was an audible intake of breath from di Monteforte; greatly discomfited, he plucked at the knots of his corded belt. 'This will not do,' he remonstrated. 'We cannot allow this. Canon Scot, what notions have you been planting in his Majesty's innocent head? To what dangers have you exposed him?'

'The best teaching,' he replied slowly, holding di Monteforte's eye all the time, 'is the teaching that opens up the path to knowledge. But knowledge cannot derive exclusively from tradition and authority. It depends also on the truths perceived through experience. For it is through this that we gain the capacity to evaluate whatever facts come our way.'

Di Monteforte's mouth set in a thin line. 'You are aware, Canon Scot,' he said icily, 'that his Holiness has spoken out against Aristotle on account of this very capacity to lead the faithful astray?' He rubbed his hands on his habit, as if to cleanse them of some impurity.

'The only truth that has ever been perceived through a glut of experience is the truth of eternal damnation. You would do better – both of you – to stick to your prayers. Look to your immortal souls. No good ever comes of wanting more than it is licit to aspire to. God in his infinite wisdom has made us weak and imperfect; the true Christian must accept this with humility.'

He made to leave the room, but added as if it was an afterthought, 'It is my duty to report this alarming development.' A sneer flickered over his face. 'It does not bode well for you, Canon Scot.'

For a long moment he stood looking at the door that banged after Tebaldo Francesco di Monteforte. Then he snorted. 'My time as your tutor would appear to be drawing to a hastier conclusion than we foresaw.'

The youth closed his eyes. 'Ever is it so in my life,' he cried. 'By some miracle I manage to find someone I can trust, and they are always taken from me.'

Michael Scot patted his slender shoulder. 'Be mindful,' he said with slow deliberation, 'of the parable of the talents. You have been given talents in abundance. My prayer is that you may always be able to use them. But remember also this.' He turned towards the desk and indicated Aristotle's manuscript on Natural Philosophy, open at the page illustrating the life cycle of falcons. 'Here on earth, in the world, life is a struggle for power, and this struggle comes in many guises.

Battles over territories and dominions are all very well,' his eyes grew sombre, 'but the ultimate battle is for the soul.'

Despite his wish to shield the young king, Di Monteforte's veiled threat struck deep, awakening some underlying fear in Michael Scot that he might fall foul of those in power. *The sin of pride and its rotten fruit ambition...* As he waited in the limbo of time running up to Frederick's wedding and his departure for Toledo, he brooded on this fear he seemed to have lived with all his life. What if his dreams of expanding knowledge for the good of mankind *were* merely the delusions of pride, the promptings of sinful ambition? What if he had indeed led the young king astray by encouraging rebellion in his heart?

How would he be held to account for this?

And would he likewise be held to account for any knowledge he uncovered? Would that knowledge be a part of him, and would he therefore be responsible for any use that was made of it?

*

The sin of pride and its rotten fruit ambition... Di Monteforte's words were difficult to shake off. The day of Frederick's wedding came, and still di Monteforte's words circled obsessively in his head – *child-groom and widow-bride.* He found himself caught between some dark presentiment of doom and an appreciation of the lavish scale of the festivities taking place. How could he ever forget the sight, that summer's morning, of the fleet of Spanish ships sailing into the bay of Palermo, the five hundred Spanish guests that disembarked, representing the cream of Aragonese nobility. The news that the bride's guests brought with them of Spain; talk of Toledo; the mighty work of translation going on there; the contribution of Moorish philosophers in making known Aristotle. And the music, the laughter, the revelry. The heat. The rotting fruit. The flies.

The plague that, like an eclipse of the sun, had suddenly plunged the festivities into darkness.

The new queen's brother, Prince Alfonso, was one of the first victims and was attended to by his own physician. Gone in an instant were the singing and dancing, gone the banquets; fear squeezed people's hearts, paralysing any impetus to courage or compassion.

The first few victims were looked after. But no one realised the slow decimation being worked on them from within. Under their waxy skin, dark feelers of blood appeared, sending out tendrils of purple that entwined themselves in a deadly filigree over their limbs, diseased ivy poisoning the life sap. The blood pooled and seeped into fetid yellowing clots. Bit by bit, under their swollen, bruised skin, the flesh was being corroded and falling away from the bone. A burning sensation enveloped them, bringing pain so excruciating that the gloomy silence in which the palace had been thrown was rent by agonised screams. The fiery canker then spread from their limbs to their vital organs. But this fire, capable of consuming living flesh without heat, filled them with a sensation of cold that no number of blankets could remedy. They succumbed, bloated and in agony, imploring for the mercy of a rapid death. Those who had been attending them suffered the same terrifying fate shortly after.

Soon there were dead bodies everywhere, grotesquely disfigured, swollen, blood oozing from their orifices, their eyes hanging out from the orbits. The heat of summer liquefied their pitiful remains; the stench of contagion soon made people fearful of breathing. Dogs foraged; rats scuttled. No effort was made to give the victims a Christian burial.

Fear once again stalked people's every move and thought, turning a dream of beauty into a waking nightmare. Why had this been visited on them? Had they strayed from righteous ways? Was it a punishment? Or worse – a portent of things to come for the young king and his bride?

The dead and dying were abandoned to the fate that had already overtaken them. Frederick and his new queen set off with their retinue in all haste for Messina on the far side of the island.

Yet the thought of Toledo gave Michael Scot no respite. He was free of his duties as tutor now as Frederick had come of age and married. But the young king did not wish to lose such a valuable addition to his court as Michael Scot, so before leaving for Messina, Frederick – finally in a position to exercise his will – engaged his former tutor's services as a translator and extended his patronage to the great enterprise of bringing Aristotle's Natural Philosophy to Christendom. This work of translation was what Michael Scot's deepest instincts were prompting him to pursue. Burdened with misgiving, but fired by a vision of the groundbreaking nature of this plan, he resolved to go to Toledo at the first opportunity.

*

And there in Toledo had his life truly changed. In the silence of the small locked room in the Norman Palace in Palermo, Michael Scot frowns at the memory. For in truth he still cannot say whether his life was changed for better or for worse. That far-off child has since established the most powerful monarchy in Christendom; but what has it all been for? Has Frederick laboured so only for it to be torn from him? Torn and trampled underfoot? Will all that effort lead only to the crushing vista of ruination and death that fell on him as he prepared for sleep just three nights before the brick fell on his head? Ah – and what a hopeless epilogue to his own life. Reduced to some crow of ill omen, its cawing replete with desolation.

The hour is late and the abbot has not come back for him, but he cannot worry about why this should be so. Even as he wipes the sweat from his brow, he is shaken by a fit of shivering. He must get through this night alone as best he can.

Toledo,
Kingdom of Castile

XII

AD 1210

The white foaming of the prow cutting its way through the waves; the creak of ropes and wood on the surging sea; the glitter of the sun on the vast blue expanse of the Mediterranean, and the exhilaration occasioned by another beginning: he was on the move again, after nearly ten years, being blown across the Mediterranean by a strong south-easterly – the *Scirocco*, as the Pisan sailors manning the ship called it – in a race with the westering sun.

Into the vibrant emptiness fell the keening sound of seagulls. A shout went up from the sailors, 'Land ahead!' Two dark blue masses were emerging from the heat haze in the distance: the Balearic Islands, Major and Minor. Majorca was the ship's final port of call on the western side of the Mediterranean, where it would embark a precious cargo of glazed ceramics and tiles acquired from the Moorish conquerors of the island, and then take them back for sale in Pisa. From Majorca, Michael Scot would have to board another ship bound for Valencia, and from there make his way across half of Spain, through the Caliphate and up to Toledo, capital of Christian Spain, and its famous School of Translation.

*

Where had he come to? What benighted corner of the earth was this place? Eventide was advancing, the orange rays of the setting sun melding with the same sinister tinge in the burnt and shrivelled vegetation all around him. The wind blew heat and dust in his face, until it seemed that he was walking in an open-air oven whose flames were licking at his very eyeballs. He had forced himself to get up from under the shelter of that lone cluster of trees when the sun was high in the sky, knowing that he still had a long stretch in front of him and that his water might not last until he got to Toledo. Truly, he had not bargained on this savage climate and unforgiving terrain. He ached all over, but worse by far was the pain in his head. Thirst was both his goad and weakness.

His arrival at the Moorish city of Valencia had left him on edge. It was not that he had never heard Arabic spoken before; it had been common on the streets of Palermo. Muslim dress and customs had become known to him there, too. But he had not counted on the effect that the complete reversal of proportions he encountered in Valencia would have on him. For in Valencia everyone seemed to speak Arabic; the languages of Christendom were but a fitful and hasty exchange here and there. The Arabic he had so laboriously studied in the manuscripts in Palermo transmuted into a blur of incomprehensible babble. He felt disinclined to open his mouth and speak. And it was just as well he had had the foresight to don anonymous black attire. As it was, his height and colouring seemed to attract undue attention. The red beard was pointed at.

Then, fortunately, still in the environs of the port, he had heard what he supposed to be one of the Iberian dialects. He approached the group and addressed the man who seemed to be giving out orders. By means of a mixture of Sicilian and Latin, he made his intentions known. And yes, the man could give him a lift to Toledo: he was having a cargo of salted and cured cod transported there and would let him travel on one of the wagons.

The last leg of his journey had started. The stench from the fish was nigh on unbearable, but he could ill afford to be choosy. He had found himself in the company of four others: the tradesman, the driver and two burly and taciturn types, presumably there to protect the goods.

They had set off on the wagons, rumbling noisily along the dusty track, and were within reach of the border with La Mancha and Christian Spain when they came across another party coming along the same road in the opposite direction. There had been a confabulation, a babbling of raised voices that largely passed over his head. By means of eloquent gestures, the tradesman had conveyed that they would be going no further, as there was some danger ahead. Michael Scot was at a loss. Was this a temporary delay? Would they be resuming the journey at all? At last it sank in: the tradesman's main preoccupation was safeguarding the consignment of fish; to that end he was prepared to set up camp here and sit out whatever threat had materialised further out along the road.

Who knew how long that would entail.

'It's a two-day walk to Toledo,' the tradesman informed him. 'Without water, it's not doable.'

'And we can't spare you any,' the wagon-driver added.

Michael Scot only had a day's supply of water, but he decided to trust to fate and press on by himself. There had been much rolling of eyes on the part of the men; the sound of their laughter had accompanied him for a good stretch of the lonely way. And then had come these damnable unending uplands of parched scrubland and scorched earth, windblown and empty of life. No trace here of the fabled Moorish irrigation systems and gardens, which lay farther to the south. But the traces of their military presence had come as a shock. It had not been like this in Sicily, where the Saracen presence was far more contained; they represented a different faith and a different culture, but never a military power that might suddenly rise up and overcome the other inhabitants of the island as a conquering force.

The evening journey along the Toledo Road in the southernmost part of La Mancha had shaken him. First there had been the scare with a contingent of Moorish soldiers. At least, that is what he supposed them to be. He had been proceeding along the road when a dull rumble broke the evening silence, making the ground tremble. He had paused to wonder what this might presage – a solitary figure clad in black, standing out on the empty road like a funereal stork fallen from the skies – and had actually wasted precious moments before some instinct prompted him to sprint away from the road and into the burnt undergrowth alongside it. In an ungainly crouch, he scrambled away as far as he could, eyes darting to find the longest and thickest of the yellowing blades of grass stretching away in all directions. With a pounding heart, he inched his way into them.

From over the rise in the road, the dust heralded their arrival. Turbaned and clad in light-hued garments, they passed by in a thunder of hooves, headed in the direction of Valencia. He wondered how it would go with the fishmonger and his consignment of cod.

From that point he had kept off the road, following it from a prudent distance in the whispering grasses. This had made his progress even slower. Eventually, up out of the lengthening shadows had loomed his destination, the fortress of Salvatierra – Safeguard of the Land – as a reminder of this threatening reality. It faced its opposite number, the fortress of Calatrava, on the other side of the valley, conquered by the Moors after the rout of the Christian forces fifteen years previously at the Battle of Alarcos.

It had been a welcome, if disturbing, sight, both fortresses poised massively atop hills of obvious strategic importance. The pale stones of these two outposts of different worlds rose up in a mute stand-off against the peacock blue of the twilight sky. He was headed for Salvatierra, where he was to be a guest of the knights of the Order of Calatrava. It was an arduous climb up to the top.

He had paused to survey the darkening land falling away in every direction below him, and been shaken by the sense of unease that overtook him. What was this place? What was this emptiness?

The last citadel, a bulwark separating Christendom from the Moors, the monks had told him. The Calatravan monks were attached to the Cistercian order, but this territory of nothing and everything, empty and yet replete with the threat of overwhelming chaos, had moulded them into soldiers. They were frontier monks, knights fighting for Christ. They berated him for his stupidity in venturing forth on his own into hostile territory. Had he not heard of the constant skirmishings with Muslim forces that were taking place even in La Mancha? And if he had fallen into Moorish hands, did he imagine for a moment that they would have shown him any particular regard?

Something about the place, the stalwart doggedness of the monk-knights, their quotidian expectancy of upheaval, sent a ripple of disquiet snaking through his gut. Something about it reminded him of home. Of the Borders and the relentless warring, of its patchwork quilt of geography and identity tugged incessantly this way and that, as first one party and then another vied for supremacy. Supremacy of their way of life, of their vision of life, of their tribe.

*

The following day a contingent of the monks accompanied him out of dangerous territory. He had ridden behind one of them, as they were sorry but they could not spare him a horse. He had been glad of the company, even if it had been silent. The long miles he had then covered on his own had weighed greatly on him, and his pace had been slow. Indeed, he now feared that he would not make Toledo before nightfall and what would he do then for water?

He needed to get there as quickly as possible. But when he came across a man leading a donkey and cart, his confidence failed him. Was it safe to approach them for a lift? The cart was carrying a woman and raggle-taggle children. He was still standing in the middle of the road, undecided, when a dog jumped down from the cart and began barking at him. The man caught the dog by the scruff of the neck and turned to look at Michael Scot. The children huddled round the woman, their eyes round with fear.

What they saw was a tall stranger dressed in black, leaning on a staff, whose face was mostly in shadow due to the large hat he was wearing. The stranger removed the hat and drew near, revealing a face of ghostly paleness; the pale eyes glittered like silver in the slanting evening light; the hair was brown. But the beard was red.

Michael Scot held up a hand in salute. The dog gave a low menacing snarl. He opened his mouth to say something; what could he say it in but Latin? The tentative words were met with a frown. Then a vehement shake of the head. A foreigner. The man's dismissive hand waved him off. A hostile torrent of something incomprehensible met his further attempts at communication. He took a step forward. The man released the dog and took a step backwards.

Its ears flat against its skull, the dog's head went down and it edged forward, snarling and baring its teeth. Michael Scot glanced at the man; he had a challenging sneer on his face. Then, as occasionally happened to Michael Scot, the fear that followed him like a shadow, whispering and probing with invisible fingertips, suddenly crystallised in a surge of anger that coursed through him. His eyes latched onto the dog's. There was a deep whirring noise as his staff sliced through the air and he brought it down with a resounding thud on the ground between them. His eyes still boring into the dog's, he pointed the staff at the animal; it cowered and with whining noises edged backwards out of reach of the staff. Michael Scot took another step forward and shouted. The dog yelped and, twisting round, shot off with its tail between its legs.

The man jumped up onto the cart and whipped the donkey into an unwilling canter. Still yelping, the dog chased after them.

Michael Scot stood and watched them disappear until every last sound had faded and the dust had settled back on the miserable track.

Everyone was suspicious, when not hostile. He endeavoured to see himself as they must have seen him: a solitary foreigner journeying on foot. As he was not on a pilgrimage, he must be a lunatic. For only a lunatic or a fugitive would choose to go about like this on his own.

Michael Scot made the sign of the cross, and then tried to gather his strength to get over the next hill. Leaning heavily on his staff, eyes fixed on the ground, he thought only of putting one step in front of the other. Eventually the ground evened out. His eyes flew anxiously ahead. Yes, thank the good Lord – he was saved.

There, not too far ahead and on her own imposing hill girdled by river and walls, rose Toledo, capital of Spain. A fortress surmounted by four towers dominated the city; all round it red stone turrets and buildings spilled down the hillside like a clotted bloodstain in the darkening brilliance of the sunset. Thank the Lord for mercies. He would be there by nightfall and, God willing, put a sturdy door between himself and this baleful sense of threat blowing on the wind. All day it had plucked and tugged at him, driven and harried him, reducing him to a microcosm of this country: a tattered mass of ever-shifting layers, in thrall to each gust decreeing now safety, now peril.

Thus had his sojourn in Spain begun. He would come to give the country other names, each name in a different language, and the sound of each language another chip in its mosaic of identity. But for the moment it was this wind whistling and moaning down a winding street, as he stood in front of the Cathedral School after nightfall in Toledo. A strange unsettling wind, nothing like the winds of his childhood and youth in Scotland. Surely a sound like this could only bring cold and skifting rain: it seemed past belief that such a lonely sound could come hurtling through the darkness on a breath as stifling as a furnace.

No candle flickered in the windows of the large building in front of him. No candle flickered anywhere. As if the rushing wind had extinguished everything in its quenching path.

XIII

There was no settling into the place. He waited for the sense of ease to come, at first patiently, but then with mounting anxiety. It was not a new situation to be facing – he had accomplished this kind of transition other times in the past. But in Toledo something kept eluding him. Or rather, something lurked on the outer reaches of his memory, amorphous and disturbing, that for the first time threatened here to overtake him.

The stifling heat gave way to a faded autumn of more dust and wind. In the scriptorium he endeavoured to start work again on his translation of Aristotle's history of animals, which he had entitled *De Animalibus ad Caesarem*. But the Arabic of Avicenna's version was remaining largely beyond his grasp: his undertaking required more certainties than he was at present able to muster, as his supervisor, Dom Pedro Palacio Taracón, did not scruple to remind him at every opportunity.

The door to the scriptorium creaked open and the silent concentration of two dozen scholars and translators was broken by the heavy-footed slapping of sandals on stone. The hackles went up on Michael Scot's neck as the noise resulting from this lumpish approach drew nearer. Palacio Taracón paused to retrieve a small manuscript from the shelving running the length of the wall, fiddled with the writing paraphernalia on a young scribe's desk, and then – unable to contain himself any longer – headed as purposefully as his cloddish gait would allow over to where Michael Scot was working.

Palacio Taracón placed himself just out of Michael Scot's line of vision, behind his right shoulder. It was useless to pretend to continue working; even if he had not been unnerved by the unwanted attention, the loud wheezing – brought on, it would seem, by the minimal exertion of traversing the scriptorium – that was directed at his back would in itself have precluded any further work. He placed his quill back on the desk and stared ahead.

'Still persevering with the Arabic, are we?' grunted Palacio Taracón.

Michael Scot turned round to see him wiping sweat from his forehead with the sleeve of his habit. He said nothing.

'That must be quite tricky for you,' continued Palacio Taracón, his voice an antagonistic rasp in the wary silence of the scriptorium. 'I mean, translating from a language of which one is ignorant, into another language in which one lacks even a modicum of proficiency...'

In a surge of dislike, Michael Scot regarded the younger man: the porcine minuteness of the eyes in the full-moonish flaccidity of his face, and the fleshy mouth on which two bucked teeth deposited a permanent patina of spittle. The fact that he was younger did not help either.

'Practice,' he replied with slow deliberation, 'makes perfect.'

'Then I would suggest that you keep practising.' The Spaniard pointed to the last sentence that he had been working on. 'What can you mean by this?' His finger circled an offending phrase. '*Facere rememorationem*? What kind of a barbarous use of Latin is this? Whoever would dream of using this brutish phraseology?' He rolled his eyes. 'Who indeed, except a barbarian! But what can be expected from such a remote, godforsaken corner of the earth as Scotland.' He turned round to face the whole scriptorium. 'Any civilized individual knows that it is more elegant to say, *facere mentionem*, *narrare*, or *rememorar*.'

Most of the heads went down, busying themselves in their

manuscripts. Away near the door somebody hawked loudly and spat into the rushes. The porcine eyes swivelled and then narrowed short-sightedly; having failed, however, to locate the dissenter, Palacio Taracón continued undeterred. 'We have standards to maintain here at the School of Translation in Toledo. Archbishop De Rada will have to be informed that not all the scholars enjoying our patronage appear to be up to the task.' Michael Scot was torn. He smarted under the aspersions this ignorant bigot cast on him; he laboured greatly to check the angry impulse to give the man a much-needed tongue-lashing. Moreover, he knew that Palacio Taracón was aware of these struggles and wished to provoke him into an unwise response. For if he could but goad him into insubordination, it was within his powers to have Michael Scot sent packing in disgrace from the School of Translation with no possibility of appeal.

But another, much smaller part of him grudgingly conceded that Palacio Taracón had a point. He was here at the promptings of his own ambition: he had the backing of no school of learning, the intellectual resources of no long-standing tradition from which to draw strength. And while it was true that he was here on a commission for King Frederick II, the Church sponsored the School of Translation and had many ways of circumventing a monarch's will. His intelligence had taken him this far, and on it alone he would have to rely – along with his belief in the intrinsic importance of the knowledge he was endeavouring to gather and disseminate. And as to questions of style, or the lack thereof – had not Frederick himself ordered that he stick as closely as possible to the original? A literal translation that would leave no room for mystification.

An admirable approach – until one tried to put it into practice: its awkwardness, the clumsy gracelessness of it, managing to obscure whatever content was being transmitted. He was painfully aware of that. And, it seemed, powerless to alter it.

In truth, the fault mostly lay with the ineptness of his Arabic. As yet he was but a hobbled mule.

*

It was when he took steps to improve his Arabic that Dom Pedro Palacio Taracón started actively to oppose him. The propagation of Moorish sophistry was no fit task for a good Christian. Not at a moment like this when every effort should be concentrated on expelling each last trace of their heathen impiety. It was true, he admitted, that the translation enterprise had got under way here in Toldeo with the visit of the Abbot of Cluny in 1145 and his sponsorship of a translation of the Quran. But Canon Scot must realise that this had not been so that Muslim heresy could be propagated; rather was the translation to provide the information by which the heresy of Islam could be fought. For that reason and no other. And instead, here was Michael Scot, a savage attempting to translate and propagate a heathen apostate. And a pagan blasphemer! Because, as every good Christian knew, Aristotle led the souls of the faithful astray. Had not his Holiness stated that quite clearly this very year of our Lord? God demanded instead that he put his talents – such as they were – to His service, and relinquish these arrogant dreams of personal glory. The greater good of Christendom came first. Times were changing. Canon Michael Scot would therefore be more gainfully employed in the backwater whence he came, rearing and shearing sheep. Spain no longer had any use for heathen or pagan or savage. Spain was once again to be of the Christian Spanish.

*

Logical reasoning was precisely the capacity that his dealings with Dom Pedro Palacio Taracón lacked, he decided, after yet another outburst from the man. There was no talking to him, no getting him to see what he was trying to do. Defeat and an empty-handed return to Palermo loomed.

XIV

Then, one evening after Vespers, he was approached by Dom Sebastian, a senior cleric who, despite his retiring ways, was held in great esteem in the School on account of his remarkable body of work. Placing a hand on his arm to detain him, he nodded in the direction of the cathedral library and intimated that Michael Scot follow him. Before entering, he removed a candle from his pocket and lit it from the torch above their heads. Shadows jumped and scurried across the walls of the library as he closed the door behind them.

'Canon Michael,' he began, smiling gently, 'be not alarmed.' His elderly form was shaken by the sudden onset of a fit of coughing. Eventually, he got his breath back and took up. 'Dom Pedro's vexations to you have not passed unnoticed. It is to no one's advantage that you put up with them in isolation.' Here he paused; his breathing came in short wheezes. He held up the candle and peered into the still darkness. His eye fell on a chair. 'Come,' he said, 'let us take a seat. I have need of what little strength I have for talking.'

They sat down, Dom Sebastian at the head of the long wooden table, and Michael Scot to his right. Dom Sebastian's soft words were swallowed greedily by the surrounding wood. 'You studied at Paris, did you not?'

Michael Scot leaned towards him the better to catch them. 'I did,' he replied. He was thrown by such an unassuming, mild-natured old man doing something so unexpected. There had been no real contact between them up to this point. He observed him in wary silence.

'Well then,' continued Dom Sebastian, 'you'll have heard about Amaury and David of Dinant.'

'I have not.'

'Hmmm.' There was a rasping noise as Dom Sebastian meditatively rubbed the sparse white bristles on his chin, then he held the candle out to Michael Scot. 'Would you be so kind as to check that there is no diligent soul still at work here.' Michael Scot took the candle and held it aloft. 'In particular,' added Dom Sebastian, settling back in the chair, 'behind the shelving at the far end.'

But they were indeed alone. He turned to Michael Scot and enquired, 'Do you know them?'

'I know *of* them,' Michael Scot replied carefully.

Dom Sebastian nodded slowly. 'Amaury has been condemned for heresy, and his bones exhumed and thrown into unconsecrated ground; his unrepentant followers have been burnt at the stake; and David of Dinant only narrowly escaped the same fate by fleeing. His writings were not so fortunate.'

Silence fell, overlaid by the rasping noise of Dom Sebastian rubbing his chin. Michael Scot tried to master a queasy feeling in the pit of his stomach.

'It's Aristotle, you see,' took up Dom Sebastian. He let a few drops of wax fall onto the tabletop and then stuck the candle in it. 'Such of his writings as have trickled through to the masters in Paris, seem to have gone to their heads!' He chuckled quietly. 'They are all at each other's throats, vying for the greatest influence, vying for the last word.' He shook his head. 'It's a wild goose chase, of course.' His mild eyes sought out those of Michael Scot. 'You do see that, Canon Michael, don't you?'

'But how could the divulgation of Aristotle be a bad thing?'

'In itself it is not a bad thing,' replied Dom Sebastian. 'But,' he added softly, 'which Aristotle are you talking of?'

Michael Scot placed his elbows on the table, interlaced his fingers and brought the thumbs to rest on his lips. His eyebrows rose interrogatively.

'Is it the Syrian Aristotle? The Moorish Aristotle? The Latin Aristotle? All these bear very little resemblance to the Greek Aristotle.'

There was a moment's silence. 'To be sure,' Dom Sebastian added nodding, 'we have done, and continue to do, our best in Toledo. But translation inevitably changes things.'

'When it does not actually obfuscate them,' agreed Michael Scot. 'As I am finding to my cost.'

'Yes, well, that is the point, you see.' Dom Sebastian smiled slowly at him. But then abruptly he turned away as a fit of coughing overtook him again. It was a while before he regained sufficient breath to continue. 'Where the translation is faulty, what message is getting through?'

'You mean a faulty apprehension of the meaning?'

'Precisely.'

Michael Scot shook his head.

Again silence fell; then Dom Sebastian resumed. 'The demand for this *novo sapere* is so great, you see, that it is difficult to keep up with it. Many translations are faulty in this way. And yet, the masters in Paris are willing to come to blows over material they believe is Aristotle's. Are you aware of the plethora of theories, schools and indeed sects that have sprung up in the wake of these translations?'

'Amaury and David di Dinant being but one example, I suppose.'

'Sadly, yes. Aristotle and the winds of change,' he mused. 'All the masters seem to be intoxicated with the vistas of change that Aristotle is opening up. The responsibility is great because they have not been content to keep to philosophy. They had to make it theological as well.'

Dom Sebastian shook his white head. 'Knowledge,' he said, his voice almost a whisper, 'is a very strange thing.' His eyes fell on the candle flame in front of him and grew round with gazing. Long moments passed. The more Michael Scot felt Dom Sebastian's attention slip away from him, the more the silence seemed to rear up in black folds all around them. Just as he was regretting having entered the library and conversation with Dom Sebastian, the old man suddenly turned eyes on Michael Scot lit up as if by some secret awareness at the core of his being.

He took up where he had left off. 'Knowledge,' he reiterated, 'is a worthy servant, but a terrible master.' His voice, although very low, vibrated with some hidden inner force. 'What do you say to that, Canon Michael?'

'I am at a loss what to answer. I possess so little of it, and have been distracted by so many other things, that for me I fear it is neither the one nor the other.'

'Ha!' Dom Sebastian chuckled again. Then his face grew serious and he asked, 'What do you know of Joachim of Flora?'

'That the Church looks upon him with deep suspicion.'

'Hmmm. A very diplomatic reply. But I am not testing your orthodoxy here. We are still talking about knowledge; the spread of knowledge; and the types of knowledge.' Dom Sebastian sighed at length. The spurt of energy that had animated him seemed to be ebbing. His shoulders drooped. 'Was knowledge Joachim's servant or his master?'

'I know next to nothing about Joachim of Flora.'

'Well, you see, Joachim of Flora was one of the very few people for whom knowledge is a servant. For him, it was merely a means to an end, that end so ineffable that knowledge is either direct, and subsumed into it, or it is not at all.' Dom Sebastian was wracked by yet another fit of coughing. 'Do you see?' he gasped eventually.

'No.' Michael Scot looked steadily at him. 'I'm afraid I do not.'

'The knowledge that comes from silence, not the noise and

debate that is but the clacking and whirring of locusts above a field of grain. He applied what he had seen to history. Listen and I shall try to tell you.'

Michael Scot followed the soft voice attentively, as it traced the great faith of this Italian monk. How he always thirsted for a more spiritual approach to religion, which should be less materially and temporally inclined. His vision of history, unfolding on Trinitarian lines. The Age of the Father, corresponding to the Old Testament, characterised by the servitude of humanity to the Law. The Age of the Son, which started with the coming of Jesus Christ and was due to conclude in 1260. This was represented by the New Testament and conferred on mankind the role of sons of God. Then would come the Age of the Holy Ghost, in which men would come into direct contact with God, thus achieving the longed-for freedom preached in the gospels. With this age, there would no longer be any need for ecclesiastical hierarchy and organisation, and all its temporal temptations. Only in this age would it be possible to fully apprehend the Word of God in its deepest meaning, and not just the literal one. It would be guided by the monks, and St Francis of Assisi was the shining example.

But since Joachim's death in 1202, and the full emergence of his teachings, papal support for his purity of vision had withered. His writings were condemned for their critical stance towards the Church. It was only a question of time before he was labelled a heretic of the worst kind and cast forever from the fold.

Michael Scot's eyes were riveted on the old monk sitting placidly beside him.

'Time, you see,' said Dom Sebastian, 'is an opportunity for us to exert our free will. The good Lord, in His wisdom, has allowed differences in perception to arise. But we must also remember St Paul's words. The exertion of free will or the accommodation of differences of perception should not be an occasion of scandal, least of all for the pure in heart.'

'So the Church is right to suppress ruthlessly all dissenting voices?'

There was a pause. Dom Sebastian got up from the table with difficulty. Michael Scot leaned over to help him. 'Discernment or learning, Canon Michael – which would you rather aspire to?'

They walked slowly to the door. Outside, Michael Scot turned to Dom Sebastian and asked, 'But why should I have to make a choice between the one or the other? Why not put the one at the service of the other?'

Dom Sebastian gripped his arm. 'Servant or master, master or servant.' His voice sank to a hoarse whisper. 'Have you decided?' He began to shuffle off. His voice, echoing eerily in the stone vaulting overhead, came back through the darkness. 'Come and see me again. I want to talk to you about a translator who can help you in your work.'

Michael Scot stood for a long time in the empty darkness, staring unseeingly in the wake of Dom Sebastian. Visions. What did the old monk's ramblings amount to but more visions? Visions and mystifications. He wanted no part of them.

But he would use his help to get an assistant translator.

XV

AD 1211

In the new year Dom Sebastian was as good as his word. He found for Michael Scot an assistant translator. This was brought about in great secrecy, owing to the identity of the man who would bridge the abyss between the Muslim and Christian worlds. For Andrés Alfaquir Toledanus, son of Abraham Alfaquir Toledanus the physician, son of Isaac Alfaquir Toledanus, also a physician, was a Jew. Dom Sebastian related how Jewish scholars had always been welcome at the School of Translation: the painstaking work of translation would have amounted to very little had there not been this learned presence in Toledo to turn to for inspiration and guidance. But he also expressed his regret at the turn events had taken since the arrival of Dom Pedro Palacio Taracón and impressed on Michael Scot that Dom Pedro would find a way to lay waste his plans for the translation of Aristotle and the Moors if it emerged that he was compounding his ill-advised translating activities by employing the services of a Jew. Dom Pedro refused any kind of collaboration with the *conversos*; his abhorrence of those who had not converted was proportionately greater.

In his own mild way, Dom Sebastian had been adamant. Let not the fear-induced limitations of others bring about a rejection of truth. One must thank the Lord for opportunities when they arose – and Andrés Alfaquir was the best in his field. Dom Sebastian had also taken the precaution of finding a small study where they could work undisturbed. For, as Dom Sebastian had said to him clutching his arm, this work was of crucial importance.

Over the following months this small study, tucked away in a far corner of the School, became the place where Michael Scot and Andrés Alfaquir Toledanus worked steadily on this great enterprise. To the Latin, Greek and Sicilian that he had already acquired, Michael Scot painstakingly added Arabic and Castilian. And from this collaboration the final part of Avicenna's commentaries on Aristotle's Natural Philosophy were produced in Latin, thus concluding the first great cycle of translation in Toledo, started by Bishop Raymond and brought to a pinnacle of excellence under Gerardo of Cremona.

This labour, once completed, Michael Scot dedicated to his patron: 'O Frederick, Lord and King, receive with devotion this book of Michael Scot, that it may be a grace unto thy head and a chain about thy neck.'

But before it was sent back to Palermo to await publication, Dom Sebastian paid him a visit in the study. Michael Scot retrieved the manuscript from the press where it was kept. Then he placed it on the large wooden table and divested it of its protective cloth covering. He stood back as Dom Sebastian turned the pages, poring over them with avid attention. Finally, the old man turned shining eyes on him. 'A work well done,' he said softly. 'Now you are ready for Averroës. We are in possession of these works here in Toledo, but it was necessary to wait until they could be translated properly.' He walked up to Michael Scot and laid his hand on his arm. 'That time has come.'

*

They had just started work on Averroës' translation of Aristotle and his commentaries on this work, which they had decided to entitle *De Generatione et Corruptione*, when the rumour spread of a military expedition being organised by Alfonso VIII. The King of Castile wanted to open up a route to the Mediterranean, and so with a raiding force comprised of militias from Madrid, Guadalajara, Huete, Cuenca and Uclés, in the middle of May he proceeded down the Valencia Road to attack Játiva. From the Caliphate, the Almohads retaliated by sending an expedition to attack the fortress of Salvatierra.

Very little else was talked about in the School. The attack was protracted and became a siege. It was talked about in more hushed tones. The only person who continued to express himself vigorously on the subject was Dom Pedro Palacio Taracón, and this he did in increasingly exasperated tones as the summer months wore on. To any who would listen, and even to those who found that, sadly, they did not have the time, he spoke incessantly of the recent Moorish campaigns and the devastation they had wrought. Did no one remember how they had had the wrath of God visited on them in 1195 following the defeat at Alarcos? And the sustained campaign over the two subsequent years of pillage, destruction and death that had been visited on the villages, towns and cities as far north as Madrid? Did no one recall the devastation that had laid waste the area immediately surrounding Toledo? He certainly did. He would never forget it. Lands that had last seen these heathens two centuries previously, had been overrun by them once again only fifteen years ago. He had experienced their campaign of war and marauding at first hand. He knew what they were about. Well, it was time to put a stop to it.

Then, at the end of that hot summer, Salvatierra had fallen. The School reverberated with the shock. Suddenly everyone was vociferous in his outrage. Very little work was getting done, and any that was, in a state of suspended disbelief. Michael Scot found himself thinking back to his brief stay in that formidable fortress less than a year ago. And yet it seemed more remote to him, more of an enigma, than any other place he had ever been. And then, he wondered, in their doomed struggle, which of the warrior-monks would have survived? Which would have perished...

Everyone seemed to be distracted; everyone except Andrés Alfaquir. This was the way he earned his bread, he reminded Michael Scot. As a cleric, Michael Scot had the luxury of always knowing that he would be looked after, be it through patronage at a royal court, or in a monastery. Alfaquir did not have this security: he must always work as hard as he could, in order to ensure a standard of living commensurate at least with his intellectual attainments.

'In other words,' he said, his eyes fixing on an indefinite point on the wall, 'I depend purely on my brains to fill my belly. For me there are no welcoming, not to say indulgent, arms of Mother Church to fall back into when times get lean.' An expression of disdain passed over his face. 'To that end, I require not to be distracted by news arriving from Salvatierra. Things will go as they are meant to go and dwelling on them will not put bread on the table.'

The repercussions from the siege and fall of Salvatierra were sending out shock waves far beyond La Mancha and the frontier between the Christian and Muslim worlds. From Rome, Innocent III was invoking Christian unity in the face of this unprecedented threat. In France, the Military Orders were preparing themselves; the bishops of Narbonne, Bordeaux and Nantes were amassing troops; the nobles were summoning their vassals. Knights and soldiers were on the way from Provence and as far afield as Italy. And, as Dom Pedro announced jubilantly to all at the Cathedral School, his superior, the Archbishop of Toledo, Rodrigo Jiménez de Rada, had been singularly successful in gathering Spanish royalty under one banner: King Alfonso VIII of Castile, King Sancho VII of Navarre, and Pedro II of Aragon had agreed to come together in common cause. King Afonso II of Portugal was also to be their ally.

There was a new caliph of al-Andalus, the Almohad Muhammed al-Nâsir. All through the autumn and winter of that year, the rumour of the challenge he had thrown down to Christendom was like a torch whose sparks were falling ever closer to a tinder box. For Muhammed al-Nâsir, or Miramamolín as the Iberians called him, had expressed himself as desirous of taking on all Christendom in a great and conclusive battle.

And Christendom would take his challenge up with a crusade against the heathen.

XVI

AD 1212

With the spring of 1212, the city of Toledo began to transform. It was filling up with all manner of combatants, pouring in from adjacent cities, regions and countries. By the beginning of June all the available accommodation had been filled by clerics, the Orders and the nobility. Michael Scot had taken to walking round the city and observing this mass of humanity prepare for battle.

But it was the plethora of tongues that came at him from every street corner from which he finally got that yearned-for sense of ease. For in the midst of the upheaval and the babel of languages, he felt less exposed; with this freedom, he let the city draw near to him and felt it take on a physiognomy. Along the narrow, twisting streets ran rivers of sounds, intermittently intelligible, mostly not. The Christians amassing to fight the Muslims were divided into speakers of Castilian, Catalan and its cousin, Provençal, Basque from Navarre Portuguese, French, and various Italian dialects. Here and there he heard a Germanic tongue. He marvelled that a coherent plan for battle had managed to be worked out in the face of such linguistic disunity.

Often as evening drew on and the heat dissipated, he would walk up to the top of the hill on which the city rested, up to *Plaza de Zocodover*, where the market usually took place. With its commanding view of the sheer descent to the encircling Tajo river valley, it was a remarkable theatre now for jousting tournaments among the nobles and knights.

On the western side of the city he would make his way along the narrow, winding lanes of the *Aljama* flanked by whitewashed plain walls that jealously guarded secret courtyard interiors, a hint of lemon and orange trees, intricately decorated tiled floors all glimpsed behind iron gates; and he would smile as his ear picked up and understood snatches of Andalus Arabic. From there he would proceed to the *Judería* – the Jewish quarter. And there, yet another language could be heard. While the menfolk had contact with the world outside, the womenfolk remained segregated. He overheard snatched conversations in Ladino, that mixture of Hebrew, Arabic and Castilian.

Many times he witnessed brawls suddenly break out on account of a perceived insult between one of the many contingents. The townspeople, if the truth be known, were heartily sick of the upheaval and, despite the surge in trade, wished the army gone. The ordinary soldiers were encamped in a sprawling mass outside the city walls; but the nauseating miasma hanging over this place had grown to such proportions in the still heat of summer that there was no escape from it throughout the entire city. The accumulation of filth had spilt over down as far as the river, and now the drinking water was being contaminated and clothes could no longer be washed. Bit by bit, disease was gaining a hold. Michael Scot found himself coerced into accompanying physicians from the Cathedral School on their rounds of the encampment in an attempt to contain the spread of the more contagious and debilitating of the maladies.

He had no desire to embroil himself in ailments and healings, potions and prognostications. But the multitude of humanity was so vast, and the threat of a pandemic carried such implications, that every available hand was forced into service. Despite himself, however, he found that he was becoming engrossed by the nature of a physician's work; it occurred to him that the missions of healing had shown how his translations of Natural Philosophy and medicine meshed.

There were mercenaries among the soldiers from abroad. Michael Scot began to see how it was always the more northern of these soldiers who had the least regard for the sun. They were ill disciplined and restless to embark on the amassing of booty. Whole contingents of them would have their midday meal in the open air and drink to excess; then the heat would do its work and they would fall violently ill. It was a great drain on their resources but it had to be faced. If dysentery set in, the campaign could come to naught.

Word was filtering through of the huge army that Muhammed al-Nâsir was amassing away to the south. He had summoned to his banner subjects from all over his empire – Tunisia, Algeria, Senegal, Morocco, Mauritania as well as al-Andalus – and their numbers were reputed to amount to one hundred and twenty-five thousand. Despite this unprecedented coming together of Christendom, the Christian forces still only amounted to fifty thousand. In actual fact, there was a full-scale invasion under way. Would the Christian coalition succeed in rebuffing this all-out attempt to extend the Almohad Empire right into the heart of Christian Spain? Who would emerge victorious from this epic confrontation between Cross and Crescent Moon?

At these questions, by the middle of June, eyes were shifting uneasily.

*

Perhaps it was an attempt to revive flagging stamina. Or a worrisome deficit in bravery. Whatever the reason, the mercenaries decided to start the 'Holy War' early with a marauding rampage.

They had been amassing down by the river since late morning, one day at the beginning of July, when the heat was virulent in its strength. They drank steadily throughout the afternoon and evening and the roar of drunken revelry could be heard throughout the city. As night fell, so did an eerie silence. This was broken by the tramp of heavy feet, up the winding street leading to the western part of the city. The drunken rabble was headed for the *Judería*.

As soon as the precincts were breached, a deep roar went up and the horde swarmed along the empty streets. Doors were broken down; people dragged from their beds; homes ransacked in the search for valuables. When these could not be found, the killing started.

Brutal, frenzied, indiscriminate; if the knights had not come galloping through the streets filled with the screams and blood of men, women and children torn from their beds and, swords drawn, made swift inroads in picking off the mercenaries running amok, the Jewish population of Toledo would have been far more severely depleted than it was.

Ready or not, the army would have to leave.

The knights rose at midnight, for that was the hour that Jesus Christ had risen from the dead, and heard masses. At first light the massive contingent began to wend its way down the descent from the city. The noise from the hooves of thousands of horses was an underlying rumble over which the cries of support from those of the inhabitants who had turned out to cheer them rose and fell in a swelling counterpoint. The procession was headed by the four kings: Alfonso VIII of Castile, Sancho VII of Navarre, Pedro II of Aragon and Afonso II of Portugal. They were followed by the bishops, foremost among whom was the Archbishop of Toledo, Rodrigo Jiménez de Rada. He was followed by the bishops of Bordeaux, Nantes and Narbonne. Gone were the tents of the encampment: in their place the sun glinted redly on helmets, chain mail and suit after suit of armour, and banners and standards streamed in the fresh breeze of the summer dawn.

It was a glorious start, united and strong; it lasted only until they reached the Moorish town of Malagón. There, despite Castilian opposition, the French forces razed it to the ground and butchered the inhabitants. When the expeditionary force reached Calatrava, they could not decide on the course of action. The Iberians were for pacting a surrender, while the others wished to repeat Malagón. In the end, the Iberians had the best of it and succeeded in conquering the city by pact. Faced with such a lily-livered approach to crusading, the other members of the force, headed by the bishops of Bordeaux and Nantes, decided forthwith to abandon the campaign.

Uncharitably, there were those who hinted that it was the difficult terrain and terrible heat that were responsible for this decision, rather than any lack of avenging zeal on the part of their fellow crusaders. The intense blue of the cloudless skies; the dry wind; the scree and scrublands that made travel so slow, up mountains and down into valleys, all the time under a beating, merciless sun that shrivelled everything it touched after nine in the morning until it went down in the evening. Whatever the reason, scores of the French and mercenary militias were falling victim to the scorching heat of the Iberian summer and disease was scything its way through these forces with devastating rapidity.

A depleted army pressed on south, this time headed for the plain of Las Navas de Tolosa, just to the south of the Despeñaperros Pass through the Sierra Morena, where the massive Almohad army was waiting for them. To reach the plain, the Christian army would have to pass through a narrow canyon called *El Muradel*; but the Muslims had thought to block it and so they found themselves stymied.

Hopes of a victory began to dwindle as it became obvious that either the Christians submitted to being picked off by the Muslims as they tried to force their way through the canyon, or they make an inglorious retreat. But then the truly unexpected happened: a local shepherd was found who knew of an alternative route through the mountains known as *El Rey*, which would bring them down onto the plain of Las Navas de Tolosa.

It seemed too much of a boon and yet there was no sign of either Muslim scouts or still less the Muslim army as they began to make their way through this secret pass. And so it was that on the morning of Monday 16 July 1212, the Christian coalition fell upon the unsuspecting Muslim army, taking them by surprise.

Fighting was inconclusive for a while, first the one side gaining an advantage and then the other. But some of the Christian knights and soldiers began to flee, crying out that the battle was lost. At that point two things happened. First, Archbishop Rodrigo Jiménez de Rada committed his Toledan militia to the fray, injecting it with new vigour and hope. Then King Alfonso determined that he would not submit to another crushing defeat such as had been meted out to him at the Battle of Alarcos; he would die on the field rather than endure that ignominy again. He commanded his standard bearer and some men to accompany him to the top of the hill where the Almohad contingent was stationed. The Muslims were unnerved at this apparition, as they thought a new wave of Christians was about to be unleashed on them. They began to fall back in dismay.

As the Muslim forces began to scatter, Alfonso also commanded that deserting Christian soldiers be rounded up and coaxed back into the undecided battle.

Some equilibrium on the Muslim side had been fatally lost, and increasingly they floundered. The decisive moment came when King Sancho the Strong broke through their lines and reached the caliph's fortified camp. There he came upon Muhammed al-Nâsir surrounded by a personal bodyguard of chained Nubian slaves.

These chains were broken; but the caliph managed to escape on horseback, fleeing to Jaén.

With appalling rapidity retreat turned into a calamitous rout. Left leaderless, the Muslim forces fell apart. Up to one hundred thousand of them were killed or captured. The Christian forces lost two thousand, mostly from the Orders.

Whilst [illegible] turned into a [illegible] [illegible] [illegible] [illegible] [illegible] were killed or captured. The [illegible] [illegible]

XVII

The cart jolted over a hole in the road. There was a groan from one of the bodies stretched out inside; the others were either unconscious or already dead. A tattered piece of material had been erected on sticks by way of shielding these unfortunates from the intense glare of the sunlight, but more than anything else it had probably served to stifle what little air was circulating. The buzzing of flies broke through the immense silence of the July afternoon with a demented intensity.

Michael Scot stood in against the walls of the buildings in order to let the cart get past and continue on its way up the winding street. It was headed where many of the wounded from the campaign of Las Navas de Tolosa were being deposited; the fortress at the top of the hill had been transformed into a huge infirmary and Plaza Zocodover an open-air vestibule. As he ascended the street, a deep rumble began to throb in the still air, like an approaching avalanche about to hurl itself on the city lost in heat-induced slumber.

Now he could distinguish cries and groans. The sight that burst on his eyes as he rounded the corner and stepped out into the plaza was staggering, and he stood there open-mouthed for what seemed like an age. In every direction, the wounded lay stretched out on the ground. Various canopies had been erected here and there, but a great many of them lay exposed to the sunlight. Some had womenfolk to look after them, but most did not. Michael Scot had heard that the Orders had sustained the greatest number of deaths and injuries in the battle, and these soldier-monks now had no one to care for them. No one who was not already dead, injured or still engaged in skirmishes with the enemy away to the south.

All these casualties awaited medication from within the fortress, where he too was headed, having been summoned to give what assistance he could in tending the injured. He picked a path through the mass of agony, trying not to gag at the stench hanging in the still air. He felt his habit being plucked at, and feeble rasping whispers begging for water. He had none to give.

But maybe he could make himself useful in this way. If they could spare him within, he might endeavour to reclaim from the brink those without who were being further enfeebled by heat and thirst.

In truth, he was feeling very queasy about what would face him inside. The rumours that had got back to the School of Translation of the depredations wreaked in battle were stomach-turning. And yet, he would have to get through it. The soldiers had done their part; it behoved him to honour this through whatever ministrations he could offer.

He found the principal physician, Father Ermegildo, in a small study on the second floor. His apron was spattered in blood and gore. He mopped his brow as another casualty was brought in. Michael Scot's stomach gave a lurch as he made out the shattered leg, the bones splintered and the tissue hanging raggedly from the gaping wound. It was, he noted with a sense of faintness, a dark colour. And evil smelling.

The man stared at them from unseeing eyes and ranted in the throes of delirium.

'It is as well,' sighed Father Ermegildo, 'for it will have to come off, and we can ill afford more alcohol to dull the pain.' He wiped his hands on the filthy apron and gestured that the man be placed on the long table.

'Father Ermegildo,' said Michael Scot, 'how can I be of assistance?' He quelled the sense of nausea that threatened to cut short his words.

'I have no immediate need of you here,' replied Father Ermegildo, 'I am well served by my two assistants.'

'I think there is need of someone to bring water to the injured waiting out in the plaza,' said Michael Scot. 'By your leave, I would procure water and attend to them.'

'Yes, yes,' replied the weary physician. 'A good idea. See to it.'

Michael Scot turned on his heel and left the study. But he did not make it quickly enough to the end of the corridor, for the high-pitched scream barrelled into him before he had managed to set foot on the stairs to the lower floor.

He had not bargained on the roar of want that would run through these men, agitating them in a paroxysm of hysteria, as if they had not realized their own state of abject craving until they saw the water. He forcibly enrolled the help of any able-bodied person he came across in that vast plaza, assigning them certain areas. Hours passed: bells chimed, calls to prayer rang out, and still he scooped and ladled, scooped and ladled, among these broken men.

And it would not finish here, for score upon score of them were still trundling up from the Sierra Morena, looking for healing from wounds that would leave permanent mutilations in the best of cases, and in the worst, be the death of them.

*

In this way Michael Scot found himself occupied for July, August and September, in the wake of the Battle of Las Navas de Tolosa. Now and again he came across a soldier who was not too grievously injured, and from him would glean fresh news from the south. The Christian forces under Alfonso VIII continued to harry their enemy, capturing and razing the fortified cities of Baeza and Úbeda, gateways to al-Andalus, and deporting the inhabitants into slavery; laying siege to and taking the fortresses of Baños, Tolosa and Ferral. The Muslim forces from Córdoba, Jaén and Granada attempted to come to the assistance of these wasted territories, but they were routed by the Christian militias from Toledo, Madrid and Huete.

The coalition began to feel itself invincible. But then disease accomplished what their enemy had failed to. Infiltrating their forces, death came like a noxious fog, wending its way through the army on a rank breath of dissolution and putrefaction, decimating them. It was time to return to Toledo.

Archbishop Ramon Jiménez de Rada personally carried the blue starred standard of the caliphs to Toledo Cathedral and placed it there during a triumphal ceremony. It was at this point that he put forward the idea of a new and suitably splendid cathedral for the city of Toledo, capital of Spain – a Spain growing rapidly in size before their very eyes.

*

'It's a pretty poor show,' said Andrés Alfaquir, putting his stylus down.

'How so?'

'It would, I fear, take two of us to make one of the new triumphant breed of Spaniards so much in evidence in recent times.'

Michael Scot raised an eyebrow.

'Oh yes – let us not delude ourselves. Neither of us would be particularly welcome at the celebrations taking place, for neither of us fully meets the mark.'

'The mark? What mark?'

Alfaquir's expression darkened. 'In my case, having lived here for centuries does not suffice.' He looked at Michael Scot.

'And in your case, despite being Christian, you are and always will be an outlandish foreigner.'

Michael Scot remained silent. What could he say? His recent experience gave the lie to what Alfaquir had just said. For he was aware of an increase in goodwill from some quarters, due perhaps to his efforts with the injured from the battle. He was spoken of in terms of a certain esteem now, and taunted less. But there was little point in sharing this with Alfaquir. He was vexed enough as it was, without having to confront the fact that even Michael the Scot was taking precedence over him in the pecking order. He derived no pleasure from his increasing acceptance if it came at the price of someone else's exclusion.

Acceptance and its corollary exclusion: a dynamic that shadowed fallen man throughout his life, from cradle to grave. Who or what established the criteria regulating this hierarchy of acceptance? What did it take to set oneself up as an elite? He had never been part of one, nor was he ever likely to be. For it was power that transmuted a sense of belonging into a need for acceptance. The drive to power was what formed elites, and to succeed power had to fragment: fragment any cohesive sense of belonging by setting people against each other, dividing them into camps, factions and tribes. And the fragmentation demanded betrayal.

Achieving acceptance inevitably came down to some choice that amounted to an act of betrayal: betrayal of one's conscience, family, friends or country. This faction and not another; siding with this tribe and not another; scrabbling up instead of sliding down.

It had to be admitted. Medicine was the channel through which a certain sense of belonging had come even to him, Michael the Scot, as he was now known. What he had strenuously avoided for so long had finally found a place in his heart. He could no longer pretend to himself that his experiences tending to the soldiers wounded in the battle of Las Navas de Tolosa had not made a deep impression on him; they had filled some hole at the centre of his being and this foreign land had opened up to him.

More possibilities were opening up in the translation venture. Surely the material that the Moors had compiled on the study of medicine was worthy of being translated too. Life seemed to be offering him several opportunities, several paths to be followed: if he could bring them together in some kind of a cohesive whole, there indeed lay a worthy ambition. A sense of what his life's mission could be buoyed him up: this was the work he had been put on earth to do, but it revolved around service. He would be a channel for whatever of knowledge came his way, so that in its turn knowledge would be his servant – never his master – in the quest for bringing about the greater good.

XVIII

AD 1215

It was a stunning blow. Michael Scot had not thought Rome would do as much. The ban extended from Aristotle's metaphysics to his speculations on Natural Philosophy; anybody caught teaching, disseminating or otherwise promulgating his works would be excommunicated. It was true there had already been papal censure in 1210, but he had thought that would be the extent of it. There seemed to be no way out. The vista of what might have been, the possibilities he had seen opening up, tormented him.

He and Alfaquir had already worked their way through the four books of the *Meteora*, along with *De Substantia Orbis*. Then they had successfully tackled Averroës' work on Aristotle's *Physics and Metaphysics*.

They had just turned their sights to the commentaries on *De Coelo et Mundo* when word reached them of the papal ban and of the consequent censure enacted by the University of Paris concerning Averroës.

*

By contrast, Andrés Alfaquir betrayed little consternation; his lip merely curled in derision. It was as if the long-threatened shadow of an impending storm had finally materialised, and some part of him had been preparing for it forever. It was more of the same old thing; maybe even a little worse. He would remain with Michael Scot for a very little while yet. Then, if events took the course he thought they would, he would be gone. He would leave his family, Toledo, and Spain, without so much as a backward glance and seek his fortune elsewhere. Despite what his father the physician said, there was always a call for translators.

It was then that Alfaquir introduced Michael Scot to Jacob ben Abba Mari ben Simson Anatolio. And with this came the realisation that Alfaquir held out no hope of a solution being reached on Aristotle and Averroës. For Alfaquir had singled out the younger man as his successor.

Not alone did Michael Scot have to deal with a papal ban of the material being translated, but he was also about to lose Alfaquir. He had no desire to relinquish this precious collaborator and have to build up again the trust and ease that came from a successful working relationship. Added to this, Jacob Anatolio was ridiculously young, only twenty-one. But, Alfaquir countered, his intellectual accomplishments were impressive. Samuel ibn Tibbon, Maimonides' translator, had taken him under his wing and his knowledge of Arabic was accordingly excellent.

Such was Michael Scot's sense of chagrin that he even refused to meet Jacob Anatolio, preferring to risk everything by remonstrating forcibly with Alfaquir in a last-ditch attempt to make him change his mind and stay. But Alfaquir was adamant. He had had enough of his father carping at his choice of profession; continually throwing it in his face that he had broken the family tradition of physicians. According to his father, if he had become a physician instead of a scholar and translator, he would not now be packing his bags and heading off to Cairo.

Alfaquir glanced at Michael Scot and shrugged impatiently. It was not a question of having chosen the wrong path in life – as he continually told his father. Having mastered three languages, he was in a position to command a substantial fee for his services.

Had he not been in the service of the King of Sicily and Germany on as good a stipend – if not better – than his father enjoyed? Quite simply, it was now time to move on. In Cairo it was still possible for Jews to make their way.

His father was always pointing out how important Jews were here in Toledo. Did they not fill all manner of important and prestigious positions? From physicians to notaries, to court functionaries. Their learning and expertise were everywhere in demand. How could the city get on without them?

Andrés Alfaquir's response chilled Michael Scot, for he cursed his father's stupidity. Merely because the family had been living in Toledo for generation after generation, from time out of mind, did not make them an integral part of this society. Everything his father said about Jewish learning and expertise was true. But, he added, what his father failed to see – what his overriding need to feel accepted would not permit him to see – was that the Jews were indeed everywhere needed. But nowhere wanted.

His father had accused him of wanting to break his heart. But that wouldn't hold him back either. For this city, Toledo, this land of Sepharad, this country-in-the-making of Spain, was no more home than anywhere else. And he was leaving. He could feel it in the air: there was something malignant arriving. Some great evil for the Jews, yet again. But he would not sit here waiting for it.

*

Dom Sebastian had taken the collapse of the translating endeavour to heart. Who do you know that can help, he asked over and over, more to himself than Michael Scot it seemed. Who do you know that is powerful enough to put this to rights? The only person Michael Scot knew who answered this description was Frederick. It must be a cleric, Dom Sebastian urged, coming as close as

Michael Scot had ever seen him to losing his patience. Who is the most powerful cleric you know?

In truth, he did not think he knew any powerful clerics. But then one name did come to mind. Stephen de Provins, his mentor from his student days in Paris.

Dom Sebastian's relief was proportionate to the urgency of the situation. Stephen de Provins was theological advisor to the pope and would be present at the upcoming Fourth Lateran Council. He advised Michael Scot to procure an audience with him in Rome in order to gain his protection in the translation work; he himself would set about inserting him in Archbishop Rodrigo Jiménez de Rada's retinue, which would be heading to Rome in the autumn for the council.

Michael Scot grew almost sanguine. If only he could speak to de Provins, explain the enormity of the work they were carrying out in Toledo, and the enormity of the loss for Christendom if it were to be made null and void. It was glaringly obvious which course of action the Church should undertake; surely they would not miss the opportunity for advancement being offered to them. He outlined his plan to Alfaquir, and spoke with cautious optimism of his hopes.

It was a fool's errand, Alfaquir scoffed. Winds of change were blowing over Spain; he, Alfaquir, had a special sensitivity to them. Too many of his antecedents had been caught up in the chaos that came in their wake for him not to pick up on the signals, signs and portents that presaged a change in climate. Look at Jacob Anatolio's family, forced to flee al-Andalus on account of the repressive, inward-looking nature of the Almohad caliphate; then there had been the Albigensian massacre. True, they were not Jews. But there had been that murderous foray into the *Judería* by the mercenaries in the lead-up to the battle of Las Navas de Tolosa. He could see the same repressive mindset was at work everywhere, the same utter refusal of what was different. And then, had Michael Scot not yet heard tell of the yellow badges that would soon become compulsory wear for all Jews? Word had reached him from his contacts in Rome. He for one had no desire to humiliate himself with one of these filthy badges of shame.

He was of the Sephardim; his people had been in Toledo for more than a millennium. Or, as they had once called it, Toledoth. The name in Hebrew signified 'generations': Toledoth, city of the generations, the generations in exile, a resting place for the Jews who fled to Spain following Nebuchadnezzar's conquest of Jerusalem and the Babylonian captivity. For the Sephardim, Toledoth was to be a second Jerusalem, and so they recreated a second Palestine around it. The towns of Escaluna, Maqueda, Jopez and Azeque were erected in the lands surrounding Toledoth in memory of Ashkelon, Makeda, Joppa and Azeka.

It was time to move on. After that initial exile, there could be no further exiles, as there could be no real homeland ever again. Everywhere needed, but nowhere wanted. One place was as good as another. At least until the winds of change blew up and once more stirred men's hearts to violence.

XIX

Dom Sebastian kept the long-term goal of the translation work firmly in his sights. It was true that Aristotle was under a papal ban at the moment. In the fullness of time this would change. So they had better not let themselves be found wanting or unprepared. Measures could be taken now, and work done, as long as this was kept from the arena of common knowledge and did not become a source of scandal. Urged on by the elderly monk, a chastened Michael Scot had given in and accepted with as much grace as he could muster the prospect of starting his translation work afresh with Jacob Anatolio. Dom Sebastian had personally arranged a meeting. It took place in the same small study he had given to Michael Scot and Alfaquir four years previously.

Although a little more stooped in gait, Dom Sebastian ushered Michael Scot into the study with undiminished benevolence. They found Jacob Anatolio seated on a bench waiting for them. He immediately got to his feet while Dom Sebastian gratefully took his place, taking a moment to recover his breath.

'Now, Canon Michael,' he said softly, not wanting to strain his lungs and induce a fit of coughing that would exhaust him, 'I have the honour of presenting to you Jacob Anatolio. You have been told of the esteem in which he is generally held; put him to the test and you shall see it for yourself.' He motioned to Jacob to step forward.

'Canon Michael Scot,' said the young man, his voice low but composed, 'I am mindful of the honour this position represents. Should you decide to engage my services, I undertake to carry them out to the best of my ability. Your goal shall become my goal and I pledge you my total commitment in securing the success of this great endeavour.'

It was well said, and in excellent Castilian. But the accent was foreign, that much he could tell, most likely from Provence. Michael Scot remained in silence, but he continued to observe the young man. He noticed that while Jacob Anatolio did not flinch, neither was there anything challenging in the eyes that met his assessing look. It was a face of contrasts: there was the angularity of youth in the strong lines of the jaw and chin and a mouth marked by a full lower lip, offset, however, by the straightness of its line; but the eyes were melancholy, accentuated by the eyebrows which tended downwards. He could see no sign of the weight of knowledge that Alfaquir alleged he carried round with him. The overall impression, he judged, as a sense of inchoate irritation gained a hold on him, still bespoke an over-weaning sense of goodwill and openness.

'You do not have the look of a scholar about you,' said Michael Scot.

Dom Sebastian looked into the middle distance and rubbed the bristles on his chin, his mouth puckered in disapproval.

Jacob Anatolio smiled. 'I believe the only confirmation you'll need in that regard can be found in my brain,' he replied, the downward slant of his eyebrows giving his smile a rueful touch, as if to mitigate the trenchancy of his riposte. 'But you'll have to move beyond the vagaries of my physiognomy to ascertain that.

'I should mention that it has been my privilege to study under Samuel ibn Tibbon, principal translator from the Arabic of Mosé ben Maimon – that towering figure of cultural learning, intellectual rigour and integrity. It is from him, whom I hope will also become my father-in-law, that I first learned of Maimonides' synthesis of Aristotelianism and Jewish philosophy, from him that I conceived my limitless admiration for the man. For, as my future father-in-law never tires of telling me, Maimonides' dictum was: "We must accept the truth, from whatever source it comes".'

'Well,' interposed Michael Scot, 'the truth of this matter is that none of it is of any importance for as long as there is a papal ban.'

'My family had to flee Córdoba when Maimonides was banned there. But it came right in the end. In Marseilles, where we moved to, there is no ban. And the work of dissemination goes on. So you see, I understand very well what is at stake. And you can count on my support.'

'Indeed,' said Dom Sebastian, his eyes moving between the cleric and the scholar. 'When can we look forward to work resuming?'

Both men regarded the elderly cleric: the one recalcitrant, the other galvanized.

*

Jacob Anatolio was grateful for this opportunity: it was the first concrete step forward on the life of a scholar and he was delighted to find that the remuneration was proportionate to the prestige. For he wished to be married, and the success or otherwise of his life as a scholar would mean nothing to him if he could not share it with Rebekah. But Rebekah's family had been reluctant to hand her into the care of a young man who had not as yet proved his worth.

Well, now there was a chance to make sure that he would not be just another penniless scribe with no prospects. To be in the pay of Frederick, King of Sicily and Germany, was in itself no small boast; it was what his future parents-in-law would latch onto. But what gave him particular pleasure was the idea of collaborating in such a noble enterprise. Because there was no doubt that the work Michael Scot and Andrés Alfaquir had embarked on was of groundbreaking importance.

From that beautiful house in Marseille, Samuel ibn Tibbon's words came back to him. They had been said gently, but left little doubt as to the precarious nature of his prospects with Rebekah. Jacob had been coming to the house for a year in his capacity as Samuel ibn Tibbon's assistant: six months had passed in silent adoration of Rebekah, and a further six as the two of them snatched every opportunity they could to spend a few moments together. But the nature of their feelings had become too obvious, so they deemed it wise to make a clean breast of it. Jacob requested an interview with Samuel ibn Tibbon, which was granted. Seated near the window of the family room on the first floor overlooking the inner courtyard, sipping herb cordial, he had armed himself with courage and asked for Rebekah's hand in marriage.

Samuel ibn Tibbon nodded slowly, his eyes shifting to the pile of manuscripts they had been working on. 'Well, well,' he had said, 'well, well.' There was a long pause, during which Jacob did not even dare to take a breath. 'But you see, Jacob,' Rebekah's father had continued, 'marriage is a serious business.' He paused to look down at his hands and Jacob, as silently as he could, took a ragged breath. 'My daughter is well provided for: the man who becomes her husband will have no cause for complaint. But it is my duty to ensure that the beneficiary of her dowry be in a position to provide amply for her in his turn. She too must be fortunate in her husband.'

Jacob took a sip of the cordial. His heart had been pounding so loudly that he feared he would not be able to swallow it.

He had been granted a period of time in which to establish his credentials. Rebekah was still young: at sixteen she had time on her side regarding marriage. Could he, in the space of a year, present evidence – concrete evidence – of his future prospects, then a betrothal might be countenanced.

Jacob had set out from Marseille and headed towards Toledo and its famous School of Translation. There, surely, he would find a patron, and the means to secure his own future.

And now six months had already elapsed and the need to find some way of presenting concrete evidence to Samuel ibn Tibbon had become pressing. It all hinged on this Michael Scot and the new material that needed translating.

*

Michael Scot worried him. The man seemed to have fallen into a state of lethargy. When they met now to work, the eyes that had previously unnerved him with their glittering intensity, looked through him, opaque and apathetic. This was not the demeanour of a scholar at the height of his powers, imbued with a sense of mission.

Jacob fretted that the plan to translate Averroës' commentaries on Aristotle would come to naught. Perhaps Michael Scot's reliance on Alfaquir had been such that, with his imminent departure, all fervour for the enterprise had disappeared. He knew that the commentaries and translation of *De Coelo et Mundo* had been abandoned in the little study on the far side of the monastery.

He sent word to Dom Sebastian that he had urgent need to speak to him. They met after dark in the scriptorium. Jacob was immensely relieved to see that Dom Sebastian had no need of convincing where the importance of the work being carried out was concerned, for he was just as anxious that it be brought to completion.

'But this papal ban,' said Dom Sebastian disconsolately, 'there is no way of getting round the ban on Aristotle.'

Taking his courage in his hands, Jacob suggested that they turn their attention instead to another Muslim philosopher. Why not translate al-Bitrûgi's recent astronomical work entitled *Kitāb al-haiʾa*? Perhaps this would contrive to show what was at stake, while avoiding the ban on Aristotle. He could take it to Canon Scot and try to persuade him to set to work on it.

Dom Sebastian's old hand gripped his arm with unexpected force, and his eyes shone. 'Follow me,' he intimated and, despite the darkness, found his way unerringly through the shadowy rows of manuscripts, desks and presses, the dim glow from his candle sending skittering shadows across the high-ceilinged room, until he came to a large press. He extracted a bunch of keys from his habit, their clangour an unexpected rent in the dark stillness, and opened it. The manuscript they were looking for was on the top shelf. He gestured to Jacob to take it down.

'Well, my son,' he said, his voice barely more than a whisper, 'I have every confidence in you. In God's name, get to work.'

As Jacob laid the manuscript before Michael Scot, the words came out in a rush. How he thought too much of this endeavour to stand by and do nothing. He knew work of groundbreaking importance when he saw it. He had taken the liberty of making inroads on this new manuscript himself.

For the second time since he had met him, Michael Scot looked long and hard at the young man. It was not easy for Jacob to withstand that penetrating scrutiny; for the eyes divested themselves of the opaque veneer that had lately muddied them, and plunged, it seemed, into his deepest being with assessing speed.

Michael Scot then broke the silence. 'God bless your intelligence and initiative,' he said, 'I have need of both.'

Although he did not manage to overcome the sense of awe that Michael Scot provoked in him, it was not of the kind that paralyses. They now had a goal: by the time Michael Scot was due to leave with Archbishop De Rada for Rome, they were to have finished the translation of *Kitāb al-haiʾa*. This, then, would Michael Scot bear with him to Rome as both a trophy of learning and a token of the possibilities that were opening up for Christendom. They worked unceasingly, by day and often by night. Increasingly, Michael Scot would detain him after they had concluded their work, and they talked for long hours together. He told the young man how grateful he was for his presence of mind in selecting al-Bitrûgi's work; how it perfectly filled a gap in astronomical knowledge to the present time. And, Jacob reminded him, also sidestepped the ban on Aristotle. Indeed, smiled Michael Scot. Although the system that it presented did in effect revert to the outmoded Aristotelian view of astronomy. Ptolemy's *Almagest*, translated by Gerard of Cremona in Toledo the previous century, had superseded all that. But, he qualified, his eyes lighting up, it did contain one new concept that might prove to be of lasting interest.

Jacob observed the childlike enthusiasm animating the older man. Then Michael Scot sighed. 'It brings me back to my own student days in Paris,' he said. The expression was now sombre. 'I was about your own age then, and it seemed that all you needed to get ahead was a good brain, goodwill, and a capacity for hard work.'

'So what is this new concept you perceive in al-Bitrûgi's work?' asked Jacob, sorry to see the enthusiasm fade from Michael Scot's eyes.

Michael Scot outlined the novelty with painstaking care. It was easy to see why the young King Frederick had set such store by his teaching. It introduced the theory of impetus. The theory could in all probability be traced as far back as the sixth century BC to Philoponus, and had been reiterated again in the sixth century AD by Simplicius, who had explained the continuous motion of the heavenly bodies by making their impetus exceed their gravity. The doctrine supplanted the Aristotelian doctrine of accelerated motion as caused by the surrounding air.

All through the heat of August, the balmy days of September, and on into the golden stillness of mid-October, they worked unceasingly. They also discussed Aristotle and Muslim and Hebrew learning: Michael Scot outlined the thrust of Avicenna's and Averroës' work, and Jacob spoke, at first shyly and haltingly, but then with confidence and admiration, of the work his future father-in-law, Samuel ibn Tibbon, was carrying out in translating the work of the great Jewish philosopher, Maimonides, from the Arabic into Hebrew.

In other words, Michael Scot said to him, Muslims had attempted to conciliate Islam and Aristotelianism; the Jews, too, were attempting it. But the same had still to be enacted in Christendom. His eyes glittered. God willing, the ban would be lifted on Aristotle so that their translations might be the harbinger of that great goal.

And so, armed with his translation of al-Bitrûgi, in November he went to Rome. But as Alfaquir had warned him, it proved to be a fool's errand.

Rome,
Papal State

XX

November AD *1215*

It was an autumn journey. An expedition of hope in the dying part of the year. Michael Scot and Archbishop De Rada were lodged in the large monastery situated between the massive Aurelian walls and the Basilica of St John Lateran. It was clear from the outset that this council had been conceived on a large scale. Innocent III had mustered seventy-one patriarchs and metropolitans, including the Patriarchs of Jerusalem and Constantinople; four hundred and twelve bishops; nine hundred abbots and priors; various envoys from King Frederick of Sicily and Germany, plus the kings of England, France, Aragon, Hungary, Cyprus and Jerusalem, as well as those present on behalf of other royalty.

Michael Scot had sent a letter to King Frederick, telling him that he would be present at the council. The king had said that he dearly wished to meet his former tutor again, and since he, too, would be in attendance, after five years they were to meet again in this city of popes.

Proceedings commenced on 11 November. The pope was a commanding presence whose vibrant opening speech proclaimed his own willingness to drink the chalice of the Passion for the defence of the Christian faith; his conclusion was a rousing exhortation to the faithful on the pursuit of moral probity. Then came the list of the seventy canons of dogmatic and moral theology, already formulated, that would have to be debated in the course of the council.

Sitting at Archbishop De Rada's side, Michael Scot listened as the words 'heresy' and 'heretics' clanged with sinister resonance and frequency around them. And the names Flora and Amaury come under scrutiny. Both were condemned: Flora merely as misguided, as he had remained faithful to the Church in submitting his speculations for her approval; but Amaury was condemned as insane, his ideas not even worth debating. Greater measures would have to be taken to suppress heresy wherever it occurred.

As Alfaquir had predicted, canon sixty-eight decreed that Jews and Muslims were to wear special dress to distinguish them from Christians.

His mind flying from one implication to another, Michael Scot nearly missed hearing the council give its approval to the elevation of Frederick II to the German throne.

When Michael Scot informed Archbishop De Rada that he would not be accompanying him to the following day's deliberations, the man peremptorily demanded an explanation. Michael Scot told him of his audience with Stephen de Provins. De Rada looked at him askance: what was somebody like Michael Scot doing presuming on an audience with Stephen de Provins, one of the most brilliant theologians of his time, and one of the few men on whose opinion the pope depended. Michael Scot was aware that his own superior, Palacio Taracón, who was de Rada's protégé, had spoken ill of him to the archbishop.

The presumption, if indeed it could be construed as such, he replied, was due to his personal acquaintance with the man. Back in his student days in Paris, de Provins had been his mentor. And it had been de Provins' interest and testimonial that in 1200 secured him the position of tutor in mathematics to the young Frederick II.

At this, de Rada paused and looked at him; then he shrugged and bade him do as he pleased.

As a fellow Premonstratensian, de Provins had taken a keen interest in Michael Scot's meteoric rise among the ranks of the mathematicians at the University of Paris; he had been the first person to take active steps in the furtherance of Michael Scot's career, and he felt a debt of gratitude to him. To which might also be added a residual sense of deference. At the time, Michael Scot had been twenty-five, while de Provins had been a far more assured forty. Michael Scot had gone on to be a part of the entourage of the King of Sicily; de Provins was an advisor to Pope Innocent III. Now he would be fifty-six and Michael Scot wondered what changes time might have wrought.

On a dark November afternoon, he was ushered into the spacious rooms de Provins had been allocated in the Lateran Palace. The pope's own living quarters were close by. A fire crackled in the immense hearth. The candles had not yet been lit, so his eyes did not immediately pick out the small figure kneeling at a prie-dieu over in the far corner.

The door was closed gently behind him. Stephen de Provins got slowly to his feet and with measured steps made his way across the room. Michael Scot had not entertained feelings of any great warmth for the man when they had known each other all those years ago in Paris. The fastidious aloofness that de Provins emanated, in no way attenuated by the Frenchman's habit of interspersing his pronouncements with benign smiles, had seemed to preclude anything warmer than respect. Which was still a great deal. But seeing him now, after so long, and in such different surroundings, it was as if the real essence of the man crystallised before him, and unexpectedly he found himself sinking to his knees, head bowed, asking for his blessing.

The small, pale hands fluttered in the sign of the cross above his head. In reality, Michael Scot was not that much shorter than de Provins, even on his knees. The hands then gestured at him to rise and indicated two chairs in front of the hearth where they were to sit.

By the light of the fire Michael Scot saw that, apart from the almost white hair, de Provins had not really changed. The ascetic detachment that had characterised him as a man in his prime, imparting an aura of otherworldly delicacy, had perhaps increased; but it was a more congruous presence now in an elderly man.

'It gives me great pleasure to see you once again, Canon Michael.' The voice was a gentle murmur. 'And how have you been getting on?'

Michael Scot, as he began his account of the intervening years, saw those minute, white hands, veins standing out like silken skeins of blue against the translucent skin, draw together in a prayer-like attitude and the finger tips come to rest on the lips. The light-brown eyes, flickering with intelligence, surveyed him with detached affection.

'So, you see,' Michael Scot braced himself as he came to the crux of the matter, 'I made the move to Toledo on account of the immense contribution its School of Translation has made to knowledge in Christendom.' He paused. 'It is my fervent hope that it may continue to do so.'

'Amen. And why should it not?'

'Some of the texts I have been translating have been censured.'

'That being the case, what were you doing translating them?'

'I had started work on them long before the censure came through.'

'And you are reluctant to see years of work thrown away, I suppose…'

'It is not merely a question of that, though it would of course pain me. There are other issues at stake here.'

'Indeed.' The pale fingers drummed on the armrest of his chair, the nails clicking with surprising force.

Michael Scot rubbed his forehead with the fingers of his hand, in an attempt to alleviate the sense of pressure that was suddenly making his skull throb. Stephen de Provins reached out a hand and, without actually touching him, made a patting motion. 'We are not talking only of Aristotle here, are we?'

'No. Averroës is the filter through which I am in the process of gleaning Aristotle's writings.'

'Well, well, well…' The fingers resumed their drumming. Abruptly they stopped. 'And what benefit is all this to bring us?' asked Stephen de Provins, observing Michael Scot closely.

'The benefits, so far as I have seen, are in the field of Natural Philosophy. The mysteries of God's creation are examined and discussed; everything from the flowers of the fields to the feeding habits of newly hatched falcons.'

Stephen de Provins digested this in silence; his fingers were still.

'It is an area, do you see,' took up Michael Scot, 'about which Christendom still knows little.'

Still Stephen de Provins stayed silent.

'In this respect, both the Muslims and the Jews are far ahead of us,' he added, observing de Provins to see if he was even listening to him. 'It was the case when Peter Abelard and Adelard of Bath noted the greater intellectual aperture of the Muslims in this field a century ago, and sadly continues to be so.'

'Do not disturb yourself with considerations of who is ahead and who is lagging behind,' de Provins interjected. He sat back into his chair, assuming a more upright position. 'The Lord's time is not mere mortals' time.' And then, a murmur, 'Many that are first shall be last, and the last shall be first…' He looked at Michael Scot and smiled. It did not reach his eyes. 'Canon Michael, I have no doubt as to the quality of the work you have undertaken – none whatsoever. I know you of old and am aware of the excellence of your God-given intelligence. Please bear with me.' He rose from his chair and walked over to the darkening window. There were a few moments of silence in which Michael Scot hoped against hope that what he had instinctively guessed, was not now about to come to pass. The prospect of so much wasted effort…

'It has fallen to us,' said de Provins, his voice rising as if to reach not only Michael Scot, still seated at the hearth, but unseen ears in attendance on this exchange, 'to be servants of the Almighty in these times of turbulence and upheaval.' The unaccustomed force imparted a tinny quality to the frail voice, bringing a flash of memory of lecture halls in the Schools in Paris. 'It is the Church's duty to steer a clear course through these perilous waters. She is accountable to the Almighty for the souls that have been entrusted to her.' He turned suddenly to look Michael Scot straight in the eye. 'Have you any conception of the countless numbers of misguided sheep who depend on us for their eternal salvation?' His voice dropped. 'And the weight of responsibility that this brings with it?'

He tucked his hands into the sleeves of his habit. 'The Lord's time is not mere mortals' time.' Silence fell in the room. 'Much hangs in the balance; much depends on the paths we now embark on. And the time is not right for these translations, Canon Michael. That time has yet to come.'

Michael Scot bowed his head. He could not trust himself to speak.

'Come, come,' said Stephen de Provins gently, moving back to his seat by the fire. 'Do not take this to heart. The Lord's ways are inscrutable to us.'

True enough, thought Michael Scot. But who's to say that these are not merely *your* ways. And what worth did they have in the eternal workings of the Almighty? He rubbed his forehead again. 'But, do you not see?' He willed his voice into a semblance of obedient reasonableness. 'Both the Muslims and the Jews have effected a conciliation between Aristotelianism and their faiths – through, respectively, Averroës and Maimonides. Surely Christendom should be working towards the same inspiring goal?'

'Listen here, Canon Michael.' De Provins' tone was suddenly

less amenable. The tinny quality turned to steel. 'Let us speak clearly on the matter. Both the Jews and the Muslims have suffered great upheaval as a result of this, er, inspiring goal, as you call it. You must be aware of the divisive impact it has had on their communities.' He paused briefly. 'This despite the fact that both the Jewish religion and Islam hinge on orthopraxis, rather than the orthodoxy that underpins Christianity.' There followed a much longer pause to let the import of this point sink in. 'The Jews are dealing with it as they can. Because they form small, close-knit communities wherever they go, no large-scale schismatic movements have arisen. But that is not to underestimate the extent of the damage that has been wreaked in these communities, which have found themselves divided down the middle. The Muslim situation is different. And yet more comparable to our own, if you will. They represent a major power, both political and religious, spread over many nations, countries and peoples. Their approach is worth reflecting upon, for it has proved exceedingly effective. In recent times, they have exiled those whose philosophies run counter to established beliefs, and against any recrudescence of the same, burned their books. Islam has cleansed itself rigorously of any elements that run counter to tradition, and especially the dangers that arise through misguided intellectual questing. Islam has, it would seem definitively, turned its back on the risk posed by according equal stature to reason and faith. Faith is their sole objective. Al-Khazali is the chief exponent of this: the candle burns, not because of energy, but only because Allah wills it so.' De Provins gave one of his smiles. 'You see? I am not averse to keeping abreast of these developments. And it is disarming, really, this approach, in its childlike simplicity...' His eyes shifted away from Michael Scot, fixing themselves on the dull light that still trickled in through the window. 'But ultimately,' the soft voice murmured dreamily in the gloaming, 'not perhaps the approach that we in Christendom shall adopt. I want – er, that is our Holy

Father wishes – that Christianity be a monument to the ongoing dialogue between reason and faith.'

His eyes honed in on Michael Scot. 'Ecclesia is a stern Mother. Prove yourself to be a true and obedient son. She will be mindful of it.'

*

The bedlam surrounding him barely impinged; the jostling crowd and the raucous voices selling wares reached him as if from a great remove. Head bent, Michael Scot made his way down the narrow street, the clamour in his own head propelling him along through the refuse and slops that littered the way. Tall narrow houses rose up around him, blocking the little light that still struggled to break through the low grey clouds. Shopkeepers and artisans shouted from the open porches where they did trade, the counters reaching out into the street. Further off, the spindly towers of the nobility reached up grasping fingers into the lowering sky.

He could not face returning to the monastery. And so he found himself striding along these filthy streets, going – despite the pace – he knew not where. Anywhere but the monastery. But this city, this city of Rome – what kind of a monstrosity was it? Scattered here and there, astounding relics of a distant and glorious past, round which had sprouted the higgledy-piggledy constructions of his own age: ramshackle, provisional, and so busily obtuse to this. Decay from the distant past, over which a thin layer of the already decaying present had attached itself, like the haphazard appearance of barnacles on the body of an elderly whale.

Had Paris been all that different? For him, that city would always be the city of his youthful hopes, the city that had first instilled a sense that a bright future might be something he could rightfully aspire to; there had he been made aware of what success could be. He did not recollect in Paris the filth or squalor or the persistent stench of waste that assailed him here. Nor had Palermo repulsed him in this way. In Toledo he had grappled with the present and the day-to-day implementation of his youthful hopes and ambitions; there neither had he any recollection of pervasive decay.

Everywhere needed but nowhere wanted. The phrase haunted him as he strode along the streets. Suddenly, it was as if de Rada were at his elbow, and their exchange on the topic of the proposed yellow badge for the Jews seeped into his mind. His objection to it; and De Rada's unabashed endorsement. His awareness of its power to humiliate; and De Rada's enjoyment of this. 'And why should we not avail of it?' he had concluded. 'It is not our invention, that much is true. The Arabs in Baghdad first employed it in the tenth century in order to identify the extraneous elements of the population. Yellow for the Jews and blue for the Christians. I see no reason why we should not follow their excellent example – in this instance.' He had chuckled and then added, 'Unfortunately, we shall not be able to reciprocate the compliment, as their numbers in Christendom seem to have dwindled remarkably in recent times.'

Everywhere needed but nowhere wanted. What now would he do with his life? All his misplaced ambitions had come to naught. The pursuit of knowledge had brought him to this pass: at its expense he had neglected to pursue ecclesiastical advancement; he had worked unceasingly in order to advance knowledge and learning. And the absorbing, peregrinatory, almost clandestine nature of his work on the translations meant that he had neglected to seek a Chair at a university. When the first papal ban had come through in 1210, he had thought that it would pass quickly away, that the authorities could not but come to their senses, given the intrinsic importance of the material he was translating. So he continued to work diligently. He had not even been troubled by the fact that his completed translations had remained unpublished. Now it was all too clear just how deluded this had been.

And so at forty, he found himself with nothing.

What then to make of Stephen de Provins' admonitions about Ecclesia, of the need to be her dutiful and obedient son... And suddenly it came to him: Avicenna's description of the workings of a hive of bees. Such a rigid hierarchy, exclusively for the benefit of the queen bee. A merciless taskmaster, she exacted total obedience from her drones; failing this, they were eliminated. The queen bee's capacity to exert power seemed almost an end in itself; even the production of honey was secondary to it. And in seeking out the enemies of the queen bee, the blow given was as fatal to the drones as it was to those on the receiving end of it.

That was all he was now: a drone stripped of his duties.

He stumbled as his foothold on the slimy mud betrayed him and his habit was spattered with the foul contents of a puddle. He bent down to wipe off the worst of the mess, and on regaining an upright position, found a basket of stinking fish being pushed under his nose. He was pressed to buy some. Suddenly, rage coursed through him.

Before he had time to think, his hand had gone out and hammered the contents to the ground. A yell issued from the fishmonger and the crowd swivelled to see what the commotion was about. It was the roar of disapproval that went up from the crowd that did it; it matched the surge of rage that had taken hold of him. The fishmonger was shouting at him, shaking his fist, the anger mottling his face. Incensed, and suddenly gunning for a clash, the crowd turned on him. He was possessed by a baleful sense of exhilaration and loosed two punches – one to the man's head, and one to his stomach. There was a low, menacing grumble from the crowd; they took a step back, while simultaneously forming a circle. Michael Scot found himself shaking. The realisation that it was not due to fear made him laugh out loud, and he observed the fishmonger get to his feet with a curious detachment, almost holding back, aware of such a deadly surge of violence in himself that he scrupled to charge him down then and there. The fishmonger eyed him, his mouth twisted into a snarl, and then he scrabbled on his filthy counter to pick up the knife he used to gut the fish. Michael Scot watched as the blackened fingernails closed greedily round the handle; his exhilaration ebbed, coagulating into something icier. Something that would leave more traces in him than in whatever two-bit adversary he might be facing.

He dodged the first lunge, and felt the disappointment of the crowd wash over him like gall. Twice more, he evaded the blade snaking its way towards him. And then, as he was stepping aside from the fourth, he felt the hand from the crowd behind him shove him back into its path. The sense of surprise: surprise at the lack of pain as the coarse white wool of his habit stained with scarlet. His limbs would no longer obey him; he crumpled to the ground.

The crowd surged forward – only to disperse again immediately. Michael Scot looked up. In the gathering darkness, within and without, he could just make out the tall figure of de Rada looming over him. Silence seemed to have enveloped the scene, and a lacerating pain suddenly kicked into life.

'You are a disgrace – to your habit and to the Church,' Archbishop de Rada's words, mixed with his spittle, fell on him disdainfully from above. He waved to his retinue. 'Take this fool back to the monastery.'

XXI

The two clerics stood at either side of the foot of the bed. The light from two candles, one in a wax-spattered holder at the head of the bed and the other held aloft by Archbishop de Rada, hovered meagrely in the close stillness of the infirmary.

De Rada was holding his candle at chest level; from there the flame stretched a tremulous tongue that played up the sallow contours and shadowy hollows of his face, until it, too, seemed to acquire the crumpled flaccidity of melting wax.

'May the good Lord have mercy on his soul,' said Stephen de Provins quietly. 'It would seem he is not yet out of danger. Have they told you anything?'

De Rada did not reply; his mouth merely turned down dismissively at the corners. De Provins noted the grotesque, mask-like quality this gave his face. It was disconcerting that the archbishop should be so unaware of the effect that the candle's position was provoking. 'But if, God willing, he makes it through the night,' de Provins added, turning his gaze back to the patient, 'he has a good chance of making a full recovery.'

'It's in the Lord's hands.'

'It's the infection that has debilitated him to this point – unconscious with fever for the last two days and nights.'

De Rada shrugged. Once again silence fell in the room. Then de Rada's eyes shifted from the unconscious form stretched out in the bed back to the diminutive man standing on the other side of it. His eyes narrowed speculatively. 'Should the Almighty grant him a recovery, I feel that there would be little point in his returning to Toledo.'

De Provins joined his fragile hands and brought them to his lips. Head aslant, he surveyed the archbishop.

'His behaviour was disgraceful,' said de Rada, his voice rising harshly. 'And he dishonoured his habit.'

'Be that as it may,' de Provins replied, his own voice barely above a whisper, so that de Rada's eyes narrowed again as if in an effort to hear him. 'Who among us has not dishonoured his habit at some stage?'

De Rada's eyes fixed themselves in contemplation of an unspecified spot on the opposite wall. He was determined not to be out-manoeuvred by de Provins.

'Your Grace, let me help you,' said de Provins. 'Allow me to rest the candle on this table.'

'Ah yes, the candle...' It was unclear whether the expression of amazement that passed over de Rada's face was due more to hearing himself addressed as your Grace – a recognition of his status; what could it mean? – or the fact that he had forgotten he was still clutching the candle. The expression did not escape de Provins. Smiling affably, he took the candle, let some wax drip from it onto the table, and then secured it.

'While I in no way condone what Canon Michael Scot has done,' de Provins took up, his benign smile at odds with the unsettling focus of his eyes, 'he has had his provocations. It cannot be easy having to hide one's light indefinitely under the papal bushel.' He toyed absently with the wax dripping from the candle. 'And not so much as a whisper of scandal has ever attached itself to his name before this.'

'Only our Saviour can be the judge of that,' replied de Rada, on the defensive. 'You are surely aware that his translating activities in Toledo have given us cause for concern.'

De Provins remained silent, seemingly lost in thought.

'As for this manuscript—' de Rada shook his head, exasperated. 'Such contentious material. And at a time when this manner of heresy leaves Spain open to all manner of risks. A heathen Muslim's musings on the workings of the universe – what next?'

De Provins' eye followed de Rada's hand as it extracted the manuscript in question from under his mantel. 'He has had the lamentable idea of dedicating it to you,' continued the archbishop. De Provins abruptly ceased poking at the wax; his eyes flew to the weighty tome. 'But God knows you must be above reproach in this unfortunate association.'

'Indeed,' concurred de Provins icily, his lips pursing. 'However, as you yourself have said, only our Saviour has the right to be the judge of these things.' He held out his hand.

'I will hand you over this manuscript in lieu of an assurance that The Scot will not be returning to Toledo.'

'It is an assurance I cannot give.'

De Rada held on to the manuscript. 'Let me explain to you why I must insist on this point. Spain has a mission at the present time. She must unite under a Christian banner. For this, there is need of courage and obedience. Now is not the time to fritter away resolve through all this mingling of ideas and watering down of truth. This... this—' his free hand made a contemptuous movement and his voice became a furious growl, 'wilful contamination with heathen and pagan heresy. That is why nothing must be let stand in the way of this holy objective. For we have it within our sights!'

At this triumphal disclosure, de Provins' lips compressed into a thin line. He surveyed the length of the robustly framed man in front of him – more warrior than archbishop. Certainly, he had done great things in advancing the cause of Christendom. Everyone knew of his tenacity and courage. But there were many ways of being true and courageous to the faith. 'Everything depends on the timing,' he murmured. 'It is vital to see this.'

De Rada snorted. At that moment he doubted whether this prating midget could see beyond even the end of his own nose. What could be more important than the battle that was under way in Spain to reconquer the country and snatch it back from heathen hands?

'News of your exploits at Las Navas de Tolosa reached us here in Rome,' de Provins continued unperturbed. 'And while your timing in military terms may be impeccable,' he smiled benignly, 'elsewhere, alas, it lacks acumen. Christendom does not depend only on its military might, you know. It must also seek to promote intellectual might.' He held out his hand. 'Kindly allow me to see the manuscript.'

De Rada's jaw set.

'I do not have to remind you of the keen interest our Holy Father takes in these developments.'

In a tense silence, de Rada handed it over. He watched as de Provins took the weight of the manuscript into one hand while covering it protectively with the other. Then he moved over to the table and the dim glow of the candle. Slowly he turned over the first page and perused what he saw there in silence; he murmured the words, *De motibus coelorum*, Alpetragius. He turned the next couple of pages, his pale fingers holding them with delicacy. De Rada saw the avid way those wily eyes scanned the pages. Then, gently, he closed the manuscript. 'I shall be very happy,' he said, as de Rada noted the peculiar tinny quality that had come into his voice, 'to keep this manuscript in my care. Perhaps Rome is indeed the safest place for it.' He smiled seraphically. 'It comes down, as I said, to a sense of timing. I shall be the keeper of this priceless compendium of learning until its moment arrives. For it, too, has a role to play in the greater glorification of our Creator.'

De Rada looked on in repelled silence as de Provins' hand caressed the cover of the manuscript with something akin to lasciviousness. 'That may resolve the question of the manuscript,' he objected resentfully, 'but its author still poses a problem. I – and my diocese – would be very relieved to see the back of his arrogance, stubbornness and recklessness once and for all.'

'Let us not betray our ignorance by confusing the author of this manuscript with its translator. Nor should we betray our Christian principles by being uncharitable to the latter. I know him of old and have no hesitation in testifying to his brilliance.'

'But he fraternises with all manner of undesirables,' de Rada gestured expansively. 'Jews, Muslims...' The list petered out. 'It is enough, I tell you! He keeps constant company with them. Think of the peril to his soul.'

'As to that, I have no reason to fear it presages his imminent perdition,' de Provins snapped. 'How else do you imagine he could have set about translating an Arabic text but by getting assistance from those versed in Arabic?'

'If that is the price to pay for such an enterprise, then I would rather forego it.'

'Even so, Canon Michael Scot will return to Toledo, and there shall he continue his work of translation of these Muslim philosophers. Unimpeded, do you hear? Otherwise, I shall have to report any interference to his Holiness.' The pale fingers tapped the cover of the manuscript. 'None of his translations shall be published, however. They must be kept out of the public arena for the present.'

De Rada grunted. He cast a last look on Michael Scot's manuscript, still nestling in de Provins' embrace. Good riddance to it. Alas, it was not in his power to say the same to its translator.

It was, of course, Hell. The lambent presence of flames in a suffocating murk; and the pain... Pain everywhere. Pain so excruciating that he thought he must die of it. But he was most assuredly dead already. What demons were tormenting him, gouging at his innards with pikes, cruelly twisting them in flesh red and raw. How he burned! And there was no let-up from this torture. A black mass was descending on him; what horrors would it contain? Difficult to breathe; suffocating, impenetrable.

And then the head loomed out at him, a hand's span from his own face. Terrifying, horned, leering horribly. Its eye travelled down to his bloodied belly; there was a snarl as it opened its slavering maw, bringing blackened fangs down on him.

He opened his mouth to scream, but no sound came out. He could not move. He watched in horror as the beast ripped away half his innards. Then he heard a high-pitched shriek of infinite terror. Followed by more screaming. Were other demons advancing on him? A hand on his shoulder, pulling at him. No, no. No more. But it kept pulling at him. Canon Michael, Canon Michael… He groaned.

'Canon Michael,' came the voice again, 'wake up. Come back into yourself. Canon Michael, can you hear me? You've had a bad dream. Wake up now, have some water.'

Slowly, the horror receded, and he found he could move his limbs. He opened his eyes. The gloom, the flickering light, they were all there. But so was his body; no gaping bloodied hole in his bandaged belly greeted him. The relief was so great that he started shaking.

'Canon Michael,' said the brother standing at his bedside, 'you must have had a bad dream. Have some water.' With a trembling hand, Michael Scot brought the goblet to his mouth. His throat still felt so constricted that he could only sip it. He also feared that he would not be able to keep it down.

'The fever is still very high,' said the brother. 'It would be best if you could get some more sleep. The night is not yet finished.'

'What did they do to me?' His voice was a disjointed rasp.

'You were haemorrhaging when they brought you in. The blood loss was severe. They staunched the wound as well as they could; unfortunately, an infection has developed, which has set you back.'

Michael Scot tried to nod. But it was an effort, and an effort to talk, and an unbearable effort to drink from the goblet. Slowly, he turned his head away from the brother; it was the only thing he could move without setting off a paroxysm of pain.

'Do not move,' warned the brother. 'You will open the wound again and set off the bleeding. You cannot afford to lose more blood.'

Lying there in the stillness, the pain radiated from the wound in his belly and throbbed into every inch of his body. How could he bear it? There was no respite. And he could not seek the oblivion of sleep for fear of the horrors that might bring. His existence was reduced to the breaths he took, moment to moment, in the hope that there might be some let-up in this agony.

But none came. A thudding torment blackening everything before his eyes.

Lord Jesus, in your mercy take this pain from me, heal me. Restore me to the fullness of my health and I will never offend thee again.

XXII

'Master Scot.'

The voice was that of a young man, but the cadence took him back in a heart's beat to a far-off scriptorium in Palermo. Michael Scot's head turned as fast as his aching body would allow, his eyes fastening on the figure framed by the doorway of the infirmary. The gloomy penumbra made it difficult to make out the face. He removed the coarse, woollen blanket covering him and made to rise from the pallet.

'Stay where you are.' The young man strode across the rush-strewn floor separating them.

'Your Majesty,' whispered Michael Scot. He struggled to raise himself onto his elbows, but with a groan of pain sank back down onto the pallet.

'Do not move,' King Frederick looked down on him, his face creasing in concern. '*You* must obey *me* now, you know.'

Michael Scot smiled ruefully. 'Indeed.'

'I am glad to see you, Master Scot, it has been six years since our last meeting.' He rearranged the blanket over the prone figure. 'As I mentioned to you in my letter, I am come to Rome for this Lateran Council and could not let the occasion pass without paying a visit.' He turned to the two guards that had accompanied him, motioned to them to wait for him outside, then drew up a chair and sat down.

As he did so, Michael Scot observed him. Back then he had been a beardless youth of fourteen and Michael Scot's thick red beard had been an object of some talk. But in the intervening time Frederick had become the proud possessor of a well-cared-for red beard himself, while Michael Scot's had faded and lost its lustre. Such was the way of things. Time passed. Things came into being, grew, and then declined.

'Your injury precluded the more normal manner of courtesies being observed, and so I have come to you.' The king sat forward in the chair. 'What happened? What is this I hear of a brawl?' A smile flitted over his face. 'I do not recall you being so rowdy from our days together in Palermo.'

Michael Scot closed his eyes and shook his head. 'Your Majesty, being found by you of all people in this situation goes sore against the grain. Truly, I ask your pardon.'

'Never mind, no fatal harm was done. Tell me how you have been getting on.'

'I came here to petition my mentor from Paris, Stephen de Provins. And in this I have been singularly unsuccessful.' Michael Scot reminded the king of the contentious nature of the Aristotelian material his Majesty had commissioned him to translate and related how it had come in for a papal ban. He mentioned the translation of Alpetragius' work on astronomy that he had brought with him, his hopes that it might rekindle an interest in knowledge with a Moorish provenance – and the refusal this had met. 'I am blocked, your Majesty,' he said. 'And cannot see my next steps clearly.'

'Ah,' replied Frederick, 'I too know what it is to be blocked.' He stood up and began to walk slowly up and down the room, his hands behind his back. Turning to face Michael Scot, he said, 'You and I find ourselves shackled by the papacy. And there seems to be no way to break free.' He rubbed his beard meditatively. 'Because by asserting the supremacy of spiritual authority, the pope has usurped the right to choose whoever is to be sovereign. There is so much at stake here, do you see, because this is the council where Ecclesia will select the next Holy Roman Emperor. Innocent initially gave his backing to Otto IV, but the German overstepped the mark when he set his sights on the Kingdom of Sicily and the pope deposed him. Innocent then settled on me as the best candidate to sit on the imperial throne, and now he is seeking the backing of the prelates on the matter. But he has left this momentous decision right until the end of a highly taxing council. The uproar, the shouting and the bickering has been such that he had to call a halt to proceedings in disgust and reprimand the prelates for their intemperance. I was not, of course, allowed into the hall. But the pandemonium was so deafening that I had no difficulty in following events.' Frederick shook his head. 'It could go either way. I would be grateful if you said a prayer for me, Master Scot.'

'Of course, your Majesty.'

'You and I know Innocent of old; he was my guardian.' Frederick came back over to the chair and sat down. 'He is not an unreasonable man, but he is an extremely powerful one, and he holds both our fates in his hands. I must tread carefully or years of work will come to naught.' The young king leaned forward. 'Just think what it would be like if succession depended simply on a family line passing from father to son. Think of the time that could be saved and put to better use...' He shook his head and sat back into the chair. 'So you find yourself having to submit to ecclesiastical authority, Master Scot?'

'I do. It means that what I am translating cannot be divulgated. And so there can be no recognition.'

'Yes, that is mortifying. But I would like to see what you have been working on. I would like to measure myself against this new knowledge.'

'No one better, your Majesty. But it has either been taken from me, sequestered by the Church, or put safely out of harm's way. In truth, I am not sure now what path to follow.'

Unexpectedly, Frederick took Michael Scot's hand in his. 'Never doubt my support for you – you will always be able to count on my patronage. I have not forgotten that our hope was to make my court in Palermo the wonder of the world for its culture, art and learning. Even if you have to remain in the background for the time being, your moment will come. And I will be there to see you get your due.'

He stood up and went over to the small, darkening window. 'You know, Master Scot, that I have not been back to my beloved Sicily in years. I have been wholly taken up in affairs of state. And this has been a mortification for me, for of all people you know how I love to give myself over to poetry and mathematics, art and learning. I have gone wandering over Germany, in fair weather and foul, my life an unending blur of warfare, battles, city walls to be scaled, ramparts to be breached; negotiations to be brokered, princes to be assuaged, city burghers to be flattered. I feel as if I am a lodger in the dwelling place of my own life: I must pay the rent, but so far ownership of the estate has eluded me. I float on the surface of my life, caught up in a mesh of titles, pulled hither and thither in the play for power. How is it possible to be looked at as powerful, and yet to feel like such a pawn?'

'Pawns and drones,' murmured Michael Scot.

'What is that you say?'

'I was just thinking, your Majesty. My wish is that I should continue my work of translation in Spain, bring it to a conclusion, and present it to you back in Palermo. My hope is that the innovation it offers will bring lustre to your court.'

'If I know that you are working on this great project, I can surely look forward to sharing it with you at a future date.'

'I know in myself that the translations represent a step forward, for they bridge the gap between faith and reason. This cannot but be a welcome advance.'

The young king nodded. 'You, Master Scot, bring to mind happier times, simpler times. Although a part of me knows that they were neither happy nor simple. Indeed, I think we can both remember how there were times when I even lacked enough to eat. I was but a starving orphan.'

He turned round to face the older man. 'And yet, such of happiness as I knew, I knew mostly with you.' He began to move towards the door. 'I do not forget loyalty and goodness, Master Scot. I should be glad to receive news of your progress. Remember me in your prayers.'

Toledo,
Kingdom of Castile

XXIII

AD 1219

In the years that followed they were not idle. Initially, it had been tiring, thankless work, but after de Provins' intervention, de Rada had backed down and Michael Scot and Jacob Anatolio managed to translate a great quantity of new material. They worked their way through Averroës' Great Commentary on Aristotle's *De Coelo et Mundo*, and then completed the Great Commentary on the *Metafisica*. Despite considerable mulish resistance from Master Scot, Jacob prevailed upon him to dedicate this manuscript as well to Stephen de Provins. At the end of 1217 he had it sent to him in Paris, where de Provins had returned after the Lateran Council. But he also sent a report of everything he had translated to King Frederick in Sicily.

Then they turned their attention to the Great Commentary on *De Anima*. It was Master Scot's idea, and one that instantly appealed to Jacob, to conserve the original passages of Aristotle's text as headings in his translation of Averroës' commentary. For, as he pointed out, the original 'Middle Metaphysics' was still unknown, and the headings would fill this gap. This translation would be valued for the presentation to the Latin world of a Greek text as yet to be rediscovered, and an Arabic text freshly translated.

He also sent a report on this latest translation to Frederick.

*

In 1218 the King of Castile decided to hold a great conference on astronomy in Toledo. Learned astronomers came from all over Christendom. Ptolemy's conception of the heavenly bodies was seen to be imperfect and insufficient, and discussions took place in the Alcázar of Galiana so that new paths might be explored. The resulting theories were contained in a manuscript entitled *The Tables of Toledo*. Michael Scot was one of the honoured guests, primarily due to his translation of, and hence familiarity with, Alpetragius' theories. And since Michael Scot's star appeared to be in the ascendant, he saw to it that Master Anatolio also benefited from having collaborated in this enterprise.

It was at this juncture that Archbishop de Rada did what few men have the courage to do. He changed his mind: not from opportunism, but from a clearer apprehension of what was at stake. The manuscript that had been taken to Rome to present to Stephen de Provins, the same manuscript that de Rada had excoriated and abhorred, was now seen as a means for renown. De Rada was a witness to the respect and admiration accorded by astronomers from all over Christendom to its translator, the man who had understood its contents sufficiently to want to pass on the knowledge it contained. This goodwill was extended to the collaborator, Jacob Anatolio, without whom there could have been no new manuscript. Basking in the prestige accruing to Toledo and its School of Translation, as well as the royal seal of approval of the King of Sicily, de Rada had gradually lessened his opposition to anything he had misconstrued as baleful outside influences watering down the purity of Christian Spain. The departure of experienced scholars such as Alfaquir was therefore regrettable; indeed, encouraged by the King of Castile, the archbishop set himself to looking for a way to accommodate those Jews who were so actively promoting the fame of Toledo as a cultural beacon. Words would no longer be sufficient to induce them to stay on in a place which many perceived to be increasingly hostile.

To this end he petitioned the new pope, Honorious III, to waive the obligation – at least in Toledo – for Jews to wear the yellow badge.

But during the conference itself, Jacob was unsettled to see that Michael Scot's restless, yearning mind was taking him somewhere else. The acknowledgements from his peers seemed to carry little weight. And on what had this wayward mind now bent its obsessive energies? On astrology and alchemy! Jacob had seen him poring over some incomplete manuscript he had come across, entitled *Secreta Secretorum*. When Jacob ventured to ask what it was about, his dismay deepened into apprehension. The text, he was told, outlined notions of astrology and the wondrous properties of plants, gems and numbers. It also contained an account of a strange, unified science that only the pure could accede to.

'This alchemy you have lately turned your full attention to, I suppose,' said Jacob.

'Indeed.'

'And how is the conference going? How do *The Tables* proceed?'

'Well enough,' replied Michael Scot, his brooding eyes barely registering the question.

*

They had been working in the hope that at some point in the future, all this labour would bear fruit. They were still receiving King Frederick's patronage to complete this immense task, but it was becoming a weariness of the spirit to both of them. Time and again Michael Scot recalled the parable of the talents, the parable he had taken care to mention to Frederick when he had tutored him as a youth. It was as if some part of him had already known of the years he would spend waiting, his work buried and unacknowledged. And the question that increasingly circled in his head: should he keep waiting or give up? For Christendom might never make its peace with Muslim philosophy.

Even Jacob was restless. Despite the recognition he had garnered, he still did not have a permanent position. This was not the place he wanted to bring Rebekah to as his bride. It seemed to him that place should be Palermo. But it was difficult to say what Master Scot's plans were. If the truth were known, the man was becoming increasingly erratic.

'Good morning, Master Scot.'

'Good morning, Master Anatolio.'

The study door shut behind Master Scot and he headed to the shelves holding the manuscripts, which he proceeded to leaf through in a desultory fashion. Master Scot was late for work again: Jacob saw the shaking hands pushed quickly back into the wide sleeves of his habit; and the roughened voice did not escape him. Nor did the bloodshot eyes that were not even raised in greeting. Jacob was himself abstemious, so the sour odour of the previous night's wine was an assault on his nose. In short, the telltale signs of another drinking bout were all there. His hand clenched in a tight fist; something had to be done.

But how? Talking about this to anybody was out of the question. Although, word was probably already getting round – starting with whoever was supplying Master Scot with the copious amounts of alcohol he had taken to consuming. It was tricky in the extreme: if he mentioned what he suspected – or rather, knew – to Master Scot, he risked jeopardizing their collaboration. There was no knowing what way he might take it – he could send him packing forthwith.

Painfully, he unclenched his fist; purple welts showed where his nails had dug into the flesh. Too much time and hope had been invested in this translation endeavour to see it collapse so ingloriously. And if Master Scot continued in this fashion, he would sink with him.

Jacob had no clear idea what Master Scot was thinking; he could not be prevailed upon to open up. Of late he had fallen to communicating in monosyllables, and if Jacob's probing irked him, would raise an eyebrow and quell him with a surprisingly piercing glance. In some strange way Master Scot brought about with him a sense of restless listlessness, always dallying but never settling. Perhaps, Jacob surmised, having been effectively silenced, he could no longer see the point in translating anything any more. The whole point of the translating endeavour was to communicate new material to as many people as possible, and that had been vetoed. Jacob saw with distress the sundered aspiration of the man, and was aware that what previously had come as easily as breathing now cost him painful effort. Some basic equilibrium had been lost, if not broken. How then could Jacob persuade him that this was the very moment when he needed to apply himself most?

He observed the tall spare form over by the shelves; should he broach the topic?

'Master Anatolio,' said Master Scot, turning slowly round, 'I feel I ought to talk to you.' Jacob's skin prickled; this did not bode well. The older man continued to avoid Jacob's eyes, whether through hostility or shame was difficult to decide. He sighed and sat down on a bench on the other side of the wooden desk, loosely interlacing the fingers of his hands in front of him. Knotted knuckles on tapering fingers, like a bundle of blackthorn twigs. His head was lowered and Jacob noted the contrast between the strong dark eyebrows and the pale skin, and then the faded red beard. The eyes still avoided his own. 'I realise that things have been far from satisfactory as of late,' said Master Scot, his voice a hoarse murmur. 'And I wish to apologise for that. The last thing I want to be is an encumbrance to a promising young scholar.' He continued to stare at his interlaced fingers. 'But the truth of the matter is that I think I have come to the end of the road with this translation venture.'

XXIV

Stunned into speechlessness, Jacob stared at Master Scot, whose eyes flickered regretfully in his direction. 'I think,' he muttered, 'for both our sakes, it might indeed be sheep-shearing back in Scotland for me – as was once so perspicaciously recommended.' The silence lengthened uncomfortably. There was so much Jacob longed to say that the welter of words jammed his tongue to his palate.

'Sheep-shearing…' he said eventually, nodding slowly. 'Well, I may have to join you.'

Master Scot's eyebrow lifted. 'The scholarly life has palled for you?'

'No, it has not. But, unlike you, this kind of renunciation is a luxury I can ill afford.' Jacob shrugged. 'Instead of giving up, you could face the difficulties. I was always taught that plain sailing does not make a skilful sailor.'

Master Scot snorted. 'Sheep-shearing. Now sailing.' The eyes slid away.

'Look here,' cried Jacob. 'Just because you can no longer make sense of any of this, does not entitle you to cast me aside like some old beast of burden that no one needs or wants any more!'

Michael Scot's head jerked back up. Gone was the young man's habitual assurance and composure; this was a cry from the heart. And he recognized fear when he heard it. Need and want… Wanted and needed... Where had he heard those words before? Who had spoken those very words to him with bitterness? Ah, yes – Andrés Toledanus Alfaquir.

Jacob clamped his mouth shut, regretting this outburst. He had been immoderate; it was hardly the best way to plead his case. But Samuel ibn Tibbon's words were a goad and a torment. The latest letter from Rebekah's father had been all that was considerate. But in amongst the polite inconsequentialities, three lines of real news had shocked him. After stating his certainty that Jacob was undoubtedly carrying out work of the first order and congratulating him, Samuel ibn Tibbon had remarked that, after all, four years had passed. What did Jacob intend to do? He was honour bound to tell him that another eligible suitor for Rebekah had presented himself and made his intentions very clear. And while his daughter had no wish to entertain this other young man's suit, as a father, he, Samuel, must always look to her good.

Jacob could not allow everything he wanted to slip through his fingers. Master Scot had been neutralised by his Church, but he would never be abandoned by it. He, Jacob, found himself in an altogether more vulnerable position. His mind whirled feverishly in an attempt to arrive at some kind of a rational decision.

'You have to listen to me,' he urged. 'This much you owe me. Hear me through and then we shall see where we stand.'

Michael Scot listened in silence, his only discernible reaction being some rapid blinking, but that might have been due to the dryness of his bloodshot eyes.

Well, to start with, Jacob pointed out, they were dangerous times. And the material they were endeavouring to translate was contentious. It was not an auspicious moment to start spreading the speculations of Averroës, even if they were an illustrious means of purveying the philosophy of Aristotle. For, even before they were published, they had somehow become associated with the taint of Alexandrian Gnosis, and hence of Albigensianism. An aura of heresy hung over the enterprise, which was conspiring to smother any voice that might emerge from the pages of manuscripts, ancient or contemporary, from near or from afar. So much for that.

Then there was the question of Master Scot's behaviour. He had become increasingly erratic. No real headway was being made with the translations. For, as Jacob knew – even if Master Scot tried to hide it from him – in between the sporadic bouts of work were interspersed far more consistent bouts of drinking.

It was not that he, Jacob, did not understand – he too felt all the precariousness of their position. Nevertheless, it disconcerted him greatly to see someone for whom he felt such respect debase himself in this way. Where was this wine coming from? Who had Master Scot cajoled or bribed into supplying him? Whoever it was, they too knew of his vice, and this left him open to disciplinary action. Combined with the contentious nature of the work he was carrying out, it might yet prove to be his undoing.

Michael Scot looked at him through narrowed eyes; his jaw shifted forward.

'If I am to help you,' Jacob stated with slow deliberation, 'then you must help *me*. I propose this. Make sure of our patronage from King Frederick: through it we can sit out the Church's opposition until more auspicious times and continue our translation work in reasonable autonomy. We can afford to bide our time until the taint of heresy hanging over the material we are translating diminishes. In the meantime, I shall procure for you in the *Judería* such Arabic manuscripts on medicine as have never been seen by Christian eyes. For word has got round,' – nodding, he glanced at Master Scot – 'of your skill in healing the sick and injured following the battle of Las Navas de Tolosa. These, too, you can translate for King Frederick, who will be the first Christian sovereign in their possession.'

The two men looked at each other. Master Scot's left eyebrow lifted and a smile touched the corners of his mouth.

'Agreed,' he said.

*

The year 1219 wore on into 1220. One summer evening as twilight settled over the city, Jacob came upon Master Scot in the study, lost to the world as he read a manuscript. Peering over his shoulder, Jacob saw that it was written in Latin. So it was not something outlandish that Michael Scot was going to suggest they waste their time translating. He waited for him to look up.

'You are very taken with what you are reading,' he said, when eventually the grey eyes met his own.

Michael Scot sighed at length. 'This is one of the most remarkable manuscripts I have read,' he said. 'It is a Latin translation, carried out last century by Gerard of Cremona, of *At-Tasrif* by Al-Zahrawi.'

Jacob shook his head and shrugged.

'I knew nothing of it either,' replied Master Scot. 'I cannot but wonder that such a piece of medical learning has remained in the shade for so long. It is truly astounding in the breadth of its learning and knowledge. This changes everything for me.'

Jacob looked at him askance. 'How so?'

'I must find out more. I must understand. This approach to medicine is incomparably brilliant. I have you to thank for this, Jacob – the manuscripts you found for me are even more engrossing than I hoped. There is much to be done. I must go to the city where this learned physician lived and find all the material written by him I can. This I will copy and then set my mind to putting into practice. For medicine is now my guiding light.'

The heavy silence that fell over the room must have impinged; Master Scot turned to look again at Jacob and his expression became rueful.

'The only thing I am loath to leave here in Toledo,' he said, 'is you. I have been selfish in concentrating on my own affairs. But fear not – I have been in touch with King Frederick. He wishes to inaugurate a new university in Naples that will surpass all others. As you know, they are all of them currently under the control of the Church, but this one won't be. There's bound to be an opening for you there. Look to it, and I will see you right. I have informed his Majesty that I wish to go to Córdoba and seek this medical material, and he has generously extended his patronage again. When I return, together we shall go to Palermo and I shall present you to Frederick.'

As Jacob nodded, all he could think of was how he was going to explain this latest delay to Rebekah. 'Then I shall have to visit Rebekah's family in Marseille,' he replied. What Master Scot suggested sounded good; but yet again it only amounted to future prospects. He still had nothing concrete. 'Let us make good a plan, that I may have something to show for my time spent here.'

Master Scot nodded. 'Frederick is to be made Holy Roman Emperor in November. Honorious III is trying to coerce him into setting off on crusade by elevating him to this position. He has not been back to Sicily these several years, so we would do well to get back to him in Palermo before he has to leave yet again.'

'How long do you think you will need to stay in Córdoba?'

'I would think about two months. If I am there by the end of August, two months of hard work should do it. I could be ready to leave before Frederick gets back to Palermo.'

'That means at the latest you should have terminated your work there by late October. We could agree to meet in Valencia at the beginning of November.'

'Indeed. And from there set sail for Palermo.'

*

In his mind Michael Scot passed over the wonders he would encounter in Córdoba. For there, the Moors had mastered such techniques as made falling ill almost a pleasure. It made his own treatment – and sufferings – at the hands of those Roman charlatans seem primitive. There was indeed much to be done.

And Córdoba... Had not the Germans written the previous century that it was the jewel of the world? A fabled city, a city of passing beauty. And he desired to see beauty now, he craved beauty and wonder.

Córdoba,
Caliphate of Al-Andalus

XXV

AD 1220

Córdoba was like a waking-dream of beauty. A dream, however, that would metamorphose horribly, terrifyingly, into a nightmare. Nothing had prepared him for the vistas he came upon there, not even Palermo. How was he to know – how could he have guessed – that what started out in a blaze of wonder, would end up as a whimper in the dark?

He pulled the wooden door to behind him and looked his last on this tiny outpost of a monastery, tucked away up in the heights of the Sierra Morena. Then in the early morning light he turned and finally gazed down on the opulent splendour that was Córdoba, capital of the Western Caliphate of al-Andalus. Despite the earliness of the hour, a pearly heat haze already enveloped the city's shimmering mass of golden stone, which stretched away to the south east towards the towering snow-capped austerity of the Sierra Nevada. He had heard tell it was home to over half a million souls.

The words of the monastery's abbot came back to him. The previous night, as he had shown Michael Scot into the miniscule cell reserved for travellers, he had cautioned discretion. 'Above all,' he had warned, 'do not draw attention to yourself. Do nothing that might provoke an outcry.' He had observed Michael Scot closely from head to toe. 'Your attire will pass muster. The black cloak is a good choice as it covers everything. You must be aware that it is forbidden to proclaim your status as a cleric. And,' his eyes had fallen on Michael Scot's reddish beard, 'as it is no harm to err on the side of prudence, I would advise you to keep the hood pulled up.' He had reached out a hand and pulled back the cloak. 'Yes, the cord belt will do too. Christians and Jews are not allowed to wear belts made of silk or other such materials.' He let the cloak fall to. 'But whatever you do, never display the crucifix.'

'What are the risks?' Michael Scot had asked.

'The risks...' The abbot had shrugged. 'The risks will be of your own making. Be mindful that there are restrictions. Those are not of your own making and must be observed. If you do so, you should be left in peace to go about your business. You are a guest here. Do not expect to find a welcome; but by respecting the laws, you may hope to be tolerated.'

With his Arabic, he was managing to make himself understood. The gap between what one learns through reading and writing and the spoken reality of the language was disconcerting, but he was managing to get by. First, he set about finding some lodgings. King Frederick had been encouraging of his desire to explore the famed libraries of the Moors, and had extended such patronage to him once again as would obviate financial worries for the duration of his stay there. The lodgings were pleasing without being wasteful: clean, well situated near the centre of the city, and – to his incredulity – equipped with indoor sanitation arrangements. He was advised to try one of the many public baths for his own personal hygiene.

He was told which library he must go to for the manuscripts he was seeking on medicine. It was not far from the Jewish quarter, within the Almodóvar Gate that led back into the Moorish part of Córdoba. A spacious building, with those same horseshoe-shaped arches he had seen in Toledo in the Mesquita, decorating the many columns within. It housed countless manuscripts and was provided with alcoves for reading and others for writing. Michael

Scot came armed with his stylus, pen and some parchment; his hope was that he would be allowed to copy any available material by Al-Zahrawi. At the far end of the main hall he saw a turbaned figure, bent over a pile of manuscripts. He approached.

'Peace be with you.'

'And with you,' came the reply. Then the head turned sharply, revealing a young man whose politely assessing eyes swiftly took in the bearer of this foreign accent. 'How can I help you?' he asked with distant courtesy.

'I wish,' explained Michael Scot, 'to consult and copy material in your care by Abu al-Qasim, known as Al-Zahrawi.'

'Many are those who aspire to partake of the knowledge and wisdom of this son of Kortuba. Who are you to accede to it?'

'I am Michael Scot, translator for his Majesty, Frederick Hohenstaufen, King of Sicily, Italy, Germany and Burgundy. Here is his seal of approval on my safe-conduct.' The parchment rustled as he removed the document from his woollen pocket.

The young man took it into his hand, touching it curiously. 'I have never come across this material before. It is parchment, is it not?'

'It is,' replied Michael Scot, frowning in puzzlement.

The Moor raised his arm and indicated the vast array of manuscripts stored in the library. 'We use paper here. It is something we learned from the Orientals,' a smile hovered over his mouth, 'a long time ago, and it has proved vastly more efficient and cheaper.'

Paper? wondered Michael Scot, What is this paper? But he held his counsel.

The librarian opened the document and glanced at it. 'I neither read nor write your idiom.' The dark eyes looked at him quizzically. 'After all, I have no call to do either. But I shall see if someone or other of the slaves can decipher this. Please wait here.' He indicated a long bench on which cushions had been strewn.

The authenticity of the document was vouched for, but Michael

Scot could not help wondering by whom. What manner of slave would be able to read Latin and Latin script? He was allowed to take the manuscript to an alcove and there consult whatever parts of it he found most interesting. Along with the recommendation that he procure himself a more economical supply of paper, he was also permitted to copy these parts.

And so it was that he became a regular sight at the library, arriving early in the cool of the morning and staying until the light began to fade in the evening, and copying became too difficult. Painstakingly, he copied as best he could the detailed illustrations of surgical instruments, the uses to which they could be put, and the symptoms of the various ailments that might give rise to the need for an operation. The learning and expertise of this Albucasis were beyond anything he had ever come across, above all the last volume of the treatise. The instruments presented ranged from a tongue depressor and tooth extractor, to a catheter and a complicated obstetric device – a forceps, evidently, which Albucasis had utilised only in the case of dead foetuses. The operations outlined included bloodletting, midwifery and obstetrics, and the extraction of cataracts. Albucasis specialised in the treatment of battle wounds, such as the extraction of arrows and the setting of bones in simple and compound fractures. There was an ingenious method described for righting a dislocated shoulder, along with the resetting of nasal bones and vertebrae. There was a part on antiseptics in the treatment of skin wounds: how wine could be used to clean wounds and prevent infection. And then, most interestingly, the surgical sponge used for anaesthetic purposes, composed of gall, poppy, henbane, hemlock and vinegar: this mixture was boiled and reduced; the sponge was soaked in it, and then applied to the patient's nostrils.

He thought back to the suffering he had witnessed in the wake of the battle of Las Navas de Tolosa; those horrific wounds; men writhing in torment; the screams of agony. How much of this could have been alleviated if they had but known of these techniques?

There was also described the process whereby the tonsils could be removed, how a tracheotomy and craniotomy could be performed. How a polyp could be removed from the nose by means of a hook; how a species of bulb syringe could be used for giving enemas to children; and how a metallic bladder syringe and speculum could be used to extract bladder stones. Along with this came extraordinary information for the ligaturing and cauterising of blood vessels and arteries. He had even devised the use of sutures from animal intestines, silk, wool and other substances.

Albucasis was particularly interested in the connection between the mind and the body. Depression of the mind gave rise to most of the body's ills. Michael Scot read eagerly about the opium-based compound invented by the Moorish doctor for curing depression, which he claimed 'brings levity to the soul because it banishes gloomy and wrathful thoughts, quietens the spirits, and combats melancholy.'

In truth, he might find no small use for this compound himself.

Certain ideas expounded by Averroës had been plaguing him. Ideas regarding life, the soul, and creation. They had left him feeling adrift, uneasy, at a loss. And at a time when the circumstances of his life had conspired anyway to produce these sensations. The Church which had been his mainstay, a moral guide, had sidelined him; and now the philosophical concepts propounded by Averroës had in some imperceptible way further diminished the pre-eminence of the Church in his life. He was loath to admit it, as it seemed to justify the reluctance of de Provins to publish his translations. It pointed to a corrupting influence in the material. His mind circled round the thought obsessively: if his translations had been published, would he have shrugged off the doubts insinuating themselves from them? Were the doubts a creeping mildew emerging from a lack of faith or an excess of injured pride?

And since he had come to this city, since he had placed himself beyond the bounds of Christendom, he had not been able to procure any alcohol. There was no let-up, no consolation to be found in his lodgings during the long evenings alone. Nothing for company but these incessant thoughts.

What kind of a man had Averroës been? Again and again, his thoughts turned to this enigmatic philosopher, a native of Córdoba. What exactly had Averroës believed? Why?

And what did *he* believe? Once it had been easy to answer that question. Now, increasingly, he was scared to try. He had no place in the scheme of things. Was there a scheme of things? Why was he here? What would come after?

When he prayed, who was listening? Did it make any difference?

Was Averroës right when he claimed that religion was for the simple masses, but the rigours of philosophy went beyond and should only be approached by the learned? What was this impersonal soul he spoke of? This developing eternity or eternal development devoid of the Father's hand sanctioning the act of creation?

And why did these speculations procure such a rush of solitude in him?

Perhaps he should seek out the original of Averroës' manuscripts here and measure himself again with their troubling message. He would have to ask the young man in the library to look them out for him.

XXVI

The young man's name was Yusuf ben-Yakub al-Hakim. He told Michael Scot so as they sipped a wonderfully refreshing goblet of sweetened water infused with lemon. From the shade of the library's arcaded inner patio they observed the hot sun beating down on a mass of many-hued flowers. But from the centre of the patio came the cool splashing of water from a fountain.

Noting Michael Scot's wondering expression, al-Hakim said, 'Very little that is delicate can resist the furnace of heat that ravages the city from June to September. That is why we have these water systems.'

'What do you grow here?'

'Well, apart from the usual olives and wheat, the irrigation systems we brought in from Syria have enabled us to grow pomegranates, oranges, lemons, aubergines, artichokes, bananas, almonds, sugarcane, cotton, rice, figs, grapes, peaches and apricots.'

'In Sicily I came in contact with most of these items. But in truth I have never heard of pomegranates, bananas, sugarcane and cotton. Are they good to eat?'

Al-Hakim smiled. 'I would not advise trying cotton – it would take a deal of time to chew.' He opened the folds of his long cloak and took his tunic between his fingers. 'This is cotton,' he said, pointing to the blue material. 'It is a blessing in the heat, as it helps to keep us cool.'

Michael Scot had been finding his coarse woollen tunic a terrible burden. Perhaps it was time for a change. 'Admirable. And this is cultivated? Like flax, perhaps?'

'Yes. The plant is harvested and then treated and spun to make the material.'

'And the other produce?'

'Our lemon drink has been sweetened by sugarcane. Pomegranates and bananas are delicious fruits.'

Michael Scot nodded. A brief pause ensued and then he said, 'So you cannot provide me with the manuscripts I mentioned by Averroës?'

'You mean Ibn Rushd? I am afraid to say it is no longer possible. And,' al-Hakim shook his head slowly, 'it does not depend on the acceptability of the seal of approval you bring.' He spread his hands in a gesture of regret. 'Most of Ibn Rushd's manuscripts were burnt several years before he died. There is little left here of his. It is a painful irony that what you Christians are in possession of is probably all that has been saved of his writings. What has been lost forever is incalculable.'

Michael Scot closed his eyes and pressed his fingers to his forehead. 'Burnt?'

'Burnt.'

Suddenly, Averroës became as remote a figure as Albucasis, who had lived two and a half centuries previously. There were no traces to be found of him in his native city, Córdoba. 'And what about disciples?' pressed Michael Scot. 'Is there anyone I could talk to who could explain his thoughts and flesh out the philosophy?'

Al-Hakim was silent for a moment. The smile was wry and fleeting. 'No,' he answered, 'Ibn Rushd has left no disciples, no one to carry on his great work. But,' he glanced at Michael Scot, 'if you delight in good conversation, I would like to invite you as a guest to my home, where I can introduce you to some friends of mine.'

'I accept gladly,' replied Michael Scot. 'Good conversation is always uplifting to the soul. But this news comes as a sore blow. How is it that I have come so far, to his home city, only to find his manuscripts burnt, and this empty silence surrounding his achievements?' He tried to quell within himself the sense of dismay that suddenly robbed him of strength.

He felt al-Hakim's eyes on him and looked up. The young man placed his goblet back on the tray in front of them and then, unexpectedly – disconcertingly – put his arm through Michael Scot's. 'Come, my infidel friend,' he said, and laughed. The white teeth were perfect. 'I can see there is much we can talk about together. Let us start now. God willing, the library will take care of itself for an afternoon.'

*

He took Michael Scot to the cemetery where Ibn Rushd had been buried in the tomb of his forefathers just twenty years previously. From here he showed him the Guadalquivir river, flowing west to Seville and then further on out to the Atlantic. Downstream from the Roman Gate Michael Scot looked upon a massive water-wheel, which he greatly marvelled at; it was used to raise and carry water to the caliph's palace. He saw the original Roman part of the city which the Moors called the Medina; he saw, too, how the walls of the city had been enlarged many times to accommodate the huge population; and then the immense suburbs to the east called al-Sarquiyya, protected by the most recently built walls. These walls had a more overtly defensive appearance, because, as al-Hakim informed him disdainfully, there had been an increase in the skirmishing with the northern Christian kingdoms. He commented little on Michael Scot's repeated exclamations of wonder, limiting himself to a quizzical smile; this did not change even when Michael Scot, pointing to the long, oil-filled stands lining the streets that lit them when it got dark, had professed his incredulity. Then al-Hakim pointed out the Great Mosque; Michael Scot saw a massive, relatively low structure, that spread over an immense quantity of ground. He remained silent, not sure what to think. Increasingly, churches in Christendom had a soaring appearance, reaching up supplicating arches and spires like prayerful hands to the heavenly Father. He liked the awe this vertical aspiration inspired in him. The mosque was different; the horizontal expanse seemed rather unprepossessing.

'Come,' said al-Hakim, 'we shall visit the Great Mosque together. I cannot have you exclaiming more over the street lighting than this jewel of sacred beauty.' He ran his eyes over Michael Scot and shook his head. 'But first we must procure you some decent attire; something that doesn't shout your barbarian status from afar. Follow me, monk.'

*

Clad in fresh cotton robes and resplendent in a white turban, Michael Scot followed al-Hakim with a certain awkwardness. Initially, the idea had appealed to him; but now that they were approaching the mosque, he was assailed by a strange reluctance to enter. He was not at all sure that he wanted to immerse himself in the atmosphere of a Mohammedan temple. But there was nothing for it; al-Hakim beckoned and he mounted the steps to the main entrance. He was about to step over the threshold when the young man whispered furiously at him, 'Remove your sandals, fool of an infidel!'

Michael Scot started, and then his eye fell on al-Hakim's bare feet; his sandals had been neatly placed just inside the entrance. He complied and they went in.

In front of him was a vast courtyard where, al-Hakim told him quietly, ablutions were performed before going into the mosque proper.

Accordingly, they approached a fountain of running water and washed. Here, when the mosque was too full, the faithful could still participate.

They stepped over the threshold of the mosque proper. And then it fell on him like an unexpected, refreshing spring shower: a sense of beauty so sweet and penetrating that he could find no words. He could only stand still, as his soul was brushed into a shiver of recognition. For as far as the eye could see, a forest of columns wove arch after arch of fluid rolling interconnected submission to the divine spirit. And everywhere there was such an intricacy of filigree carvings, calling the faithful to interior meditation.

It was a God at once remote and abstract, and yet simply grasped; reticent in any outward manifestation, yet immanent in the sense of beauty. And undeniably present.

*

That evening Michael Scot went to al-Hakim's house in the Medina. Two friends were already there, reclining on large cushions that had been spread over a rug. In the middle was a low table, on which an intricately ornate lantern, lit from within by a single candle, glowed in the gathering darkness. There was a glazed pitcher of wine and four goblets. Introductions were made. Ibrahim al-Jazzar stared unabashedly at Michael Scot, while Abu al-Biruni was more circumspect.

'Well,' said al-Jazzar to al-Hakim, 'you seem to have provided the foreigner with most of your wardrobe.'

Al-Hakim smiled briefly and nodded.

'The unclean made clean,' mused al-Jazzar.

'Where do you hail from?' asked al-Biruni, handing Michael Scot a goblet.

'Originally, Scotland, but I have travelled extensively over the years.'

'Scotland...' Al-Biruni glanced at his friends. They shook their heads and sipped their wine. 'It is in the far North, is it not?' he pursued. Then his eyes lit up. 'Beside – what is it called, yes, I have it – England!'

The other two pursed their lips and looked judicious.

'Yes,' added al-Biruni, 'a savage climate, I believe. Endless darkness, cold and rain. A calamitous lack of civilised amenities.'

It was hard to know what to say. These charges could not in honesty be denied. But curiously for Michael Scot, who normally had little inclination to trifle with the truth, distance from home seemed to provoke a proportionate sense of defensiveness of the same. 'Have you been?' he enquired tersely. He downed most of the contents of his goblet.

'No,' replied al-Biruni placidly, 'but I know of a soldier taken captive by your infidel crusaders who wound up there. He eventually made good his escape, this sojourn having relieved him of any pressing inclination to stay on.'

'And now there is another of these crusades on the go,' said al-Jazzar. He had a curious way of communicating; the words were undoubtedly uttered for Michael Scot's benefit, but he directed them at al-Hakim, as if he were a bridge spanning a gap that al-Jazzar himself could not quite manage. 'That brings the grand total of crusades up to, what is it? Six, seven?' His eyebrows receded most of the way up his forehead, forming two indignant semicircles, like bristling caterpillars poked at by a stick.

'In actual fact,' replied Michael Scot, 'the crusade sanctioned by his Holiness the Pope last year is the fifth.'

Al-Jazzar's hand traced a dismissive circular gesture. 'You Christians are a fanatical lot.' He turned to his friends. 'You recall the spate of Christian suicides that afflicted the caliphate for a while?' Al-Hakim and al-Biruni nodded. 'The only way they could find to manifest their hatred of us was by committing suicide. They were given every chance to save themselves, yet one after another, hoping to undermine the caliphate, they put themselves in the way of death.

How many of them were there? Do you remember?'

'Forty-eight, I think,' replied al-Hakim.

'You refer,' enquired Michael Scot, 'to the Movement of the Martyrs?'

'I believe,' replied al-Biruni, 'I spoke of Christian suicides. The difference is not just a question of words.'

'Be advised,' interjected al-Hakim, refilling any empty goblets with the dark red wine, 'that, like most of the Christian suicides, Michael Scot is in fact a monk. We don't want him needled into joining their ranks.'

Al-Jazzar's eyes narrowed; al-Biruni's widened.

Michael Scot plunged ahead. 'I see them as martyrs. Their land had been invaded – the equivalent of a crusade, if you like – and their right to practise their religion curtailed.'

'Precisely, monk,' replied al-Biruni, 'curtailed – not forbidden.'

'Although maybe it should have been,' interjected al-Jazzar, 'and the problem extirpated at the root. Do you remember how, until the authorities found a way of weeding out and suppressing the seemingly blameless Christians who were fomenting this violence, we had no peace? Praise be to Allah, it is all in the past.'

Al-Hakim drained his goblet. 'But we all know that there are far more unsettling things afoot at the moment than Christian suicides and Christian crusades.'

Michael Scot's ears pricked up. What could be more threatening than a crusade or Christian martyrs. 'Namely?'

'Regrettable as your shambolic crusades and marauding armies undoubtedly are,' said al-Biruni, 'ultimately they are of little importance. They pale into insignificance when compared to the devastation Genghis Khan is visiting on the empire in the East. For the Great Khan is making his inexorable way over the Asian Steppes, leaving a trail of death and destruction in his wake, the like of which has never been seen. The East, from which comes all light, now threatens to engulf us in a shadow of oblivion.'

The other two men nodded silently. Al-Hakim added, 'He is as efficient as he is merciless.'

For Michael Scot, the name Genghis Khan was but a murmured menace. But then again, he had difficulty in even placing the Steppes.

'This Khan is an ill omen indeed,' said al-Jazzar. 'I fear that his avenging wrath will not spare us Muslims, even here in the far West.'

A veil of melancholy fell over the company.

'May Allah protect us,' said al-Hakim softly. 'If it is our destiny to be spared, we shall be spared. But if He wills otherwise, there is nothing any mortal can do to change this.'

'It is even as you say,' murmured al-Biruni. 'And sometimes it seems to me as if we ourselves have already initiated this process. What we have frittered and squandered away may yet be taken from us wholesale.'

'How do you mean?' asked Michael Scot. 'I am at a loss to understand how anything could be lacking in this city of celestial beauty.'

'Alas for you, foreigner,' al-Biruni's expression contrived to be both scornful and wistful, 'that you did not see Kortuba in its days of glory.'

'For they are surely gone,' added al-Jazzar.

'It is October in Kortuba.' Al-Hakim nodded slowly. 'The weather is still holding, but the grapes have been harvested, and a chill wind is whipping up.'

The three men drank long and deep. Michael Scot finished the contents of his goblet as well; the strong wine had gone to his head.

And that was when al-Biruni pulled a pouch from his cloak and laid it on the table. 'I think it is time for the opium and hashish.'

XXVII

Careful fingers unwrapped the poppy leaves from round a number of small, dun-coloured stumps. Al-Biruni leaned forward and inhaled; the pungent odour reached Michael Scot's nostrils as well. The candle was held beneath one of the stumps, which proceeded to burn with a steady flame. 'See?' murmured al-Biruni. 'The quality is the best.' Abruptly, he removed the candle and placed it back in its holder on the table. 'Did you procure the hashish?' he asked, turning to al-Hakim.

Another small pouch was placed on the table; its contents revealed a number of pellets the size of chickpeas. The men smiled.

'What are those?' Michael Scot enquired, indicating the pellets.

'They are not for you, infidel,' replied al-Jazzar. 'They are the means by which we shall glimpse the joys of the eternal paradise awaiting us, the true believers.' All three men laughed.

'Opium,' explained al-Hakim, pointing to the stumps, 'and hashish. The hashish has been roasted and rubbed by hand, and then mixed with peeled sesame seeds and sugar. The one will be dissolved in the wine and drunk, and the other chewed.'

As he spoke, al-Biruni lifted a couple of the stumps and crumbled them into the pitcher of wine. This he stirred and then poured into the four goblets. Michael Scot watched him intently.

'It is an aid to good conversation, monk. Do not look so scandalised!' Al-Biruni raised his goblet and drank. 'It will give ease to that nervous disposition and calm those questing eyes. We have been taking our ease with these substances for more than two centuries and are none the worse for it. Drink, and be at peace.'

Michael Scot did not know whether to be more taken aback at the invitation to drink this opium – the very substance he had hankered after the other day – or at his unflattering portrayal as fidgety crank. And he had thought he had passed himself off tolerably well... He drank. 'What is all this you say of autumn and chill winds?' he asked. 'I can see nothing but perfection here. What, in your opinion, has gone amiss?'

Al-Biruni began to speak. Michael Scot settled more comfortably into his cushions, letting the words wash over him. He understood with an ease that previously he had had to struggle for. And his body felt for the first time as if it were truly in repose. He listened and heard of the Muslim conquest of Kortuba, in the year the Christians call 711. He heard how the pinnacle of beauty and civilisation had been reached two centuries later. For this was the century that saw the building of the Great Library, which would house over six hundred thousand manuscripts, and the Royal Palace, which did not have its equal in splendour and magnificence. Then the Alcázar was built, and then the Great Mosque. There were over one hundred thousand houses in Kortuba, and most of these had marble balconies for the heat of summer, and hot-air ducts under mosaic floors for the chill of winter. Paper abounded: there were hundreds of libraries and bookshops. Hundreds of public baths. Only Baghdad was a fitting rival to this city and court.

And then, during the following century, the decay had set in. The attacks had started, presages of imminent civil war. First the Great Library had been devastated, its priceless contents either destroyed or scattered all over the peninsula. The Berbers brought about the downfall of the caliphate shortly afterwards, ransacking and demolishing the Palace, Medinat al-Zahra. At that point, Kortuba lost its pre-eminence as capital of the Caliphate of al-Andalus, and the area fell a prey to a succession of warring *Taifas*, or kingdoms. The cohesive grandeur and vision of the past were lost.

They lived on in a fragmented fashion, still showing the odd, sporadic recrudescence of the old brilliance. But it was as if Kortuba had become a chimera, a dream of itself.

Silence fell. The three men finished their wine; Michael Scot did likewise. Then they each took one of the pellets and chewed slowly and deliberately for a time. Michael Scot wavered. What to do? Should he take one too? Al-Hakim caught his eye and gestured at him to take one. He reached out.

Time passed; how much was not clear to him. But while the three Kortubans retreated more and more into a blissful silence, Michael Scot felt himself invested with renewed impetus. He started to question them. And yet, he said, in the century just gone by, Córdoba produced two of the greatest minds the world has seen: Maimonides and Averroës. Was this not indicative of vigour? And they answered him, slowly, ruminatively, patiently. Yes, it was indeed true that these two distinguished philosophers had been born in this city. And yes, they were an adornment to the same. But regretfully, they were isolated phenomena: Maimonides had been hounded from the city by the Berber rulers because of his Jewishness. And Ibn Rushd had met a similar fate – he, too, had been hounded from the city; but not before he had been stoned by its zealous inhabitants within the mosque. One wondered indeed what these illustrious personages made of Kortuba, the city of their birth.

'And how so?' persisted Michael Scot. 'Surely the city would have been proud of these sons.'

'Alas for Kortuba! Alas for philosophy! The Asharites won and all has been undone.'

'And who are these Asharites?'

'The Asharites and the Mutalizites, the theologians and the philosophers; crudely simplified into faith and reason, respectively.'

'Faith and reason, reason and faith, this indeed is a conundrum.'

'No, no – not faith and reason, but faith versus reason. Either the one or the other. And if one opted for reason, one likewise risked a stoning in the mosque by Kortuba's zealous inhabitants, who had frequent recourse to this particular method of solving problems. Ibn Rushd had attempted a rebuttal of the theologian al-Ghazzali's *The Incoherence of the Philosophers*; he had put everything into his defence, *The Incoherence of the Incoherence.* But to no avail. And most tellingly, when the caliph had sensed which way the wind was blowing among the people, when he sensed the overwhelming hostility of the ordinary populace towards the rationalist position of Ibn Rushd, he had abandoned his protégé, leaving him to face public opprobrium on his own, and then exiled him. Ibn Rushd had had to leave Kortuba in disgrace, not knowing if he would ever be allowed to return, but knowing that most of his manuscripts, his life's work, had been thrown onto a bonfire.

'Although, it was also rumoured that Ibn Rushd had done himself no favours by speaking so disparagingly of the caliph's Berber background. But why had he been betrayed in this way by the caliph who, after all, was also his father-in-law? Alas, alas, alas.

'So, the Asharites had won, even here in al-Andalus, where reason and the philosophers were greatly prized by the educated. The populace, spurred on by the theologians, would not countenance equal status being given to religion and philosophy as systems for explaining the cosmos.'

'Well and indeed, for it is a dangerous proposition.'

'One, nevertheless, that we had grown used to here in al-Andalus. And to the undoubted benefit it brought to the caliphate.'

'It is still a disquieting proposition.'

'There are many here who would agree with you, infidel.'

'And not only here. In Christendom, such a proposition would confound most of the faithful.'

'Listen carefully, monk. The claim is not being made that Allah can be known through philosophy; not even the theologians have the right to arrogate that capacity to religion. As systems of apprehending the cosmos, however, they should have equal status. Ibn Rushd was right. And that is why one has to be careful. Here in Kortuba, there is little point in discussion any more; if one's point of view is not acceptable theologically, if it offends orthodoxy (in Islam a deliberately nebulous standard, unfortunately vulnerable to manipulation), one can be destroyed and see the work of a lifetime demolished in less time than it takes to say 'blasphemer'. That leaves direct knowledge, and the refuge and solace to be found in seeking after the hidden mysteries of the Divine. What better way to accomplish this than by enhancing the mind's perceptiveness and receptivity through these substances?'

But the Moors' words clanged round Michael Scot's head like bells tolling a funeral procession. He shook his head, as much to free himself of what seemed to be a ringing in his ears as to disagree. 'Who knows where this might take us?' he said anxiously. But where had he heard those words before? A white-haired figure slid in at the back of his mind, the hands fluttering in a blessing, far away, an age away, in a room in Rome where the gloaming advanced. His limbs went slack. Why did he now find himself echoing the prudent, the fearful? What was this sense of imminent dread slithering round his gut? Yet more thoughts poured into his head; ideas crowded together; questions jostled for attention. They centred on that enigma, Averroës. To say nothing of the confusion regarding the greatest enigma of them all – God.

'The unknowability of God became a Christian dogma at the Lateran Council of 1215: God cannot be imagined with any accuracy, and any words used about Him are more inaccurate than accurate. A sanctioned mystery.'

'As I said, monk. Philosophy cannot fully explain Allah; nor even theology. But philosophy may go some way towards making sense of the cosmos He has gifted us with.'

'Indeed but I do not like this unknowable, impersonal God at the centre of His cosmos...'

He gave voice to his fears, listing painstakingly the evils that would ensue should Averroës' stance be given way to. And with every distressed thought, with each febrile enunciation, the Moors withdrew increasingly into silent indifference. He wondered how they could fail to grasp the enormity of what he was pointing out to them; indeed, why had he not perceived it himself before now? They wondered when he would desist and let them sleep.

*

It was not far to his lodgings from al-Hakim's house. He should have been tired and yet he was not. Thoughts tumbled through his mind; bringing them under scrutiny was like trying to stitch together shredding clouds in a blustery sky. There were so many of them, clamouring for attention, demanding answers. He inhaled; the air was balmy. But it was of no help. If anything, the rush of air suddenly made him feel nauseous. He stopped to regain his composure, leaning against one of the apparatuses used for street lighting. Undoubtedly sorely needed, as he suddenly realised he was having difficulty remembering the way back. At least he would not have to pick his way through potholes and filth – the street itself was paved and clean. But which one should he take?

He moved away from the light stand and the dizziness fell on him like a blacksmith's anvil. He staggered. Shadows jumped around him; were they his own, or was he being followed? He endeavoured to bestir himself, terrifyingly aware of his vulnerability. More shadows flickered and jumped. And then there was a cawing.

As if there were a weight attached to his head, it took an immense effort to turn it around and see where the noise had come from. He could see nothing.

He moved off, and with a sense of relief so great that he staggered again, recognised the street where his lodgings were. Once more there was a cawing, raucous and mocking. And then, out of the corner of his eye, he saw it: an ungainly black shape, scuttling along a few paces behind him, hopping grotesquely from one scaly leg to the other, in and out of the shadows. The talons made a clicking noise on the paving. Then it stopped, cocked its head, and fixed a glittering eye on him.

XXVIII

Then began the voyage to lands where time ceased to hold sway. A place of terror, a nightmare made manifest, as easy to fall into as it was difficult to emerge from. And although he did indeed return, those swampy labyrinths would suck some part of him away forever, leaving a murky sediment in their wake. Things would never again go easy with Michael Scot, for back with him did come the whiff of sulphur.

*

The windows were all closed and shuttered, and yet that hateful cawing could still be heard, as if at a certain remove. He lay down on his bedding and pulled the cover up over his face as a fit of shivering overtook him. He desperately wanted to sleep so that he would not chance to lay eyes again on that baleful shadow hobbling and clicking along in pursuit of him. And then would come the blessed morning, with its holy light, and he would not need to fear any more.

Suddenly, he felt exhausted; he could no longer feel his extremities. But the clamour inside his head gave him no let-up. There could be no worse sensation: a mind enforcing wakefulness on a derelict body. And yet, bit by reluctant bit, something stronger than the wayward chaos of his thoughts swamped him, heavy wave by heavy wave. It must have been sleep; it might have been a waking nightmare.

It rolled over him and he acquiesced.

Then came the hands. Hands that came clawing out of the darkness, clutching at his throat. His eyes flew open and he beat them away. He gasped as a massive weight lowered itself onto his chest. And then fingers wrapped themselves round his throat once again. He opened his mouth to scream, but no sound came. The thought burned itself into his mind that he had to bless himself – he had to make the sign of the cross or he would perish. But the weight paralysed him. His mouth was a gaping hole, a silent blackness of horror in the darkness, within which all sound was trapped.

There was a crackling in his head as, with a supreme effort he finally managed to open his eyes. Or had they not already been open? He could no longer say with any certainty. He clambered from the bed and scrabbled frantically for the candle. He attempted to light it in the cold embers of the fire; it refused to take. He cursed, panic bringing him to the point of screaming as the hairs on the nape of his neck rippled and the skin on his back crawled. Sweat drenched the cotton tunic he had not bothered to change out of. But then, from the depths of the embers, a glow intimated hope. A flame guttered and slowly acquired strength. His eyes flew to the corners of his room; nothing could be seen. There was nothing else visible in the room with him. Nothing to explain what he had just experienced.

It was even more terrifying.

Every coherent thought now fled his mind, which became an emptiness quivering to the intimations of some nameless fear. There was the jug of water over on the small table by his bed. He poured some into a goblet and blessed it; with jerky movements, he splashed it all round his bed, muttering prayers. The candle he secured on the table as well, and then slid back down under the cover. He reached for his crucifix and placed it on his chest.

The same rolling, oppressive heaviness overtook him again and his eyes closed.

At first it was imperceptible, but slowly, agonisingly, he realised what he was hearing. Whispering. It increased in volume, and now the hostility washed over him with needlepoints of venom. It rushed at the bed, and his dread was such that he thought he must die of it. He clutched the crucifix and brandished it at the dark; and the dark bore down on the bed, crushing him.

From somewhere there came a high-pitched sustained howling.

Respite. Sweet respite. Then the whispering started again and he felt his gut twist. Every nerve in his body tensed, and he listened intently. But this time it was different: he could not perceive the same hostility, and the waves of malevolence were absent. And there it was again; this time the words were audible. *You seek for me, but do you truly know what this entails? What is it you want to know? Are you ready to know it?* Michael Scot covered his face with his hands, but the whispering voice continued. *I cannot answer you, imprisoned like this.* He kept his hands over his face and his breath came loudly and raggedly through his nostrils. Then, right beside his ear the voice hissed, *Free me! Come to the tomb and set me free. You I have chosen to liberate me from earthly bondage. If you succeed, I will share the secrets of the knowledge you would possess. Bestir yourself... Arise...*

He followed the whispering guide through the sleeping city, past shuttered houses, out as far as the cemetery where Averroës was buried. He found the tomb. It loomed before him, a mass of secrets in the stillness of the night.

Where had the whispering voice faded to now? He stood under a cold and impassive moon and waited for an indication of what to do next; but none came. All was quiet, empty, every presence fled.

Suddenly, he could not bear it any longer, and he flung himself against the tomb, railing. Where was he now when answers were needed? Why so many questions if there were no answers? The echo of his voice was blunted against the immense silence.

And then his eye lit on a large stone to one side of the tomb; he picked it up and smashed it against the entrance. He would make him give some answers, make him put his mind at rest. He continued to smash the stone against the tomb for some time until, in exhaustion, it tumbled from his hand.

There would be no answers.

He returned to his lodgings in a flurry of avenging rage. He would not be mocked like this. The prospect of answers to his questions, of knowledge, had been held out to him; he would take what was his due. Enough of this tantalising. He wanted to know what was beyond knowing.

Once inside the room he pushed back the table and chair, creating an open space at its centre. Then he fetched the candle and positioned it right in the middle. Next, he filled the jug with water and slowly poured a trickle all around him, creating an invisible circle. He kept inside it. When he had completed the circle, he stepped over to where the candle was placed and raised his arms above his head. *I call on you, spirit of Averroës. I summon you here. I command you to reveal the secrets you are privy to, the knowledge you hoard. Obey, come, show yourself.*

Into the shadowy silence of the room came a deep whirring. And then, like a runaway wild boar emerging suddenly from the forest, some force barrelled into him like a blow to the stomach. His arms crumpled to his side and he slithered to the floor. There was a crackling and his arms jerked back out. His head felt as if the top of it had been sliced off, and all the contents gushed out, spilling over the floor. The candle guttered and went out.

But then came bliss. A vision of beauty infused with joy. He rose above himself, saw his body stretched out on the floor below, and floated, cradled by the joy in the very air about him. Everything was near, everything throbbed with life, even the simple furniture in the room. Outside the window, the sky sparkled and the stars were epicentres of life at the end of his fingertips. He was at one with it. His finger brushed the nearest star; to his horror it exploded. A dark emptiness took its place. Ah, the sorrow – one by one all the stars exploded; bit by bit the bright night sky was overtaken by an impenetrable darkness. The lights were all disappearing. Darkness engulfed him. He could not come back; he was a floating speck in an ocean of blackness. All was emptiness, nothingness. He whimpered and that, too, was swallowed and there was nothing at all. Infinite, unending.

*

'Yes, Master, come up and see for yourself!' Beckoning at al-Hakim with gestures that betrayed his agitation, the man who had rented Michael Scot his lodgings led the way up the stairs to his room. 'For, Allah protect us all, I assure you, we have none of us heard the like of it before. Praise be to the Almighty that you have come by, for we did not dare open this door. The djinn surely visited this place last night; we all of us heard the uproar.' The eyes in his plump face were rounded in fright as he mopped at the copious flow of sweat on his face. Al-Hakim placed a hand on the door; it was not locked and opened. The man took a step back.

Within the room was an uneasy stillness. In the middle of the floor Michael Scot lay motionless, his face hidden. The innkeeper gasped. Al-Hakim strode over to him; the innkeeper followed at a prudent distance. Then he took in the disarray, the broken furniture and his hands flew to his face. 'Oh,' he lamented, 'the damage, the damage! Look at the condition of this room, the furniture has been ruined!' That explained the shrieking, the roaring, the sounds of a struggle that had kept him and his terrified family awake last night… What had possessed him to rent his property to a barbarian Christian?

Al-Hakim stooped down over the unconscious figure on the floor and exclaimed sharply.

'What? Allah protect us, what is it now?'

'I should have thought of it before,' muttered al-Hakim, vexed. 'I forgot that he had never taken...' His voice drifted away.

The innkeeper's eyebrows rose and his mouth pursed.

Al-Hakim ran a hand over Michael Scot's clammy forehead and lifted it to his nostrils. Yes, the odour was unmistakable. Opium poisoning. To say nothing of what the hashish might have done. On top of the alcohol... He clicked his fingers at the innkeeper, who was glumly contemplating the devastation. 'Help me shift him onto the bed.' Reluctantly, the innkeeper complied. Al-Hakim brought his thumb and forefinger up to the bridge of his nose, and thought for a moment. 'I want you,' he said quickly, turning to the innkeeper, 'to prepare the following decoction immediately. Immediately, do you hear?' Rapidly, he listed the ingredients: dill, radish, salt and honey in water. Vomiting had to be induced as quickly as possible, or this was a sleep that Michael Scot would not wake from. The innkeeper dallied by the door, a disgruntled expression on his face. Al-Hakim exclaimed in annoyance, 'Go, you fool! Do not worry about the damage now. I myself pledge to make it good with you. Now go!'

The innkeeper took himself off and al-Hakim observed the sleeping form in the bed. Michael Scot slid in and out of consciousness, as the flickering of his eyes indicated, but there was no doubting the gravity of his situation. And just at that moment came a muttering. Al-Hakim started, but he could make no sense of it. The muttering grew louder, and the distress of the speaker was evident. There was a groan, and then al-Hakim distinguished the word quite clearly.

'Jacob,' cried Michael Scot.

Al-Hakim moved swiftly up to the head of the bed. 'Jacob who?' he pressed. No answer. He squeezed Michael Scot's arm;

the tunic was moist. 'Tell me, monk,' he urged, 'who is this Jacob you call for?' Still there was no response. 'Where should we send to for Jacob? Where can we find Jacob?'

He had almost despaired of getting an answer when the eyes began slowly to open. Finally, in a voice that bespoke a parching thirst, Michael Scot rasped, 'Jacob Anatolio. Toledo.'

XXIX

He had been thrown from some immense height, falling falling falling, plummeting down through the dark air like a travesty of the angels cast out of Heaven, to hurtle into the ocean, down down down into the waters, waters that were ever colder and murkier. His scream of refusal had been as silent as the bubbles that escaped his mouth, all swallowed by the crushing weight of nothingness around him.

And then, as if he had been spewed out of the belly of the abyss, he found himself washed up on an island. Exhausted, he lay motionless in the darkness on soft sand and let the gentle sound of lapping water soothe. Presently he stirred and propped himself up on an elbow.

Over in the heavens to the east pulsated the blessed dark radiance that marks the turning of night into day. Ah, the joy of the approaching dawn! A serene, sapphire luminescence presaging the return of glad hope.

Once again he found himself falling, but this time it was a far easier passage, no matter how burdensome. He became aware of weariness in his eyes as they opened slowly on the pale light of early morning. For a moment he could not recall where he was; the unfamiliarity of the room and its furnishing threw him into confusion. But then it fell on him like a weight: Córdoba.

Instinctively he closed his eyes again in an effort to block the memories swamping him; but he knew it would be best to stay awake and face whatever the day brought with it. He stirred, attempting to raise himself on his elbow. A throbbing in his head made him groan and he sank back onto the bed. It was only then that he noticed the shadowy figure sitting in the chair over by the table, for at his cry it too stirred.

Michael Scot froze in fear. What was this? An intruder or another demon come to torment him? But as the figure approached the head of the bed, he reached out a hand and sighed, 'Jacob, Jacob Anatolio, is it truly you?'

'Yes, Master Scot, it is I.' A hand rested on his forehead, and then, 'How do you feel?'

'I – do not know – how I feel.' The words came out disjointedly. 'In truth, I do not know – anything any more.'

'I will help you,' said Jacob. 'The Moor, al-Hakim, has been very good. It was he who sent for me. I came as quickly as I could, but,' – Jacob shook his head – 'you have been very ill. Very, very ill.' And very, very imprudent, he thought to himself. He looked down at Michael Scot: there were streaks of white in his hair where before it had been chestnut brown. The eyes were bloodshot and the pallor of his face was disturbing. In addition, he had lost an inordinate amount of weight. If the Moors had not been possessed of their skill as physicians, Michael Scot would have passed to the other world. It was a miracle that he was still here. But perhaps it was not the moment to tell him this; he looked too fragile. 'You must rest and regain strength. Then I think the best thing to do would be for us to set off for Palermo. We do not want to find ourselves stuck in Córdoba.'

'Yes,' muttered Michael Scot. There was a pause. 'But Jacob,' his voice was flat and spent, 'I have had such dreams, such night-mares.' He turned haunted eyes on the young man. 'And all of them seemed so real…' He related the dream where he had gone in search of Averroës' tomb, on the far side of the city. But he could not bring himself to tell of the others: the crow, the exploding cosmos, the black emptiness... It was too horrifying.

'Do not fret about those dreams now,' replied Jacob. 'They are gone, a thing of the past, and you will never be troubled by them again.'

Michael Scot's eyes slid away; his knuckles showed white round the crucifix resting on his chest.

Silently, Jacob repeated his words to himself. We do not want to find ourselves stuck in Córdoba. Seized by a sense of anxiety, he started to pace up and down the small room; Michael Scot observed him for a few moments, and then let his head fall back down onto his pallet. He closed his eyes and was soon overtaken by sleep.

It was late October and the heat had gone. They could hope to travel in benign weather conditions. They had to leave now, whether Master Scot was fully recovered or not, otherwise they would surely find themselves stuck here. A winter passage to Palermo would become rare. Jacob cast his eyes round the room, and they came to rest on the press in the corner. It was unlocked and the door swung open to reveal Mater Scot's woollen habits and a black cloak. Jacob rummaged further until his fingers closed round what seemed to be parchment, yet felt subtly different. There was a large quantity of it and he stooped down to scoop it up with his arm.

Carefully he placed it on the table. Yes, he was looking at the result of Master Scot's two-month stay in Córdoba, and he had not been idle. Medical treatise upon medical treatise, along with notes and even some diagrams. This would all have to be brought with them. Jacob shifted one last piece of this strange parchment and the words *Secreta Secretorum* jumped out at him. So Master Scot was still dabbling in this morass of astrology and alchemy. What a mass of contradictions the man was. Jacob sighed. And something about the journey to Averroës' tomb didn't sound quite right either. He'd have to look into that too.

But the first thing to do here was to enlist al-Hakim's help in procuring horses and directions for their journey. A packhorse would also be necessary for carrying Master Scot's materials. They needed to get to Valencia and from there try to find a ship bound for Palermo.

There was a moan from the sleeping figure on the pallet. With a suddenness that took Jacob by surprise, Master Scot's arms began to flail feebly in the air in front of him; it looked as if he was trying to ward something off. 'No!' The sudden cry tore through the silence of the room. 'No!'

Swiftly Jacob moved over to the pallet and placed a restraining hand on Master Scot. But this only served to make him writhe more. 'Master Scot,' cried Jacob, 'Master Scot, wake up. It is me, Jacob.' With unsettling abruptness, Master Scot's eyes opened. But they rolled back into his head and then his mouth formed a dark, gaping hole. From it came an unearthly moan that grew in intensity. Jacob was powerless to quell the uproar until he clamped one hand over Master Scot's mouth, managing at least to lessen the volume. With the other he kept tugging at Master Scot's sleeve, trying to bring him round. After an age the seizure subsided and Master Scot's eyes, round with terror, darted all over the room. 'Tell me, Jacob,' he whispered eventually, 'am I alive or dead?' His eyes bored into the young man. 'For if I am dead, then you are in Hell with me. And why would someone like you be in Hell? Why?'

'Of course you are not dead, Master Scot,' Jacob endeavoured to keep his voice steady. 'We are both of us here in Córdoba.'

'Well, and is not that hell enough?' Michael Scot slumped back down onto the pillow. The terror seemed to seep away, leaving him jaded. After a while, in which Jacob could find nothing to say, Michael Scot turned to him. 'Jacob,' his voice was a hoarse whisper, as if he feared being overheard, 'thank the good Lord it is you.' He scrabbled for Jacob's hand, the long, knotted fingers clutching at him like a scuttling crab. 'Do not leave me,' his eyes latched onto Jacob's, 'I beg you will not leave me. It is horrible, too horrible!'

Jacob had to remain in that position until Michael Scot finally allowed his eyelids to close again in sleep. And even then he could not extricate his hand from the iron grip that held it.

When Michael Scot awoke, Jacob broached the idea of Palermo to him and the necessity of getting there as soon as was feasible.

'Yes, Jacob,' he said softly, 'Palermo – I need to see something familiar again.' He nodded slowly. 'And to have you face this journey with me would gladden my heart.'

'Do not forget, Master Scot,' added Jacob, 'that we have much still to accomplish. There are great manuscripts still awaiting our translation.'

The raised eyebrow directed at Jacob made him smile; it reminded him of Master Scot in easier times.

'But I have not forgotten, Jacob, about the new university in Naples.'

The joy that filled Jacob's being took him by surprise. Only now did he admit the extent to which he had feared the demise of hope.

His anxiety about Rebekah had been growing with every passing month. The year was winding inexorably to a close and he still had nothing concrete to offer. He had sent off a missive to her, knowing full well that her parents' eyes would scan it first. He had outlined his intentions: departure for Palermo with Michael Scot and the procurement of a position. He would pursue two avenues of possibility: one as Michael Scot's assistant in Palermo; the other at the soon-to-be opened university in Naples. Either of these would mean the attainment of a stipend enabling him to bring Rebekah to the Kingdom of Sicily as his wife.

At nineteen, Rebekah would soon be considered past the optimum marrying age, and they had been betrothed now for four years. An unconscionable amount of time for her mother, whose main concern was that her daughter not still be unmarried at twenty, for that would lay her open to the ridicule of disappointed hopes. If things did not go as he hoped, not alone might he lose the girl he loved, but he had no doubt that Rebekah's mother would also pursue him with a vengeance for breach of promise.

Michael Scot coughed. His disquieting eyes, two penetrating silver beams observing him, caused Jacob to shiver slightly. Then the older man seemed to shake himself out of a trance. But his voice was kind. 'You are distressed, Jacob,' he said, 'but it is understandable.' The long bony hands smoothed the cover on his bed. 'Yes,' he added pensively, 'your future depends on what transpires in Palermo. However,' – the assessing eyes reached into his being – 'be assured that I will do all in my power to assist you once we are there. You will be able to bring your bride to your new home.' He turned his face to the window and said no more.

Jacob froze, unsure what to say. His head crowded with all manner of doubts. He had no recollection of discussing Rebekah with Master Scot. Had he even mentioned her name to him? It would never have occurred to him to speak of his matrimonial prospects with a cleric. He could not account for it.

Eventually, Michael Scot turned back to him, frowning slightly. 'Stop tormenting yourself. The future awaits you.'

But it was in the Moorish city of Valencia that Jacob's suspicion was confirmed. Something untoward had infested Michael Scot and was making its disquieting presence felt.

XXX

In Valencia they were to seek out a Pisan trading ship that would take them eastwards over the Mediterranean to Palermo. They took leave then of the courteous al-Hakim, but both Jacob and Michael Scot rode out from the glittering city on their Arabian mounts, the baggage-laden cart trundling after them, without so much as a backward glance.

The route al-Hakim had advised them to take to Valencia proved a good one and the journey passed off without mishap. Even the weather was accommodating: still very hot during the middle of the day, but mild in the mornings and evenings. And they did not have to contend with the freezing cold that came at night time in the central uplands during the winter. But they spoke hardly at all. Jacob determined to keep his observations on the rocky dry terrain they were passing through to himself. Now and again they came across some farms and estates, all of which appeared to make extensive use of irrigation systems that filled Jacob with wonder. Once outside these cultivated areas, however, the landscape was harsh. As they plodded along the dusty track, Jacob observed Michael Scot; indeed, he did not even have to trouble to camouflage his scrutiny. For so intense was the other man's concentration on whatever thoughts were circling darkly in his head that he appeared not to take in anything of what surrounded him. It was disconcerting, for he contrived to seem more distant than Jacob had ever perceived him, and yet did he loom up more largely within his own mind, like a white amorphous fog expanding silently into every corner of it. It was as if a veil were separating Michael Scot from the rest of the world; from beyond this veil, however, some arcane power emanated that ever drew his eyes to rest uneasily on the form ahead of him swaying rigidly on his horse as it picked its fastidious way over the rocks and stones that littered so much of the track.

They were yet a day from Valencia and had stopped in lodgings for the night when Jacob finally put into words what had been troubling him since they had left Córdoba. Did Master Scot intend travelling to Palermo in the Moorish garments that he now wore?

Michael Scot nodded slowly. The habits required a good deal of darning and mending. He could not account for it, but they had become sadly tattered. He had therefore stopped wearing them. Even as he watched him, Jacob could see the attention beginning to wander, the eyes turning in on themselves, retreating to whatever place it was now swallowed most of his thoughts. 'But,' Jacob ventured, 'will you be wearing these same garments upon your arrival in Palermo?'

'Yes, yes,' Michael Scot replied. 'Why wouldn't I?'

'Do you think it wise?' Jacob persisted. But it was too late; he could see that his words no longer impinged on the man. For he merely sighed and murmured, 'Wise is it, now? Whatever that amounts to.'

They halted on a hillock overlooking the city of Valencia before beginning their final descent, and gazed out onto the immense expanse of azure sea stretching away in front of them. Michael Scot breathed in deeply. 'Ah, I can smell the vivifying pungency of the sea. It is a joy to the heart.' He took a deep breath. 'We are leaving, then. I feared I would not arrive at this point, but we will indeed make good our departure.' An aura of renewed vigour seemed to invest him and he smiled slightly, turning to Jacob. 'Do not torment yourself.' He looked back out to sea again, and suddenly his voice deepened, acquiring a peculiar resonance. 'Your courage shall pay dividends. This voyage shall not be for nothing. The post you desire shall indeed be yours. You have your youth, your intelligence, and no one to answer to except your own conscience.'

The hairs on the back of Jacob's neck rose; he tried to convince himself that it was on account of the breeze.

From a little behind he anxiously observed as Michael Scot stopped the man and asked him for directions. Now that they found themselves in another Moorish city, surrounded by foreign sounds, foreign smells and strange sights, it was probably just as well that Michael Scot's Moorish garments had not been discarded in favour of the tattered Premonstratensian habit. As it was, Jacob was trying to contend with the irritation brought on by a pervasive sense of vulnerability. More than ever, he was aware of how little it took to draw unwelcome attention to themselves. He watched as the man gesticulated down towards the end of the pier to the large ships docked there.

The horses clopped along and the cart trundled heavily behind them. Finally, they came to a halt in front of the vessel that would transport them to Palermo: a homecoming of sorts for Michael Scot, and a leap into the unknown for him. It was a large, sturdy ship, flying a Christian flag: a white quadrilateral cross on a red background.

'It is a Pisan ship,' said Michael Scot out of the blue, 'the cross of the knights of St Stephen is the emblem of their city.'

Jacob's eyes darted from the flag and back to Michael Scot; but he had already turned his attention to the figure that had just appeared on deck. From under his turban, his eyes narrowed as he sized him up.

The man drew near to the side deck. 'What do you want?' he shouted down in Arabic.

'We wish to negotiate our passage on your ship as far as Palermo,' replied Michael Scot in Sicilian.

The man paused, evidently taken aback at the linguistic turn of events. He shaded his eyes and looked again at the two men standing on the pier. 'Palermo, eh?' he grunted. Then he hawked loudly and spat into the strip of sea separating the ship from the pier. 'We're full,' he stated, switching to Tuscan. 'There isn't room for another Christian soul on this ship, let alone anything heathen.' His belly shook as he wheezed in enjoyment of his own wit.

'I wish to speak to the captain,' said Michael Scot.

The man abruptly stopped wheezing. 'I *am* the captain,' he replied sourly.

'I have been commissioned by King Frederick of Sicily,' stated Michael Scot, 'to bring work of the utmost importance back to him from Spain. It would be foolhardy to hinder that.'

'With all due respect,' the captain hawked again loudly into the seawater, 'his Majesty's whims are nothing to me.' His tone became sneering. 'I'm from the Republic of Pisa and bow to no man, king or otherwise.'

Michael Scot sighed. Then with slow deliberation he covered the gangway and gained the deck. Jacob watched these proceedings in disbelief. If the other sailors materialised, they would surely meet an untimely end.

The captain looked warily at Michael Scot and then barred his way. Although his words were incomprehensible, the tone of voice left no doubt as to their threatening nature. Master Scot stood his ground, but he never took his eyes off those of the captain. He appeared to be saying something, but it couldn't be heard above the captain's shouting.

Master Scot was deluded if he thought he could browbeat that truculent boor into complying with their wishes. But, open-mouthed and silent, the captain had gone very still and was now just looking at him. Master Scot murmured again; the man nodded.

Still holding the man's eyes, Master Scot shouted down to Jacob from the deck. 'Start loading our luggage on the ship. We have a passage to Palermo.'

*

What did Jacob remember of their sea voyage to Palermo? He had never experienced such an expanse of sea, and it did not much agree with him. But he was grateful for whatever boons came their way, and luckily he was untroubled by seasickness. He registered the beauty of the intense blueness of sky and sea, unmarred by a heat haze; and he gave thanks for the benign winds of that late October, enabling them to glide over the immense surface of the sea ever closer to their destination. But the seagulls were their undoing.

He had little difficulty in persuading Michael Scot to keep out of sight as much as was possible. Naturally, the man could not be expected to spend the entire voyage in the rank darkness of the tiny space apportioned them for sleeping. For himself, his only wish was to keep out of the way of the surly captain, in case whatever aberration had induced him to change his mind about the passage wore off. When they had been at sea for a couple of days, Jacob deemed it opportune to accompany Michael Scot up on deck to get some fresh air in the late afternoon. He chose his time deliberately, as it was generally the time when Michael Scot was at his best. Mornings could be reduced merely to the exhausted aftermath of a tormented night, and evenings to the prelude of a much-feared night. But so far, the voyage was proceeding smoothly.

They emerged on deck into the brilliant sunshine. Michael Scot staggered and Jacob steadied him. With both hands, he leaned on the rim of the side deck. 'The light is blinding, even with my eyes closed,' he murmured.

'Two days below deck in the gloom is quite a while,' said Jacob. 'Make allowance for it.'

They remained like that for a while, and then Michael Scot raised a hand to his eyes and shaded them. Slowly he opened them, his hand a slatted blind. He breathed slowly and deeply.

'Look,' said Jacob, pointing to the left, 'a fishing vessel.' There, away in the blue distance, a boat was sailing back towards Valencia, followed by a flock of keening seagulls.

No sooner had Michael Scot turned his head to look than his face blanched and some paralysing fear made his mouth hang agape.

'It is the crows,' he whispered, 'they are seeking me out and will surely find me.' He started to shake. Then his head jerked back and the eyes rolled, showing the whites. Jacob's heart plummeted. A seizure. Rapidly he took in their surroundings: no one was in the immediate vicinity; perhaps he still had sufficient time to get Michael Scot below deck before it took full effect.

Without saying a word, he bundled Michael Scot back down the narrow wooden steps and along the cramped passageway to their allotted space. The fetid air closed in around him as soon as he pulled back the blanket that partitioned it off. For one moment, he was assailed by an overwhelming urge to roar himself; to smash his fist into the hanging he had just let fall behind him, which afforded them all too little protection from the hostile crew beyond it.

But he willed himself back into a state of apparent calm. Michael Scot had collapsed shaking on the few items of clothing they could spare that acted as a pallet, his back arching. If it came to it, Jacob decided, he would have to gag him, or they risked being thrown overboard by the crew. Jacob hovered over Michael Scot as his hands began to flail, his mouth an open hole from which mercifully no sound emerged.

In this manner did the sea voyage pass off. Subsequently, Jacob thought it was the closest he would ever come to losing his sanity himself; but time and events wrong-footed him there too.

After the seizure, Michael Scot retreated into himself, to a distance beyond Jacob's skill to reach. Now, however, Jacob too lived in fear: fear of the crew getting wind of the vulnerable situation they found themselves in, and the unpredictable way they might react to it. Each morning at first light, he would make his way up silently on deck and negotiate their ration of food and water for the day. But, because of the volatility of Michael Scot's behaviour, he would first have to tie him to the wooden bars across the tiny aperture that looked out on the sea. He hesitated at gagging him, fearing that it might bring on suffocation. He gave thanks for the small supply of monies they had, but fretted also that the sailors might get it into their heads to rob them of it. So he always struck the meanest bargain he could, accepting swill that the sailors disdained, in order to seem more down-at-heel than they actually were.

Days passed by as he stared at the barred aperture: he watched as the light waxed and waned. He watched through nights bereft even of moonlight, his greatest dread that the silence of this darkness would be broken by the moaning that sometimes came with one of Michael Scot's fits. Nights passed in a blur of semi-conscious, semi-vigilant trepidation. He was weary beyond normal tiredness, and time had never lain so heavily on him.

And then the shout had gone up. 'Land ahead!' He wept quietly. He was in a frenzy to be off this stinking vessel as quickly as possible. Michael Scot sat in front of him, slumped against the wall, staring into the gloom. He was calm, and had been so for the past day, but the eyes were vacant. A muscle worked in Jacob's jaw, making it twitch. He had to see where they were, had to know how much longer he could expect to have to stay cooped up in the bowels of this hulk.

It was a risk he just had to take. He stood up and took a last look at Michael Scot, before pulling back the hanging and going up on deck.

When he managed to adjust his eyes to the brightness, he anxiously skimmed the horizon, until he made out the outline of mountains in the distance. At last! He shouted over to one of the sailors, 'How much longer until we sail in to Palermo?' The sailor shook his head; evidently Castilian was beyond his powers of comprehension. 'Palermo,' shouted Jacob again, gesticulating wildly at the horizon. 'When?'

A slow nod of dawning comprehension on the lardish face in front of him, and then the single word, 'Tomorrow'.

His heart sank. He could not contain himself any longer; another day – and night – was more than he could contend with.

Slowly, he headed back down below board.

In a fever of anticipation, Jacob watched those mountains, but they never seemed to draw any nearer. All day they inched over that enamel sea, without seeming to move. And all day the mountains remained as elusively distant as ever. Jacob was beside himself; he honestly felt that it would be he, and not Michael Scot, who would take to howling at a certain point and have them both thrown overboard. He fell to wondering if what still separated them from land was within swimming distance...

At nightfall they still appeared to be no closer to their destination, and Jacob fell into a fitful sleep. It was not until first light that the real extent of their progress became apparent.

At last! At last!

He shook Michael Scot. In silence they made their way above deck and then craned their heads to get a view of the bay. Michael Scot turned back to Jacob; his eyes were no longer vacant. 'I know this,' he said softly, 'I know this.'

In silence they observed the panorama spread out in front of them.

Right in front of him was the bay of Palermo, over which a majestic mountain rose up sheerly. Michael Scot's knuckles showed white as they gripped the rim of the side deck. Slowly he shook his head and murmured, 'Can this be a homecoming?'

Palermo,
Kingdom of Sicily

XXXI

November AD *1220*

Pier delle Vigne exulted. This could make the difference to his career, this could be the turning point between plodding mediocrity and the success that had so far eluded him. His pace flagged as the steep rise in the narrow street took its toll on the short legs of his stocky frame. But before the news of this sighting was conveyed to Archbishop Berardo di Castacca, he had to be sure that he had indeed seen the right person. The description fitted only up to a certain point: passing tall, a real longshanks, unusually pale-skinned. But he had been unable to tell the colour of the hair, hidden as it was under that turban. And the silver-grey eyes he had been told of had been lost in shadow. But, sure enough, the Mohammedan garb they had spoken of in scandalised tones had been well to the fore. Furthermore, this longshanks had been in the company of what appeared to be a young Jew.

He paused at the top of the street to regain his breath, propping himself up against the wall of a building. Late afternoon at the end of November, and although the weather was mild, already the streets were emptying as the dusk gathered the city into a shadowy hush and its inhabitants scuttled home. Pier delle Vigne's intermediary with the archbishop and direct superior, the cleric to whom he must first relate the news of this sighting, was Tebaldo Francesco di Monteforte. They were both anxious not to disappoint Archbishop di Castacca. Di Monteforte was spurred on by a personal antipathy towards the object of their search, but he had pinned his hopes of advancement on managing to be of use to these two men. If he had indeed run their quarry to ground, they would surely entrust him with other, weightier assignments.

The pounding of his heart had lessened and he resumed his journey. He was headed for the cathedral. The archbishop had summonsed di Monteforte and him only two days previously; yet already the directives given to him had been accomplished. He was keenly aware of the great favour he had been shown by the archbishop in being invited to Palermo, for, at thirty years of age, and despite his degree in law, he still had not managed to find a patron. Until the archbishop's invitation, his education had merely been a mocking reminder of just how far short of his aspirations he had fallen. The risk of lifelong poverty had been a miasma that followed ever closer on his heels.

The archbishop had told him he showed promise: if he continued in this way, it would be in his power to introduce Pier delle Vigne to Frederick. He sighed. At last, a worthy patron. And farewell to the grinding poverty that had been the source of such humiliation – to him and his mother. She had not lived to see the beginning of his ascent; together they had mostly shared dishonour, shame and degradation. Now was his opportunity to avenge the miserable life fate had reserved for her.

Frederick had but a week ago been crowned Holy Roman Emperor by Pope Honorius III in Rome and was even now on the road back to his Sicilian kingdom. He must make the most of the opportunity the archbishop had put in his way.

*

To Jacob it was beautiful. There could be no doubt about that. As beautiful, perhaps, as Córdoba: the same luxurious gardens, basking in the tepid, slanting rays of the late autumn sun, with their miraculous fountains of running water, citrus groves and palm trees; the same elegant buildings of inlaid stone. Large, imposing streets and small, winding lanes; elegant piazzas. It recalled also Toledo in the manner in which synagogue, church and mosque were to be found in such close proximity. And yet there was something subtly different about it, something that conferred an alien quality on this teeming city, in which, Jacob suspected, resided its innermost spirit. Underneath all the superficial beauty lay a vigorous energy, an impulse and a drive, like the quiver of muscles running beneath the mantle of a large feline. Palermo seemed to him like a leopard about to spring: a creature of incontestable beauty; but the very strength that made it beautiful must necessarily place it forever at a remove. This unbiddable spirit, or maybe it was intractableness, or was it wilfulness, he had already come up against in his travels to various cities; he had come across sensuous beauty, too. But never the two together in this disconcerting way.

He felt the beginnings of some great melancholy insinuate itself into his gut; it twisted sharply when he arrived at the Jewish quarter of the city. In through the gate, with its Arabic inscription, *Harat al-yahud*, and round the narrow streets. The most important Jewish centre in the world, it was said, after Toledo, from which had emerged a merchant class that transformed the silk industry. And then had come the expulsions in 1147 under Roger de Hauteville; the steadily dwindling population, down to 1,500 heads of households in 1170; further reduced now to this sad conglomeration of abandoned homes alongside the few still occupied ones.

And so it was that the palpable beauty he saw around him served only to aggravate some dormant sense of loss. Where had he come to? Could he ever make this place into a home for Rebekah and him? Would he be allowed to?

*

They had been living frugally now for nigh on a month in their lodgings in the Jewish quarter of the city. Michael Scot had directed Jacob to this area. It was important, he said, that they keep away from the area up round the palace, for there also was the chancellery, as well as the area round the cathedral. I am in need of my forty days in the desert, Michael Scot had said, to Jacob's consternation. The previous months had hardly been an oasis of serenity and pleasure, so what could this possibly mean?

Jacob had not known what to expect from Master Scot. During the crossing on the Pisan ship, his eyes had taken on that haunted yet vacant look that had characterised them for most of their stay in Córdoba. He had wondered if they would ever emerge from the nightmare realms that encroached more and more. So he watched over Michael Scot. And once again some stubborn streak in the man seemed to draw him back from the brink. He armed himself with his crucifixes and his amulets, but this time he repeated obsessively: 'Lead us not into temptation, but deliver us from evil.' And 'Lord, I believe; help You my unbelief.'

Michael Scot's return to this city of the leopard seemed to restore in him a degree of serenity. What for Jacob was still disturbingly alien was, after all, familiar for him. The 'forty days in the desert' mostly entailed prayer and rest in their lodgings, and of this Jacob wholeheartedly approved. It denoted an instinct towards self-preservation that boded well for the future. Master Scot said quietly that he had need of solitude to come back into himself: he would have preferred to go to a church, indeed the routine of collective prayer would have been a great consolation to him. But he feared he was not up to it yet; besides, his attire precluded it.

Jacob had thus found himself with a measure of freedom he had not enjoyed for quite a while, free to come and go as he pleased.

On his wanderings round the city, he set his mind to picking up the Sicilian idiom: he could put this enforced leisure to good use and not come unprepared when at last he was presented at court. In this way, bit by bit, he picked up news. The latest news was that Frederick was on his way back to Sicily. In Germany he had put his father's kingdom to rights. Then he had stopped off in Rome, where he had been crowned emperor by the pope. From what Jacob managed to gather, there were mixed feelings about this in Palermo: the ordinary people were glad that he was returning, for surely he would bring his protection with him and put an end to the tyranny of the barons and the raiding incursions of the Muslims.

Jacob relayed this news to Michael Scot, who went to the trunk containing his belongings and opened it. He extracted two crumpled and tattered habits, laying them carefully on his bed.

'I ought to get these mended,' he remarked. 'The time has come. We have been here for more than a month now, and soon I will have need of these habits again.' He shook his head, looking at the ragged and worn garments. 'They have seen better days...' He frowned and then looked at Jacob. 'Do you think you could bring them to the Benedictine monastery at Monreale? The monks there would mend them, and I would be ready to present myself at court for the emperor's arrival. I am most anxious to present you to him, for I have a debt of gratitude towards you that will not soon be repaid.'

So it was that Jacob found himself making the short journey to Monreale and handing over the habits to be mended. But he was closely questioned and treated with no small amount of suspicion. What was a Jew doing in possession of two Premonstratensian habits? How had he come by them? And so he had to give Michael Scot's name to them, and explain that he was lately returned from Spain on the emperor's business, where he, Jacob Anatolio, had been his assistant. The stony silence that had met these admissions induced such a feeling of unease in Jacob that he felt a sudden and impelling need to recount of a misadventure at the hands of Iberian bandits. He and Michael Scot, he explained, the lying words spilling off his tongue with disconcerting facility, had fallen victim to marauding thieves and – here he shook his head – they had not desisted even before Canon Michael's habit. They were, of course, Muslim bandits, who not only had robbed them of the few valuables in their possession, but, disgusted at the paucity of their takings, had set upon Michael Scot and beaten him to within an inch of his life. This tale had served its purpose: a common enemy had clearly been divined. The monks huddled round Jacob Anatolio in appalled fascination. The habit had been held up for horrified inspection. Tattered, but not bloodstained. Interrogative eyes were turned on him.

The injuries, Jacob clarified quickly, his stomach lurching, had been to Canon Michael's face. For the most part. Severe bruising to the body...

'And the other habit? What had befallen that?'

Jacob cast his eyes to the ground, staring at the square tiles. He pursed his lips, and then quickly looked back up. The bandits destroyed anything they disdained to rob, he explained, shaking his head sadly at such impiety.

'The two habits were beyond mending, it seemed. New ones would have to be made. Could the costs be met?'

'They could.'

'Well then, Canon Michael Scot would do well to come and collect his new habits himself when they were ready.'

'The costs of the new habits could be met because Canon Michael Scot had so far managed to avoid spending his money on other clothes. If he was obliged to present himself in Monreale, he would have to expend money on garments in order to get there in decency. He would prefer to stay in Palermo, complete his convalescence, and have his habits brought to him. Which service he, Jacob, could best render him, as his assistant.'

This suggestion was grudgingly acceded to. But the habits would take another fortnight to make.

The emperor was due back in Palermo in less than a week.

*

'But are you sure it is indeed he?'

Pier delle Vigne observed Tebaldo Francesco di Monteforte in silence for a moment. He allowed himself a slight shrug. 'As sure as I can be – given that I have never met the man and have only your description to go on with.'

'Well, in that case, perhaps you should take me to the place where you claim to have seen The Scot. I will know beyond a shadow of a doubt whether it is he or not.'

Pier delle Vigne groaned inwardly. It was late; he was tired. He had spent the day tramping the length and breadth of Palermo, searching for this individual. And just who was this Michael Scot to have excited such antipathy? He longed for the comfort of his lodgings and a good meal. 'I would ask you—' he started, 'that is, if I might make so bold as to point out—' He paused to clear his throat as di Monteforte irascibly folded his arms. 'Whoever it is,' he took up more briskly, 'he will not disappear between now and tomorrow morning.'

Di Monteforte opened his mouth to object, but Pier delle Vigne smoothly brought home his point. 'It is dark. Who would be out and about at this hour? And even if he were so foolhardy as to be out and about, we would not be able to see him.'

Di Monteforte's mouth closed.

'I will take you there at first light tomorrow, and we shall wait and see.'

Di Monteforte nodded. Pier delle Vigne's stomach growled in the silence.

'So you see, your Grace,' said di Monteforte, 'it is of the utmost urgency that we have this disreputable individual summonsed before the emperor. Only in this way can we hope to show conclusively the depths of heresy – nay, apostasy – to which he has sunk.' Di Monteforte surreptitiously wiped the sweat that had collected on his upper lip and wiped his finger down the side of his habit.

Archbishop Berardo di Castacca's eyes remained fixed on him for a few moments longer. Then he frowned and looked away. 'It is passing strange,' he murmured, almost to himself. 'Who could have imagined such a thing.' He turned back to di Monteforte and Pier delle Vigne. 'You have done well in finding him so quickly,' – Pier delle Vigne bowed his head in what he hoped would pass for unassuming modesty – 'but I cannot believe that Canon Michael Scot has joined the ranks of the heathen Muslim.'

'But I can,' di Monteforte interjected. Pier delle Vigne could see the effort the man was making to keep his composure, the breath he had to take before speaking again. Whatever unchristian feelings he harboured in his breast, they would have to stay there, well out of sight, or Archbishop di Castacca would dismiss him. It was di Monteforte's awareness of this that was placing such a strain on him. Once again, Pier delle Vigne wondered who Michael Scot was, or what he had done, to have become such a focus of ill-will.

'Your Grace,' took up di Monteforte, 'in my capacity as overseer of the young Prince Frederick's studies, I had many an occasion to come up against the baleful influence Canon Michael Scot exerted on my charge.' Pier delle Vigne watched as the sweat broke out once again on di Monteforte's upper lip. 'It was disgraceful, I tell you!' The strident echo of this pronouncement bounced off the high ceiling in the archbishop's room; di Monteforte looked the most startled of the three of them. He coughed. 'That is to say,' he continued, his voice suitably lowered, 'it was terrible to have to behold. The constant doubt that the prince's soul was being endangered because of some dubious notions that The Scot was planting there. Your

Grace must understand this – you had the prince's best interests at heart from the beginning.'

The archbishop remained silent for a moment. Then he said, 'The matter does not convince me.' Di Monteforte's eyes widened. 'Nevertheless, it is my duty to ensure that no damage accrue to Frederick, our Holy Roman Emperor.' He sighed. 'Therefore, we shall proceed as follows. I will supply you with a summons before the emperor for Canon Michael Scot, which you shall deliver to him. In this way, he will have the opportunity to explain himself. And we shall then know what the best course of action is.' He stood up. 'Speak to my secretary; he will draw up the summons for you. But,' – he held up a warning finger – 'discretion is of the essence here. We must avoid any hint of scandal for the emperor.'

The two men bowed and left the room.

'Fortunately,' said di Monteforte, his eyes cast meekly on the floor of the corridor running alongside the bishop's quarters, 'we are not bound by any such scruples towards The Scot.'

XXXII

The banging echoed round the lane of the Jewish quarter, shattering the dark silence of the night. The guards hammered on the door once again. Shutters were opened cautiously. A head appeared from an open window on the upper storey of the lodging house. 'What do you want?' came a querulous voice.

'We are here on the emperor's business,' replied Pier delle Vigne. He stepped out of the shadows. 'Open up immediately or it will go ill with you; we have a summons for Michael Scot.'

There was a fearful imprecation from the window and the shutter was closed. Presently keys rattled in the front door. The guards burst in, their shadows leaping over the walls as they swarmed into the narrow entrance passage lit by a single candle held aloft by the terrified owner of the lodging house.

'He is above in his room,' he blurted, the jerky movements he made with his arm towards the stairs making the flame of the candle jump. The guards took the rickety stairs two at a time.

Pier delle Vigne cursed his short legs and the humiliating delay as he walked into Michael Scot's room well after the guards. His eyes flew to the tall figure over by the bed. Yes, it was he. And he was indeed wearing the Mohammedan attire.

'I have a summons here,' – he extracted the parchment from the folds of his pocket – 'signed by Archbishop di Castacca, to bring you before the emperor.'

Michael Scot's eyes flew to the door, seeking those of the young man blocked there by the guards. Wordlessly they looked at each other.

'This very night,' insisted Pier delle Vigne. 'You must leave now with the guards.' He indicated the stairs; the guards began to prod Michael Scot with their spears.

Suddenly, the young Jew's voice was an urgent torrent of babbling noise, washing over all of them in the small room. Only Michael Scot appeared to understand, however.

'Listen carefully!' cried out Jacob in Arabic. 'Tell them that you had to wear these garments because you were set upon by Muslim bandits on your return journey from Toledo. Tell them,' – he gasped as one of the guards struck him in an attempt to stem the flow – 'they beat you,' he took up hoarsely. 'Senseless.' He fell to his knees as another guard brought his spear down across his back. His head bowed in pain, he still managed to grate out, 'Anything not stolen was destroyed.' He coughed. 'Including the other habit.'

'Silence!' roared Pier delle Vigne.

'Monreale…' whispered Jacob. 'The new habits…'

Pier delle Vigne waved to one of the guards. 'Bring our zealous friend; I am curious to see if he prattles on in this fashion before his Majesty as well.'

Pier delle Vigne contemplated the four figures in front of him: two guards, the young Jew, and the man he had been directed to summon before the emperor – Michael Scot. The slope in the street that led from the Jewish quarter down near the seafront up to the palace was taxing, and he had fallen behind. But no matter, this was a job well done and he could feel satisfied. He wondered what lay ahead for this Michael Scot. For his own part, he still had not made up his mind what stance to take on the matter. Di Monteforte had his own reasons. 'What has this man done to deserve your revilement?' Pier delle Vigne had asked him, just before setting out to take Michael Scot by surprise in his lodgings. Di Monteforte's lips had twisted. 'I do not like him,' he had replied coldly. 'And that is reason enough.'

It certainly was. But Pier delle Vigne also saw that the archbishop was not set against this Scot. The archbishop was acting purely from a desire to safeguard the emperor's reputation. And the archbishop was di Monteforte's superior. He was also his own means to a worthy patron. Clearly, he would be more advised to take the archbishop's line. Indeed, that was why Pier delle Vigne had not added his signature to the summons. That honour he had left to di Monteforte and the bishop's secretary. If trouble arose from this episode, he did not want it traced back to him.

On a personal level, he would wait and see what the emperor's reaction to this foreigner was when he presented himself at court in Mohammedan garb. Then, and only then, would he decide if he too did not like Michael Scot.

*

This was the place he had only looked on from afar. In any case, as Jacob now saw, stepping over the threshold of the Norman Palace, he would not have got in due to the presence of armed guards at the entrance.

Jacob tried not to give in to the feeling of dread that threatened to overtake him; but it was difficult, especially when the thought flew through his mind – fleeting and piercing – of Rebekah. What hopes he had placed in Palermo. He turned to Michael Scot; his expression was morose.

He did not wish to alarm Michael Scot any further, so he just said, 'Michael, remember what I told you, and let us hope for the best.'

Michael Scot grimaced. 'The foxes have their holes,' he said softly, 'and the birds of the air their nests; but the Son of Man has nowhere to lay his head…' He shook the guard's hand off his arm. 'I can find my own way to the Green Hall,' he said. 'Unlike yourself, I am no stranger to his Majesty's gatherings.' The guard attempted to catch a hold of him again, but was quelled by the look Michael Scot cast on him. 'Come, Jacob.' His eyes narrowed. 'Let us face the assembly.'

The loud rumble of many voices met them as they walked down the torchlit corridor. And there ahead was the entrance. Jacob felt Michael Scot's fingers momentarily clutch his arm, heard the shaky intake of breath. Then he walked into the Green Hall. Jacob had not even time to take in his surroundings, for gradually the assembled courtiers, functionaries, nobles, knights and clergy turned to look at Michael Scot as he made his way up through the hall, and a stunned silence fell over them. By the time Michael Scot had reached the dais where Frederick was seated on his throne, it seemed to Jacob that the only audible sound in this vast space must be the beating of his own heart.

Jacob followed at a certain remove; the skin on his back prickled as he moved over to the side of the hall, in against the wall. He glanced in the direction of the throne, and then steeled himself to look at the emperor: he saw a slight man, about the same age as himself, richly attired. Pier delle Vigne came hastening after them. He paused to draw breath and then in a loud voice announced, 'Your Majesty, pray accept the homage of Michael Scot.'

The emperor started. As the figure in front of him regained an upright position, he leaned forward and squinted through short-sighted eyes. 'Can it be true?' he said, the slowness of the enunciation betraying his incredulity. 'Can this be Canon Michael Scot?'

The intake of breath round the Green Hall was as softly ambiguous as the echoing wash of the sea. It bespoke consternation mixed with pleasurable anticipation of the chastisement certain to fall on the head of the perpetrator of such an outrage. Silence fell again.

Pier delle Vigne took in the astounded expression on the emperor's face; his eyes flicked back to Michael Scot.

'Your Majesty,' Michael Scot's voice rang out strong and sure among the gaping assembly of the Green Hall. Jacob was glad of it. 'I apologise for my unseemly appearance.' He paused; the silence was absolute. 'Should his Majesty wish, I can account for it.'

The emperor rubbed his thumb along his bottom lip, back and forth. 'I think you had better,' he said eventually.

'I thank you, your Majesty. I am only lately returned from Toledo, where I brought to a conclusion the task you assigned me. There I translated the works of Aristotle, and that great philosopher's Moorish interpreter, Averroës.'

At this name, a murmur broke out among the assembly. A Moorish interpreter? That explained the clothes. It grew in volume. Michael Scot the apostate!

The emperor held up his hand for silence. Michael Scot then turned on the gathering, and with slow deliberation his eyes roamed over the sea of faces, lingering on some in particular.

Some took a step backwards; others, mouths agape, remained stock-still. But all instantaneously fell silent. Perhaps it was because of his own nerves having been rubbed raw on account of the tumultuous events of the past few weeks; perhaps it was his awareness of the knife-edge he and Michael now walked on; perhaps he was just succumbing to hysterical superstition like everyone else; but from his vantage point at the side of this great hall it seemed to Jacob that some battle was being waged: with a shadowy rush, two spirals of smoke seemed to take each other on, coiling in and around each other, each seeking to swallow the other, until finally one of them succeeded in getting the upper hand.

The haze slithered away. No longer did the hall feel tainted with a vicious sense of expectation; somehow that unruly herd instinct for blood had been cowed.

Jacob could not say how, but he knew without a doubt that

it was Michael Scot who had willed this. He was swamped by a sense of suffocation; a feeling of helplessness such as he had never experienced fell on him. God preserve him – surely he too was not about to lose his reason and succumb to visions and seizures. This was what came of spending too long in the company of a deranged individual. Truly, things had come to a sad pass when he had to be glad of this kind of devilry.

For his part, Pier delle Vigne noticed the slight smile that had appeared at the corner of the emperor's mouth. 'So, Canon Scot,' took up the emperor, 'or maybe I should call you Master Scot for so long as you are thus attired – you have carried out the task we set you all those years ago. I congratulate you!' He smiled.

Pier delle Vigne's mouth set in a thin line.

'But what of the account you said you could give for your attire?' pursued the emperor.

'Your Majesty,' replied Michael Scot, 'I was waylaid by Muslim bandits near Valencia, on my way back to Palermo. They beat me to within an inch of my life, destroying my habit in the process. Anything else they reputed of no value met with a similar fate. That included my second habit. I had to accept such charity as was given to me in those Moorish lands, of which the clothes you see now are evidence. I am here by the grace of God, for which I give much thanks.'

'Indeed, I can see now that you are the worse for wear. Draw near to the throne, that I may salute you.'

The emperor rose and extended his hand. Michael Scot made his obeisance and kissed the imperial ring. 'I am glad to see you again, Master Michael Scot,' the emperor said, laughing. 'I have missed our talks.'

It was then that Pier delle Vigne's complacent detachment towards Michael Scot slithered down some muddy slope into a swamp of jealous hostility, from whence it would never more emerge. In the emperor he had discerned a patron that he would dedicate his life to. And he would share him with nobody.

XXXIII

December AD 1220

Don Filippo flinched as the floor creaked in the room overhead. He was seated at the table in the main hall on the first floor of his townhouse, endeavouring to take his breakfast in peace. It could mean only one thing: that barbarian was up, and about to foist his unwelcome presence on him. Along with his unwelcome assistant. Such an imposition! He still had not got over the shock of it.

He placed the morsel of soft white bread in his mouth, noting with regret that the loaf was now finished. Certainly, it was delicious: so exquisitely delicate. The Lord knew when the cook would get round to making some more. Not until the following week in all likelihood, what with the shortage of refined white flour and other delicacies from the Saracen-held lands. So he would have to make do with the usual roughage. But, he reflected with a certain acid pleasure as he finished off the creamy goat's cheese, this meant there would be none left for the foreigners. Good enough. His home was not a receptacle for waifs, strays and other undesirables. What could the emperor have been thinking when he issued the disposition obliging him to take these men into his own home?

He saw what it was, and not without bitterness. Yet again he was being penalised for not being married, for not having a family. For what disturbance could the presence of this Scot create in an empty house?

That was not the point, of course. The point was that all eyes at court, malevolent and otherwise (and they were mostly malevolent, as he knew to his cost) had now honed in on his quiet existence in this unassuming townhouse in Palermo. The court wanted to see exactly what manner of an oddity The Scot was, and this meant closely following his progress now he had come into Don Filippo's orbit.

It was a most unwelcome scrutiny. He was not used to it, having always done his utmost to avoid drawing any undue attention to himself. It did nothing for his equanimity.

The heavy drape hanging over the entrance to the hall was pulled back, and Don Filippo started at the sight that met his eyes. In the shadows created by the gloom of a winter morning, a ghostly presence seemed to have glided into the hall: pale and white it was, from head to foot. Don Filippo blinked rapidly and looked again. Well – at least those scandalous Mohammedan garments had disappeared. They had been replaced, he noted approvingly, by the white woollen Premonstratensian habit. But the combination of the white hair, the pale skin and the habit gave such a spectral aura, although the faded red beard did stand out. For a moment he thought he saw the silver eyes glitter. But surely that had been his imagination. And in The Scot's wake came his Jewish assistant.

From being a decorous place of refuge, his home might as well now be a lodging house of ill-repute, its doors flung open, ready to receive the scrapings of the streets.

As The Scot advanced upon the table, with alarmingly long strides, Don Filippo noted, and on ludicrously large feet, he recalled the rumours circulating in hushed tones among the courtiers about those eyes, the unsettling powers that some of them had begun to insinuate they possessed. He blinked rapidly as The Scot came to a halt in front of him.

'I thank you for your kind hospitality, Don Filippo.'

'Er, quite. I mean – yes. That is – I – er...'

Michael Scot's eyebrow arched. He smiled slightly and looked away. 'I have reason to believe that our stay here in your house will shortly be drawing to a close.'

Don Filippo's eyes swivelled towards The Scot's; they looked back at him with an openness that gave the lie to any of these scaremongering rumours. Indeed, Don Filippo thought he detected in them a certain detached friendliness. Rumour, he reflected, was a poison that shrivelled all real communication. 'How is that?' he asked.

'I have spoken to the emperor,' replied Michael Scot. 'And here I know I can rely on your discretion; this must not be repeated outside your house.'

Don Filippo nodded in complicit approval.

'The emperor is in the process of procuring a new Cistercian abbot for San Giovanni degli Eremiti. As soon as this has been completed, I shall make my home there.'

'I see.' It might at this juncture be construed as indelicate to enquire further as to when precisely this desirable event would take place. In any event, he reflected, his fingers relaxing round the bunched-up material of his tunic he had been clutching under the table, he could ask elsewhere. He looked down at his tunic and smoothed its crumpled pleats.

'And lodgings have also been found for Master Anatolio. I am going to the palace now and shall return late this evening. Do not disturb yourself in providing a meal.'

The Scot saluted him and walked back over to the entrance. Don Filippo's eyes followed him, their expression at once baffled yet mollified.

*

Together with Jacob, Michael Scot set off for his private audience with the emperor. It was encouraging to hear that they were to be received in Frederick's own chambers; but this was marred by the displeasure he felt when his eye fell on Pier delle Vigne, the unctuous minion who had manhandled Jacob and him, dragging them before the emperor in that high-handed fashion. Delle Vigne had settled himself to the right of the chair the emperor was sitting in, stylus in hand, ready to comply with the imperial wishes.

'Canon Scot,' said the emperor, as Michael Scot bowed before him. 'Well met!'

'Your Majesty, I come bearing a gift that may be of interest to you.'

'Apart from your most excellent translations, Canon Scot?' The emperor smiled. Michael Scot noted how at the mention of his translations delle Vigne had ceased his scribbling, his eyes darting to the emperor. 'Yes, I have had occasion to read some of them and it would give me great pleasure to discuss them with you at a future date. My secretary will arrange a time for us.'

'That is most gracious, your Majesty. It would be an honour. But,' – Here Michael Scot stuck his hand into his habit and there was a rustling noise as he carefully extracted what looked like a manuscript – 'would it please you to examine this artefact?' He held out the manuscript.

The emperor bade him draw near. 'What is it?' he asked. 'It looks like a rather commonplace manuscript.'

Michael Scot opened it and passed his hand over the page. 'Feel this, your Majesty.' He handed it to the emperor, who also rubbed it. 'This,' he added, 'is paper.'

The emperor's eyebrows lifted. 'Ah,' he said slowly, observing it more closely. 'And what can you tell me about it?'

'We came across it,' Michael Scot paused for a moment to indicate Jacob, who had been standing in silence well to the side. He motioned at him to move forward; nervously, Jacob did so and bowed low. 'My assistant, Jacob Anatolio,' said Michael Scot, 'without whose help, my endeavours in Spain would have come to nought.' The emperor regarded the young man before him and then nodded. 'But,' continued Michael Scot, 'as I was saying, we came across it in abundance at a place in Spain called Xátiva. There the Moors, with great ingenuity, did run a place they called a paper mill.' Michael Scot shook his head. 'Because of the vast quantities of this stuff they contrive to produce, with little trouble or expense, you would not believe the number of manuscripts and writings of all types that circulate in their lands.'

'Indeed,' mused the emperor.

'The Moors have perfected the techniques required for its production, and it has greatly added to the circulation of knowledge in their society.' Michael Scot paused and looked directly at the emperor. 'In such a centre of learning as your Majesty's court, perhaps the time has come to initiate its production here as well.'

The emperor passed his hand over the manuscript, rubbed it and then lifted it to his nose to smell it. 'Good work, Canon Scot. Once again you have served me well.' He held out the manuscript for it to be taken, and with surprising deftness Pier delle Vigne stepped forward to relieve the imperial hand of its burden. 'See to it,' the emperor said curtly to delle Vigne's recumbent form.

'Your Majesty,' added Michael Scot, 'there is one further matter I wish to bring to your attention.' He indicated Jacob. 'Before you stands a young man of exceptional ability; I have known him for nigh on six years and can vouch for it. Jacob Anatolio has such projects in mind as would without doubt bring glory to your Majesty and his court. Were you to consider involving him in the new university you are in the process of founding in Naples, I am sure that he would prove his worth there as well.'

The emperor was silent for a moment, then he looked up. 'I have every reason to trust the esteem in which you hold Master Anatolio. Unfortunately, it is beyond my power to grant him a position at this new university. For, despite my wish that the university be secular and beyond the reach of clerical influence,

I find myself continually enmeshed in obligations and laws and ordinances extracted from me by the papacy. In short,' Frederick made a gesture of regret, 'Jews have been barred from university and my hands are tied on the issue.'

Jacob froze; this was the end of all hope. His aspirations were undone. It had all been for nothing.

'And yet,' took up the emperor, 'I am reluctant to part with somebody of whom Canon Scot speaks so well. Let me know what Master Anatolio's fields of interest and specialisations are, and we shall procure a suitable position for him here in Palermo.'

Not trusting himself to speak, Jacob could only bow as low as he could.

XXXIV

It was just as Don Filippo had feared. Not only had his house been invaded by barbarians and foreigners, but now he would have to put up with the scheming scrutiny of the chancellery and the Church. And at such a late hour. He glanced over at Michael Scot and his assistant, who had themselves only just arrived back from the palace, noting that they, too, looked put out. Schooling his face to blankness, he bade his servant let the two callers enter.

The servant ushered in Pier delle Vigne and Francesco Tebaldo di Monteforte. Don Filippo determined to do and say nothing until one or other of them apologised for intruding at this unseemly hour.

'We ask your pardon for the lateness with which we impose on your hospitality,' began Pier delle Vigne.

Impose, yes, thought Don Filippo, but his hospitality was something they would not be seeing. 'And it could not have waited until tomorrow?' he enquired.

'His Majesty has also ordered that an appointment be made for Canon Scot to discuss his translations,' announced delle Vigne.

Di Monteforte, his face a study in rigid contempt, added, 'We also have a letter from his Majesty that urgently needs signing by The Scot.'

'However,' he paused and his lip curled as his eye skimmed disdainfully over Michael Scot, 'the discussion of the translations with his Majesty depends on their being removed from his possession and taken into safekeeping in the chancellery.'

'What?' The cry burst from Michael Scot. 'How can that be? His Majesty said nothing of it to me.'

'Well, he's not obliged to, is he?'

'I won't be handing over anything to you until his Majesty tells me to do so.'

Di Monteforte reached into his habit and removed a sheet of parchment. His expression changed from contemptuous to smug as he proceeded to show it to Michael Scot.

'As you can see,' pursued delle Vigne, 'there is a very clear order here to hand over the translations for safekeeping to the chancellery, signed by his Majesty.'

'This is preposterous!'

'I don't follow,' murmured delle Vigne. 'Are you saying that his Majesty's orders are preposterous?' In silence, two sets of eyes bored into Michael Scot. Jacob moved discreetly forward and placed a restraining hand on Michael Scot's arm.

'Canon Scot said nothing of the sort,' he said firmly. 'What he meant was that your part in this has caught him by surprise.'

Di Monteforte shot him a scornful glance. 'Our part, as you say, is determined entirely by his Majesty.'

'And,' said delle Vigne, 'we need hardly remind you that such contentious material as this is a liability for him.'

'Precisely,' interposed di Monteforte. 'Having been placed under a papal ban, the emperor has no choice but to confiscate it.'

'His Majesty also recommends that you abandon the study of any matters relating to Muslim philosophy or philosophers and pursue instead only those relating to medicine, for which at least there is some use.'

There was no reply from Michael Scot, who had gone very still. Jacob glanced at him and saw that his eyes were closed. Suddenly they opened, and he brought them to bear first on delle Vigne and then on di Monteforte. 'Read the letter from his Majesty again,' he said. With a sense of mounting unease, Jacob noted a change in his voice, which seemed to have deepened. Behind him, Don Filippo stirred restlessly.

Di Monteforte moved forward and, unfolding the letter, held it out for delle Vigne to read from. But he had only got to the end of the first sentence when, with a startled cry, di Monteforte cast it from him and both men recoiled in horror.

'What ails you now?' asked Michael Scot.

The two men looked at each other in consternation. 'N-nothing,' stuttered delle Vigne.

'I thought for a moment you might have been confronted with a vision of what your scheming ways look like to the Almighty,' said Michael Scot, staring at them all the while.

Jacob placed himself between Michael Scot and the two men, his eyes flicking from one side of the confrontation to the other.

'No such thing,' cried di Monteforte. 'And how dare you to presume either on our having schemed or to any knowledge of how the Almighty judges us.'

'Finish reading then.' Michael Scot moved to retrieve the parchment on the floor. Don Filippo intervened. 'The hour is late,' he said, a tremor in his voice betraying his distress. 'Why don't we adjourn and take this up in the morning when we are all better disposed?'

'I agree with Don Filippo,' said Jacob.

'I'm afraid this can't wait,' replied Michael Scot with the touch of mulish obstinacy that always riled Jacob. 'Here you are, gentlemen.' He handed the parchment to them and, folding his arms, stood back to listen.

With a palpable sense of reluctance the two men resumed reading. And yet again di Monteforte had not got beyond the second sentence when delle Vigne shrieked 'Snakes!' throwing his hands in the air and backing away. Ashen-faced, di Monteforte cast the parchment from him.

'It is infested with serpents,' he whispered. 'What did you do to it?'

Michael Scot regarded them imperturbably. Jacob shook his head and glanced over at Don Filippo, who had sat down rather heavily on his chair. This was going to be tricky to explain away.

'The work of the devil is going on here,' hissed di Monteforte. 'You have not heard the last of this.'

Silence settled on the room. Michael Scot looked as if he were lost in his own thoughts and Don Filippo seemed lost for words. Jacob frowned. The effort of speaking weighed too heavily on him; what could he say that would not require an out-and-out lie, and he had no head for the invention of a lie at that moment.

Suddenly, Michael Scot groaned. Jacob glanced over at him, his stomach giving a lurch of fear. He knew what that particular sound presaged. They were undone.

Michael Scot pressed his hands to his head and gave another and louder groan. Don Filippo was regarding him, his face frozen in an expression of appalled shock, while delle Vigne and di Monteforte had both gone stock-still. Before Jacob could even attempt to usher them from the room, Michael Scot had collapsed on the floor, his body sprawling out to its full length. With jerking movements his back arched and his eyes rolled back into his head until only the whites showed. Spittle flecked his open mouth.

There was a whimper from Don Filippo, who retreated behind his chair; delle Vigne and di Monteforte, while never taking their eyes off Michael Scot, took a few steps backwards. Only Jacob rushed to cradle Michael Scot's head and soothe him.

Eventually, the convulsive movements subsided and his eyes returned to normal.

'You had a seizure,' said Jacob.

Michael Scot's eyes closed; wordlessly he turned his head to the wall.

'I knew it…' said di Monteforte, self-righteousness vying with gloating, 'the work of the devil.'

Jacob looked down at the drawn face on his lap. Despairingly, he watched delle Vigne and di Monteforte hasten from the house. There would be no recovering from this.

XXXV

AD 1221

For the first time in his life, Pier delle Vigne admitted the possibility of happiness. With a patron this powerful, surely he could hope to put himself beyond the reach of those who sought to keep him down. For the emperor was indeed all powerful, and he would render himself indispensable in maintaining this state of affairs.

He set about acquainting himself with all the events, details and intricacies that had melded to form the life to date of Frederick Hohenstaufen of Swabia, Holy Roman Emperor. In Sicily he learned how the barons had long been undermining the emperor's power. They were being supported in this by the island's Muslim enclaves, above all to the west and south of Palermo. Saracen-occupied Mazara had become a byword as a hotbed of violent uprisings.

It was a festering thorn in the emperor's side, and Pier delle Vigne began to see how it had come about. The young Frederick had been orphaned of both parents by the age of six. Archbishop di Castacca, who had known Frederick since he was a baby, spoke to Pier delle Vigne of this time with evident distress and delle Vigne listened carefully: listened to how the young prince's childhood had been blighted by personal neglect and constant fear as anarchy had been unleashed on the kingdom in the period of upheaval that followed his father's death; listened to how Marcovaldo von Anweiler had attempted to usurp his throne, plunging the island into chaos; how the barons had been only too glad to exploit this in order to reaffirm their own power, condemning the populace to even greater hardship; and how the retreating Muslim population, dwindling more and more into isolated communities as the Norman and then German conquerors set their mark on the land, but unresigned to this change in fortune, reacted with constant skirmishings and occasionally a devastating full-blown uprising. And all the while, encouraged by the absence of a centre of power, the commercially minded Genoese and Pisan city-states had artfully played their own game, establishing trading outposts that amounted at this stage to colonies.

A firm hand was clearly needed, so Honorious III's request for a crusade, extracted just before Frederick's coronation, could not be acceded to. The emperor would just have to play for time and hope in the benevolence of his Holiness, who, in effect, seemed well disposed.

For his part, Frederick would undertake to maintain the status quo. He was the ruler of an empire split in two by the Papal States: from Rome over as far as the Adriatic coast, the temporal assets of the papacy amounted effectively to an obstacle to the complete unification of the northern and southern parts of the Holy Roman Empire. An empire neither Roman nor holy, as Frederick was wont to say, but for the moment he would leave this be. In order to maintain the status quo with the papacy, he would not pursue what amounted to a natural aspiration: he would abstain from seeking to unite the two sundered parts – the Germanic and the Mediterranean – of his empire.

But the papacy continued to pressurise the emperor into regulating the various creeds within his Sicilian kingdom. Legislation was to accord Christianity the pre-eminent position that was its natural due.

Sicily, therefore, would have to be seen to be a bastion of Christendom; the papacy trusted that the emperor would see to it that his Jewish and Muslim subjects complied fully with this.

And so, reminded of the importance of the statutes of the Lateran Council, Frederick went to Messina in the spring of 1221 and there enacted the ordinances requiring Jewish men to wear a beard, and thus render them recognisable as such. The Muslims, less assimilated, were instantly recognisable in any case.

*

The new epistolary work he had been charged with had taken quite a while, but in his freshly promoted capacity as notary in the imperial chancellery, Pier delle Vigne had set to it with all the zeal of a neophyte. And it had led to the successful outcome he would shortly be able to parade before Archbishop di Castacca.

Before leaving on yet another campaign in the spring of 1221, this time against the insurgent barons in Alifa, the emperor had left instructions that San Giovanni degli Eremiti be handed over to the Cistercians. Pier delle Vigne had listened as Frederick enumerated the virtues he found in this order: the austerity, the lack of attachment to worldly goods and worldly ambition, the sincere pursuit of the Christian ideal. It had, remarked the emperor, given rise to a distinctive form of religious devotion that struck him very favourably.

For this reason, the Cistercians would be a trustworthy foil to the more opulent Benedictines out in Monreale. Frederick did not want to find himself having to lay siege to that monastery as well if it got above itself in worldly pretensions. Which, he added, his blue eyes narrowing, was not beyond the bounds of probability, given the state of insurgency most of his subjects with even a jot of power had demonstrated in Sicily, and given the wealth Monreale had always been intent on hoarding. All he needed was for it to come to the papacy's notice, and he would find himself with an outpost of the curia on his doorstep.

And so the emperor would show great favour to these ascetic Cistercians. He would be their patron and the abbot would be his personal confessor. He had chosen his candidate from a list that Pier delle Vigne had taken infinite pains to covertly engineer. The result of all these painstaking manoeuvrings was indeed a judicious choice. At forty, Hugo de Clermont was a man in his prime; but this prime was limited exclusively to the field of learning. Born in rural Picardie, he had attained fame at the University of Paris as a scholar of Greek, a subject, reflected Pier delle Vigne, with pleasingly abstruse connotations and applications. As far as he was aware, Hugo de Clermont's reputation had no other reason to exist except for this scholarly aptitude for Greek. And a talent – for as such did the emperor see it – for shunning worldly advancement. He had never been the abbot of an order before, never occupied an administrative position. If, mused Pier delle Vigne, he could be kept tolling his beads and perusing Greek manuscripts, the more pernicious attempts by the Church to control the emperor's temporal affairs might just be curtailed. The new abbot would also be a means of keeping The Scot and his devilry in check. And if *he*, delle Vigne, could be the means of bringing this about, so much the better.

XXXVI

Pier delle Vigne's first impression of the new abbot of San Giovanni degli Eremiti put him in mind of a mirror version of himself. The same stocky build, which in Pier delle Vigne at thirty still had to run to fat, had already done so in the new abbot at forty, for Hugo de Clermont was possessed of an unmistakable paunch. Pier delle Vigne allowed himself a quick smirk and thought that it did not point to particularly frugal eating habits. But he did not care for those round, pale blue eyes, which Hugo de Clermont turned on him with candid yet penetrating intelligence.

He had, however, been reassured by the unmistakable air of trepidation which the new abbot had not managed to suppress, for all his chilly reserve. He wondered how it might best be exploited.

The meeting between de Clermont and the Archbishop di Castacca had gone smoothly and Pier delle Vigne basked in the evident satisfaction the archbishop had shown while talking to the abbot. He had outlined the nature of de Clermont's responsibilities, laying great emphasis on his role as confessor to the emperor. Sadly, di Castacca went on to explain, it was a duty that he personally could no longer carry out, given the overwhelming burden of work he had to face as archbishop. In the past, it was a duty he had counted as his most important. The emperor was always in need of a counsel of wisdom; it now fell to de Clermont to see that this was indeed what he got. Was he up to the task? Di Castacca turned assessing eyes on him.

De Clermont's face had remained impassive as he replied in the affirmative; but the whiteness of the knuckles clutching the crucifix on his scapular did not escape Pier delle Vigne.

'Then, of course,' added Archbishop di Castacca, 'there will be the choir monks and lay brothers under your care in the monastery itself. They should number thirty-five.' He paused. 'And now to the topic of Michael Scot.' The archbishop paced back and forth, and then turned to de Clermont. 'Canon Michael Scot, I should have said, for this man is a Premonstratensian.' Di Castacca paused and frowned. 'However, I should warn you that he has been a cause of scandal here in Palermo. And we suspect even in Spain, where he went as a translator for the emperor. Here di Castacca glanced at Pier delle Vigne; his eyebrows rose and he shook his head.

'I am not one of those who see in him the personification of the devil.' His eyebrows descended rapidly. 'And I deplore all this rumour-mongering. You should know that Canon Michael Scot is especially esteemed by the emperor – and not without reason. But it also has to be said that he constantly runs the risk of giving rise to scandal. The reason for this is not so clear to me, but it must not be allowed to get out of hand. And that is where you, Father Abbot, will be able to assist. I ask you to afford particular guidance to Canon Scot, and in so doing avoid the taint of scandal that he seems to bring with him wherever he goes. I feel that the rigorous application of the Cistercian monastic rule will be of great benefit to him.'

*

Hugo de Clermont glanced at Pier delle Vigne, who was escorting him to the monastery where he would meet Canon Michael Scot. All his instincts were against the man, so he maintained a resolute silence.

'The archbishop,' said Pier delle Vigne, breaking in on his thoughts, 'is a man of outstanding Christian charity.' To this piece of presumptuous banality, de Clermont chose not to reply. 'So much so,' pursued delle Vigne, 'that I feel an extra word about The Scot might be in order. Purely in the interests of keeping you fully abreast, of course...'

Again, de Clermont did not reply, but he felt the curiosity rising, despite his best intentions.

'You see,' took up delle Vigne, 'what his Grace omitted to mention – undoubtedly through an excess of Christian charity – was that the word increasingly associated with The Scot is "necromancy".'

De Clermont's head swivelled; he saw the fleeting smirk of satisfaction on delle Vigne's face. 'Necromancy?' he echoed.

Delle Vigne nodded dolefully. 'Unfortunately, yes. It pains me to have to say it of a man of the Church, but so it is.'

'I can imagine,' replied de Clermont acidly. 'I seem to recollect, however, that his Grace did mention the word "rumourmongering" – and his aversion to it.' He paused, and then added quietly, 'I am sure this, too, springs from his Christian charity.'

Taken aback, delle Vigne took in the momentarily unveiled hostility in the hooded eyes on a level with his own. Perhaps he had underestimated de Clermont.

'Even so,' took up delle Vigne with slow deliberation, 'as the new abbot, you would be advised to keep abreast of events regarding the clerics under your supervision.' He pursed his lips; de Clermont observed him in impassive silence. 'And so, I shall relate to you the latest circumstance that throws a questionable light on The Scot.' He sniffed. 'There are many more of these circumstances, but for the sake of brevity—'

'Quite,' interjected de Clermont.

'—for the sake of brevity, I shall limit myself to the latest.' Delle Vigne paused, allowing an expression of disdain to pass over his face. 'Not even a week since, Michael Scot—'

'Canon,' snapped de Clermont. 'Canon Michael Scot.'

Delle Vigne here allowed himself a regretful smirk.

'As you wish, Father Abbot. Canon Michael Scot. Well, as I was saying, Canon Michael Scot not a week past accosted three notaries from the chancellery. He came upon them in their place of work, accompanied by his Jewish acolyte – maybe you should look into that too – and proceeded to issue absurd demands as to the type of equipment he would be requiring in his laboratory. But these requests have to pass through the correct channels, and this takes time. Canon Michael Scot was not at all pleased, immediately becoming unreasonable and imputing all manner of deficiencies to the chancellery. The three notaries informed him that their duties for the day were terminated and that he would have to leave the room. At which point, Canon Michael Scot looked at them, looked at the multitude of parchments lying on the table, and then issued what can only be construed as a threat. He warned them – and I quote – that "if they were not careful, the wind would take their damnable scribblings and blow them to hell." And before the notaries' horrified eyes, this is exactly what happened.'

Pier delle Vigne took a deep breath. 'Yes – it is a sinister scenario, is it not? In an enclosed room, a sudden gust of wind blew through it, scattering the notaries' work everywhere, creating complete havoc. And then, just when the notaries were about to give way to panic – more than justified in the circumstances – when they looked again, the room and table had returned to normal.'

This time Pier delle Vigne enjoyed the silence that fell between them. 'I personally spoke to the four witnesses involved in this disquieting episode.' He shook his head regretfully. 'They all concur.'

They had arrived at the library, and it would now be his task to present The Scot to his new abbot.

Keeping his eyes focused ahead, de Clermont offered a silent prayer. Dear God in Heaven, grant me patience and strength, for I shall surely have need of both.

XXXVII

The library in the monastery attached to San Giovanni degli Eremiti was possessed of a meagre number of manuscripts; this paucity was in stark contrast to the abundant quantity of wooden shelving. It all spoke of an erstwhile aspiration to literary expansion, subsequently abandoned. The abbot sighed inwardly and moved slowly to the far end of the room. Pier delle Vigne followed and then busied himself rummaging in the satchel he was carrying.

The abbot had no idea what to expect and trepidation that he might fall short of what was required hunched his shoulders. Pier delle Vigne suddenly ceased his rummaging and a wary silence washed over the abbot like a hot breath; his skin prickled.

Over by the entrance, a tall figure stood observing him. Even in the gloom of the library, the man's appearance was striking. This must be Canon Michael Scot, and for once rumour had not exaggerated. In a few long strides he covered the ground separating them, and the abbot felt as if some unnameable force was bearing down on him: the overwhelming impression was of paleness; but two things registered with a shock: the faded red beard, and the eyes. Which was strange, because as Canon Michael Scot drew up in front of him, the abbot saw that the eyes, too, were pale, of a silvery grey. But from their glittering depths they exerted some uncanny hold over him. And they never deigned Pier delle Vigne with so much as a passing glance.

The abbot had to strain his neck in order to look up at the man. Unflinchingly, he looked into the eyes still holding his own. He wondered at the unquiet soul regarding him.

And then, unexpectedly, Canon Michael Scot fell on one knee and asked for his blessing. Over his head, Hugo de Clermont's eyes flew to Pier delle Vigne. Stylus poised over a wax tablet, he looked as nonplussed as the abbot.

The abbot extended his hand and the ring was kissed. He blessed the kneeling form.

'Rise, Canon Scot.' The abbot took a step backwards and gestured to him to take a seat on a bench running the length of a large table. He took a seat on the one opposite.

'Your place, Canon Scot, is in the monastery.' The abbot placed both hands palms down on the oak table. 'I expect you to transfer here immediately.'

'Of course, Father Abbot. I shall be glad to do so.'

The abbot observed Canon Scot keenly, but he could detect no trace of guile. Well, that was one obstacle surmounted – there had been no outward opposition to the summons to the monastery. But what if Canon Scot were going to reserve his opposition for inside the monastery and make things difficult for the newly fledged community? Hugo de Clermont interlaced his fingers and rested his chin on them.

'You will be expected to observe the monastic duties here in full,' he took up. Then he paused and added quietly, 'Nothing must come between you and these duties. Is that clear?'

'It is.'

Again, a surprising lack of opposition. The abbot felt emboldened to probe further. 'No matter what work you may be carrying out at the moment, nothing can take precedence over these religious duties.'

'I understand.'

'What work are you engaged in?'

'It is work of signal importance. But in truth I shall be glad to be a part of collective worship again.' Canon Scot glanced at the abbot, who wondered how the grey eyes could have made him feel so on edge such a short time ago. For now they were nothing but pools of tired humility.

Hugo de Clermont brought himself up sharply. Maybe that was precisely the intention of this individual: to beguile him into a false sense of security and then manipulate him as he chose. 'Quite,' he said brusquely. 'Vows are vows – made to be kept.'

To this, Canon Scot made no reply. He merely folded his hands in his lap and looked down at them with a distracted air.

'So,' took up the abbot, 'what *precisely* is the nature of your work?'

Canon Scot's eyes seemed to travel back from some great distance and he slowly brought them to bear on Hugo de Clermont. With an effort he murmured, 'Medicine.'

Silence fell. The abbot frowned. 'Medicine? Can you be more precise?'

Canon Scot glanced over his shoulder at Pier delle Vigne, who was busily scribbling at a table nearby. He looked up at the unexpected hiatus and saw two sets of eyes observing him. He tapped his stylus on the wax tablet and waited.

The abbot perceived the other cleric's unwillingness to speak in front of Pier delle Vigne, but he did not want to let him off the hook just yet. 'I am waiting, Canon Scot.'

The grey eyes bored into him. 'My assistant and I are endeavouring to perfect a system of scientific diagnosis by applying Avicenna's *Canon*. We work in isolation, alas, for there is nothing else like it in the Latin-speaking world, where one depends more on theology for a prognosis. I was involved in the translation of some of Avicenna's work in Toledo.' He looked down at his hands and his expression became rueful. 'My translating days are over. With your permission, my assistant and I would turn the theory of the medical texts we came upon in Spain into practice here in Palermo.'

Before Hugo de Clermont could utter a word, Pier delle Vigne interjected, 'My Lord Abbot will of course be aware that the assistant in question, the assistant that Canon Scot is happy to collaborate with, is one Jacob Anatolio.' He paused and then added, 'He is a Jew.'

'Like Our Lord Jesus Christ,' the abbot replied coldly. 'I trust that your instinct for collaboration with *him*, at least, is all that it should be?'

Michael Scot's head jerked up; the grey eyes flickered. There was a grunt as Pier delle Vigne stooped to retrieve his stylus, which had fallen to the floor. He was overtaken by a fit of coughing. When it subsided his face was scarlet, whether through annoyance or exertion was not clear. 'Canon Scot,' he said hoarsely, 'tells us that one cannot depend on theology for a patient's diagnosis. Does that mean that the astrology he sets such store by takes precedence over theology?'

The abbot's eyes flew to Canon Scot's. Head bowed, he was rubbing his forehead. 'It does not,' he said, making no attempt to disguise his hostility.

'And,' added Pier delle Vigne, still smarting from the abbot's words and anxious to press home his advantage, 'the medical texts Canon Scot and Master Anatolio came upon in Spain are of Moorish provenance. Is my Lord Abbot sure that we in Christendom need to have this material foisted on us?'

The abbot was aware of both men observing him closely; he kept silent. Eventually, he looked up. 'We shall discuss this further, Canon Scot, when you have moved to the monastery. Which, I trust, will be as soon as possible.'

Michael Scot got to his feet. 'It will.' He bowed his head and left the library.

Hugo de Clermont looked after him. He had not been able to bring himself to make any allusion to the episode in the chancellery.

XXXVIII

From the security of the laboratory the emperor had put at Michael Scot's disposal by way of a sign of preferment, Jacob heard of these developments in his newly ratified capacity as Canon Michael Scot's assistant. It was a precarious equilibrium; but one that had nevertheless enabled him to return to Provence as a scholar in the pay of the Holy Roman Empire and finally claim his bride. Rebekah's parents had asked for two months to finalise the details of her dowry, after which time he was to return there for the wedding. Together they would then set out for Palermo and Jacob would bring her to the house he had found for them in the Jewish quarter.

Jacob's main fear had come to nothing; he was managing to make his way in the world and he had succeeded in securing the hand of Rebekah. But there were other things that niggled away at his peace of mind. It was true that a great weight had been lifted from his shoulders when Master Scot had returned to the religious life within the monastery; the abbot had made it quite clear that this was what the emperor wished, and what he, Hugo de Clermont, saw as a duty to be enforced. Canon Michael Scot was to receive the support and discipline that the monastic life necessarily imposed on its followers. Master Scot himself had embraced this development with surprising fervour, and it would leave Jacob free to start out in married life without the added responsibility of having to look out for Master Scot.

As they progressed in their work on Avicenna, he began to perceive what he felt was an unhealthy interest on the part of Master Scot in alchemy, on top of the astrology which seemed to obsess him.

He could not reconcile these elements with the work they were doing in the field of medicine, in which Master Scot excelled. Grudgingly, Jacob could bring himself to admit that this proficiency might be due to the way in which Master Scot could draw on the rational through his learning, yet go beyond that by seeing with his heart, arriving thus at diagnoses and prognoses that eluded the skill of most of his contemporaries. Jacob knew of the pull of the esoteric; there was a part of him that knew Kabbalah. But there was another, and stronger part, the part that cleaved to Maimonides, that chose not to engage with it. He had heard tell of the indications for spiritual transformation contained in the esoteric teachings of Kabbalah, the word itself meant 'received tradition'. Surely there was material enough for the righteous man to be going on with in the Torah and the Talmud, without resorting to the labyrinths of the esoteric.

But every fibre of his being revolted at astrology. As Maimonides had said, 'Astrology is a sickness, not a science. It is a tree under whose shade thrive all sorts of superstitions.' And alchemy seemed to be an offshoot of the same ilk: fatuous musings seeking to give themselves a specious veneer of the rational.

*

One Spring evening as twilight settled over the palace and their work for the day was done, Master Scot expressed his admiration of Kabbalah. 'Does it have a place in your life, Jacob?' he asked. Shaking his head, Jacob replied, 'It is not for me.' Michael Scot added, 'It is in the process of being committed to writing under the title *Zohar*.' Animated by his enthusiasm, he took out a bottle of cordial and filled two goblets.

Jacob shook his head; their inclinations and approach could not be more different at this stage. Increasingly, Master Scot was given over to the esoteric, while he cleaved to the rational. 'Kabbalah,' he said, 'may just be an attempt on the part of the anti-Maimonists to undermine the rational approach to faith. For me, however, faith should never be sundered from man's rational faculty. The only way to come to God is through rational study and long years of education. In itself this is an elevation of the soul. There are no shortcuts; there is no magic that will accomplish this.'

'No,' replied Michael Scot, 'perhaps not. But the soul, for me, is my guardian angel, simultaneously in matter and yet above and beyond it. A guide out of time, back to the realms of eternity where we shall partake of the Divine. This is what I feel. This is what I was shown. It came from somewhere outside myself to offset the mere workings of my brain, which would have had me cleave to the ascetic purity of the Gnostic and Albigensian stance. But they are chilling, and merciless. I feel this too. What I have not yet managed to do is make my vision personal: this unity of the mortal and immortal parts of each soul, linked by a gossamer thread of latent divinity. To give it meaning I need to bring it into my own life circumstances.'

'You are a shaman in a cowl,' said Jacob, smiling.

'And this from a rabbi in a pleated Greek tunic,' replied Michael Scot.

'But,' added Jacob, 'while you have been hunched over the Kabbalah, I have been busy with biblical exegesis. And this has focused my mind greatly on Hebrew. The more I study it, the more wondrous it seems. For it encapsulates the non-said within the said. The absence of vowels means that it both is, and is not, it contains nothing within everything. In this way it is peculiarly suited to evolving meaning.'

'Write, Jacob, write. Write down what you understand. Share it, circulate it, and be not afraid.'

XXXIX

AD 1224

'You are very quiet this evening, husband,' Rebekah regarded Jacob with affectionate eyes, from which a certain shyness still had not disappeared. 'Did you not enjoy your supper?' She had taken special care with the evening's meal, recreating the dishes she had grown up with, even if they were countless leagues from home. Jacob had eaten everything – the leek soup, the lentils and spiced mushrooms, the *fougasse* she had baked at the communal ovens – but he had done so in an unusual silence.

He looked up from his bowl and wiped the breadcrumbs from the thick beard he had grown since moving to Palermo. She noted the troubled expression in the dark eyes, normally so gently humorous. She had learned to read their changing expressions. She had blossomed in the appreciative understanding they usually turned on her, but over the last few days, since they had returned from the synagogue in fact, Jacob's expression had been apologetically evasive. Rebekah felt sure that this did not stem from any conflict between them as husband and wife; the conflict must come from outside the home, it must have its cause in her husband's work. She would leave him be; it was not her place to pry.

'Supper was delicious,' replied Jacob. 'Do not trouble yourself, I have some matters on my mind, that is all.'

Rebekah stood up to collect the empty dishes. Jacob looked at her belly and noticed that she was beginning to show. A part of him was gratified. They already had a daughter, long since in her cradle asleep, and now he hoped for a son. But he also felt anxious.

It was strange how the satisfaction of accomplished objectives had evaporated so quickly. Jacob needed to remind himself that he had indeed achieved a great deal: by dint of hard work and perseverance, he could claim as his patron the Holy Roman Emperor. He had finally been able to marry Rebekah and bring her with him to Palermo, where they had taken lodgings in the repopulated Jewish quarter. He was inundated with commissioned work – the translation of Maimonides and Averroës into Hebrew – and had undertaken to carry out biblical exegesis. His official position was assistant to Michael Scot, and this had opened up the horizons of medicine and experimental science.

There, however, was the rub. He was all too aware that the experimental science Michael Scot and he were carrying out under the patronage of the emperor was termed in a far less benevolent manner by the chancellery and courtiers. Somehow experimental science had degenerated into necromancy. He saw the furtive glances sent their way, heard the whispers, felt the hostility.

He of all people abhorred anything with a whiff of superstition; the occult and all its meretricious blandishments were anathema to him. He had been wary of Michael's approach, for he had wanted no part in anything connected with the swamp of esoteric babble that purported to be science. But, despite some of Michael's more questionable ideas, the field they had set out to explore together did not appear to have anything of the arcane about it. They were endeavouring to apply Avicenna's *Canon* to medical prognoses in a rational, scientific manner. Over the three years they had been working here together, he had learned much and developed the same passionate belief as Michael in what they were doing.

The alchemy they had more recently embarked upon was different. Here he had misgivings, and yet he could not put his finger on any precise thing that was objectionable in the practice of it. In actual fact, he was finding the enterprise very stimulating. And it was his intimate conviction that scientific investigation was essential for the true comprehension of religion. 'I shall light a candle of understanding in your heart, which shall not be put out.'

But he was all too aware, given his own misgivings, how this alchemy must appear to the ill-intentioned.

He was a family man now; he had taken his place in the world. Or rather, he was attempting to take his place in the world. But to help him in this he had taken to going ever more frequently to the synagogue. He needed some centre of truthful serenity in his life. And he had been asked to give lessons to the congregation, drawing on his work in biblical exegesis.

That was why the hostile reception to his lesson this past Sabbath had caught him off guard. Increasingly, in his dealings at court, he had found himself defending Jewish thought, Jewish custom, the Jewish religion. While regrettable, perhaps it was only to be expected in an alien environment. The synagogue had become for him a place of refuge, a place where he had hoped not to have to continue defending himself.

So the attack from Mordechai Chaim ha-Cohen – for attack it had been – had thrown him completely. He had been expounding on the benefits inherent in the rational approach to knowledge exemplified in Aristotle, and the re-elaboration achieved by Maimonides. Mordechai Chaim ha-Cohen had accosted him afterwards. The hostility unleashed was such that it had robbed him there and then of the power of any kind of a coherent answer. The answers he should have given had been circling uselessly round in his head ever since. Just what danger could there be in assimilating the genius of the Greek philosopher into the Jewish religion? Why should the Jewish religion have to remain untainted by outside influences? Why were outside influences necessarily a taint?

Did not this approach place them on the same lamentable level of fearful ignorance as the bigoted gentiles it was his sorry lot to have to deal with elsewhere?

Some balance had crumbled. He could sense an instability weaving its way through his aspirations and work, and he now feared he would not be allowed to achieve the vision of unity he had aspired to. It had to be faced: he was not finding his place in the world; the world was leaving its mark on him.

*

'And so you are leaving?'

'So it would seem.' Jacob looked at Michael, who was replacing a manuscript in the press beside the window. Jacob would miss this laboratory. He spread his hands. 'What can I do? I followed your advice and committed my thoughts to writing. On the basis of these books the emperor has commissioned me to translate Averroës' Intermediate Commentaries on Aristotle into Hebrew, and I am to carry out this work at his court in Naples.'

'Do not fear, Jacob,' Michael Scot replied, 'I of all people would never wish to hold you back. You must go where your interests will best be served.' He paused and looked directly into Jacob's eyes, something Jacob was aware he did not often do. And suddenly the incessant treadmill of thoughts in his head seemed to dissipate and Jacob felt lighter. 'Your steadfastness to me in times both good and bad,' said Michael Scot gently, 'has been a great consolation. My blessing upon you, Jacob Anatolio; now go and follow your star.'

Jacob could say nothing. The two men looked at each other in silence.

Michael Scot reached out and gently pressed his arm. 'Listen to this prayer-poem, Jacob. *The Canticle of Brother Sun* by that remarkable man, Francis from Assisi. Let me recite it for you, it is in the Umbrian idiom of central Italy, and I have found it worth committing to memory.' Michael Scot looked away. Then, his voice deepening and yet hushed, he began:

'Most high, all powerful, all good Lord! All praise is yours, all glory, all honour, and all blessing. To you, alone, Most High, do they belong. No mortal lips are worthy to pronounce your name.

Be praised, my Lord, through all your creatures, especially through my Lord Brother Sun, who brings the day; and you give light through him. And he is beautiful and radiant in all his splendour! Of you, Most High, he bears the likeness.

Be praised, my Lord, through Sister Moon and the stars; in the heavens you have made them bright, precious and beautiful.

Be praised, my Lord, through Brothers Wind and Air, and clouds and storms, and all the weather, through which you give your creatures sustenance.

Be praised, My Lord, through Sister Water; she is very useful, and humble, and precious, and pure.

Be praised, my Lord, through Brother Fire, through whom you brighten the night. He is beautiful and cheerful, and powerful and strong.

Be praised, my Lord, through our sister Mother Earth, who feeds us and rules us, and produces various fruits with coloured flowers and herbs.

Be praised, my Lord, through those who forgive for love of you; through those who endure sickness and trial.

Happy those who endure in peace, for by you, Most High, will they be crowned.

Be praised, my Lord, through our Sister Bodily Death, from whose embrace no living person can escape. Woe to those who die in mortal sin! Happy those she finds doing your most holy will. The second death can do no harm to them.

Praise and bless my Lord, and give thanks, and serve him with great humility.'

XL

AD 1225

All round the Green Hall of the Norman Palace, clusters of nobles, clerics, courtiers and functionaries chatted with a cursory air of distraction. They were waiting to pay homage to the emperor, who had just returned from a prolonged sojourn in Puglia, and then submerge him with their petitions. Hugo de Clermont observed the silent figure by his side. It was a strange time for Canon Michael Scot: his tall thin figure exuded a palpable sense of solitude in the midst of this gesticulating, circulating mass of courtiers. And how could it be otherwise? The abbot was aware of the loss that Jacob Anatolio must represent for him, so he had taken precautions to ensure that a discreet eye always be kept on the man. To this end the abbot had come in his dual capacity as the emperor's confessor and Canon Michael Scot's superior. The surreptitious glances these sly courtiers cast their way here in the Green Hall did not escape the abbot's notice.

Presently a knight and his wife came and stood beside them. The man briefly saluted Canon Michael. Hugo de Clermont glanced at him curiously; the glance was returned. Canon Michael bestirred himself and made a concession to court etiquette. 'My Lord Abbot, may I present Don Ruggero della Rovere?' He turned to the stranger. 'Don Ruggero, this is Hugo de Clermont, abbot of San Giovanni degli Eremiti.'

The two men saluted each other. Canon Michael continued,

'You have only recently returned from campaigning with the emperor, Don Ruggero. How does peacetime suit you?'

'It suits me very well, I thank you.' The large burly man's sun-weathered face broke into an unexpected smile. 'I have got through so many battles at this stage with nothing worse to show for it than this,' – he gestured to the recently acquired purple scar running the length of his right cheek – 'that I deemed it necessary to find me a wife before my luck ran out.' He gestured with a shy gentleness, oddly at variance with his appearance, to the slip of a girl standing a step behind him. 'May I present Madonna Adelasia?'

The two clerics acknowledged the young bride. But before anything further could be said, Pier delle Vigne entered the hall and announced that the emperor had been delayed; he would join them as soon as his work with the emissaries from the curia was terminated.

A murmur ran through the assembled courtiers, rising and then quickly falling back into the usual decorous patter of inconsequentialities. Pier delle Vigne was approached by Tebaldo Francesco di Monteforte; they whispered together for a moment, and then Pier delle Vigne clapped his hands for silence.

'In order to pass the time not unpleasantly,' he began, 'I propose that we entertain ourselves in this interval.' Hugo de Clermont noticed that the scheming lackey appeared to be standing on his toes in a doomed effort to add something to his meagre height. 'To that end,' Pier delle Vigne continued, 'let us put our knowledge to the test.'

A subdued murmur ran round the hall. Hugo de Clermont did not care for the glance that passed between Pier delle Vigne and Tebaldo Francesco di Monteforte. 'Who better to start with,' took up Pier delle Vigne, turning a provocative smile on Canon Michael, 'than our resident man-of-learning. Don di Monteforte has a question to put to you.'

Di Monteforte stepped forward. 'Here is a question for you, Canon Michael Scot. It draws on your mathematical knowledge, which we are assured – mostly by yourself alas – is second-to-none. I realise that you have dedicated yourself to other more questionable areas of learning in recent times, but precisely because of the ambiguous nature of these areas – heathen philosophy, alchemy and medicine – we feel it more in keeping with your role as a cleric to delve into the store of your mathematical learning. There at least not even you can contrive to make it any less pure.'

There was a sharp intake of breath from Hugo de Clermont. But before he could say anything, Canon Michael had stepped forward. Silence fell among the courtiers; an air of expectation brought an intense stillness to the hall.

Hugo de Clermont was furious. Despite his vigilance, the very situation he had come in order to circumvent was materialising. He could do nothing now that would not be an open admission of fear, and taken as an implicit admission of guilt. His fingers closed round his crucifix and his lips formed a silent prayer. It was hindered by a loud rasping noise from beside him.

Don Ruggero was rubbing his hand over the considerable growth of stubble on his chin. Men of learning? he growled. Testing knowledge? What was this buffoonery? He had work enough to be doing on his estate without frittering away the little he could dedicate to it on these lamentable goings-on. Why could they not speak directly to the emperor and then be on their way?

Momentarily thrown by the vehemence of this frank outburst, the abbot turned back in time to see Canon Michael's eyes latching onto di Monteforte's, holding him in a silvery beam. 'What would you ask me then?' he said quietly.

Hugo de Clermont wondered if his own eyes had misled him, or had di Monteforte indeed shivered.

'Calculate for us, if you can,' said di Monteforte with difficulty, his voice having unaccountably dwindled to a squeak, 'the height of the ceiling in this room.'

'It shall be done.' Michael Scot strode up to the top of the hall, the courtiers opening before him like the Red Sea before Moses. At the top of the hall he turned suddenly to face them; a few took a prudent couple of steps backwards. 'Before I carry out this calculation, I require your attention for a moment,' he added. The courtiers looked at him expectantly. He stared back at them in silence. Then he raised his hand; all eyes were drawn to it. 'And now,' said Michael Scot, his voice deepening, 'I am ready to carry out the calculation.' His hand still held aloft, he paused and then added, 'Is anyone willing to assist me?' He gestured towards the frescoes of animals on the wall behind the throne. 'Or rather, any *thing* willing to assist me?'

Hugo de Clermont's skin prickled as the assembly collectively exhaled, the sound falling somewhere between a wail and a gasp. All heads swivelled upwards, and then at the same moment ducked. That was when the screaming started.

'Oh, the Lord have mercy on us!' cried Don Ruggero's terrified wife, clutching at her husband.

'What is it, woman?' he said gruffly. 'Why do you discompose yourself so?'

'Do you not see it?' she whimpered. 'Look! The royal eagle from the fresco, come to life. It flies like a demon over our heads.'

Hugo de Clermont and Don Ruggero looked at each other aghast. At that moment Michael Scot held out his arm, fist closed, as if waiting for something to alight on it. 'And now,' he said, his voice rebounding off the walls of the hall, 'who would hear what the height of the Green Hall is?'

Some fled; others sobbed uncontrollably; still others fainted.

Hugo de Clermont looked around him mystified. What devilry was this? What had Canon Michael Scot got up to? Why this outcry? He turned to Don Ruggero, but he was bent over his wife, trying to revive her.

'I do not understand,' said Hugo de Clermont. 'What is the meaning of this? I saw nothing to justify this pandemonium.'

'Nor I,' replied Don Ruggero. 'But my wife insists that an eagle flew out of one of the frescoes, apparently finding the time to communicate the height of the ceiling to Canon Michael Scot...' An expression of scornful disbelief curled his lip.

'An eagle!' expostulated the abbot. 'It is preposterous.'

Don Ruggero lay a restraining hand on his wife's arm. 'True enough. All I saw was Master Scot walk up to the throne and wave his arms about, and then all hell breaks loose. What ails these fools?'

'That is precisely what I saw,' agreed the abbot. It was unaccountable; two completely different versions of Michael Scot's actions were emerging. He would have to get to the bottom of it, for the episode had about it all the sulphurous whiff of sorcery. What in God's name had possessed the man to go and do something like this? It made the rumours about him seem true. He *was* dangerous, then, and versed in sinister arts. Evidently Pier delle Vigne had not been exaggerating when he warned him of this. He caught Canon Scot's attention and beckoned him. 'It is time for us to be going back to the monastery,' he called out, his voice tight with suppressed fury. Rigidly, he waited until Michael Scot had made his way back down the hall, and together they left it.

The uproar followed them all the way out as far as the main entrance to the Norman Palace.

XLI

'And so you do not believe that occult arts were used?'

'Your Majesty, we were all stunned by the episode. But as far as I have been able to ascertain, black magic was not used.'

The emperor sat into the high-backed chair, placing his hands on the carved oaken armrests. Hugo de Clermont paused as a servant entered the emperor's private chamber, bringing two goblets of wine on a tray. As soon as he had left, the emperor continued, 'The rumours flying about are very discrediting. They are saying that he is in league with the devil, and that this is the result of his contacts with the Moors in Spain who, they assert, are all adepts in necromancy.'

'I can imagine.'

'Every day reports reach me of some new charlatan robbing an endless stream of gullible fools with promises of supernatural remedies for everything from boils to cuckolded husbands. It falls to me to prosecute them. But with this latest episode I lay myself open to the charge of wanting to remove the speck of dust from my neighbour's eye, while passing over the plank in my own.'

'And,' replied the abbot, 'Canon Michael Scot has put himself on the same level as these charlatans by bringing himself to the court's attention in this lamentable fashion.'

'Indeed. What explanation did he offer for this exhibition?'

'It is getting more and more difficult to get him to talk.

Added to this was my own prejudice, and hence anger. For I was terrified lest one of the clerics under my supervision had tainted himself with dabbling in the dark arts.' The abbot shook his head. 'Eventually, he opened his mind a little to me, and what I gathered is this. Canon Michael Scot, while he was in Spain, and in particular down in the far south in Córdoba, fell into a delirium as a result of the excessive heat he encountered there. This delirium unbalanced his mind for a while, but he was lucky to have been looked after by his assistant Jacob Anatolio.' Here the abbot paused. He was reluctant to continue; the explanatory words he had repeated to himself on the issue suddenly seemed unconvincing, futile even. What would the emperor make of them? He steeled himself. 'When finally he recovered, he found that he had acquired the ability to look into men's hearts and understand what lies there.'

'You mean that he had gained an increase in understanding?'

The abbot paused; he rubbed his nose. 'Yes.' A long drawn-out syllable of grudging agreement. 'Let us call it an increase in understanding.' His fingers sought the crucifix round his neck. Then he added quietly, 'It would also seem that when he looks into men's eyes, he can make them follow his bidding.'

'How do you mean?'

'Apparently, he can bend their will to his, and make them see what he wants them to see.'

The emperor's fingers drummed the armrests. 'He could do that when I was a boy. The force of his thoughts had little difficulty in overpowering my own. Certainly, if he has added still more to this capacity, one can see how it might be…'

The abbot nodded slowly. 'But it must not be seen to happen again.'

'Absolutely not.'

'And I still cannot understand what would have driven him to do such a foolhardy thing. He could offer no explanation either.'

'I shall have to remove him from Palermo. He is too compromised here.'

'I am at one with your Majesty on this.'

'I can ill afford any taint of the heretical. There are those in the curia who seek any pretext to have me excommunicated. I must pre-empt this.' He rose from his seat and began to pace up and down the chamber. 'I shall take him with me to Puglia, where I intend to remain for the coming months.'

The abbot nodded slowly. 'Do you think it wise, your Majesty,' he asked, 'to leave him without my supervision?'

The emperor stopped his pacing. 'I do not.' He looked directly at the abbot. 'You shall accompany us.'

*

In the event, it was not the problematic figure of Michael Scot who brought down an excommunication on the emperor's head.

Life at the court of the Holy Roman Emperor was proving to be complicated. Hugo de Clermont wondered for the umpteenth time what exactly it was that had made him seem a suitable candidate for the role of confessor to the emperor. Personally, he felt singularly unfit for it. And then there were his pastoral duties at the monastery to add to the sense of unease.

'Yet another bride for the emperor chosen by a pope.' Frederick's words, and his vexed expression as he said them, jabbered away in the abbot's mind. He could not rid himself of them, for they contained the crux of the emperor's looming difficulties. And what an invidious position he himself had been put in: how in conscience could he give absolution for the sins that were sure to come about because of the position the pope was putting the emperor in?

Honorius was hobbling Frederick on two fronts: marriage and a crusade. Following the death of the emperor's first wife Constance of Aragon in 1222, who passed quietly away, largely ignored both by Frederick and the populace, the pope had expressed himself forcefully on the topic of marriage, recommending that Frederick remarry as soon as possible. To that end he personally had selected the bride. Yolanda de Brienne was thirteen years of age and eminently eligible.

Here Frederick had looked bleakly at the abbot. This eligibility did not extend to her looks. She had none. But her father was Jean de Brienne, King of Jerusalem. 'And that,' Frederick sighed, 'brings us to the other noose being tightened round my neck. Honorius is demanding that I set off on the sixth crusade as soon as I have married Yolanda, and claim the City of God for Christendom once again. What am I to do?'

The Papal See was now in the process of exacting from Frederick the dues owed for its guardianship of the emperor's young person and stewardship of his kingdom. Hugo de Clermont could see how these dues might put paid to the emperor's vision of glory for his empire.

In the space of a couple of years, peace and the stability it brings, from a mirage longed for by a weary populace, were now beginning to flourish. The emperor's policies were leading to an eagerly awaited prosperity and a sense of achievement ran through his kingdom. As the emperor's confessor, the abbot had become privy to Frederick's imperial ambitions: his great desire was to unite the German and Italian parts in one vast empire stretching from the North Sea to the Mediterranean. Standing in the way of this were the city-states of the Centre-North of Italy – and especially the Lombard League – and the Papal States that cut a large swathe from Latium right across to the Adriatic Sea.

Frederick would have to play his cards very cleverly, as neither of these forces had any intention of accommodating the imperial designs.

As the autumn faded into the dull chill of November, the royal retinue set off for Puglia, where Frederick was to marry Yolanda, thirteen-year-old daughter of the King of Jerusalem, Jean de Brienne.

The marriage took place in the cathedral in Brindisi. Hugo de Clermont observed the wan child standing beside the thirty-year-old emperor: plain, and possessed of no particular talents or intelligence – nothing in short that could recommend her to her future husband, a man with more than his fair share of both these endowments – the abbot deplored the level of interference that had brought about this union. It was patently a mismatch, and as the emperor's confessor, it would be his sorry task to have to sit through the litany of sins that would accrue from it.

Alas, Hugo de Clermont did not even have to wait until the same time the following day before the ill-advisedness of the match revealed itself. The emperor's new father-in-law approached him as the highest-ranking cleric in the emperor's immediate retinue, demanding that Frederick be brought to book over the outrageous slur perpetrated against his daughter's honour on her wedding night.

Yolanda's more enterprising cousin and lady-in-waiting, Anaïs, had put herself in the way of the emperor, and he had decided that this unblushing courtesan was a worthier object of his attentions than his bride of a few hours.

There was nothing the abbot could say that would placate the offended father-in-law's sense of grievance. Slighted in this blatant manner, his daughter – despite her reddened eyes and the small, pale frightened face – promptly became an object of scorn for all the courtiers. Jean de Brienne took his grievance to the pope himself, who carefully stored up this information, holding it in reserve for some future time when the emperor might need to be brought to heel. The humiliated father's pride was restored through a large sum of money taken from the papal coffers.

Once again the pope reminded Frederick of his promise to lead a crusade to the Holy Land. And the curia reminded the imperial chancellery that the threat of excommunication would not be held in abeyance indefinitely.

Andria, Kingdom of Sicily

XLII

AD 1226

The lord of the ascendant (Aries) for the interrogating emperor was Mars, and that of the seventh house for his enemies, was Venus. But Mars was just entering Leo, while Venus was five degrees farther on. And this separation signified separation of will on the part of those rebels in making peace with the emperor, not from love, but from fear. Furthermore, Venus was two degrees away from conjunction with Saturn, and so was going from bad to worse, since Saturn in such a case signified prisons, lamentations, labours, plaints, sorrows. All this was in Leo, a fixed sign, indicative of slowness, but also of stability and firmness. On the one hand, this conjunction was in the fifth house beyond the fourth degree, signifying that the decision lay with the emperor when to end persecution and bring this tribulation to an end. On the other, it signified that the hostile party would commend itself to a certain old man to escape the hands of the emperor. Added to this, regal Jupiter was retrograde in the sign of the ascendant.

Michael Scot cradled his brow in the palm of his hand for a few moments; then he raised his eyes from the chart he had drawn up with painstaking care and rubbed them. He sat back into the chair and stared unseeingly at the bare wall in front of him. Hardly auspicious as a response. It would fall to him to tell the emperor that the Diet he had convened at Cremona was likely to turn out a humiliating failure.

Frederick had convened the Diet for Easter, and that time was nearly upon them. It was an open secret why he had done this. Honorius' demand for a crusade had to be complied with; but, reasoned the emperor, this imposition might yet be exploited as a means of bringing the Lombard cities to heel. The crusade could be turned into an opportunity to draw these recalcitrant city-states, heedless of their own good, back into the imperial fold. He chose the city of Cremona as the seat of this gathering because it had amply demonstrated its faithfulness to the emperor; to it he then summoned the other less amenable Lombard cities, ostensibly to pass their troops in review and evaluate how he was placed militarily for the crusade. They would, however, be made to realise their natural status as his vassal states.

The emperor had invited all the feudal aristocracy, the bishops and magistrates, and his son, Henry VII, who was journeying down from Germany.

Michael Scot got up from the writing desk and went over to the window. A sea of trees stretched away from the castle, giving way to softly rolling hills and Mediterranean scrub. He knew the species of trees – mostly evergreen oak and maritime pines, interspersed with olive groves in red tilled earth. The hazy light of a mild spring evening came in gentle waves through the narrow window. It brought with it the scent of sage and the more pungent rosemary. He peered again and, in the empty landscape falling away from this castle on a hill, saw a cloud of dust in the distance, probably someone riding towards the castle. Whoever it was, they were covering the ground at a great speed.

How many places could the heart become attached to? Had he already reached his limit? In truth, he did not know what to think of Puglia: it had roused no great feeling in him, for good or for bad. It did make him despondent however. He looked out again on the alien landscape, almost flat, empty of hamlets, strangely monotonous, except for the lone rider making his way with demented speed in the direction of the castle. He could not understand the emperor's attachment to the region, the store he set by this small town, *Andria semper fidelis*. The castle was handsome in its austerely practical Norman way, a solid shimmer of massive white stone against the grey-green of the uplands. Michael Scot was loath to uproot himself once again and carve out a niche in yet another hostile environment. He was weary of it.

He was weary on many levels. Not the least because his sleep was being robbed from him by the most distressing dreams. In actual fact, they were nightmares, and left him with an unnerving sense of impending catastrophe. The emperor and his imperial aspirations came to him in these dreams as a castle perched on the top of a cliff; a storm could be seen arriving from the sea, a rolling wave surging like a mountain towards them, and a dark mass of clouds gathering billowing momentum, driving down on the precarious castle on the cliff. The two would combine forces to submerge the castle and sweep it away.

And during all this he saw himself looking on in horror, a solitary figure out on the cliff itself, exposed to the turbulent elements, futilely brandishing what seemed to be a staff at the advancing tempest. And then he was struck by lightning.

It was unaccountable. Evidence of the success of the emperor's policies was before everyone's eyes. Peace, stability, well-being – all these had been brought to his kingdom. Frederick was in the process of extending these virtues to the rest of the empire. Why then this sense of ill omen?

His thoughts broke off as, in a clatter of hooves, the rider came to a halt at the castle gates. He declared himself as an imperial envoy and was let in. He asked for the emperor; but the emperor was out falcon hunting. The envoy's horse was led away to the stables, and another was saddled up for a scout to go out and inform the emperor.

As Michael Scot followed these proceedings, the sense of unease slithered through his guts again. He would have to look harder at what the stars were pointing to. Surely in this way the emperor would be better prepared, could take the necessary countermeasures...

It was imperative to broach the topic of the bedevilled Diet of Cremona with Frederick.

*

Silence enveloped the cathedral. Outside dusk was gathering and the altar was suspended in a darkness broken intermittently by the fragile flames of votive candles. Despite this atmosphere most conducive to prayer, Hugo de Clermont's mind jumped incessantly from one thought to another. Foremost among these was the emperor; Canon Michael Scot loomed on the fringes like the soughing of the wind.

He shook his head. Today there would be no gain from trying to harness his unruly thoughts through an act of will. Better to ask the Lord's pardon for his weakness and try at least to bring some order to the chaos of worries in his head. On top of it all, he had deep misgivings about how the monastery in Palermo would be faring in his absence. He had left Father Bernardo in charge: while he was a good man, he was all too prone to letting himself be manipulated. He could only hope that he would not return to find his community riven by internecine squabbling. And about the most futile of issues: who had not carried out their cleaning duties; who had eaten more than their fair share outside mealtimes; who had not risen at the designated hour for Vigils... Well, it was in the hands of the Lord. He could do nothing here. And it was here to this far-flung region of Puglia that the emperor had summoned him as his confessor.

That, at least, was the pretext. The real reason was to make sure Canon Michael stayed out of trouble. And after all, he was also Canon Michael's confessor.

It was a difficult situation. The emperor was evidently going to spend increasing amounts of time in Puglia, largely due to the presence here of Bianca Lancia. He could not be torn away from her. But maybe it was just a passing infatuation. He did not, however, hold out any great hopes of the empress Yolanda providing a legitimate counterbalance to the undeniable charms of this Lancia woman. He would have to ensure that the emperor did not lose his head and put his kingdom in jeopardy by giving Jean de Brienne, his father-in-law, any further pretext for attack.

Before leaving for Puglia, the abbot and the emperor between them had come up with a way of rehabilitating Canon Michael's much tarnished reputation following the debacle in the Green Hall and the alleged presence of flying eagles. At the unwelcome memory, the abbot twitched on the pew.

An evening had been organized where, it was announced, Canon Michael Scot would be put to the test by the emperor, who was anxious to ascertain the extent of the man's purported breadth of learning. The veiled threat had not escaped the court, which therefore thronged the Green Hall once again, in hopes of seeing The Scot given his just deserts by the emperor.

The abbot nodded in satisfaction at the memory. For they had been disappointed. And he had, despite himself, been impressed by the demonstration of knowledge that Canon Michael had delivered to the waiting hall. It was all very far removed from the Greek that he had dedicated himself to studying, and as such, most of it eluded his understanding. But he had nevertheless felt the full force of the charged nature of the questions the emperor posed; they were questions that seemed beyond the power of answering.

Such had been the emperor's satisfaction with Canon Michael's answers to his questions that he had engaged him in a lengthy discussion afterwards. The abbot had looked on as they talked animatedly, glad for all their sakes of the positive outcome.

They debated the way Natural Philosophy and alchemy came together in this account. Canon Michael reminded the emperor that astrology was also an intrinsic part of the cosmos. Then he had delivered himself of a warning. He had recommended that the emperor take special care two days later if he was having his hair cut by the royal barber. For Saturn was in Sagittarius, which was square with Mars in Pisces; and to all this must be added the negative aspect of the waning moon in Aquarius. In other words, Canon Michael had informed the emperor, this distribution of the stars points to a potential accident (Saturn in Sagittarius), involving cuts, injuries, inflammation of the blood (Mars) to the feet or toes (Pisces), corroborated by the waning moon in Aquarius, pointing again to accidents to the ankles or feet and blood poisoning. Your Majesty might be advised, he had concluded, to postpone the visit to the barber. The emperor had looked at him askance, and their conversation had drawn to an abrupt close.

The abbot still remembered the dismay he had felt when, two days later, news circulated round the court that the emperor had met with an accident while being shaved by his barber. The ham-fisted oaf had let his razor slip, and it had fallen on the emperor's foot, slicing open a vein. The main worry was that an infection of the blood might set in; the emperor had called immediately for Canon Michael Scot.

There had been much grumbling about this among the courtiers. Who was The Scot to muscle his way into the emperor's good graces with his quackery? Into what disreputable hands was his Majesty placing himself?

Their sense of pique was mollified somewhat by the vengeance the emperor exacted on the hapless barber, who found himself thrown into prison minus his remiss hand in less time than it took The Scot to concoct a healing potion for the imperial injury.

This had marked the beginning of Frederick's reliance on the astrological and medical skills of Canon Michael Scot. From being an embarrassing encumbrance, he had transmuted into one of the emperor's most precious assets, chosen repository of the hidden secrets of the future and wise dispenser of that most elusive of blessings, good health.

XLIII

The envoy galloped away into the dusk. He had been in the castle for less than two hours: obviously, he had conveyed to the emperor news of a serious nature and the reply had been carried away immediately. The abbot decided to go down to the main hall and see if word had begun to circulate among the courtiers.

The first person he saw was Pier delle Vigne; he grimaced, but there was nothing for it – he had to know.

'We have had news from Northern Italy,' stated delle Vigne, 'and alas it is not good. Yesterday, the sixth day of March, in open defiance of the emperor's wishes, a large number of rebellious Lombard cities renewed the Lombard League for a further twenty-five years.'

A gasp went round among the group of listeners that had quickly clustered around him.

For once, Pier delle Vigne's expression bore no trace of sly complacency. He looked worried. 'It is tantamount to throwing down the gauntlet to the emperor. There can be no Diet of Cremona now, and he will have to deal with these upstart yokels. The timing is particularly unfortunate with the crusade to the Holy Land looming…' He fell silent.

'And who knows,' a voice added, 'what opportunity this will give the pope to drive a wedge between the emperor and the breakaway city-states.'

'A divided empire and a strengthened papacy.'

*

'What do you advise?' The emperor looked at Pier delle Vigne. 'The situation is serious.'

'It is, your Majesty,' replied delle Vigne. 'Above all because there are not sufficient imperial troops in the area to allow for an unequivocal military response.'

'We run the risk of being defeated by this League.'

'Yes. They have managed the situation very artfully. With the Veronese blocking the mountain passes and holding off your son Henry's army getting through from Germany, there is no other force to assist you in fighting the other communes, who are waiting for your arrival from the south. Indeed, word has it that the opposition from the Veronese has been so fierce that Prince Henry is in the process of retreating.'

'It does not go well for us,' said the emperor. Then softly, as if to himself, he added, 'This is what Canon Michael Scot foretold not even a week since. I should have listened more carefully.' He fell silent for a moment, rubbing his thumb along his bottom lip. Then abruptly he announced, 'I cannot allow the upstart pretensions of these traitors to cheat me of my imperial objective. As we are not placed well enough to dominate the situation militarily, we shall have to fall back on political manoeuvrings.' He motioned to Pier delle Vigne to take note. 'Annul the Treaty of Costanza and outlaw the Lombard communes.'

*

'Well, Canon Scot?' demanded the emperor impatiently. 'Will the empress give me an heir?' His fingers drummed on the arm-rest of his chair; the noise echoed dully round the empty hall they had adjourned to in order to discuss this personal matter.

'We have been married now for nigh on six months, she is young, and yet she has not managed to conceive.'

Michael Scot looked down at the rush-strewn flagstones. The silence was so protracted that the emperor stopped drumming his fingers. He fixed the tall figure in front of him with penetrating eyes. Eventually, a pair of grey eyes were lifted to meet his own, but he could not make out the expression in them. And then he saw that they were not looking directly at him, but somewhere beyond. For a brief moment, or maybe it was a trick of the evening light, they seemed to float, to dance like pinpoints of quicksilver; then Michael Scot blinked slowly and began to speak.

'My Lord Emperor,' he said, 'the Empress Yolanda will give you children.' The grey eyes bored into the emperor, and his voice rose. 'And it will be a time of joy and then sorrow. There will be another christening and a funeral.'

The emperor slumped back into the chair. He covered his face with his hands and then rubbed it, as if to rid it of a great weariness. 'More afflictions,' he murmured.

'And yes, the empress is young,' continued Michael Scot, seeming to ignore the last comment, 'but in truth, perhaps too young. She is barely more than a child herself. As you ordered, I examined her yesterday and found her to be of a sickly constitution. Allowance must be made for these factors.'

'So, Canon Scot, what do you propose?'

'That your anxiety on the matter not be conveyed to the empress; it will be but a further impediment. However, I can advise you as to the most propitious times for begetting a child.'

The emperor looked at him distractedly. 'Most propitious times for...? His voice trailed off. 'But if you have just intimated that the outcome is ill-fated?'

'My Lord Emperor, this is what I have seen. I do not know how much faith to place in this vision. We must always remember that God has given us free will, and a soul, which is the perfection of the body. For the soul exists only by the will of the Supreme Creator, and is not subject to the stars as the body is. In short,' – Michael Scot extended his hands, palms upwards – 'your Majesty must pursue his destiny.'

'Whatever that is. Let us hear these propitious times, then.'

'If a woman has sexual intercourse under a waxing moon, especially when it is in a mobile sign and one like itself, she will conceive more quickly, and conceive males sooner than females, and the delivery is easier then and less painful.

'As you are the interrogator, my Lord Emperor, I have taken your ascendant and its lord, Mars in Aries, and,' – here Michael Scot extracted a sheet of paper from his habit and spread it on a nearby table – 'as your Majesty can see, I have examined the disposition of the moon to it. I have also examined the empresses' seventh sign and its lord. I have found that both lords are in conjunction with the lord of the house that signifies sons and daughters. Finally, as the moon is waxing, and will be in Pisces in two days' time, I would suggest that this is the most favourable time.'

'So be it.' The emperor looked at him for a long moment in silence. Then he said, 'The pope has little talent as a matchmaker. Would that I could have chosen my wife myself.'

*

In January of 1227 the Empress Yolanda was delivered of a baby girl, who was christened Margherita. The infant princess did not live to three months.

Michael Scot had felt the weakening pulse of the newborn with a sickening feeling, as long-buried memories flooded his mind of a far-off time in Scotland when a lone woman had tried to save an ailing infant and met a savage death. And here he was peddling his visions and his cant; what end would he come to?

All the while Pope Honorius had been working behind

the scenes, mediating between the emperor and the Lombard communes. He set too much store by the impending crusade to run the risk of alienating the emperor; nor, however, did he want to alienate the interesting specimens of upstanding Christianity that Lombardy was producing. In the event, he managed at the beginning of February 1227 to arrive at a compromise that brought peace between the opposing sides.

This proved to be timely, as Honorius died on 18 March. He was succeeded barely a day later by Cardinal Ugolino dei Conti di Segni, a relation of Innocence III, who was elected with the name Gregory IX. The election of an eighty-two-year-old pontiff might have seemed like an interim solution, but the indomitable will and vigour that Gregory IX brought to the office enabled him to outlive most of the doubters half his age.

The pontiff set about bringing all his weight to bear on tipping the scales of Church and Empire in his favour. From relatively small beginnings, the effects of this overt policy of domination began to amass against the emperor.

XLIV

AD 1227

It was another long hot summer in which implacably blue skies gave way to oppressive nights without a breath of wind to lift the heavy suffocating air. The date for departure on the crusade was upon them. It had been arranged with Honorius that Frederick would set sail for the Holy Land with his army no later than 15 August 1227. The emperor had wanted Canon Michael Scot to accompany him there as his astrologer and physician, but Hugo de Clermont intervened on his behalf, pleading a recrudescence of the heat-induced nervous exhaustion that had overtaken Canon Michael in Córdoba. He was in no condition to travel, still less be of any kind of use.

The emperor had had to yield to the abbot.

And so it was that Hugo de Clermont and Michael Scot set off back for Palermo while the emperor was encamped in the malaria-infested flatlands of Brindisi, waiting to set sail in torrid heat. Soon malaria began to devastate his army. The departure was postponed to 8 September, but when Frederick did set sail, he himself fell ill. His followers were dismayed, taking it as a bad omen for the campaign. They coerced him into turning back, and he landed in the white city of Otranto.

This was but unacceptable shilly-shallying for the pontiff, who promptly excommunicated him.

The abbot and Michael Scot had settled back into San

Giovanni degli Eremiti in Palermo when word reached them of this excommunication. Gregory IX was not possessed of the same forbearance as his predecessor, and not even the emperor's illness could persuade him that the failure to set sail for the Holy Land was anything less than an act of rebellion towards the Holy See. No one could rebel against God's representative on earth, not even the Holy Roman Emperor. It was time to redress the balance of power, which had tipped dangerously in favour of the emperor. But he, Gregory, would bring this wayward monarch to heel and make him learn his place in the scheme of things.

From Palermo Michael Scot learned that somebody else, some other physician among the multitude of courtiers that gravitated round the emperor, had looked after him in his illness. Somebody else in the white-stoned city of Otranto had cured him of the dangerous bout of malaria he had fallen a victim to in Brindisi.

And then the terrifying visions returned.

Alone in his cell one still, clammy night in the middle of September, Michael Scot had been kneeling by his pallet, the sheepdog of his will rounding up the bolting sheep of his thoughts to pen them in prayer. The hairs on the back of his neck had stood up, although there was not even a breath of wind inside or outside the cell window, and drops of sweat had formed on his forehead. His fingers clutched the pallet and he pressed his eyes tightly shut. A lurid scene burst in on his mind's eye.

As if in a primordial cave of quietude, the living darkness pulsed all around him. Far ahead a small point of red rippled like a blossoming rose and an explosion of stars glistered in short-lived splendour. A sigh like the soughing of the wind, then with a crackle a pale sphere was pierced by a comet. It lit up and oscillated gently until it was cradled in the enfolding darkness.

A pale belly, swollen, distended. A pale face, that of a girl, distorted in cries of agony, her legs splayed on a bed surrounded by a mill of shadowy figures. Her fingers clutched spasmodically at bloodstained sheets; hands were wrung in the darkness around her; a wail went up.

And then a cascade of numbers. 16... 3, 8, 1227... 25, 4, 1228...

In the grey light of dawn Michael Scot prepared for Lauds. Sleep had eluded him. He was still undecided whether or not he should tell the abbot about this vision. He had no doubt what it presaged. The number 16 was the sixteen-year-old Yolanda; 3, 8, 1227 was the date she had conceived before her husband set off on crusade; and 25, 4, 1228 was the date that there would be a birth and a death, a baby boy and a widower father.

Hugo de Clermont could see from his demeanour that something was troubling Canon Scot. The red-rimmed eyes that slid uneasily away from any real contact with him, the silence in which he seemed to have enfolded himself, an intangible barrier keeping everyone at bay. From a distance the abbot observed all this, alertly vigilant.

Then came the cry in the night that the abbot had expected and feared. His cell was right next to Canon Michael's and it sounded as if he was in the throes of a nightmare. The abbot had taken to leaving a candle alight for just such an eventuality, so he was up like a shot and into the next cell.

Canon Michael was muttering in his sleep, his legs jerking convulsively while his arms swatted at something. And then came the cry. 'Jacob,' moaned Canon Michael, 'Jacob! Where are you? I cannot find you in this darkness. Jacob! For pity's sake! Ah, the pain... I am undone. It is finished.'

The abbot did the best he could to soothe Canon Michael. But once he had awoken from the nightmare, he avoided the abbot's eye and retreated into silence.

'I will stay here with you, Canon Michael,' said the abbot. 'Try and get back to sleep.' No protest met this offer. But neither of them slept more. In the frail flickering light of the candle Canon Michael stared silently ahead of him, locked in some solitary vigil of his own.

The abbot was aware that Canon Michael was spending more time than usual in the laboratory he had shared with Jacob Anatolio in the Norman Palace. 'My experiments in alchemy,' he had murmured evasively. But the abbot had only the vaguest of ideas as to what exactly these experiments entailed. He was torn between a wish to do the right thing by Canon Michael's intelligence and the fear that there would be a return of the episode when, with horrifying ease, he had held the courtiers to ransom in the Green Hall.

Not a week after the nightmare, he spotted something else besides the hood of his cloak covering Canon Michael's head. How bizarre that the man would have covered his head with the woollen hood in the heat of September. And then, from under the woollen material came a glint of metal.

'What is this I see?' The abbot put out a restraining hand on Canon Michael's arm as he walked past him. 'What is that under your hood?'

The abbot had felt the tension in Canon Michael's arm as he replied stiltedly, 'It is nothing. A little item I devised to keep my headaches in check.'

'Your headaches?'

'Indeed. Lately they have been severe and this helps.'

The abbot raised his hand to remove the hood, but Canon Michael backed away. 'Do not place your hand anywhere near my head,' he said very quietly. The abbot's hand fell back down by his side. 'But Canon Michael,' he said after a pause, 'how can I justify this breach of the rule? How can I let you be any different from all the others? It will not do, you know.'

Canon Michael stared at him. The eyes were a curious mixture of obduracy and fear. Something was eating away at the man.

'Father Abbot,' he said after a pause, lowering his eyes suddenly, 'this is not a whim, despite appearances. The—' his voice faltered for a moment '—the properties the metal skullcap contains are of great benefit to the headaches that plague me night and day. This skullcap is all that stands between me and far worse.'

Palermo,
Kingdom of Sicily

XLV

February AD *1230*

He becomes aware of his own breathing. And then the solid feeling of the settle under him. The immense inner distances he has travelled through recede and his eyes slowly bring the windowless room back into focus. There is no way of knowing what time of the day or night it is. But from the silence Michael Scot suspects it is far into the night. In the end, of course, the skullcap had not been able to come between him and far worse. If he were to die this night… Well, if he dies this night, he will at least have managed to look back over his life; he will at least have been granted some time to try and make peace with this shadowy entity called his life, the reach of which continues to elude him.

He rises slowly from the settle and walks over to the table. He is glad now that the abbot left some water and a goblet. He takes a long and refreshing draught and then notes with a rush of relief that there is no pain in his head. For the moment he is in no danger of a seizure.

Revisiting his life has not brought on a seizure; that, surely, is worth being grateful for.

But, with a sense of unease, the circumstances leading to his being in this small fortress-like room trickle back into his consciousness. What fate awaits him outside? What has transpired among the emperor, the abbot and Pier delle Vigne?

Suddenly, the sound of a key turning in the lock breaks through the silence. Hugo de Clermont puts his head round the door. 'Canon Michael, how are you?'

'I am well, thank you.'

'I am sorry that I had to leave you on your own for so long, but I have not been idle.' The abbot draws near and looks closely into Michael Scot's face. 'Yes – you seem to be bearing up all right.' He smiles slightly. 'It is just as well, for a long night awaits us.'

'What has happened?'

'Don Filippo informed me that an envoy had arrived from the pope for his Majesty. He overheard delle Vigne and da Messina. Apparently, they are behind this communication and they intend to use it to damage you, above all with the emperor.'

Michael Scot shakes his head. 'Is there no end to their conniving?'

'And, as if the battle for the emperor's ear over imperial policy were not enough, remember that delle Vigne knows you have seen into the future and found him wanting. He now has even more reason to wish you removed from the scene.' The abbot looks closely at Michael Scot again. 'Are you up to this encounter?'

Michael Scot nods.

'I am glad. Follow me now in all haste; we must intercept his Majesty before he gets to King Ruggero's chamber and warn him that delle Vigne lies in wait for him there.'

The sumptuousness of the décor in King Ruggero's chamber occasions Pier delle Vigne intense sensuous pleasure. The different surfaces – the marble of the wainscoting and the gold leaf of the upper part of the walls – register in Pierre delle Vigne's mind as physical sensations. The delicacy of execution displayed by the frescoed hunting scenes excites his imagination, while the symbolic nature of the hieratic animals alternating with these scenes is a solemn reminder of the dizzying heights to which he has risen. He looks up at the peacock, symbolising eternity, and the lion, representing regal strength, with satisfaction: he, too, is now a part of this world.

If he deals with this situation judiciously, there could be a double advantage. First of all, the emperor will be moved to safeguard in all possible ways the future of his empire, for he will see the extent of the threat it is under. And secondly, they will finally be rid of that necromancer, The Scot.

He thinks with satisfaction of the contents of the dispatch from his Holiness. Of course, such a communication has required a great deal of behind-the-scenes manoeuvring on his part – but it looks as if it is going to be worth it. His Holiness is most anxious to return finally from Perugia, where the Romans effectively banished him two years previously because of his stridently anti-imperial pronouncements. So his position is relatively weak. But the pope is still the pope, and he is looking to reforge the alliance between Church and Emperor in order to regain some strength. The emperor's crusade to the Holy Land having been a resounding triumph – despite the excommunication hanging over his head at the time – his Holiness is now anxious to partake in this aura of glory by embarking with him on another type of crusade. Their common target now is to be heresy.

To that end, his Holiness has been most vehement that no trace of heresy can attach itself to the emperor.

And here is the rub: in the dispatch his Holiness expresses himself as being surprised at some of the goings-on which he has been informed are making themselves the focus of public attention at the Cistercian monastery in Palermo. Striking the right balance between exciting his Holiness into outright punitive action on this score and a complacent dismissal of it as trivial on the other had been rather tricky, but he and da Messina had managed it adroitly. The upshot is now that his Holiness requires reassurance that no taint of heresy attach itself to the emperor through his contacts at the monastery. So, reasons Pier delle Vigne, if things begin to go badly for him at this interview, he will give them the explosive news that his Holiness is sending an envoy from the curia to investigate. It is not written in the dispatch, but he has been assured that it could soon be arranged. And it may be enough to just hint at this possibility to bring the abbot and The Scot to heel.

Pier delle Vigne smirks. It is a risky game to play, but one that should pay dividends. His eye inches to the centre of the ceiling, coming to rest on the imperial emblem. In its talons, an eagle grips a writhing hare.

An inoffensive enough little creature, he can see no reason why the eagle should single it out over other and worse animals for such a horrible end. But such are the inscrutable ways of royalty. A cold drop of sweat trickles down his back; he shivers and looks away.

He had kept a vigilant eye on the emperor throughout the banquet, and as soon as his Majesty had eaten his fill – which was regrettably soon, for his Majesty is abstemious in his eating habits – he had quickly slipped from the hall himself so as to precede the emperor to King Ruggero's chamber. He has already relieved the envoy of his precious dispatch and he holds it now, waiting for the emperor.

Footsteps can be heard in the corridor outside; the guards stand to attention; the door is opened.

'Your Majesty,' replies Pier delle Vigne, bowing very low, 'please forgive my intrusion, but given the urgency of the situation in Rome, time is of the essence. A dispatch has just arrived from his Holiness and it is imperative that you see it right away.'

Only then does Pier delle Vigne's eye fall on the silent figures of the abbot and The Scot in the doorway. He notes the glance that passes between the emperor and the abbot. This spurs him to even greater persuasiveness. 'Your Majesty – before you listen to anything else or anyone else, I implore you to give this your undivided attention.'

The abbot steps forward. 'We, too, urgently wish to speak with your Majesty.' The curtness of his delivery sends a ripple of warning through the air to delle Vigne.

'I shall look at it presently,' says the emperor.

'Hermann of Salza, Grand Master of the Teutonic Order, has agreed to act as your representative in Rome,' presses Pier delle Vigne. 'You need to reply to his Holiness immediately.'

'I understand your haste, Master Secretary, but there are other issues to weigh up before any answer can be given to his Holiness.'

'As his Majesty prefers.' Pier delle Vigne's eyes dart towards The Scot, whose expression is inscrutable. 'Your Majesty,' he takes up, 'be of good cheer. This is a very positive development, which you can exploit to your own advantage. You find yourself in a position of strength.'

'Regretfully, your Majesty,' the abbot interjects, 'Canon Michael has discovered reasons for doubting the trustworthiness of Master Secretary's recommendations.'

Frederick turns cold, assessing eyes on Pier delle Vigne, who clears his throat and replies, 'Your Majesty, you know that I am motivated only by the pursuit of your interests and those of your empire. This is slander of the basest order—'

'I have no time for this kind of bickering,' the emperor's voice rises.

'No, your Majesty. But to gain a sense of perspective on this slander, you need also to be aware that The Scot's antics have drawn attention to San Giovanni degli Eremiti and, despite his Holiness' determination to strike up an alliance with you, there is now a distinct risk of a visitation from the curia to investigate the rumours that have reached their ears.'

Silence greets this pronouncement.

'And how could news of these so-called antics have reached the ears of the curia?' the emperor asks after a pause, his eyes fixed on him.

'I have no idea, your Majesty,' Pier delle Vigne replies, his face a study in guileless puzzlement.

'I hope for your sake that this is the case,' says the emperor.

'Because if word gets to me that you had any part in this,' his voice sinks menacingly, 'I will have your head on a platter.'

'Or perhaps your eyes…' murmurs Michael Scot.

'Now leave us,' orders the emperor. 'I have things to discuss with the abbot and Canon Scot.'

Pier delle Vigne looks crestfallen. He bows and begins his exit from the chamber. At the door, his forehead creased with concern, he adds, 'Be of good heart, your Majesty. It will come right with the pope.'

XLVI

Three large wooden chairs have been placed in front of the imposing fireplace, in which a fire burns. The emperor gestures for the abbot and Michael Scot to take a seat.

'How are you, Canon Scot?' enquires the emperor. 'I have had very conflicting reports of your health.'

'By the grace of God, I can sit here before your Majesty,' replies Michael Scot. 'How long I may continue to do so is a moot point.'

The emperor glances at the abbot.

'Canon Michael has sustained a serious injury that may yet prove fatal.'

The emperor sits back into the chair and places both hands on its armrests.

'I wish to make a request, your Majesty,' says Michael Scot.

The emperor leans forward. 'Speak, Canon Scot.'

'Free me,' he says slowly and softly, 'from my obligations to you here in Palermo. Free me that, in the little time I may have left, I might serve you better in other great centres of learning in Europe.'

The emperor frowns. 'How so?'

'By circulating the knowledge of Aristotle contained in my translations of Averroës.'

The emperor chews speculatively on his bottom lip. 'All in good time, Canon Scot,' he says eventually.

'That, sadly, is a well I shall not be able to draw from much longer.'

The emperor sighs and looks away. 'But the time is not yet right.' He pauses, and then rises from the chair. He heads to the massive open fireplace and warms his hands at it for a few moments. The golden thread in the embroidery of his mantle gleams in the light of the flames.

'No,' resumes the emperor, 'Aristotle is too provocative. The pope would take it amiss, and the last thing I want to have to contend with is another excommunication.' A glance in Michael Scot's direction finds him staring at the ground. 'You must see,' the emperor adds, 'that this is the moment for a rapprochement with the papacy. Gregory has never been in such a vulnerable position, and he is anxious to build up his alliances again.' The emperor shakes his head. 'His ill-advised, nay – unchristian – pursuit of temporal power makes him undeserving of any indulgence on my part; but I do not wish to bring about the collapse of the papacy by visiting my military might upon it. The pope represents one of the two pillars that support law and order in our world; no one desires to overturn the system by doing away with one of the pillars. One might wish, however, that the spiritual pillar would be just that, and leave temporal matters to those to whom Providence has entrusted them.'

'Your Majesty,' the abbot also gets to his feet, 'what you say is undoubtedly true. However, by all accounts the winds of change are sweeping through the northern universities, especially Paris and Oxford. Theology is no longer the be-all and end-all of university curricula. The pope himself is behind these changes. Indeed, the time may be ripe for this *novo sapere*.'

The emperor turns to look at him and nods pensively.

'And,' the abbot presses home his point, 'in any case, Paris and Oxford are well out of the immediate reach of Rome, nor have they any direct bearing on the empire.'

'Your Majesty,' says Michael Scot, 'I ask this of you most earnestly. It is not some passing whim. The time has come for me to see my birthplace again.'

The emperor shakes his head. 'You put me in a difficult position, Canon Scot. I know you well and long enough to realise that you are not given to whims.' He extends his hands palm-upwards towards Michael Scot. 'But would you have me put your needs – however deserving – before those of the empire? The empire must come first. You know that. And I have need of you here.'

Michael Scot bows his head and then clutches it with both hands. A muffled groan escapes him. In the light of the torches beads of sweat glitter on his forehead. 'Useless,' he mutters, 'it's all useless. You don't understand, you cannot understand. You haven't seen what I have seen.' He gets unsteadily to his feet and his eyes dart round the chamber. 'It's all round us, waiting for us everywhere.' His arms make a circling motion and then fall to his sides. 'No matter what decisions are made or what actions are undertaken, the outcome can only be one.' His voice falls to a whisper. 'Death.'

The word falls into the silence like a stone plummeting into mud.

The emperor opens his mouth to speak. No sound emerges.

'Death,' cries Michael Scot, twisting his head from side to side, as if in great pain. The word obtrudes with ugly force once again on the silence in the room. The emperor brings his fist down on the table. The abbot starts. 'Control yourself, Canon Scot,' cries the emperor. 'What ails you that you must bandy about such a word?'

Before their appalled eyes, Michael Scot crumples to the floor. He grips his head and curls up into a foetal position. A long low cry escapes him. 'Ah, the pain. It is too much. Enough, enough.'

The emperor hurries to Michael Scot's side and stoops to get him into a sitting position. Rushes from the floor have stuck to the rough tunic. Another moan escapes him.

'Fetch him a glass of wine.' The emperor gestures impatiently at the abbot.

'No, no,' mumbles Michael Scot. 'I am addled enough with pain. I can ill afford fuddled wits as well.'

'Headstrong, infuriating man!' The emperor's voice rises again. 'For once in your life, do as you are bidden. Take the wine and be done with it.'

The abbot moves quickly to help the emperor, who is leading Michael Scot back to his seat by the fire. He hands the goblet to the emperor, who puts it to Michael Scot's lips. He takes a long draught, before sinking into the seat.

'Canon Scot,' says the emperor, a deep frown cutting across his forehead, 'this accident is indeed serious.'

There is a pause as Michael Scot regains his composure. 'The long and the short of it is this,' he says eventually, his voice a hoarse whisper. 'I need to set out once again for my place of birth. The hope being that the good Lord spare me long enough for it to become my place of death.'

'You are sure?'

Michael Scot attempts a laugh, but it is short-lived. He cups his head in both hands. 'As sure as an astrologer ever can be.'

'But what shall *I* do without my astrologer? How am I to face the perils of government without my trusted astrologer to guide me?'

'Canon Michael,' intervenes the abbot, 'relate the content of your visions to his Majesty.'

Michael Scot struggles to his feet. Some colour has returned to his cheeks, the abbot notes, undoubtedly on account of the wine. But it is the change in Canon Michael's eyes that is most striking. The abbot both fears it and is in awe of it: when they glitter in that way, God's cosmos no longer seems like a knowable place. And yet it is still God's own cosmos. Some strange force has taken hold of Canon Michael; gone is the broken man of two minutes previously. He stretches up to his full height and his voice rings out with a peculiar resonance into the echoing chamber. 'Beware, my Lord.'

Unblinking, the emperor's eyes bore into him.

'In the year of our Lord 1235, the higher planets will come together in the sign of Libra, and there will be a land peace treaty of great justice and integrity. But in the year 1236, there will occur an eclipse of the moon, followed by a fire-coloured partial eclipse of the sun, both in the Mars-ruled sign of Aries. Beware. For then shall come forth the treachery of the Lombard League and the serpentine plotting of Parma. And their venom will mix with the smoke issuing from the dragon hoarding treasure in Rome. Beware the papacy. And in this same year when the planets are drawn together by God's command in Scorpio, in a dark and unfathomable sign, then will appear the dragon's tail, and war will begin. Calamities will visit themselves with great destructiveness on the opposing forces. And the eagle will extend its protecting wings to all peoples; but its beak will rupture on hard stone and in this way it will no longer be able to feed itself. Most of all, your Majesty—' Michael Scot breaks off to look at the emperor; a tear rolls down his haggard cheek. 'Most of all, my Lord, beware certain gates of iron in a city named after Flora.'

The emperor retreats into a pensive silence. Hugo de Clermont puts an arm round Michael Scot, whose face has returned deathly pale, and assists him back to his seat. He passes him some water from a jug on the table, which Michael Scot hardly has the strength to sip.

Abruptly, the emperor gets to his feet. 'Well, Canon Scot, you have told me more in this brief interview than I could hope to learn in years of diplomatic manoeuvrings.'

The emperor shakes his head and sighs. 'So much is at stake, and mistakes are so costly.' Almost to himself, he continues, 'There are times when it seems to me that no matter how well meaning my intentions, no matter what decisions I make, no matter what plans I lay,' – he glances at Canon Scot – 'events conspire to land me in precisely those situations I had most wanted to avoid. No man is ever totally in charge of his own destiny. How much more burdensome is this, then, for me, being responsible for so many destinies.' He rubs his forefinger over his bottom lip; and then the eyes seem to come back from a great distance, focusing on Canon Scot with their customary incisiveness. 'And so, in the name of our long and fruitful acquaintance, let us come to an agreement that may be mutually beneficial. Complete a written record of these visions, and you shall be free to go. I shall then furnish you with a testimony that will enable you to take your translations wherever you please.'

Michael Scot looks up at the emperor and nods slowly. 'I thank you, your Majesty.'

'I shall be sorry to lose you, Canon Scot,' says the emperor. 'With Fibonacci gone, and now you, to whom shall I talk about mathematics and science?'

A sad smile flickers over Michael Scot's face. 'My Lord Emperor, if it were possible to escape this mortal destiny of ours by dint of learning, no one would deserve it more than you.'

'Well, see if I don't cheat you out of your prophecy of death. Henceforth I will make it my business never to set foot in Florence.'

A melancholy silence now falls on the room. The emperor again grows restless. 'So, Canon Scot,' he says, rising from his seat, 'your journeying starts again.'

Michael Scot struggles to his feet too, and attempts to bow. So does the abbot.

'Send in Master Secretary, who will doubtless be cooling his heels out in the corridor.'

'Doubtless,' echoes the abbot. 'My advice, your Majesty, is to disregard any nonsense he comes out with about the risk Canon Michael poses in your dealings with his Holiness. In any case, with Canon Michael's departure there will be no case to answer.'

'And remember, your Majesty,' says Michael Scot, 'that betrayal comes when least you expect it, and from the least expected quarters.'

The emperor closes his eyes and bows his head. 'Ever has it been so, Canon Scot,' he replies wearily, 'or it would not be betrayal.'

Salerno,
Kingdom of Sicily

†

Confessio
May AD *1230*

The predictions were duly consigned to the chancellery and Frederick released me from his service. Bit by bit, stage after stage, and laid low by my maladies, I have made my way here to the Medical School in Salerno on this the first leg of my return journey. I am to read from my translations of Averroës' commentaries on Aristotle's De Anima. *After all these years of enforced silence, it will be a strange sensation to make my work known in such a public manner.*

Yet this opportunity to exhibit my translations leaves me mostly indifferent, for it comes too late; and a part of me still fears the censure I may bring upon myself, despite the fact that I am dying. These are volatile times.

The headaches come on sudden and fierce and are a torment to me. Since the accident, my brain has become as a manuscript from which the ink has faded: I turn page after page, but can make out nothing. Anger then shrivels and scorches even this void.

And my powers—

Such as they were, my powers have deserted me.

Finally, I shall meet again my stalwart friend Jacob Anatolio. The beneficiary of an imperial appointment, Jacob left Palermo for Salerno six years ago. How will he have fared in the meantime? What shall I respond to him when he asks me the same question? Indeed, I fear to meet him – fear his pity, and my own anger. What shall I tell him of the plummeting of the wheel of my fortunes and its stubborn refusal to rise again? Its sentence of death?

To what else can I attribute this sentence but the wheel of fortune? How could this be Your doing? Source of all life and goodness – how could You be responsible for this blight and destruction?

And yet, and yet – thus do You seem to me now: both Creator and Destroyer. These words circle each other endlessly in my addled brain, now the one, now the other gaining the upper hand. Creator of life and Destroyer of hopes. You have stripped me and left me with nothing. Not even the desire to live.

And yet here I am.

So not even the horoscope has turned out to be true. A further humiliating instance of my ineptitude. No doubt the predictions concerning Frederick will show themselves to be as charlatanical as those regarding my own death. Truly I know nothing, am sure of nothing any more. The circumstances have lined up, but headstrong, wilful time will be harnessed by no man.

Of my life's work, only the translations now seem to me to have merit. Perhaps, indeed, because they carry so little trace of the translator. In them I am merely a conduit for others' originality.

The voices I have filtered are voices of real knowledge and will last; my essence in them is but a ghostly presence. For that is what my life now seems to have amounted to: an agonising preparation for becoming a ghostly presence.

XLVII

Yet another place. The vivid blue of the Mediterranean sky overarching this wide bay of Salerno, the green of its mountain trees tumbling down into turquoise waters. Michael Scot has always loved nature; he presumed even to study it. But there will be no settling in here. No growing familiarity with the soul of a place, no gradual love for its contours and colours. That is all over and done with. The beauty of the vista pricks him now like an irritation, the splendour of its buildings seems but a mere distraction.

He sits down at the top of the flight of white marble steps leading to the cathedral, where Lombard and Saracen styles have come together. Despite himself, his eye follows the white blocks of stone in the new campanile right up to the very top, which is surmounted by a small rounded cupola. Inside it is the same: the soaring white aspiration of the stone building softened by the lateral flow of the rounded arches in the courtyard. The Medical School in Salerno is the oldest of its kind in Christendom and dates back to the Lombard era. It has notched up four centuries of history. The University of Naples, opened lately in 1224 under the auspices of the emperor, has been offering some competition; this indeed was the emperor's aim. But no one doubts the excellence of the work still being carried on in the Medical School.

Suddenly, the late spring sunshine makes his eyes water; he shields them with his hand. A stab of pain so acute that there is a crackling noise in his ears robs him of sight. His breathing becomes shallow. Tentatively, his hand fumbles with his cowl; he manages to cover his head, warding off the unbearable sunlight. Let it not begin again, please Lord, let it not begin again. The last attack was just a matter of hours ago, and he is still drained from it. He dares not even rock back and forth for fear of upsetting some precarious equilibrium – the infinitesimal step that still separates him from a plunge into an abyss of pain. A low moan escapes him.

'Michael?' A hand is placed on his shoulder. He attempts to look up, but a shower of stars breaks before his eyes, and again that crackling noise in his ears.

'Is it you, Jacob?' he whispers.

'It is, Michael, it is.' He is lifted gently to his feet.

In silence they make their way to the Medical School.

*

Inside the shadowy stillness of the building, Michael Scot feels himself drawing back from the brink. The sense of gratitude brings tears to his eyes. Mutely, the two men observe each other.

Jacob Anatolio notes his wretchedness with distress. Word had reached him that the man was but a shadow of his former self. Even so, he cannot reconcile the old man hunched in front of him with the imposing figure he had once looked up to – in every sense – as a youth. 'My brother Michael,' he murmurs.

'Brother Jacob,' returns Michael Scot, his voice a hoarse whisper.

They embrace each other.

'I know,' says Michael, drawing away, 'I'm hardly a sight to gladden the heart.' He pats the younger man's arm. 'I live on borrowed time. And the interest on it is exorbitant.'

'It's good to see that your intellect has been untouched, Michael.'

Michael Scot's eyebrow rises, then he winces. 'No more about myself. How are you? I warrant you have things enough to tell me.'

'Alas, not all of them good.'

'I may be able to offer you some consolation then.' A smile flickers across the wintry paleness of the grey eyes. 'My brother Jacob, I have sorely missed your company and our talks.'

Jacob sighs and pulls Michael's arm through his own. 'Lean on me and come now to the lecture hall. I want you to sit and rest there while I get you some water. Your lecture is avidly anticipated; indeed, people can talk of little else. You cannot imagine the hornets' nest your arrival has stirred up here.' His eyes glint in enjoyment. 'Although – maybe you can.'

'However much I seek to elude it, the buzz of dissension follows me always.'

'Pay no heed; your conscience is clear. What have you done but carry out work that needed doing? Let us be practical here – you need to keep your strength up for the lecture. Rest, therefore, and be at peace.'

They progress slowly down the length of the vaulted passageway and come to a stop before the largest of the lecture halls. 'They are worried,' smiles Jacob, opening the door, 'in case even this hall is not big enough to seat the crowds who are coming to hear you.' His voice echoes in the cavernous space, empty except for themselves.

He closes the door and opens a smaller one a little further down the corridor. It leads into a small study. 'Take a seat here.' Jacob indicates the large, high-backed wooden chair over by a window. 'There is still a good while before you are due to begin, so rest yourself.'

He sits and Jacob observes him, adding, 'I know just the cordial to have made up for you. Valerian, peony, mugwort, thorn-apple and some common henbane. Wait for me here.'

*

From the back of the lecture hall, Jacob observes Canon Michael Scot as he brings his reading to a close. He is impressed, happily so, at the transformation he has undergone. For there is no comparison between the frail, broken-looking individual of barely a few hours past and the compelling presence at the lectern on the dais whose voice, while a little hoarse, still effortlessly commands attention. There before them all stands the man whose work will allow Christendom to learn of the Muslim philosopher Averroës, the illustrious intermediary through which Christendom will re-acquaint itself with the Natural Philosophy of Aristotle. It is a momentous event, and Michael has proved himself worthy of the occasion. But Jacob fears what physical repercussions may come in the wake of this effort.

The faces in the packed hall are turned towards Michael: some are frowning, some wide-eyed. But all are giving him their undivided attention.

Michael's concluding words fall into silence. Suddenly, a murmur breaks out, which rapidly becomes a deafening roar. There is clapping, some banging on wooden bench tops. Groups form and begin to argue animatedly. A number of them converge on the dais where Michael is now leaning on the lectern.

Jacob notices the sagging shoulders, the sudden pallor, and hurries towards him. As he moves over to offer his congratulations, a young man steps forward and monopolises Michael's attention.

'I am Friar Eric Toldenstraeng,' he announces. Michael looks him over and a frown settles on his face. 'Your choice of subject matter,' adds Toldenstraeng, 'was contentious.'

'Contentious is how the ignorant see anything that stimulates their fear.'

Toldenstraeng rearranges his long, black hooded cowl. 'We

Dominicans hold heresy to be an abomination; your reading seemed to parade it under the guise of philosophy.'

'Firstly, I cannot be held responsible for Averroës' views. Secondly, the fact that he is of another faith does not preclude knowledge from him. And the pursuit of knowledge surely cannot constitute grounds for heresy.'

'The pursuit of knowledge…' murmurs Toldenstraeng. 'Yes – that is it. I get the whiff of Gnosis, and by extension, the foul stench of the Albigensians. This, you see, is where these readings lead.'

There is a babble of comment from the throng that has pressed up against the dais. Some agree, some dissent.

Michael Scot pulls himself up to his full height. His eyes glitter from under his thick, still-dark eyebrows. His expression is contemptuous, his tone icy. 'Well, you Dominicans can congratulate yourselves on a job well done. You appear to have ambushed the highroad to heresy with your bonfires.'

Silence falls.

A beam of sunlight falls on the pink skin of Toldenstraeng's tonsure; it lights up the lank blond hair running round it. The young man is tall, at least as tall as Michael was in his prime. From this exalted height, to those standing below him off the dais, the sunbeam makes him look as if he has a halo. The timing for this sign of divine preferment is unfortunate, reflects Jacob. 'One must always,' says Toldenstraeng, his hazel eyes running over the throng before him, quelling the murmur building up, 'be vigilant.'

'So, Friar Toldenstraeng,' enquires Michael, 'what does your vigilance stretch to?' He sits down slowly on the chair that Jacob has placed behind him. 'Are there to be bonfires in Salerno, too?' A snicker runs round the group. 'And are my manuscripts to provide,' – Michael looks up and the same sunbeam catches his own eyes, causing them to glitter – 'the kindling?'

The Dean of Studies steps forward. 'Not at all, not at all,' he says heartily. 'Friar Toldenstraeng came here with far more benign intentions.

Did you not?' Without waiting for an answer, he continues, 'We are all most grateful to have heard you this day, Canon Scot. Indeed, young Toldenstraeng had wished to consult you on Arabic in order to finish his treatise on bloodletting.'

'Ah.' Michael raises an eyebrow. 'Am I, perhaps, to take his outburst as a way of recommending himself? As such it was clumsy. Because, according to Friar Toldenstraeng, no matter how worthy this material is, through contact with the heathen philosophy of the Muslims, it will lay even so exalted a soul as his own open to a charge of heresy.'

Toldenstraeng looks at him with sudden loathing. 'I will have a care – nay, it will be my most special mission – not to endanger my soul with any filthy taint of Mohammedanism.' He pauses. 'There are those of us,' he says with quiet contempt, 'who can come in contact with heresy and heretics, and know them for what they are.'

All eyes turn to Michael Scot, but he has closed his own and appears not to have heard. Jacob's skin prickles and he takes a half step forward. Michael groans and cradles his head in his hands. A murmur builds up.

The Dean of Studies extends a hand towards Canon Scot, but then seems to think the better of it. Instead, he turns on Toldenstraeng. 'See where your intemperance has got us?' he says nervously. 'This is your fault. Take him to the infirmary down the passageway, examine him, and see that you put this right.'

Toldenstraeng looks down at the ground.

The Dean of Studies heads for the door. 'That would be all we need now – the illustrious scholar Canon Michael Scot pays a visit to the Medical School in Salerno and, while under their care, falls ill and dies. Can you imagine the rumours and the jibes?' He turns back to look at the assembled group before walking through the door. 'I hold you responsible for him, Toldenstraeng. I await a full account of your examination when you have finished.'

XLVIII

The infirmary is small but well appointed. Wooden cupboards contain row after row of labelled jars storing medicinal herbs. The shutters have been pulled to, leaving the room in a soft penumbra. On a settle under the window, Michael Scot sits with his eyes shut.

'Well then, Toldenstraeng,' his voice cuts through the tense silence; it sounds fatigued but he enunciates his words clearly, 'how do you intend to proceed with this examination?'

The young physician pauses. He is aware of his unwelcome patient's reputation: the alleged brilliance of his skill in medicine, astronomy and mathematics. 'It would not be fitting,' he begins, but his voice comes out as a rasp. He clears his throat. 'It would not be fitting,' he takes up more loudly, the surge in volume making up for the plunge in self-assurance, 'to presume to tell you anything you have not already worked out for yourself.' He is further unsettled by the sudden aperture of the patient's eyes, which scrutinise him, latching onto his own with an intensity that makes his stomach give a lurch. The rumours surrounding the man about his skill in sorcery flit through Toldenstraeng's head. He breaks away from the beam of The Scot's searching eyes, moving over to one of the wooden presses. 'I shall proceed as I have been taught, but I welcome any directions you may see fit to give.'

Michael Scot nods. 'And so, in the name of God, let us begin.'

'Amen.' Eric Toldenstraeng carefully observes the patient.

'Let us start with your appearance, as an indicator of the internal situation.'

'Wouldn't you be more advised,' interrupts Michael Scot, 'to measure my pulse before your prognostications bring about any unnatural alterations?'

Toldenstraeng wipes his hands on his habit. 'Of course.' He takes the bony wrist between his fingers. A rapid pulse. 'It would point to the type of temperature associated with an excess of black bile,' he says quickly.

'Yes,' replies Michael Scot. His frown eases a little. 'That is so. Now proceed with the examination.'

'Yes. Your appearance—'

Michael Scot sighs at length. Two dark eyebrows come down again over his pale eyes. 'What are they teaching here these days?' He shakes his head. 'A good doctor always interests himself in eliciting an account of his patient's symptoms. No matter,' he adds coldly, 'how little store he may set by it.'

Toldenstraeng's mouth twists in chagrin. 'Of course.' It is true – he ought to have elicited a first-hand account. Even though he already knows the background to the case, word having reached them here in Salerno of the calamitous occurrence that had incapacitated The Scot. Well, first things first. 'What was your precise location when the accident befell you?' he asks. 'And, in order to draw up your decumbiture chart, I shall require your ascendant sign, along with the month, day and time of the mishap.'

'My decumbiture chart...' repeats Michael Scot meditatively. There is a pause.

'Yes,' says Toldenstraeng, frowning, 'To establish the sixth, seventh, eighth and tenth houses.'

'Admirable. Obviously, you feel that is not possible from an account of the merely physical symptoms. You still haven't asked about them.'

Toldenstraeng rubs his forehead with his fingers. A muscle twitches in his jaw. 'And they are?'

The account he is given is terse. He invites The Scot to sit up and then takes his skull in his hands.

For all that the accident happened a full three months previously, there is still a lump and a scar on the crown of the head, bluish-black in colour, semicircular in shape. He prods it gently. Hard and rounded. His hands fall back down to his sides as Michael Scot observes him.

'The wound itself would also seem to point to an excess of black bile,' he says. 'What is the nature of the pain you are experiencing?'

'Its nature is to cause me as much pain as it can. Could you be a little more specific?'

His university examinations had been less gruelling. 'Where is this pain located?'

'Ah, well, I would have to say in the front half of my head.'

'Is the pain low and continuous, sharp, or beyond bearing?'

'Intermittently severe.'

A moment's silence. 'Again, I find there are symptoms corresponding to an excess of black bile. Let us turn now to any alterations you have experienced in the animal, natural and spiritual faculties.'

A raised eyebrow greets this.

'Alterations in your sense of taste?'

'Yes. Flavours unaccountably seem to have acquired a vinegarish taste.'

'And your appetite?'

'Decreased. With a preference for what is hot and stewed.'

Toldenstraeng frowns. 'What about your breathing? Is it deep and frequent?'

There is a pause; Michael Scot's lip curls. 'On no account,' the voice drops, yet gains in menace, 'should a doctor suggest to a patient what his symptoms might be.' Toldenstraeng has to master an impulse to shiver. 'And no,' weariness seeps into the tone, 'it is not deep and frequent. It is shallow and frequent.'

Toldenstraeng looks down at the ground.

'Aren't you forgetting,' enquires Michael Scot blandly, 'to say something about my appearance?'

Toldenstraeng's hand has clenched itself into a fist; he unclenches it. He observes the excessive thinness, the gauntness, the slowness of movement. This points to the prevalence of bile in the system. But the complexion presents problems. It is neither ruddy – which would have indicated normal bile – nor dark and bluish – an indicator of black bile. It is extremely pale. 'How are you sleeping?' he asks.

'I'm not.'

Of course, reflects Toldenstraeng. And there can be no doubt as to the man's rigidity of character. 'Your appearance also points to an excess of bile,' he says, 'but we shall have to corroborate this.'

'Indeed.'

'The excretory functions,' says Toldenstraeng, gesturing to a ewer on the table. 'I need to examine your urine.'

Michael Scot gets to his feet and retrieves the ewer. He turns his back to Toldenstraeng. The smell of urine fills the small room.

'Leave it there on the cupboard.' Toldenstraeng indicates. 'As soon as you give me the details of your horoscope, I shall draw up your decumbiture chart, and then proceed with the prognosis and remedies. An unguent for the headaches. A cordial for the insomnia. And some directions for clearing the air in your rooms. Last of all, I shall endeavour to deal with the protuberance on the crown of your head.'

'You will need to administer these remedies yourself, I suppose,' enquires Michael Scot gloomily.

'Yes,' replies Toldenstraeng, equally unenthusiastic.

*

'Come now to my lodgings,' urges Jacob. 'My wife and I will look after you there.'

'I thought you were settled in Naples?'

'So did we – but more of that anon.'

Michael Scot looks back towards the study where Toldenstraeng is sweating over the remedies for his ailments. 'No doubt the young ignoramus is exerting himself as best he can. Not that it matters, for you have already given me any prognosis and medication I need. But we must keep the Dean happy.' His eyes roll heavenwards. 'I am afraid he will have to accompany us to your lodgings.'

'Of course, Michael. I left word with Rebekah to expect visitors. Let me explain to him where the lodgings are and he can join us as soon as he is ready.'

Jacob Anatolio surveys the tall, lanky young man standing on the far side of the room. The hazel eyes that return his gaze betray an expression he has long been familiar with.

'Thank you for the invitation to dine at your lodgings,' says Toldenstraeng distantly. 'But would it not be more—' His voice trails off as he searches for the right word.

'Kosher?' supplies Jacob helpfully.

'More in keeping,' takes up Toldenstraeng with the slow deliberation of someone measuring his words with infinite care, 'with the rules Canon Michael Scot and I are subject to as men of God, if he were to return to the monastery and allow me to proceed with his cure there?'

'No doubt it would be,' replies Jacob, 'but an affliction for the soul, nevertheless. As such,' he adds briskly, 'hardly something that any good physician would wish to visit on an ill patient...'

A muscle twitches in Toldenstraeng's jaw and his eyes strain at Jacob Anatolio, as if betraying the words he has had to bite back.

'We'll see you in the Jewish quarter when you have finished,' adds Jacob, turning on his heel.

XLIX

Michael Scot steps over the threshold of Jacob Anatolio's lodgings. The physical tension recedes as his eyes welcome the relative darkness of the vestibule. He removes his sandals as Rebekah Anatolio places a bowl of water on a small table. Her kindly face looks up at him as she tips the water from the ewer over his hands and into the bowl. She smiles as she hands him a linen *salvietta*. 'Canon Scot, it is such a great pleasure to have you again as our guest. My husband has been talking about meeting you these ages. You are most welcome.'

She addresses him in the idiom of Campania, which she has picked up in the five intervening years since last he saw her. In this interim she has changed from a shy young girl into a wife and mother of three. She bustles around him, removing the *salvietta*, ewer and bowl, picking up the shoes he has left at the front door. She has imparted the feel of a home even to these temporary lodgings. Michael Scot is caught between a desire to recoil from all the over-abundant evidence of feminine domesticity, and the unexpected sense of ease that slides over him with this rediscovery of comfort.

'I shall leave you to talk now,' she says brightly, 'as supper won't be ready for another while.'

The glance that she exchanges with her husband on her way back to the kitchen is pensive.

Michael draws back from the bright afternoon sunshine pouring in through the open window of the room Jacob uses as his study; he rises and goes to draw the shutters to. The light is now filtered in soothing rays onto the rushes and fresh herbs strewn across the floor. The noise from the street below is unabated.

'Thank you,' says Michael. 'Sunlight has been having a very adverse effect on me recently. Truly, it is time for me to be going back to Scotland; I am not anticipating the same problem there.'

Both men smile briefly, and Jacob sits down facing his friend. 'So, Michael,' he says, 'you are on your way back to Scotland.'

'I am.'

Rebekah can be heard humming in the kitchen, and from farther off in the house come the shrill excited cries of children playing. Both men gaze at the floor, lost in thought, wrapped within an expectant silence. 'Michael,' says Jacob, his brow creasing in concern, 'how goes it with you?'

Michael does not reply immediately. The sound of women's laughter comes on a breath from the kitchen, where Rebekah is being helped in her preparations for the evening meal by the servant-girls. Then slowly, hesitantly, the words begin to elbow their way out of the morass in his head. The intrigue at court. The backbiting and pettiness. The impossibility of getting any serious work done due to the officious intrusion of court functionaries who had their own protégés to push ahead, their own policies to pursue. There is only so much struggling a person can do; when the odds are overwhelming, it is wiser to desist.

'Overwhelming?'

'Yes, overwhelming. You know nothing of the visions I have had. Betrayal. The spectacle of destruction visited on all hopes and endeavours. The stench of death everywhere. Frederick's. And my own.'

'Your own death?'

'Yes, indeed. I have lived for the past three years in the knowledge that a piece of falling masonry would procure me a fatal injury to the head.'

'And this has come to pass?'

'It has. But, despite appearances,' – Michael pulls at the tufts of wild white hair sticking out of his head and sucks in his cheeks, further emphasising their sunken nature – 'what sits before you is no ghost.' He chuckles quietly. 'For the moment, at least...'

Jacob smiles. 'Well then, I am delighted that this is indeed a visit, and not a haunting.'

Suddenly, both men begin to laugh. Jacob briefly catches a glimpse of the man that so inspired him more than fifteen years ago, and who now lets himself be cradled in the easeful serenity that comes with trusted company.

Michael winces and places a hand on the crown of his head. 'Ah, Jacob,' he sighs, 'what has it all been for? Frederick's plan for an illuminated, humane and universal empire will come to naught. The name of the place where he will die was given to me in a vision: in the city of the flower, *florentia*, before certain gates of iron.'

Jacob observes him in stunned silence. 'When?'

'That is obscure to me. But say nothing of the matter to anyone.'

'You have my word.'

'Let us hope that it may prove merely to be the rantings of a sick old man, and nothing more. But enough of me. What of yourself? Why these allusions to adversity?'

A great heaviness descends on Jacob when he thinks of his life over the last few years. 'What can I tell you, Michael, of backbiting, pettiness and betrayal that you have not yourself already experienced? There is so much to say, but I can make no sense of it. Even now.'

'Start at the beginning,' replies Michael. 'It may be that by the end we will still have made no sense of it. But the telling alone carries its own significance.'

At first haltingly, but then with ever greater urgency, Jacob begins to tell of the relentless opposition from his own community. In the end it had broken him.

'Broken?'

'Yes, broken. Brother Michael, such was the persecution visited on me, that at one stage I contemplated taking my own life. Me – Jacob Anatolio, champion of the rational. For truly the world seemed devoid of any refuge, any rationality, and I no longer understood what I was doing in it. All I could do was ask myself, Why do I labour so? What has it profited me? I have become as a stranger to myself and the world has darkened before my eyes.

'The anti-Maimonists have used any means at their disposal to discredit my work and studies. My pursuit of Averroës' commentaries on Aristotle, translating them from their original Arabic into Hebrew, has worsened my position. The Jewish community already settled here sees no reason to share my admiration: external ideas should not be permitted to contaminate the purity of Jewish thought, and they fight bitterly against the spread of the corrupting influence of these philosophical developments.

'If I had not had the patience and fortitude of my wife to lean on, and the thought of my family to spur me on, I do not know what would have become of me. As it was, I found myself confined to bed for two months following a complete nervous collapse. My wife nursed me back to health.'

Michael shakes his head. 'Alas that I should hear this. But, as you alone know, I understand your plight all too well. And yet, I see you here, apparently in the full of your health.'

'Yes, thank God. It has been a tough lesson, but well learnt. I refuse this mortifying life, always having to be on the defensive – against the Gentiles and against my own. I reject this fear of knowledge. I will not buckle under it. I should not be forced to choose between betraying my sense of truth and justice by renouncing the quest for knowledge, or betraying my family's need for a peaceful existence.

'If you cleave to your conscience rather than your tribe, even the opposite factions of a society will contrive to come together in order to eliminate you, in an unholy alliance of fanaticism. But I have come to the conclusion that I might as well be hung for a sheep as a lamb. So now I do not limit myself to merely translating Averroës' *Intermediate Commentaries*; I comment on them in my turn, offering criticism where I deem it necessary. Just as Averroës engaged with and criticised Avicenna. In this way, and despite the fanatics, I still pursue the furtherance of knowledge.'

'Good, brother Jacob, good. I would urge you to write something of your own, too. Something that contains all your considerations on the fatuousness of this specious purity.' Michael smiles and then adds, 'Let this book be a permanent thorn in the side of those who would limit knowledge in the name of religion and race. You have the freedom to do this – to be a reminder of their futility, a goad to those who have retreated into orthodoxy. How would this come in Hebrew?'

Jacob reflects for a moment. '*Malmad ha-Talmidim*.'

'Get writing, then! Since last I saw you I have written three books of my own. The *Liber Introductorius*, the *Liber Particularis* and *Liber Physionomie*. In them I have put my own ideas,' – Michael gestures disparagingly with his hand, left eyebrow raised – 'which may only have served to nullify any value they might have aspired to. Even so, it is a satisfaction.'

'What are they about?'

'The third one, *Liber Physionomie*, speaks for itself. But the first two are a compendium of my obsessions: astrology, astronomy and alchemy.'

'Not the most rational of pursuits,' muses Jacob. He shakes his head slowly. 'But I have changed my opinion on a great number of things since last we talked in Palermo. Since I found myself in the grip of the irrational, despite all my best intentions. Since, that is, I so narrowly missed committing the most irrational of acts and found that The Law had become a thing of dread. Since that time the shadowy has become more real, the irrational has acquired substance, whether I like this or not. And I have had to try to accommodate it in my life. But this thought has remained with me – that faith should never be sundered from man's rational faculty. The only way to come to God is through rational study and long years of education. In itself it is an elevation of the soul. There are no shortcuts; there is no magic that will accomplish this. Rational processes are the highest path man can aspire to: rationality is needed to fully understand the Divine. Not magic. Remember – there are no shortcuts.'

'I have used every faculty at my disposal in an effort to understand what it is that binds all these things together,' replied Michael. 'Be they obsessions or interests, they are all the fruit of a plethora of laws. Is it the nature of this world to be a fragmented jumble of laws? Or does one unifying law underpin everything?'

'The Law,' said Jacob, 'is something that resonates within the Jewish heart. For The Law to acquire personal significance it has to encapsulate not only regulations and speculation, it must also be a mainstay of experience. Regulations, speculation, experience: this is real education for me. But it has proved to be a far more mysterious process than I first thought.'

'Amen. In truth, all that is apparent to my fallen eyes is an immense fragmentation.' Michael's eyes wander to the window. 'Angels and mankind, men and women, languages, races, religions, empires, kingdoms. And knowledge… theology, philosophy, mathematics, astronomy, Natural Philosophy, medicine, alchemy…

'Alas, real discernment has eluded me. There is so much that I do not even begin to comprehend. At the end of my life's work, the field of knowledge stretches away like an immense forest; I am like a deluded beaver, gnawing and chewing away at pitifully few trees – and the end result a ramshackle leaky dam.'

Rebekah quietly pulls back the heavy drape separating the

room from the rest of the house. 'There is a man here to see Canon Scot.' Her expression is vexed. 'He says he will not be staying, so there is no need for him to take off his sandals, but he insists on entering.' She wipes her hands in her apron and looks at Jacob. 'Will you kindly attend to him?'

'That must be the young ignoramus, come blustering into your house.' Michael shifts testily on his seat. Jacob rises and goes out to the vestibule.

It would be very easy, reflects Michael, to give full vent to his dislike of the young Dane. His conscience tells him not to; but when has that ever sufficed to stem the tide of antipathy that overtakes us towards certain people? As a member of this newly founded reforming order of the Dominicans, Toldenstraeng enjoys the benefits of full papal endorsement. But their kind of reform is all too simplistic: reform through a dogged refusal of change. Reform that purports to protect some citadel of purity by digging a moat to keep out the new and throwing down into it any internal dissenters. This kind of reform has always been able to count on the inward-looking conformity and paralysis that fear brings with it.

The Dominicans have already acquired fame in the few short years since their founding as preachers, but above all as avengers of heresy. The word sends a shiver along his spine. For, fortified with the papal blessing, in 1209 they had descended on the Albigensian community in the South of France and decimated them. By the time he had arrived in Toledo in 1210, the Albigensians and their chilling creed were teetering on the brink of annihilation. Persecution continued in sporadic purges, the thoroughness of which attested to the Dominicans' overweaning determination to extirpate all traces of heresy. Many in Toledo had been attracted to the new religion – in truth, he had not been immune to some aspects of it himself. But he had not forgotten the horror and fear that overcame these individuals as the full extent of the persecution took its toll.

And here is Toldenstraeng reminding him of all that. And fuelling his antipathy, of course, is the fact that Toldenstraeng is young. Not alone has he embraced a new order, but even his pursuit of knowledge possesses an aura of something new. Michael and his friend Jacob – despite his being some twenty years younger – represent the last of the encyclopaedists: the drones who spend their time amassing facts, accumulating others' knowledge. Toldenstraeng represents the new, the specialised: he will probably break new ground in his treatise on bloodletting. It brings home to Michael the extent to which he has limited himself to following in others' footsteps.

Raised voices can be heard from the vestibule; they draw near.

L

'Because, as a guest in my house, it would be a courtesy,' Jacob finishes up, holding back the drape for Eric Toldenstraeng.

'I did not require to be your guest,' he replies stiffly.

'Well, you need not fear that removing your sandals will be a source of contamination,' says Jacob.

'But it is not a custom of mine.'

'There, indeed, is a boast.'

Friar Toldenstraeng glares at Jacob. His jaw shifts forward.

'Come now,' Michael bestirs himself, 'let us sit down together and you can tell me what kind of a cure you have devised.' He indicates the other end of the bench he is sitting at, running the length of the wooden table. 'What is your prognosis?'

With difficulty, Toldenstraeng removes his eyes from Jacob's face. There is a tense pause, and then finally he takes a seat. He shoots one final hostile glance at Jacob, and begins. 'The pain you are experiencing, and indeed the nature of the accident itself, are borne out in your decumbiture chart. Mars in Aries in your sixth house cannot but signify a serious injury to the head. After reflecting on your symptoms, however, I believe that the protuberance is not due to an injured nerve; it must be caused by an accumulation of humours in that region. Therefore, I propose the following cure: let an onion be cooked in ashes and cleaned of its skin with rue, salt and cumin; then proceed to chop it up and cook it in oil. Later this evening, it should be applied lukewarm to the swollen area. Towards midnight, when it has cooled entirely, it should be reheated and applied once again. On the morrow, you should find that the swelling has gone.'

'And if it has not?'

'In that case, the humours must have gone putrid and it will be necessary to proceed with the following compress. Galbanum must be softened on a hot brick and then placed on a sheet of paper, from whence it should be applied to the injured region throughout the night. This will bring about a rupture of the skin, and the putrid material should be expelled. A second and third application may prove necessary.'

'I see. That sounds satisfactory. But what is your prognosis?'

Toldenstraeng's eyes slide away. 'It is difficult to say. Let us hope that we are dealing here with an accumulation of humours – putrid or otherwise – as a build-up of hardened material would be more difficult to resolve.'

'You mean a tumour?'

A pause. 'I do.'

'I do not think that will be necessary,' says Michael, waving away the offer of a cordial for his insomnia. 'Evidently, I shall be enjoying an eternity of sleep in the near future.'

Toldenstraeng looks down at the floor. It has not escaped him that The Scot has admitted he will not be taking his place among the blessed in Paradise, contemplating the Godhead in an eternity of bliss. An eternity of sleep sounds like Limbo, where the lukewarm, the indifferent, and all the lost souls go. Souls like The Scot, who through frequenting unbelievers and heathens, have lost the certitude of the true way. There are those who wonder if The Scot did not at some stage become a Mohammedan.

'Not so hasty, Michael,' intervenes Jacob. 'Even if you have no use for it, I do. I cannot remember the last time I enjoyed an unbroken night's slumber. Let me hear.'

'Proceed, then, in this manner,' says Toldenstraeng frigidly. 'Prepare a poultice by crushing the seeds of hensbane, portulaccus, and a double measure of poppy. Mix this with rosewater. Then, with the aid of a cloth, apply this poultice to the forehead and temples.' He pauses for a moment. 'Ah, yes – chopped green poppy seed applied to the same area is also most effective.'

'Thank you,' says Jacob, 'I shall indeed try this remedy.'

'There is one last thing it might please you to carry out,' adds Toldenstraeng, turning to Michael Scot. 'Have you thought about clearing the air where you sleep?'

Michael shakes his head. Jacob gestures at him to continue.

'It involves creating a sort of artificial rain,' says Toldenstraeng. A raised eyebrow greets this. 'Artificial rain,' takes up Toldenstraeng hurriedly, 'that will refresh the room. For this, some jars will be necessary, and in the jars should be bored several miniscule holes. The room itself should be cleaned and fresh herbs strewn on the floor. Then the jars should be hung near the bed where the sick person is lying and water poured into them. It is greatly restorative.'

Michael snorts. Toldenstraeng glowers. 'No, no,' says Michael placatingly, 'I find your remedy most ingenious. I was just comparing it with what it was usual to do in Scotland. I wonder if it was the same in Denmark.'

Toldenstraeng stiffens.

'It was customary, do you see,' Michael continues, turning to Jacob, 'to burn the head of a pig, then place it under one's pillow and sleep on top of it.'

'Yes,' says Toldenstraeng warily, 'it was customary to do that where I come from, too.'

Jacob cannot keep the amazement from his face. 'And who actually had the temerity to find this outlandish remedy useful?'

Toldenstraeng looks at him with a fresh impetus of hostility. He can reveal nothing of himself, but it is ridiculed by these Southerners. And a Jew, to boot. It has been a relentless struggle to get himself taken in any way seriously, to the extent that he has questioned the wisdom of coming here at all. Undoubtedly, he has learned much – but at what cost? He has had to deal with their sneering assumption of his innate inferiority, purely because of an accident of birth. Why should his country of origin mark him out as a dolt and a dullard?

'It is the custom in this part of the world,' he says, looking rigidly ahead of him, 'to presume that nothing of any worth can come from Northern Europe. I beg leave to differ.'

'Well, that is true,' says Michael, 'in so far as it goes...'

Toldenstraeng folds his arms.

'You see,' takes up Michael, 'I have encountered the same difficulties as yourself. You may have a clear idea of where and what Scotland is. But in this part of the world, it is just one of the many barbarous lands with which the North abounds.' He shakes his head. 'When I was a young man, about the same age as you are now, trying to make my way in the field of astronomy and mathematics, I came up against great opposition.' Michael nods at him. 'Oh yes, I was told to take myself back to the wilds of Scotland and stick to sheep-shearing. Educating a barbarian was as useful as teaching a dog to ride a horse.'

Toldenstraeng smirks, in spite of himself. 'Unfortunately, it has also been my own experience. I encounter prejudice in my every endeavour.'

Michael raises an eyebrow. 'And yet, forgive my pointing it out, for one so young you appear to be forging ahead remarkably well. Therefore, I wouldn't wish you to wallow in sterile self-commiseration. Realise that the prejudice you encounter is what comes of being born in an impoverished, backward, superstition-ridden country, with no established tradition of learning. Realise also that your lone efforts may be laying the foundation for a tradition. Are you up to the task?'

'Of course I am,' shoots back Toldenstraeng.

'Well, there is no doubt that what you lack in background, you make up for in singularity of purpose.' Michael looks assessingly at him. 'Think carefully, young man, if you wish to further knowledge. To do this you must come in contact with other peoples and other tongues. In this way you will put yourself forever beyond the bounds of easy assumptions. And you will learn much, and perhaps even be allowed the privilege of furthering the course of knowledge. Know that this will automatically place you outside the confines of the orthodox, and occasion you great weariness of spirit. You will be a voice for the aspirations of humanity, but may never enjoy their fruits.' He shakes his head. 'I was advised once to choose between knowledge or discernment. In truth, they have both eluded me.'

Friar Toldenstraeng looks at this elderly man, and sees in him an example of what he will not become. The moral flaccidity repulses him. An apologist for the heathen infidel. A frequenter of Jews. And then the lack of a sense of pride in his country of origin: why would he stoke the fires of scorn that these Southerners are all too ready to shower on them? And as for the Jew – the devil take his damnable posturings on hygiene and the washing of hands. Clean hands will be of little use to him when he is cast into Hell as a Christ-killer.

But he will say nothing of this to them. He will bide his time. He will acquire all the knowledge he can from these corrupt and loathsome Southerners and all their acolytes, and separate it from the taint of degeneracy that is their hallmark. Soon he will take it back with him to the integrity and uprightness of his own country. They think they are so superior, with their sneering ways; but the Day of Judgment will come also for them. In the meantime, he will find tuition in Arabic from less compromised persons.

'I have, as you say, singularity of purpose,' says Toldenstraeng. His words have a peculiar staccato quality, as if they are being reined in at every syllable. 'I have learned much here, and seen even more... I will make sure that it serves me well when I return home.' Toldenstraeng gets to his feet. 'For home will never be here.'

Michael and Jacob exchange a glance.

'I'll see you out so,' says Jacob, drawing back the drape leading out to the door.

*

'His training has been good,' said Michael. 'His grasp of matters is not bad. But as a person, he will always be an obtuse oaf.'

Jacob sighs. 'The roll-call grows long...'

Nearby a bell starts to ring for Vespers. Michael blesses himself and bends his head in prayer. Jacob listens to the shrill cries of swifts cutting through the warm air of early evening. Michael makes the sign of the cross again, and says, 'I remember where last I heard those very words, "Home will never be here".'

Jacob glances over at him.

'At the house of Andrés Alfaquir,' murmurs Michael, 'in the *Judería* of Toledo. I wonder if he ever found his heart's ease.'

*

The leave-taking is painful. It is the last time the two men will see each other. Jacob Anatolio will have to find the strength to step onto the winding road of knowledge once again and see off the attempts to waylay his intelligence; Michael Scot, to look down a short alleyway, the end of which beckons with grim finality.

There is a ship sailing for Marseille on the morrow and Michael Scot must be aboard it. From there a merchant's caravan will provide him with transport as far as Paris.

†

Confessio
June AD *1230*

Life is as it is. Simply, it is the most astounding gift and has its own ineffable dynamic. Knowledge helps us to understand and appreciate the extent of the gift that God has entrusted to us, for it, too, comes from God and its purpose is to remove fear from our experience of life.

It is God who inspires us, God who wants us to share in this divine plan for His creation. For surely, without knowledge, life is reduced to mere existence; fortified with knowledge man can begin to perceive the extent of the miracle that is life.

Where did it come from? How can it be accounted for? And where is it headed?

Life is a gossamer web of paradox. For as long as my eyes are fixed on God, knowledge helps to give this intricate whole meaning; as soon as knowledge becomes an end in itself, it is as if the thread holding me had separated from the whole. And I must then cling to it all the more desperately, at any moment fearing to fall.

It is not God's wish that we hide from knowledge. He gave us the parable of the talents. If we hide from knowledge, we hide also from the truth. We should always be mindful of the ultimate purpose of knowledge; I was not, and it shrivelled me.

Therefore must I relinquish the expectation that I can

control events: knowledge moves through me, and on; it does not stop with me. This lack of control is the price we pay for free will: the only control we have is over the choices we can make from moment to moment, day to day – the consequences of which overarch the months, years and decades and give shape to a lifetime.

For I, too, am part of this whole, and with humility I must accept my place in it. With the same humility I must acknowledge that I do not know what that place is.

Lord Jesus Christ, be with me, stay with me. Help me to discern that I am cradled always in the palm of Your hand.

Paris, France

†

Confessio
July AD *1230*

Like a salmon I continue my journey to the source. It has brought me now to this great city, the city of my first youthful triumph, and the memory is bittersweet. For I know that I return with none of the promise of those long-gone days fulfilled. I return, not to spawn, but merely to die.

Your ways are truly inscrutable. I know not whether You would have us cowed into submission or awakened into readiness, for this strange life abounds with both instances.

Is it the limits to our knowledge that bring about submission?

Is it the extent of our discernment that enables readiness?

I am an orphan; I have been alone in the world for as long as I can remember. I have had the comfort of neither wife nor child. I have learned to do without kith or kin. I am a witness to my clan's ruthless butchery of what did not conform. I made this bitter discovery a cornerstone in my life, and put myself forever beyond my kinsmen's reach. Surely the world could have no harder lesson.

And indeed the world did not; but the lesson has come at a terrible price. Homelessness, rootlessness and fear. Always fear.

I still find it unbearably painful to say the word 'mother'.

And yet the hunger for a sense of belonging has never abated. But over the years I have come to welcome it in whatever transient form it has all too rarely transpired.

What is home? Where is it to be found?

Of what are we fashioned that the need for it should be so strong? What half-intuited desires drive us to seek for it always? This has seemed more of a source of torment to me than anything else. That what we want, what we continue to hanker after, should be the cross we must carry around with us.

Dying is a lonely business. I should be used to this sensation, as I have been alone all my life. But I am dying even as life on this earth goes on; in the face of the abundance of life all around me, dying seems like the aberration. A disgrace that affects only the few. And the sense of vulnerability this brings unmans me. The ultimate reality strips you of everything – all hypocrisy, all pretensions, all dignity.

And yet I know You have been there before me.

So I am moved to thank You for the blessing of a friend such as Jacob; meeting him again has given me unexpected joy. The quiet joy that comes with talking in amity and truth to a kindred soul. It has saved me from my own despair. Jacob has been a consolation in my life, this I know, this I feel. But my heart is so shrivelled that it also cannot help but wonder why.

For this friendship to have such redemptive power, of what are we formed?

Jacob is right. There are no shortcuts. No secret paths traced by alcohol, opium and hashish; no manipulation of learning through recondite initiations leading to a hidden elixir of life. What else was astrology but a fear-driven pursuit of the elusive coordinates of existence, as a safeguard against the capricious dictates of fate. All arrogant delusion. Astrology burgles the future of free will, for the stars are only signs and not causes of the future, just as the circle hanging before a tavern is not wine, but the sign of wine. What is the point in spending one's life trying to foresee events that may not arise, and procure answers to questions that properly have none?

There are no shortcuts to our dreams. And if the dream transmutes into an obsession? In truth, astrology has been as nefarious an enslavement as the orthodox conformity exacted by religions. A crippling observance is extorted that shrivels the soul.

Rules and laws; laws and rules... Life cannot resolve itself in laws, just as life never remains in the realm of mere right and wrong. There has to be some miracle of Grace – for Good and Evil do exist, and they are cosmic forces to be reckoned with. How can a creature as feeble as man hope to overcome the repercussions of evil if not through a miracle? Left to his own devices he has not sufficient time or strength on his side. But a miracle subverts all known laws and out of compassion grants us not what we deserve, but what we need.

The greatest, most scandalous miracle of all is You, Lord Jesus Christ: through Your life and sacrifice You have subverted all cosmic laws. Free me, I pray, from the terrible justice that would be my lot should the Law run its inexorable course.

For I am at a complete loss. What has my faith amounted to but a fear-induced cleaving to burnt-out formulae; while my reason has been wasted on fear-driven pseudo-scientific posturings that owe more to my own woeful inadequacies than any objective apprehension of reality.

LI

He had forgotten the airy lightness of a northern summer. Forgotten the light-tinctured white clouds piling up in the distant blue reaches of a mild sky. He smiles as he makes his careful way up to the entrance of the Cathedral School. Despite the maze of narrow streets he has had to find his way through, some only wide enough to allow for the passage of a man, the upper stories of the houses jutting out, blocking still more of the precious sunlight, and the odour of excrement everywhere, all he can think of is the sky and the breeze-blown clouds. His memories of Paris are too dear to him, too much like a hidden trove of treasure, for any grumble to pass his lips. It has been his fortune to visit this city once again; he will have to leave it, and everything else, all too soon. Everything about it now seems painfully dear.

He is shown into the library where he is to meet Stephen de Provins. He does not immediately notice that his host is already waiting for him, until he hears a voice.

'Canon Michael!'

He turns slowly in the direction of the window to see a small figure making its way towards him, hands outstretched.

'Canon Stephen,' he says softly. He never raises his voice now above a loud whisper; it seems to help keep the headaches at bay. Then again, it could also be that the enforced calm that whispering necessarily imposes on one's dealings with others has been the real boon. He makes to genuflect, but surprisingly those outstretched, delicate hands make actual contact with him.

'No, my son,' says de Provins, his voice gently firm, 'come over and sit by the window. We shall enjoy the balmy air while you rest yourself.'

Michael Scot nods and smiles, letting himself be led by this man fifteen years his senior over to the large chair. He reflects that the level of unexpected solicitude in de Provins' demeanour is probably proportionate to the anxiety his appearance arouses. He must look as if he is on his last legs. Which indeed he is. He sits down and looks out of the window to his right, reflecting with calm satisfaction how this realisation no longer procures him the feeling of anger it had the power to do until very recently. He smiles slightly again as he looks across at de Provins. At seventy, the hazel eyes are undimmed by age, and regard him with the same detached intelligent affection as always. The hair has turned pure white, and he is slighter, with something of the gnome in the crafty expression that occasionally flits across his face; but here is somebody who will undoubtedly still be to the good even in ten years' time.

'So, Canon Michael,' he says, his voice muted in bland sympathy, 'you have been put to the test.'

'I have.' Michael Scot's eyes take in the other man's feet, which dangle from the chair he is sitting on, well short of the floor. 'But then again, are not we all, sooner or later?'

'That is true,' de Provins smiles affably. 'But be mindful that from those to whom much has been given, much will be expected.'

Michael Scot nods in silence.

De Provins gets down from the chair, and with unexpectedly nimble celerity begins to pace up and down the room. Michael Scot does not follow his movements; it might bring on a crick in his neck and make him giddy. He sits placidly in the chair, glad to take the weight off his feet. The boniness of his knees shows through the homespun wool of the habit.

'And to you, Canon Michael Scot.' He lifts his head as the tinny quality and increased volume in de Provins' voice alert him to something of import about to be communicated. 'To you, much has been given. I am as aware of this now as I was when first you showed promise at the University of Paris. Rest assured that neither your work, nor your humble obedience, has gone unnoticed.' De Provins pauses to look over at Michael Scot. 'There have been developments with regard to Aristotle.'

He draws up to the chair Michael Scot is sitting on; their eyes are level. His manner has a subdued ebullience about it and he blinks rapidly before resuming. The tinny quality melts away as his enthusiasm for what he recounts takes over. The meeting with Gregory IX. The pontiff's desire that a commission be instituted to evaluate the works of Aristotle, above all those pertaining to Natural Philosophy, where the most insidious traps might be lying in wait for God-fearing Christians.

'For you see,' – de Provins' hand hovers over Michael Scot's arm while never actually touching it – 'his Holiness is all too aware of the changes taking place in Christendom. The world we live in is no longer divided between *Regnum* and *Sacerdotium*: a new order is making itself felt in our midst, that of *Studium*.' The hand is withdrawn and the pacing resumes.

De Provins' pallid fingers, a little curved with arthritis, punctuate his account, fastidiously stabbing the air in order to press home his points; he draws a composite picture of the situation with all the meticulous precision of the vigilant theologian. Step by step he pulls into shape the tangled threads of the approach to knowledge up to the present time. Michael Scot's lifetime of endeavours are but one – if even – of these many threads. De Provins forges on, and Michael Scot listens desultorily, his eyes drawn to the spectacle of the late afternoon sun irradiating the white clouds outside the window.

He is apprised of the great changes taking place within the

university, the struggle for power between the chancellor and the masters, in particular the masters of the Arts Faculty. Their elected representative is the rector, and through this person they have shown the greatest acumen in creating an administrative body willing and able to take on the authority of the bishop. These masters have played a political game, and, it has to be admitted (de Provins here permits an indulgent smile to flit across his features), so has his Holiness, Pope Gregory. The masters wish to disenfranchise themselves from the bishop's stranglehold; but in his capacity as advisor to the pope (de Provins lowers his eyes deprecatingly), it has been his privilege to acquaint his Holiness with the most far-sighted policy the Holy See might take in this regard.

The fact is that ever greater sections of Christendom will gain access to learning. The Church has already been instrumental in opening up the benefits of learning even for the poorer among her flock. But these numbers are bound to increase and the Church has no desire to alienate any of them. To this end he, Stephen de Provins, has advised his Holiness to come to an agreement with the masters, even if it means going over the head of the bishop.

And this is being done. Gregory has managed to maintain his power as supreme arbiter of what should and should not be studied, while managing not to alienate anyone. The only faction to emerge badly from this struggle has been the bishop and his representative within the university, the chancellor. The balance has tipped in favour of the masters and their representative, the rector, and away from the bishop and his. The supreme power, however, remains the same: the pope. The end result of all this is the paradoxical situation that, while the Theology Faculty is undoubtedly the most prestigious in the University of Paris, it is now the one with least power, dependent as it still is on the chancellor and bishop.

Michael Scot idly follows the progress of a pigeon as it flies in a wide homing circle back to its perch in the eaves of the Cathedral School.

'But,' says Stephen de Provins, 'it is all in a good cause. The pope is mindful of the immense advantage to Christendom of the correct dissemination of knowledge. And that,' he concludes in tempered triumph, 'includes Aristotle.'

Michael Scot sighs and turns his gaze slowly on de Provins. He says nothing.

'Are you not glad of this?' De Provins blinks rapidly, rather taken aback at the cool reception given to his announcement. 'The time for this knowledge has come.'

'I am. I hope that it will be of great benefit to those coming after me. It can be of little benefit to me now. My time, alas, is up.'

De Provins compresses his lips. With measured steps he approaches Michael Scot's chair once again. 'Canon Michael, you have proved yourself a true and obedient son of Mother Church. Please be assured that your time will never, er, be up, as you say…' As de Provins turns away, Michael Scot catches a flicker of restrained exaltation that lends a momentary lustre to his eyes. He is not surprised to detect the tinny quality in the declaiming voice again. 'For it is your privilege, Canon Michael Scot, to exist now on a glorious threshold: you approach the eternal.' De Provins resumes his perambulations at a more sedate pace. Then he adds, 'And let us not forget the end we are all working towards here on earth: the good of our fellow Christians. There can be no thought of personal advancement.'

'Of course.'

Silence falls in the library. De Provins returns to his chair opposite Michael Scot. He joins his hands and rests his lips on the tips of his forefingers. He seems lost in prayer. Presently he breaks the silence and says, 'I suppose you heard about the masters all leaving the university this year gone by?'

'Something garbled reached us in the Kingdom of Sicily.'

'Well, in an effort to induce them to come to Toulouse, the university there announced that the masters would have unfettered access to the texts of Aristotle they had been banned from looking into in Paris.' De Provins opens his hands slightly. 'That is when I advised the pope that it would be better to re-examine the previous papal ban. And he has agreed to this. On the strength of this initiative, we have been able to entice the masters back to Paris. Aristotle is of paramount importance.'

'He was once for me. But I lean more to Plato now.'

De Provins joins his hands once again; his eyes fall to the floor. After a pause he says, 'This just goes to show that, despite having spent so much of your life in the company not only of Aristotle, but also his Muslim transmitter, they have not succeeded in making a convert of you – still less a fanatic.'

'As far as Averroës is concerned, I do not agree with his views on the soul. And I most heartily disapprove of his thoughts on women.'

'Which are?'

'Well now, if I remember correctly, he wrote that Muslim society allows little scope for the development of women's talents. They are destined exclusively for childbirth and the care of children and husbands, and this state of servitude has destroyed their capacity for larger matters. It is for this reason, he maintains, that women seem to lack moral virtues; they live their lives like vegetables, devoting themselves to their families. From this stems the misery that pervades Muslim cities, for women outnumber men by almost double and cannot procure the necessities of life by their own labour.' Michael Scot pauses and the two men look at each other.

'Most questionable,' says Michael Scot.

'Indeed,' replies de Provins. 'Shockingly radical. But no more than what one would expect from a morally suspect society.'

'I have seen Córdoba,' says Michael Scot softly, his face turned to the window. De Provins observes the profile, reflecting that the deterioration in what had been such a striking appearance is startling. His own excellent health affords him a sense of comfort, such a gratifying manifestation of the Lord's favour. But then Michael Scot turns to look at him, and he is thrown by the glittering eyes that hold his own. 'You have not been privileged to behold the splendours of that wondrous city,' Michael Scot continues with slow deliberation. 'I imagine it must be difficult to talk of a society when you are not familiar with its works.'

With an effort, de Provins looks away from those compelling eyes. 'It is not something I feel as a lack,' he says.

Michael Scot smiles. 'Be that as it may,' he replies, 'both Abelard and Adelard of Bath acknowledged the superior capacity of the Muslims for intellectual questing and reasoning, especially in the field of Natural Philosophy. Indeed, Adelard stated that it was the Muslim thinkers who helped him to use and make the most of his faculty of reason.'

'Is it true then that Averroës holds that the existence of God can be proved by reason independently of revelation?'

'I was told in Córdoba that religion and philosophy have equal status as systems for explaining the cosmos.'

De Provins joins his hands again, resting his lips on the forefingers. But he does not reply. Michael Scot is in no hurry to obtrude upon the silence. In truth, it is wonderfully restful.

Eventually, de Provins bestirs himself and enquires after the emperor's library in Palermo. 'There must,' he says, 'be quite a store of learning amassed there by now. But it is deplorable the way the emperor has provoked his Holiness; such a misguided attempt to gain the upper hand. Society is changing; new forces are shaping the way of things to come. The merchants in the centre-north of Italy, for instance, are showing that they can do very well without the yoke of the empire. And the Church will win out in the end.'

Michael Scot shifts on his chair. 'But so too is the Church changing. Or rather, it is *having* to change. Increasing numbers of the faithful have shown their dissatisfaction with the endemic corruption, and the ferocity of the massacre of the Albigensians has horrified still others. I personally do not esteem the Dominicans, and from what I hear, the Franciscans are already succumbing to the usual corruption. Nevertheless, the Church would have found itself in a very difficult position if the Mendicant orders had not arisen, to give at least the semblance of fresh impetus. Certainly,' Michael Scot glances at de Provins, the hint of a smile on his mouth, 'Premonstratensians like ourselves have been sidelined. And that is borne out even here at the University of Paris, where the Theology Faculty is the one with the least power. And if that model were transferred to society at large...'

De Provins compresses his lips. 'I would hate to think you were bitter, Canon Michael.'

'So would I.' Michael Scot gets slowly to his feet. Stephen de Provins observes him with surprise. 'Please pray,' he adds, 'that the Lord guide my footsteps, inner and outer. I must be on my way.'

De Provins gets to his feet as well. They move towards the door.

'I shall not see you again,' de Provins murmurs.

'No. But to you I entrust such of my manuscripts as I dedicated to you. In this world, everything starts, goes on, and then passes away. Even knowledge. And now, on this the last stage of my journey, I ask your blessing.'

Stephen de Provins is disconcerted by the sharp sense of sadness that grips him. He looks at this man and wonders why it should be so. He raises his hand and makes the sign of the cross.

Scotia

†

Confessio
August AD 1230

I have reached the pewter skies. I did not think I would live to see them again. The tarrying twilight of an August evening, a soft grey expanse of sky acquiescing to an advancing darkness. The plangent cries of curlews out over the rolling moorland, the purple of the heather fading as night falls.

It is a homecoming. And one that has enveloped me with such ease that it was as if I had never left this place. As if a veil had fallen away, I resumed living with sensations that belonged to the distant past. It is, therefore, a homecoming for my memories, a chance for them to live again, an opportunity to see, smell and hear things that seemed dead. Within my Gethsemane, the glimmer of a resurrection.

Yet there is a part of me that remains at a distance. A part of me that still hovers on the fringes of this easeful familiarity. It is the part that remembers the illness, the visions, the power – unasked for – over others' wills. No matter how much I may wish to forget this part, it is there, claiming my attention. Perhaps I could still work my magic. Perhaps I could still add to the pearls of sheep excrement that pass for the fruits of my knowledge. But it wearies me. And, in truth, my attention – the obsessive focus it would demand – keeps wandering. Wandering to the skies, to the clouds, to the wind that hums of half-intuited riddles.

I can no longer find it within myself to speak of what my destiny is or ought to have been; I cannot separate it from all that surrounds me. And it seems to me that it is our destiny, in the miniscule amount of time granted to us, to exist as a chip in the cosmic mosaic, the beauty of which, the purposeful design of which, lies ever beyond our grasp.

Let me give thanks then for these things which also have made up my life: the friendship of good men like Jacob Anatolio and Hugo de Clermont; the respect of great men like Frederick; the marvels of this world which I have seen with my own eyes, the efficient splendour of Palermo, the beauty of Córdoba; the zest for learning in Toledo and Paris; and everywhere Your creation in its bewildering variety, its mysterious unquenchable thirst for the miracle of life – an unending conjuring into being of something where there was nothing.

This sense of gratitude is like being rocked in a cradle-web of gossamer and brings its own peace. And now I can feel my guardian angel pulling on the part of my gossamer strand that resides in the eternal.

I have left the searing sun of the south far behind me and in the opalescent twilight of a northern evening stand now on a threshold. Here the dying of the light is gradual, a gentle yielding to shadow that hints at the proximity of unperceived realities.

Not an end but a beginning.

Paris,
France

†

AD 1240

I, Canon Stephen de Provins, do hereby testify that, out of a keen sense of scruple to our Mother Church, I did send to Scotland another of our Premonstratensian brethren, Canon Jean de l'Église, scribe of this missive, to ascertain what material, if any, had remained in the possession of Canon Michael Scot. I charged Canon Jean to gather this material and convey it here to me in Paris, where I then read it.

I can confirm that, with one exception, Canon Michael's most significant works were indeed left in my care. Others are to be found in Palermo. I am pleased to add that his translation endeavours have borne such remarkable fruit, which is why I sent Canon Jean to Scotland. There is such a demand for these translations that we were in hopes there might have been still more awaiting discovery. Here in Paris the names of Aristotle and Averroës are on everybody's lips; word has even reached me of a young Italian, a certain Tommaso d'Aquino, who is making his name by providing a rational philosophical framework for Church doctrine, centred on Aristotle's thought. Averroës has proved contentious, but that is as it should be.

Yet, a decade past when Canon Michael returned to his native Scotland, returning to his Maker very shortly after this, who would have thought this rational impulse centred on

Aristotle would have taken on such importance? Who could have foreseen the thirst for the exotic philosophy of Averroës?

I have read Canon Michael's Confessio *and am saddened by the evidence of the struggles he faced. He was sorely tested. And yet, the rational impulse that I see emerging in the universities cannot but be a motive for satisfaction when contrasted with the morass of uncertainty that astrology and all the other necromantic activities plaguing Canon Michael's life are concerned.*

It is my duty, therefore, to set in writing, before a witness, that of the predictions mentioned by Canon Michael, none has come true. I investigated these claims through correspondence with a certain Giovanni da Messina, master secretary and personal assistant to the emperor's prime minister, Pier delle Vigne, at the court in Palermo. Da Messina was able to inform me of the precise nature of these predictions, as they are stored in the court chancellery. In particular, I can testify that the prediction alluding to the emperor's death in front of iron gates in a city named after Flora, has proved to be singularly inexact. Frederick II is still in the whole of his health (like myself, praise the good Lord) and continues to be a thorn in the side of the papacy. Following the mutinous betrayal by his son Henry, and defeat at the hands of the Lombard League in 1237, he has become increasingly despotic and cruel. It is not to be wondered at this stage that our Holy Father refers to him as the Antichrist.

I am glad to see that Canon Michael found a measure of peace at the end of his life, evident in the gratitude he expressed to his Maker for the good things his life had bestowed on him. I was, however, pained not to see my own name among the people who meant most to him; for I remember Canon Michael Scot. And it is a very strange thing: the more time passes, the more he stands out in my memory, until at times he seems more real to me now than he was in life. He was an enigma to himself and those who knew him. A gifted man, but a troubled one.

Nevertheless, one who did much to advance the cause of Christendom.

The world is a strange place. It is Mother Church's task to guide us through its snares and traps. And this is both her strength and her dilemma: she is ever caught between the aspirations of the individual soul and her duty to nourish the entire family in order to keep it together.

Let us bow our heads and ask for the Lord's guidance and protection.

Amen.

†

AD 1250

With this missive, an addendum to the previous, dated 1240 by Canon Stephen de Provins, I, Canon Jean de l'Église, give testimony that the predictions of Michael Scot regarding the Emperor Frederick II have proven themselves true. For not a fortnight past the emperor did take ill and, in the city of Fiorentina di Puglia, in an iron bedstead, died before his physicians could do aught to save him.

Thus passes away the scourge of Christendom.

It is incumbent upon me to write down what I know of this story, for many versions are being circulated, mostly by people who neither knew those involved nor had any contact with them. As for myself, I was sent a decade past, and two since the demise of this Michael Scot, to his resting place in the wilds of Scotland, that I might retrieve such of his writings and manuscripts which my master, Stephen de Provins, was anxious to acquire before other and less scrupulous hands snatched them forever from the jurisdiction of the Church. There I did hear with my own ears the stories that circulated about this sorcerer. And in particular, from those who witnessed his death.

Before he died, Michael Scot was heard to murmur, 'I surrender to you.' All those present concurred that he had finally been won over by the devil, and his soul carried off to eternal perdition. For how can you surrender to God if, as a cleric, your whole life should have been given to Him in the first place?

The devil came for his own, they said.

I remember the rumours that Michael Scot was a necromancer and had died, they said, while compiling a book of magic, Almuchabola. *So, along with Michael Scot's* Confessio, *I removed this book and a few other of his writings, in case they should prove to be incriminating. But in the space of these ten years, the content of this* Almuchabola *has been understood, and it has been seen to be a book of algebra that Michael Scot was translating when death overtook him.*

Herein there is aught of magic, save whatever of newfound knowledge confounds us.

Michael Scot's predictions about the fate of the empire have also come true, since it now teeters on the brink of destruction. Frederick II was betrayed, not only by his own son, but also by his prime minister, Pier delle Vigne. The facts are difficult to ascertain, but I have done my best by making direct enquiries to the chancellery in Palermo. What was related to me is passing strange, but I set it down here by way of a record.

The prime minister was charged with treason. There are those who say it was on account of greed: Pier delle Vigne misappropriated what was not his. But there are also those who hint at a darker reason. They point to a plot hatched between Pier delle Vigne and a certain Giovanni da Messina to assassinate the emperor's physician and astrologer, Michael Scot.

They paid an urchin skilled in hunting hares, birds and game with slings and stones to climb up onto the roof of the chapel of San Giovanni degli Eremiti and loosen some stones there. They had marked Michael Scot's stall with red paint, and the urchin was to use his expertise to gauge which stone to dislodge that would fall directly onto his head. This the urchin did, and with remarkable accuracy. Delle Vigne and da Messina had taken care to remove the red mark from Michael Scot's stall before the morning service. And the rest we know.

But the urchin could not resist boasting of his feat. And soon all Palermo knew of this act of wickedness. Eventually, it made its way even to the emperor's ears. His vengeance was absolute. First da Messina was summarily executed. Then he had Pier delle Vigne conveyed to a tower, where he was tortured and his eyes plucked out. He was being led to a place of cruel execution in an open cart before a taunting populace, when suddenly he fell from this cart, receiving a blow to the head from a large stone on the roadway. The blow was of such gravity that he expired before reaching the place of execution. There are those who say, however, that the fall was not an accident; Pier delle Vigne took his own life rather than endure any further torture or humiliation at the hands of the emperor he had served so faithfully.

No emperor; no prime minister; no successor. Soon there will be no empire.

The Lord is not mocked.

But truly this Michael Scot was an enigma. Where he was accused of necromancy, there appears to have been none. But where he was laughed at for a charlatan, there has confirmation come of a disturbing proficiency.

I judge not, that I may not be judged.

Amen.

Author's Note

Since my university days I have had a fascination with Frederick II. What reeled me in was the meteoric trajectory of his ill-fated attempt to build an empire as a bulwark against the over-weaning power of the thirteenth-century Church. But it was when I came across the figure of a Scottish monk, Michael Scot, who became physician and astrologer to the emperor, that I knew there was a story to be told.

A Matter of Interpretation is the story of this indomitable Scotsman's quest for knowledge and meaning. The quest takes place against a backdrop of momentous historic events that point to this era representing a tipping point in the approach to knowledge and its dissemination. For a brief time in the Iberian Peninsula and Sicily – the period known as *Convivencia* – Christians, Jews and Muslims came together to promote scholarship and learning across all manner of divides. Ultimately, Christendom and Islam travelled along different routes in the stand-off between philosophy and theology, between reason and faith, and this can be traced back to choices made around the beginning of the thirteenth century.

In *A Matter of Interpretation* I mix fact and fiction. There are several accounts of Michael Scot's life, but the one I felt would best serve the purposes of my novel is *An Enquiry into the Life and*

Legend of Michael Scot by Rev. J. Wood Brown (David Douglas 1897). There are other accounts, such as *Frederick II: A Medieval Emperor*, David Abulafia (Pimlico 2002) and *Michael Scot* by Lynn Thorndike (Thomas Nelson 1965). *Frederick the Second 1194-1250*, Ernst Kantorowicz, trans. E.O. Lorimer (Constable 1931) presents a different timeline concerning the events in Michael Scot's life. So, while I make no claims to offer the most accurate historical retelling of Michael Scot's life, I hope I have managed to offer the reader an account that opens up the greatest opportunities for storytelling. As far as the other historical figures are concerned, I have tried to maintain historical accuracy.

For period detail I accessed the website www.stupormundi.it and explored Toledo's Jewish past thanks to Benjamin R. Gampel's essay 'Jews, Christians, and Muslims in Medieval Iberia: *Convivencia* through the Eyes of Sephardic Jews', in *Convivencia: Jews, Muslims, and Christians in Medieval Spain*, ed. Vivian B. Mann, Thomas F. Glick, and Jerrilynn D. Dodds (George Braziller Inc 1992). I also referenced Jozef Brams' *La riscoperta di Aristotele in Occidente* (Jaca 2003).

Acknowledgements

My thanks and gratitude go to my family, Luca and David, for their unfailing support. Thank you also to sister-in-a-million, Sarah, my first reader and woman of many talents.

I am enormously indebted to my wonderful editors at Fairlight Books, Louise Boland and Urška Vidoni, for their vision and skill in helping me do justice to Michael Scot's story. A big thank you also to my eagle-eyed copy editor, Alison Howard, for her painstaking and invaluable work.

A special mention for fellow writer Siobhán Mannion, whose generously-given input and support were much appreciated. Thanks to all my friends and family who journeyed with me and supported me.

Fairlight Books

ALAN ROBERT CLARK

The Prince of Mirrors

Two young men with expectations.
One predicted to succeed, the other to fail...

Prince Albert Victor, heir presumptive to the British throne, is seen as disastrously inadequate to be king. The grandson of Queen Victoria, he is good-hearted but intensely shy and, some whisper, even slow-witted.

By contrast, Jem Stephen is a renowned intellectual, poet and golden boy worshipped by all. But a looming curse of mental instability is threatening to take it all away.

Appointed as the prince's personal tutor, Jem works to prepare him for the duty to come. A friendship grows between them – one that will allow them to understand and finally accept who they really are and change both of their lives forever.

'A gilded cast of characters parades through this sumptuous tale. A clever mixture of history, psychology and sex.'
—Alastair Stewart OBE,
ITN anchor

FIONA VIGO MARSHALL

Find Me Falling

She bought a house where you can hear the sea, murmuring on the edge of consciousness...

Bonnie, a traumatised concert pianist, finds refuge at the edge of England, in a cliff-top house haunted by memories and broken dreams.

When Dominic, a road sweeper who is visited by neurological hauntings of his own, gives Bonnie a ring he finds on the street, elemental forces are unleashed that neither is able to control.

'The evocation of the eerie alternate realities that are just a few misfiring neurones away for us all stays with the reader long after the last page is turned.'
—Dr Sallie Baxendale, Consultant Neuropsychologist, Department of Clinical & Experimental Epilepsy Institute of Neurology, UCL London